The Sins We Seek

THE DARK ABYSS OF OUR SINS • BOOK THREE

The Sins We Seek

THE DARK ABYSS OF OUR SINS • BOOK THREE

KRISTA D. BALL

DEDICATION

For those who fight from the shadows.

THE STORY SO FAR...

THE DEMONS WE SEE

ALLEGRA, CONTESSA OF Marsina, had no interest in Cathedral politics. On her journey to Orsini to officially decline the post of Arbiter of Justice, she encountered Mrs. Ansley, a mage harassed by local officials. Allegra extended her protection to the woman. However, they were set upon by local militia accusing Mrs. Ansley of being an elemental mage. Unable to do anything against the assault, Allegra and her escort raced to Orsini, where she accepted the post of Arbiter, and ordered the Holy Father's Own Consorts—her escort—to find Mrs. Ansley. They never did.

Angered by the clergy's role in the growing mage rebellion, Allegra relocated the office of Arbiter to Borro Abbey. Several members of the Consorts formed her protection detail, including Captain Stanton Rainier and Lieutenants Lex and Dodd.

Knowing she needed to make a show of support for mages, she sent Dodd and Lex to find Walter Cram, the de facto leader of the elemental mage rebellion. Walter's arrival at Borro Abbey enraged many on all sides, and she granted Walter and other elemental mages legal immunity while at Borro Abbey.

During the winter, hundreds of refugees made the perilous trip to Borro Abbey in hopes of protection. The abbey struggled to feed people, to stop bread riots, and to control the hatred between everyone. Allegra was assaulted by a mage slave owner, and security around her was tightened.

One evening, Allegra accidentally opened a demon portal in the abbey's undercroft. Walter managed to close and dispatch the demons; however, he caused the ceiling to collapse. Several people died and Allegra was caught in the rubble.

After rescue, Allegra adjusted to the reality of demons being real. Walter's presence was a strain on the peace talks, and her growing feelings for Stanton added to her personal stress. Allegra struggled to control her magic and Lex discovered she was an elemental mage.

General Bonacieux and Queen Portia arrived at Borro Abbey for the peace talks. Fractures between the abolitionists began to show, even as Allegra and Walter repaired their friendship.

Bonacieux began hiding troops just beyond Borro's boundaries. Allegra confronted Queen Portia about this and threatened to remove them all from the peace talks.

A local boy called Little Ferret stole a loaf of bread and was sentenced to hang. The elemental mages freed the boy, and a riot broke out fueled by Bonacieux's men. Walter Cram defended the Consorts and Allegra, and as many townsfolks as possible, against the slaughter. In the end, nineteen people died.

Days later, Allegra hosted Borro Abbey's peace talks ball. She confessed to Stanton that she was an elemental mage. She thought he would arrest her, but instead he promised to keep her secret and they declared their love for each other.

A couple of weeks had passed in relative quiet when a massive demon came through Queen Portia's bedroom. Bonacieux killed Portia for being an elemental mage, and left Lex for dead. Then he and his men tried burning down Borro Abbey, before Walter collapsed it on top of the demon portal.

Walter, Dodd, and Allegra escaped into the mountain paths, while Stanton managed to get as many out as he could, and began the trek toward Orsini, with an enemy army behind him.

THE NIGHTMARE WE KNOW

SEPARATED FROM THE main convoy, Allegra, Walter, and Dodd were presumed dead. They were rescued by Princess Imogen, sister to the King of Amadore, who helped escort them ahead of Bonacieux's army.

Lex arrived at the Cathedral gravely injured, but with healing and doctoring, was declared to be out of danger. Lex told the senior cardinals that General Bonacieux had killed Queen Portia, and covered for Allegra's use of elemental magic.

Once Allegra arrived at Borro Abbey, she discovered the mages who'd escaped Borro Abbey treated differently than wealthy escapees. She ordered the fair and equal distribution of food. She also faced obstruction from several members of the senior cardinals. She confronted Cardinal Vittorio about his involvement in hampering her ability to access her personal money, causing her to not be able to purchase bread for the refugees. Cardinal Vittorio justified it by saying she should not have brought mages into Borro Abbey.

Rupert and Pero suffered marriage troubles, as tempers flared over mage rights. Pero moved into Father Michael's new bedroom, causing the priest to move in with Walter Cram, who had a larger room.

General Bonacieux demanded Allegra be handed over to him. He had elemental mages tortured until they would serve him without question. In desperation, Francois considered allowing the cardinals to vote to hand Allegra over, causing a rift in their lifelong friendship. Walter and Stanton both threatened to kill anyone who tried to take her.

Tiny demon portals opened up in the back alleys of the Cathedral, near where the servants and infirmary entrances were located.

While the cardinals debated handing Allegra over, she, Father Michael, Stanton, and the Consorts, plus her servants and assistants, handed out writs of freedom in Orsini's main courtyard to both slaves and elemental mages. When confronted by the Holy Father and the senior cardinals, she declared the place the Courtyard of Freedom. Francois slapped her and declared she had been stripped of her Arbiter's power.

When Allegra finally agreed to discuss the matter in private, she was whisked away with her entourage to the Holy Father's private suites. She drank his best wine while the cardinals argued about what she'd just done and how they'd punish her. However, it became quickly obvious the wine had been poisoned and Allegra fell unconscious for a day.

After Allegra's poisoning, Walter advised the senior cardinals that all water needed to be tested, for fear that Bonacieux had been behind it, since he'd done this to mages before. Bonacieux had left with his cavalry and some of his mages to chase after Grand Duchess Katherine who was rumored to be returning to Cartossa to take the throne. He left some of his infantry behind. Allegra had been temporarily reinstated as Arbiter, since Katherine had declined the role, which was the last letter that she'd gotten out to them.

Little Ferret (now known as Little Gopher) alerted Walter, Lex, and Dodd that a barrel of water was found to have been surrounded with dead rats and a demon mark was found next to the area. Lex and Dodd discreetly looked into it further. However, they came to a dead end.

After some quiet nights without Bonacieux's army attacking, Allegra and Stanton were awakened in the middle of the night to the news that demon portals had been opening up on both sides of the walls.

Allegra worked to secure as much of the inner Cathedral as possible with Cardinal Rigi, but ended up trapped in the infirmary where a fever outbreak was being contained. Allegra fought a demon who'd attacked her servant, Calm Seas, and beat it to death with a bottle. Eventually, they locked themselves in to wait out the battle.

Pero and Father Michael were helping evacuate the elderly clergy while Rupert was getting everyone else to safety in the deepest parts of the Cathedral, away from windows. Pero and Father Michael set off to find the nursery and get the children to safety.

Dodd and Princess Imogen fought at the north gate, trying to control both the crowd and deal with the demons. Lex, still too injured to fight, was tasked with escorting the fleeing people inside Orsini's buildings and into safety.

Stanton was with Walter, who was closing the demon portals before they merged and allowed larger demons to come through.

Several elemental mages joined the fight. Eventually, Walter and Stanton both passed out from exhaustion and smoke inhalation.

Once all of the fissures had been closed, they became aware of how dire the situation had been. Many mages were dead. Several elemental mages sacrificed themselves to close the demon portals nearest Bonacieux's men, in an attempt to stop large demons. All of them died—the mages and the soldiers.

The aftermath was difficult on Allegra, who felt partially responsible for what had happened. Some of the Consorts declared they would never arrest another elemental mage without reason, even if they had to refuse orders and risk punishment. The main gates of Orsini had been ripped off by demons. Most of Orsini's windows were shattered and even the most inner parts of the Cathedral had a coating of soot.

Cardinal Devonshire finally arrived and called a full conclave with Allegra there. Allegra declared she would leave the conclave and free every single person inside Orsini's walls unless they stripped her of her power. One of the younger cardinals pushed Cardinal Giso, injuring him. Devonshire silenced them by destroying a speaking stone.

Devonshire had Cardinal Vanida, one of Allegra's staunchest critics, dragged from the chamber kicking and screaming, and dissolved the entire conclave. Under Orsini law, she created the Orsini Assembly and placed the senior cardinals in charge, along with Princess Imogen as the Colonel of the Militia, and Allegra, newly installed as the Constable of Orsini. From there, all decisions would be for them to decide and only them, until the danger has passed.

Word came quickly that Cartossa had descended into civil war, with Grand Duchess Katherine now under siege near the border by Bonacieux. Dodd and Lex debated if they wished to be more than friends, while Walter and Father Michael became lovers. Rupert and Pero began patching up their marriage, though it remained uncertain if Rupert and Allegra will be friends again.

DRAMATIS PERSONAE

MAIN CHARACTERS

Allegra, Contessa of Marsina. Arbiter of Justice. Constable of Orsini. Known as Her Ladyship and Contessa.

Captain Stanton Rainier, Duke of Barrington: A war hero long before he'd become a Consort. Lover of Allegra. Prefers to be known as Captain Rainier.

Walter Cram (also known as Lancaster Rivers): Unofficial leader of the mage rebellion.

Lieutenants Lex and Dodd: Senior Consorts, they are tasked with investigating who is behind the portals.

SERVANTS AND STAFF

Nathan: Allegra's financial and legal assistant.

Serafina: Allegra's day-to-day secretary.

Nadira: Allegra's trusted maidservant.

Kia: One of Allegra's young servants.

Calm Seas: One of Allegra's young servants. Recovering from extensive burns.

CONSORTS AND MILITIA

Her Highness, Imogen: Sister to the King of Amadore, temporary Colonel of the Militia. Also known as Ginny to Allegra.

Rahna and Martin: Consorts appointed as Allegra's personal guard.

Beatrix: Consort.

Little Gopher: Cathedral runner. Previously known as Little Ferret before getting in legal trouble at Borro Abbey.

SENIOR CLERGY

His Holiness, Francois (real name Rupert): The Holy Father, Francois is a moderate. Childhood friend of Allegra, and married to Pero, an abolitionist.

Father Michael. Bishop of Orsini. Formerly Bishop of Borro: A country bishop for many years, and friend of Allegra's and Stanton's. Recent lover to Walter Cram.

Cardinal Devonshire: An elderly woman, head of the censure board. A moderate.

Cardinal Giso: An older cardinal and a staunch abolitionist.

Cardinal Vittorio: A staunch conservative.

Cardinal DeLancey: An elderly, frail woman who generally sides with the status quo.

Cardinal Vanida: Former member of the senior council. Kicked out by Cardinal Devonshire for inappropriate behaviour. Has a hatred of mages.

Sisters Bianca and Margarite: The two clergy who assisted Allegra while escaping the destruction of Borro Abbey.

AND NOW, THE CONCLUSION OF THE *DARK ABYSS OF OUR SINS* TRILOGY...

CHAPTER ONE

THREE WEEKS HAD passed since the last demon sighting, and all was calm. Not a whisper of even the smallest demon marks. There were no portals spewing screeching, winged creatures. There were no evil generals at their gates, nor armies poised to murder them in their beds. The wells had not been poisoned. The food riots had been avoided. The coughing sickness had abated. No mages had been burned at the stake.

Overall, it could have all been much worse.

On days like these, Allegra fought the temptation to lock herself away, to foster the illusion that all was normal and calm. She forced herself to walk in the sun every day, to face the restoration efforts, to see the bodies covered in sooty cloth, and look into the haunted eyes of Orsini's residents, be they permanent or transitory.

Most days she made the trip outside of Orsini's north walls to where the market had relocated, both for its own safety and to not hinder clean up and reconstruction efforts. It was safe there, or at least as safe as anywhere could be.

Today, Allegra followed Ysabeau through the labyrinth of back alleyways. She had hired the young woman to assist Nathan, who was currently chest-deep in documents, finances, and Cathedral law. The young woman rambled on about how honored she was to work for the Arbiter of Justice. Allegra did not bother to correct her on the most recent title change. Contessa of Marsina? That she would always be. The rest were merely jobs.

The two women passed by an alley that had a line of bodies in the street, all wrapped in soot-smeared sheets. In this part of Orsini, workers were still pulling out the dead—be they demon or people—from collapsed buildings. Though grim, it was better than the early days, when the uncovered bodies had been tossed into piles like firewood; there were simply too many for anything else.

Three workers tipped their hats respectfully as she walked by before resuming the work of tossing demon corpses into a cart. The pyres outside the city walls were still burning the demons, though not as many now. She watched the work for a moment. She saw the expressions of the workers, their pain evident even through the dirt, soot, and bandages. In her heart, she knew well enough that none who had survived the demon attacks would ever be *fine*, not in the truest, purest sense of the word. It had marked their souls forever.

All she could do, all any of them could do, was to move forward, step by painful, tedious step. Unfortunately, that could not happen so long as they were still pulling out the dead.

Ysabeau pointed at a building ahead and they crossed the alley to stand in front of it. It has a symbol painted on its front, announcing the building unsafe. Most of the roof was missing. One side of the building was scorched, and there were visible demon claw marks, where something had tried to rip off the front door.

Allegra shivered as her mind reconstructed the scene here from her own wealth of memories. The black stains on the side of the building were where a demon's brains had been splattered. She knew how that sounded and smelled. She could hear the cries of the helpless roaring in her ears, drowning out Ysabeau. Even now, she felt the bottle in her hands as she prepared to crush a demon's skull.

"Your Ladyship?" Ysabeau asked, seemingly for not the first time.

Allegra was sweating, and far more than a woman of her rank was ever allowed in polite company. Nevertheless, she smiled and said, "My apologies. I find myself unusually fatigued this morning. My attention faded. Please, repeat back what you said."

"Your Ladyship, there is nowhere to put the residents of this building once we evict them." Ysabeau sighed. "The people inside do not wish to be displaced from the building that saved their lives, even if it has been condemned and must be pulled down for safety's sake. Her Highness will not issue the order to forcefully remove them. Captain Rainier has also refused. However, Brother Eagle is insisting they be removed, and housed in the north tents. The people inside object. I had hoped you could moderate the situation."

Allegra pulled her attention from the stains and realized the building had no windows. Most of the glass in both the Cathedral and Orsini's wealthier buildings had been destroyed in the attack, but this was a poor building that never had glass. Only cheap, double shutters, in and out. This design would be used for all of Orsini's new buildings and the repairs, though sliding glass windows would be installed between the protective wooden layers.

She wondered if any of them would trust plain glass windows again or would they all rely upon inner wooden shutters for the security for both their bodies and souls.

"Your Ladyship," Rahna said to get her attention. She never went anywhere without her guard now. Rahna stepped closer and pointed down the alleyway. "Captain Rainier."

Allegra turned in the direction Rahna indicated and smiled when her eyes landed on Stanton. He gave a slight, awkward wave, and she motioned for him to join her. Rahna retreated back to a respectful distance, and Allegra turned her attention to the current crisis.

"Why are we making poor Orsini residents sleep in tents?"

"Brother Eagle feels strongly that the main residential floors cannot handle an influx."

Allegra made an exaggerated gesture of looking over her shoulder and craning her neck skyward. There, the Cathedral's largest dome glimmered and glinted in the morning sun. She turned to Ysabeau and raised one eyebrow.

"I know, Your Ladyship. I know." Ysabeau blew a strand of hair from her face. "Normally, I would ask Nathan, but he's been preoccupied with Cardinal Vittorio. Apparently, the cardinal has been screaming at him since before dawn."

Allegra gave Stanton a wide smile when he approached. He unwrapped the cloth he carried to reveal two knotted rolls decorated with seeds and spices. One was formed into a circle, and the other was a larger twist. "Pick whichever you prefer."

She snatched the larger one and gave him a wicked grin. Before taking a bite, she asked, "What did Nathan do now?"

The young woman shrugged. "You know what the cardinal is like, Your Ladyship."

Yes, she did. She took two bites of her roll, which was still warm. Now that they were in Orsini, and it was late spring, the variety of ready food had improved greatly.

"Ysabeau, forgive my bluntness, but my roll grows cold in the morning air. Where should these people go, and who is blocking your work?"

"Well, Your Ladyship, to be equally blunt, Brother Eagle is blocking my attempts to move these people into the old priory."

"The blue house?" Stanton asked. When Ysabeau nodded, he added for Allegra's benefit, "They're still pulling bodies out of there."

Allegra took another bite of her roll. It was perfectly baked, and still had enough warmth to send a puff of steam upward with every bite. "I am not certain that is the best course of action. Are they not traumatized enough?"

"It was their suggestion to move to the Old Town."

The "Old Town" was the oldest part of Orsini's housing, not to be confused with the oldest parts of the Cathedral, which were historical and religious marvels. The Old Town was a set of semi-dilapidated buildings that were often used for storage and little else.

"The Old Priory has no windows, or so I'm informed. These people were trapped in here, in this building, and the lack of glass saved their lives. They are right to be fearful of being in open tents, with all that happened to them." Ysabeau shivered. "I truly do not know how they are managing to hold up so well."

Ysabeau had been one of the lucky ones. She did not see the demons swooping down to murder friends and foe alike. She had been escorting Devonshire, helping with the elderly cardinal's paperwork. They had only seen the aftermath. A little voice gnawed at Allegra that the apathy she felt at the suffering of these poor residents was not good for her soul. Ysabeau's reaction was how she should feel.

She took another bite. Not today, though. She did not have the fortitude for it. However, she could still help others. Allegra motioned at Ysabeau's ledger. She pulled the tiny pencil from its leather sheath, flipped to the page marked with the ribbon, and wrote her approval to move the residents into the Old Town. She signed it with her name and rank.

Ysabeau accepted the ledger and closed it. "Thank you, Your Ladyship. I will have the occupants help with preparing the priory. I am certain they will feel safest there. Will you get into trouble with the cardinals for doing this?"

Stanton snorted. Allegra managed to keep grunts and snorts to herself. "My dear girl, how long have you been away? The cardinals held a vote, only weeks ago, to determine if I should be hanged from the front gate. I'm confident I can endure some ruffled robes."

Ysabeau's mouth formed several silent words before she mumbled polite words and hurried off inside the building. Allegra took another bite of her roll. Stanton's guard blended seamlessly with her two guards, all keeping the respectful distance.

"You told me you weren't bitter about the vote," Stanton said.

With Stanton, she had no qualms about snorting in a decidedly unladylike manner. "I find time has stewed the bitterness, though I aim not to be so in public. Bad for the reputation and all."

He gestured around them. In general, people left them alone, but any eye contact brought tips of hat brims, waves, and smiles. "I believe this is the very definition of public, my dear."

"I did say I would *try*," Allegra said. After chewing another bite, she said, "I will never speak ill of Borro Abbey, but I missed Orsini's ability to get sesame seeds."

He laughed. "Enjoy it, for I suspect there will be no more until the autumn."

"The Almighty giveth and the Almighty taketh away. Blessed be the name of the Lord God Almighty, who cruelly created agricultural seasons and import logistics."

After lamenting how Orsini had finally run out of the winter store of potatoes, they fell into a comfortable silence as they turned to walk to the main Cathedral steps. They both had long hours ahead of them, with tedious reports, reconstruction efforts, and the general unrest that comes when terrified, common people pressed against the will of terrified, powerful people.

At Stanton's suggestion, they detoured to inspect the southern gate. The portcullis had been repaired and reinstalled. The powers that be had taken the opportunity to build new outer gates, since the old ones never worked anyway. These replacements were being carefully mounted into place as they watched. The inner gates were double the thickness of the previous ones. Heavy bands of metal zigzagged across it to reinforce the entire thing. There were piles of rope nearby, as well as large bracing beams. They would never be caught off guard again.

She found herself wondering if magic could be used to encase Orsini within a massive demon-proof dome, or perhaps some form of demon trap. Probably not, she concluded, but the daydream was comforting nevertheless.

She glanced at where dozens of elemental mages had given their lives to close the portals. Guilt flooded her, as it always did. She had been safe inside one of the chapels, locked up for hours with the sick and scared. She had not been out here fighting for the lives of Orsini's residents. She'd not closed a single demon portal. She'd not done a damn useful thing.

Her vision turned blurry, and she accepted Stanton's offered handkerchief and dabbed at her eyes. Once finished, he found her hand with his and squeezed.

"How is Walter doing with the list?" Stanton asked quietly. He'd taken to calling him by the more friendly first name these days. When pressed, Stanton had said Walter grew on people like a bad rash. She'd laughed when he said that.

"He wants to double-check that he has everyone accounted for," Allegra said.

Rupert had requested a list of the mages who'd died defending the south gate against the demons. The Holy Father wanted a plaque engraved with their names, to remind future generations that mages had died on that spot. Walter said it was a nice idea, but she felt so empty when thinking about the gesture. It did not wash away the transgressions of the past, nor did it change that they were still, this very moment, debating if elemental mages were allowed to exist in the world alongside everyone else.

Orsini might suddenly not have enslaved mages, but that did not change the reality that just beyond their battered walls bubbled a civil war. That the war was spilling over to their side of the border. That there were more and more refugees every day, fleeing the conflict, and seeking the protection of the Lord God Almighty.

And the Arbiter of Justice.

The Constable of Orsini.

Contessa of Marsina.

She knew titles meant nothing, and yet in moments like these, they could mean everything. Nothing because what use was a title when the true heroes fought and died. Everything because it was only people with titles who could remember those heroes. She turned her head away from the memories, both hers and the images conjured by the stories of others. She wished her mind could not see clearly, for it would be easier for her in moments like these.

"Your Ladyship, Captain, forgive me, but..."

Allegra turned her attention to the gate's guard, who informed them that another wagon train of refugees approached from further down the south road. They were in bad shape, so the report said, and needed admittance into the courtyard. They had injured children. There was no time to fall apart and replay decisions and regrets. There was still a war happening beyond their walls, and a demon summoner in their midst.

She and Stanton both gave the order to get the children inside.

IT WAS PROVING difficult not to stab Lex. Not because Dodd ever wanted to stab his oldest friend in the world—for one thing, his mother and Lex's mother would band together to stab him in his own bed if he did something so carelessly stupid—but rather, Lex insisted Dodd not go easy during sword practice, when it was absolutely clear to Dodd that he needed to go easy.

Every morning for two weeks now, Lex insisted that they come outside at the ass crack of dawn to practice swords, brawling, running, climbing, and whatever else Lex decided. The other Consorts or the Orsini militia took turns joining in, and even some of Her Highness's soldiers when they had time. Some mornings they practiced in the Old Town, dodging around the buildings while people either took bets or shouted at them (or both). Other times, they practiced where the market used to be. Then mornings like this one, they practiced outside of the north gates where trees and rocks and bugs got in the way.

Dodd easily dodged an attack from Lex and blocked the next swing of the sword, all the while listening to his stomach grumble and growl that he'd not eaten yet. Worse, his stomach knew that, by the time they finished here, there'd be nothing left of the dining hall's breakfast beyond dried out bread.

Dodd stepped around Lex, meaning to only give a slight kick in the calf. Lex tripped over his own feet and lost his balance, hitting the ground with a forced exhalation and wince. Lex held his middle and moaned a bit.

"That's it, we're done," Dodd announced. "If Cardinal DeLancey sees us doing this, she's going to tan both of our hides."

Lex scowled and swore, but finally accepted Dodd's outstretched hand. He was fine with helping Lex to his feet, but did not bend down to pick up Lex's dropped sword. Even though Lex winced, and grunted, and staggered trying to straighten up, Dodd knew better than to help with this one. For whatever reason that only the Lord God knew, Lex insisted on practicing bending down and stretching his insides to pulp, so he let Lex have his way on this one.

Finally, Lex straightened his back, shook out his shoulders, and gripped his sword. "Again."

Dodd sheathed his sword. "I'm done."

Lex scowled at him. "Oh, come on. The surgeon said I need to work out the scars and skin. I have to practice, or I'll never use a sword again."

"I'm just saying this seems excessive," Dodd said. "Look at you. You're sweating."

"So are you," Lex said.

"I'm sweating because I thought it was going to be cold out and I put on my wool liners, and now I'm going to die of heat exhaustion. You're sweating from pain. There's a difference."

"It is rather warm," Lex commented. Then he sighed and said, "My guts hurt."

"I bet they do," Dodd said. "You're doing too much first thing in the morning. Why not do a bit first thing, then some more at luncheon, and some practice in the evening?"

"I'm always tired in the evening now," Lex complained.

"That's because you're doing too much in the morning," Dodd said. Before Lex could protest, Dodd pointed and said, "There's Cram. Come on, let's see if we can get him to fight me."

"How will that help heal my guts?"

"Laughing until you vomit is exercise," Dodd said confidently as they walked toward the mage.

Once in complaining distance, Cram turned an accusatory gaze at Dodd. "What have you done to him? He's about to pass out!"

"We were practicing," Dodd said, rather more defensively than he'd meant.

"Practicing?" Cram demanded. "Lieutenant Lex looks like he needs a surgeon *and* a healer."

"I'm supposed to exercise," Lex said. Dodd knew him well enough that he was feeling defensive, too, just by his tone.

Cram stared at them both. "I thought I'd bring you both some breakfast, thinking I was being nice. I didn't realize I couldn't trust the two of you alone without an adult in charge. Come on, let's go eat. Lex, can you even walk?"

"Of course, I can fucking walk," Lex snapped.

None of them commented on how slowly Lex was walking, as even Walter Cram, demon lover, seemed to know when it was best to keep his damned mage mouth shut.

They made their way inside the gates and Lex insisted on climbing up the scaffolding to sit and eat. Dodd complained, but he was overruled. It wasn't that he was afraid of heights. It was that he didn't see the point in sitting two stories higher than everyone else just to eat some tarts. It wasn't like people would steal from them.

Cram took the cloth off his basket and Dodd's stomach growled loudly. Tiny fruit tarts, just two bites each, were stacked in one corner. The middle of the basket had something lumpy wrapped in another cloth, and Cram revealed it to be beignets in one pouch, and steamed buns in the other. Next to that was wilted kale leaves with wooden sticks visible from one end. Those were the grilled meat.

Most days they ate in the dining hall together at least once, but Cram announced himself to be in an uncharacteristically generous mood. Cram claimed he'd paid for it using real coin, too. There was a time, and not that long ago, when the merchants wouldn't even let the mage talk to them, let alone take his money.

Now, some of the merchants were offering Orsini's most notorious demon lover discounts.

Discounts.

No one ever gave Dodd a discount.

Assholes.

However, he wasn't going to spit on free fruit tarts, nor would he turn down three of the tiny pastries. He wouldn't have turned those down anyway, but especially not now when food rations were reduced to two meals a day to ensure everyone ate, no matter their position, rank, or wealth. And it wasn't that Dodd was against free food for the poor. His issue was merely that thin soup with unbuttered bread was a winter snack, at best, and certainly should not be called a meal.

As ever, the conversation turned to the investigation concerning the demon attacks. In Dodd's expert opinion, this job was a steaming pile of horseshit. There was no plan, unless "find the bastards who tried to kill us all" was a plan. Which Dodd felt very much was *not* a plan so much as bravado or possibly a protest slogan when the inevitable pitchfork-wielding mobs arrived. They were no further ahead, there were no leads and too many leads at the same time, and he had to spend all of his waking moments with Walter fucking Cram.

Who, Lord God help him, he was actually starting to like.

"Well?" Cram demanded between chews. The man had inhaled three meat sticks, several tarts, and even more of the pastries in what seemed to be mere moments. Dodd had never seen any person love food the way Cram did; maybe it was all of that running he seemed to do.

While Lex talked to Cram about their pathetic progress, Dodd found himself staring at Lex. And, despite what Cram said, it wasn't in a "I want to fuck you up against the inner sanctum's frescos" way but more in a "holy shit, you were stabbed in the guts and are still alive" way.

Dodd noticed that Lex's hands still had an edge of a tremor; they got like that whenever Lex pushed himself more than necessary. Against Dodd's preference, which he'd not stated out loud because he was a supportive friend, Lex was now refusing all healing items, insisting they be distributed to those injured during the demon invasion. Lex's reasoning made sense, in a cold, calculating manner: the most recently injured would need the items more. But that meant Lex now relied on human recovery, medicines, and herbs alone, and those things took fucking forever.

"You going to stare at Lex all day or answer the question?" Cram demanded.

Dodd didn't hear Cram ask a question, but he rolled his eyes and said, "Ya know, I think Lex is finally starting to gain back his weight again."

Cram gave Lex a quick scan and nodded. "I guess a little. Here, have another tart."

Lex accepted the tart and popped it into his mouth. After a quick chew, he said, "We need to do up a list of everyone who was at Borro Abbey, but also here when the attack happened. Then, we need to interview everyone."

"We've already interviewed people," Dodd said.

Lex shook their head. "No, I mean *everyone*. From the chambermaid to the Contessa. Map out the timeline. Speaking of maps, we should mark where everyone was located when the attacks took place, where people saw things, whatever. It's time we did it that way."

Cram sucked in a deep breath. "I understand what you're saying, and why, but listen to me. You're asking us to make a list of *us*. All of us. Ally, Rainier, the two of you, Michael, Nadira...I don't like names on paper. People like me always get hurt when we're on lists."

"*Michael* is it?" Dodd asked between bites. "Not Bishop Michael. Not the Bishop of Orsini. Not Father Michael. Just plain ol' Michael."

"Oh, go fuck yourself," Cram snapped.

"I'd ask for help, but I hear you're too busy with Michael," Dodd said, drawing out the name. He batted his eyelashes.

Cram rolled his eyes, but the blush was evident in his face. And his throat. Dodd grinned and took this as confirmation of the latest rumor that the Bishop of Orsini was taking late suppers with the notorious Walter Cram.

Lex snorted, but was too busy with his jam tart to say much. Finally, though, Lex decided it was time they were all professional again, which was disappointing, as Dodd was hoping to get details from the mage. "Let's start with us, our friends, and then work our way out. So, Cram, where were you the day the demons attacked Borro Abbey?"

Cram shot Lex a dirty look. "Fine, we can do it this way, but I'm telling you right now that mages aren't going to answer questions like that from the likes of you two."

"That's why we have you," Dodd said.

They finished their meal first before the threesome of friends—yes, Dodd had to accept they had probably adopted Cram like some kind of lost kitten—relocated to Cram's suite.

And yes, suite was the proper term. Cram had been moved four times since arriving at the Cathedral, and finally the powers that be decided the safest place for him was deep within the Cathedral, past the barricades that kept the rabble from wandering the halls. Up on the eighth floor of the main Cathedral. Cram didn't have much of a view beyond that of the bell tower and he didn't have a veranda. Still, Dodd whistled.

"So this is the new room, huh?" Lex said, spinning in a circle and taking in the suite. "I'm still sharing bunk beds with Dodd."

Cram dropped his basket in the corner behind the door before heading over to one of the two desks that were pushed together under the large, glass window that dominated the wall. Both desks were piled high with scrolls, letters, and ledgers. While Cram dug around his desk, mumbling about how "it was here somewhere," Dodd had a bit of a snoop.

Cram's suite was a long, fairly narrow room, but the servants had managed to make a sitting room at the front by installing two sets of accordion decorative screens. Dodd poked his head beyond the first set to see another in front of what appeared to be a dais for the bed. He couldn't quite see because of the privacy screen.

He *did* see a shirtless man further into the room, bent over to grab something off the floor. Dodd jerked his head back; his mother always said his curiosity would get him into trouble some day.

Cram hadn't noticed Dodd, at least, and was seated with his back turned to him, having had found whatever he'd been looking for. He was chatting with Lex while setting up his writing implements and Dodd caught the end of it.

"Rainier said it was too much work protecting me, so they stuffed me up here."

"We're all stretched pretty thin after the attack," Lex said.

"That's what Rainier said. So if I'm here, they don't need a guard on me constantly to watch my every move."

Dodd stepped over to the window and rubbed the gauzy curtains between his fingers. Even Cram's curtains were better than anything in the barracks. "I think you meant to say if you're here, the Consorts don't need to be risking their lives constantly protecting you."

"No, I'm pretty certain I meant exactly what I said," Cram said.

Dodd had not expected to see Father Michael of all people step from behind the privacy screen. He'd heard the rumors, of course; everyone had. But he'd not recognized the shirtless man on the other side of the suite as the priest.

Dodd said rather too quickly, and a little guiltily, "Oh, hi, Father Michael. Walter didn't say you were here."

Cram made an annoyed sound. He always did whenever Dodd or Lex called him by his first name.

Father Michael smiled and gestured at the sofa. "Would I be in your way, my child?"

"Stop calling me that," Cram chided automatically, even though Father Michael was speaking to Dodd and not Cram. "If we are going to do this Lex's way, we need a list of everyone who was at Borro Abbey and then whoever was here during the recent attack."

"We should divide everyone up. Like, servants, refugees, townsfolk, whatever, so that it's easier to check later if we're missing someone," Dodd said.

"Good idea," Cram said, and he began writing on the tops of pages.

Father Michael smiled at them. He'd not sat down yet. "Shall I leave the three of you to your sleuthing?"

"Oh, you can stay, Father Michael," Dodd said.

"Bishop Michael," Lex corrected. "He's an extremely important person now."

The priest waved a dismissive hand at them. "No, I shall always prefer to be called Father Michael, even if the Lord God Almighty were to return to personally appoint me Holy Father. The Almighty desires humility and I shall never be one not to follow His will."

Cram stopped writing to glare. Following a dramatic sigh, he asked, "If you insist on staying, can you at least help us with the names?"

"Of course. *Lancaster.*"

Dodd had seen Cram angry plenty of times, but the irritation that crossed Cram's face was a new one. Enough so that Dodd felt almost sorry for him. "You know I hate that name. You know why. Stop showing off, and either help us or fuck off."

"Whatever you say, my child," Father Michael said sweetly.

Lex buried his laughter better, and so Dodd got the death scowl from Cram. Father Michael went to the second desk, clearly now explaining why Cram had two desks in his room. That second one wasn't in the old room, Dodd knew that. The priest began digging around for paper and pencils, and handed those out, all the while bickering with Cram endlessly.

When Dodd took a seat next to Lex, he whispered, "They bicker more than Pero and the pope!"

Lex gave a smug look and said, "I think this has been going on for a lot longer than the last couple of weeks."

"Since Borro? Really?" Dodd whispered.

"I'm just sayin', Cram is sure touchy about anyone asking him his whereabouts."

Dodd's eyes grew wide, and he sucked in a sound of glee. "I thought it was because he was afraid we'd accuse him of being the bastard mage who got us all into this mess."

Lex gave a knowing glance at the couple—who were clearly a couple in Dodd's eyes, seeing them here together for the first time—bickering about how the priest had his own room and why couldn't he go there during the day like they'd agreed.

"It would explain a lot, though, wouldn't it?" Lex whispered.

"Oh for the love of the Lord God Almighty, would the two of you stop whispering!" Cram shouted. He crossed his arms and glared. "I could be out there liberating mages and burning Cardinal Vittorio's estates down to the ground, but no. I'm stuck here with the Bishop of Orsini farting all night long and eating my food, and I don't need the two of you gossiping and whispering in my own room."

"To be fair, you were farting more," Father Michael said. He grinned at Dodd and Lex when he said it. "Allow me to go fetch you all tea. Some of you are grumpy today."

"That's because you were farting all night," Walter muttered.

"I believe most of the smell was from your own body." Father Michael stood from his desk and inquired if Dodd or Lex would want tea. They both agreed, and he said he'd see what he could find. "And I will see about writing desks for both of you. Surely there must be some to be found."

Dodd waited until the door clicked shut before he began the close interrogation. "Cram, what is going on?"

"None of your business," Cram snapped.

"Dude, seriously," Lex said. "You're sleeping with the Bishop of Orsini!"

WALTER HAD KNOWN it would eventually all come out, but he'd hoped to avoid it for a while longer. He'd been relying on the Orsini gossip mill to focus on Pero and Francois's marriage. Plus, with all of the reconstruction and constant relocations, and just the traumatizing after-effects, many people were sleeping communally for comfort and support. No one blinked an eye at it.

What's more, Walter taking this specific suite had been a blessing to others. It had three large glass windows that could easily allow one of the large, winged demons inside. Too many of the important people feared windows now. No one wanted this room, not even the footmen, who Walter insisted be offered the room first.

He took it with the footmen's blessing, and four of them happily move into his old, windowless room. If that gave them comfort, then he'd live in this unnecessary luxury. He was not afraid of windows, nor of the demons, nor of fire. What Walter feared, deep in the quiet parts of his soul, was not the fire, but the people who started them, who break the windows, who open the world to demons.

Now, he and Michael were living along the same corridor, inside the thick, wooden doors that had saved the lives of so many very important people.

Children, Walter reminded himself. The doors saved children.

At first, no one seemed to find anything odd in Michael being in his room in the evenings. They were neighbours. They'd spent the winter together at Borro Abbey. Everyone had been through a lot. No one should be alone. It was normal. No one gossiped.

But then, Michael decided to stay overnight, and the morning servants saw him naked in Walter's bed. He probably could have lived that one down if Michael had not decided to do it again the next morning. And the morning after that.

And then because that wasn't enough, Michael had the servants bring his desk across the hallway so that they could work together in the evenings.

"Well?" Lex prodded.

"It's nothing," was all Walter managed to say.

Lex raised an eyebrow and said, "It sure as shit doesn't look like nothing."

It wasn't nothing. Or, maybe it was. Walter didn't know. He leaned against the edge of his desk and sighed. He ran his hand through his hair, which desperately needed to be cut or he'd have to start braiding it. "We're just lonely."

"Right, but you're sleeping with Father Michael," Dodd said.

"Yes, I am aware," Walter snapped. He drew in a breath and said, "Why are you both giving me such a hard time? Neither of us can have a normal relationship, not right now. We've known each other a long time. He asked. I said yes. It's not a big deal."

He was confused by the glance that was exchanged between Dodd and Lex. Finally, it was Lex who spoke. "Listen, Cram. *Walter.*"

That's when Walter knew he wasn't going to like what these two were about to say.

"I'd take a sword in the guts for Father Michael, I just want to say that up front. But sleeping with a bishop, and not just some nowhere one but the fucking Bishop of Orsini, is asking for trouble." Lex sighed. "People in power don't like you, but a lot of that is because of what you represent."

"And you can be an annoying ass," Dodd interjected.

"Thanks," Walter said dryly.

Lex made a frustrated sound. "I'm worried that someone ambitious could use your reputation to...well..."

"Well what?" Walter demanded.

Dodd blurted out the point: "He might be using you to make cardinal."

Walter snorted. "He was only made Bishop of Orsini in the last month! Besides, he was already a bishop."

"Yeah. Bishop of backwater nowhere. Bishop of Orsini is *very* different, and you know it," Dodd said.

"I just want you to be careful," Lex said.

"We don't want you to get hurt," Dodd said.

Walter stared at the two children and he realized many things all at once. First, he was getting old. Second, he was making friends and he did not like that. Third, and most importantly, he'd already started to wonder if Michael had developed a taste for Cathedral life.

He was old enough to have been used before, and nor was he so innocent to think he'd never used someone himself, including when that involved someone warming his bed. And on both accounts.

So when he spoke to the two earnest, but young, people in front of him, he felt no anger, no shame, and certainly no remorse. "If Father Michael is able to leverage sleeping with me into getting him wrapped up in cardinal robes, then he absolutely deserves the position. Be it the one in the Cathedral, or the one in my bed. Now, are we done here? I want to get to work."

"You've taken all of the fun out of it," Lex said with a pout.

"Love is dead," Dodd complained.

"It died for me a very long time ago," Walter said. He realized after he'd said it that they probably thought he was talking about Ally. He was not, or at least, it wasn't what he meant. She was the last time he'd fooled himself into thinking he could make love and his life work together. He was older, and smarter, now. Love didn't exist for Walter Cram. "Lex, this was your idea. How do you want to run these lists of yours?"

Mentally splashed with cold water, they began working. The basics of Lex's list turned out to be complicated and convoluted, so Walter wrote notes on loose paper first, before adding to his journal, after Lex and Dodd corrected, commented, and complained as necessary. Consorts, militia, servants, guests, clergy. All the names they could remember, and a few whose names they couldn't recall but could describe.

Michael returned some time later with several servants in tow. Two carried a tabletop writing desk each, while two more carried small tables for the desks to be placed upon. Still two more servants carried a simple wooden chair each, and a final pair of servants carried food, an iron cauldron, and tea implements.

As the servants organized the items, Walter demanded, "Where am I to put all of this?"

Michael held out his hands, gesturing at the entire suite. "I have full confidence in the staff."

Walter grew angry watching the half-moon tables set up for Dodd and Lex. This was his suite. This was his space.

This was *his*.

Walter did not want to vent his anger at his friends, so he stepped over to the window under the guise of getting out of the way of the servants. He could not afford attachment, not to this room or to people. All of this could be snatched from him by nothing more than a low-level clerk. He should let them place the tables and tea pots wherever they wished, for this was not truly his. Men like him never ended up in such places, not permanently. Those like Walter Cram only ended up tied to bundles of dry sticks.

Michael stepped next to him, choosing to lean against the window frame. In moments like this, it was hard to remember he was a bishop, anointed by the Lord God Almighty, and all that rot.

When Walter didn't speak to him, Michael asked in a quiet voice, "Have I pushed too hard?"

Walter turned his head to look at the man who'd been sharing his bed too frequently. He had been too reckless, even by his own standards. He had always liked Father Michael's company. Oh, certainly, the man irritated the life out of him, and always had, but never, not once, had the man betrayed him. That counted for a lot to a man like Walter.

He could not say all that. Instead, he said, "Everyone's talking."

A snort escaped the priest. "I thought Walter Cram, demon lover and rebel mage, did not care about the opinions of others."

Walter glanced at Dodd, who was helping a servant pour a bucket of water into the small tea cauldron that now hung in the fireplace. "I don't like gossip."

"The Lord God does not like it when we lie, Walter." Michael's eye twinkled as he leaned closer to whisper, "You love gossip, my friend. You simply hate being its subject."

That made Walter burst out laughing, drawing the attention of the love birds, who were determined to waste the best years of their lives dancing around each other because it might ruin their friendship.

"Friends," Walter muttered. At Michael's questioning glance, he said, "Like anyone can be *just* friends anymore. Enemies. Lovers. Allies. Former lovers. Former enemies. There is a Lord-forsaken warzone outside our door, and they want to be friends. Who has the luxury of time for that?"

Michael smiled at him. "Those who aren't designing to die upon the scaffold?"

Walter sighed dramatically and said, loudly, "Now that we've refurbished my home, can we please get back to work?"

Lex and Dodd requested that Michael stay to assist with the list, and he clarified titles, rank, and added several other names to their list. However, soon they had to face the names of the dead and missing. When Lex started sniffing and Dodd's eyes were red and swollen, it struck Walter that perhaps this had been the reason to avoid the list in the first place. They all had to face the names of the dead now, and no one wanted to face even more grief with what had just happened outside of their doors.

He had already done such a list of the dead mages, for the pope's engraved plaque. He had not considered the others had not taken such an opportunity. He poured them tea and listened to their stories of the dead. It was the normal custom. He'd forgotten not everyone was as used to death as he had become. His wounds no longer oozed pain, but that was only because he'd built up so many calluses. He only shared when prompted, focusing instead on the culprit's identity.

Walter found that to be the more painful path. It was someone with unquestioned entry to so many spaces. Someone who faded into the crowd and never raised suspicions, no matter if they were in a dirty alley or the pope's dining room. And as loathed as he was to suspect Nadira or Rainier, or even Allegra, it had to be someone, and more and more, it was clear to Walter that it was someone he knew and trusted.

"Who has access to the Holy Father's rooms?" Walter blurted. At the confused expressions, he explained, "We never caught who drugged the pope's wine before the demon attack. It's connected. It has to be."

"Why does it need to be?" Michael asked. He didn't look up from his desk, where he scribbled away on a sheet of paper.

Walter paced between the sofa and the window, shaking his finger as he sorted through his jumbled thoughts. "We are searching for an individual with significant access, both at Borro and now here. That's how the pope's wine was poisoned."

"There is no guarantee those events are related," Michael said. He was still scribbling down names.

"I maintain whoever had access to his apartment would also have access to all of the places we found portals or demon markings," Walter said. He stopped pacing to stare at them. "Even if those two events aren't connected, following the trail to those with access would help us. I'm sure of it."

Dodd made a displeased sound. "I still don't think it's a servant."

"Maybe not, but I'm not comfortable accusing folks like us," Lex added. "Because, has anyone realized we're all the best suspects? Like, all of us in this room right this minute?"

Michael finally stopped writing and looked up. "My dear child, we all know it wasn't you."

"How can you be certain?" Lex asked. "It could've been me. I could've summoned the demons at Borro. I could've poisoned the pope's wine. I could be behind all of this. You don't know, do you? That's why I don't like accusing people of shit."

Walter scoffed. "Lex, trust me when I say, if you were a mage, we'd have known by now. You would not have had any control over yourself between your night terrors and the drugs they were putting in your wine."

"Oh," Lex said sheepishly.

Walter pointed. "That is a good thought. Yes. Wait, I want to write that down."

Walter hurried, took his seat, and moved his ledger. He began writing.

Regarding Lieutenant Lex: It is our opinion (Lieutenant Dodd and Walter Cram) that Lex could not be the mage in question. The high doses of sleep and pain additives would have caused any but the most experienced mage to lose control of their powers. No portals were found at any time in Lex's room or in Lex's immediate area. Lex was never alone from the journey from Borro Abbey to the Cathedral (as confirmed by Father Michael, Bishop of Orsini). Demon markings and open portals were found around Orsini while Lex was still under full observation.

"Is it necessary to use my full title?" Michael complained.

"You make it sound like I was dying," Lex complained.

"That is because you were dying for a while there, my child," Michael said.

Once satisfied the ink was dry, Walter put a ribbon marker in the book and closed it. "One of us should interview your guards and some of the sisters, then we can officially rule Lex out. It's just one person, but it's something. What do you think?"

Lex shrugged. "I'm happy to be ruled not the murderous mage, that's for sure. But yeah, I like this. It's something I can help with, too, especially when I'm not feeling so amazing. Which is right now."

"I told you to stop fighting Dodd in the streets," Walter said. "All right. Lex, you're in charge of eliminating me, Dodd, Rainier, and Michael from the list. You okay with doing that?"

"I wasn't even around the entire time," Dodd protested. "I was with you!"

Walter had no intention of accusing anyone unless he was absolutely certain and could prove it, and he wanted to ensure no one could accuse him.

"Dodd, your entire attitude toward mages makes you likely to be one of those self-loathing mages who live in secret and lash out at other mages. We'll need to investigate you further and rule you out."

Dodd glared. "I don't lash out at mages. Just you."

"I'm honored. You're still on the list," Walter said dryly. "How should we split up the clergy?"

"I can interview some of them," Michael volunteered.

Walter waited for Dodd and Lex to give their opinions on the matter, as Allegra had not given her permission to bring others into the mix, though it was probably assumed they would require the assistance of others to thoroughly investigate the situation. They did not seem to be bothered by Michael's offered assistance.

As the others talked out their plans and lists and such, Walter found himself scowling at the sofa. Not the people on it, but the actual sofa. His mind conjured up the fresh memories of that morning, and what the priest had started when he was sat there drinking his morning tea.

"Why are you scowling at us?" Lex demanded.

Walter needed Michael out of his life for no other reason than the distraction he was causing. "The three of you are getting on my nerves."

"We're just sitting here," Dodd said defensively.

"Oh, do not mind him, my children." Michael used that irritating, patronizing voice he often used whenever he was doing priestly things. "Our friend, Walter, carries many scars upon his person. I believe joy opens the wounds more than he'd like to admit. And I believe it hurts him knowing that we consider him our friend."

Hot anger surged in Walter's heart, so strongly that the papers on the desks danced. He glared at Michael, feeling nothing but contempt for the man who just dared to speak openly about *his* wounds. His nightmares were his alone, known only to those who had shared his bed. They were not meant for public display. He was fucking Michael, not confessing his sins to him.

"Walter!" Dodd shouted at him, now standing. "Walter, calm down."

The teacup on Walter's desk danced on its saucer, the expensive porcelain chattering against more expensive porcelain. He should steal the cups, and the silverware, and run from this place, and never return. The priest did nothing but stare back, calmly, without reproach in his expression. Not even a challenge was in his expression. That angered Walter more.

The teacup and saucer fell off the desk, but Lex caught them in time.

"Walter Cram!" Lex shouted. "Stop!"

Dodd shouted out his name, and then punched Walter in the gut.

Walter buckled over, gasping for air. With his gaze off Michael, he gathered his wits about him, even while unable to suck in a full lung of air. A hand pressed against his back, and Dodd apologized profusely for attacking him.

"I didn't know what else to do," Dodd was saying.

Walter closed his eyes and focused on the breathing. The tremble within him ceased, and the magic faded away once more to be locked away safely.

He stood up straight, put up a hand to separate himself from Dodd. "I need some air."

Walter turned his back to the protests, and he did not press a hand against his stomach, even though he desperately wished to. Dodd really could have pulled his punch more. He slammed the door behind him, catching the attention of several people in the hallway outside his room. Yes, they would all be talking about this now. It didn't matter. He had to escape from that room. The three of them could stay to work, or gossip, or summon the abyss for all he cared.

He gulped down his anger enough to head toward the closest passage, where he could take a shortcut straight outside, and avoid the main doors. He needed air, and wide, open spaces. And to not be near that fucking prying priest.

His secrets were his alone. They were not for sharing, and the damned priest knew that.

CHAPTER TWO

ONE LOOK AT Walter as he collapsed in the chair across from Allegra's desk told her all she needed to know concerning his mood. She let go of all expectation that she would accomplish any work and settled in for what proved to be a rather long monologue of complaints. Walter mumbled his way through all of his sighs and groans, until she got the sense they were soon approaching the true centre of his grievances. Her busy office was no place for whatever Walter needed to discuss next, and so she ordered everyone out. Servants and assistant-clerks alike all gathered their things and quietly escaped the room. Walter simply hung his neck over the back of the chair, as if he was awaiting the release of his head from his shoulders.

When the last person left the room and the door firmly closed behind them, she said, "We are alone now. What is the matter?"

Walter didn't change position. "I miss being chased out of town."

She chuckled. "Surely you are more comfortable than in some dirty, underground cellar hiding with a dozen mages who have not washed in months?"

More groans. "It does not feel like it with Michael stinking up my room."

"Ah. It is true, then?" He groaned more. That was confirmation enough for her. "I confess I'd have never guessed that one."

Allegra topped up her teacup. The delicate porcelain tea pot was wrapped in a thick, hand-woven cozy that clearly had magic woven into it, for it could keep tea warm for hours at a time. She had never considered such a project for herself and wondered if she could accomplish it. She would have to either knit or embroider cloth—she did not know how to weave wool—but with some small modifications and the time to concentrate and practice, she believed she could create such a magical item.

Unfortunately, she would require quiet and concentration, with hours free from distraction and terror, so she supposed it might be some time before she could create such an item.

She took two sips of her tea, allowing Walter the opportunity to offer up more complaints. However, when he slipped into little more than grunts and sighs, with little else by way of words, she decided it was time to dig. "I realize how inappropriate it is for me to ask this, but I must ask why *him*."

"I thought you liked him."

"Oh, I think Father Michael is a wonderful man. I would do anything for him, and I am delighted if he is so. I truly want *you* to be happy, though. He is not that much older than you to make the gossips to even take note, and he can offer you protection." She sucked in a breath, trying to bide time to choose her words carefully. "You do not need to stay with him if protection is your only reason. Stanton and I can ensure your safety. You do not have to...prostrate yourself if that is not your first choice."

"The dear captain should not be forced to babysit your former lover," Walter said. He tried to add bravado into his voice, but his expression faded to one of sadness. Then he looked her straight in the eyes, and the years of hardship finally showed in his expression. He hid it well most of the time, but not in that moment when he said, "Ally, I'm so lonely. When I'm with him, I don't feel so alone anymore."

That was a feeling she could understand well. She had had plenty of those nights when the cold and the darkness seemed endless, and her body and spirit cried out for the warmth and comfort of another human being.

Then Walter snorted. "Of course, after a few hours with him, I'm reminded why I've been alone most of my life. I don't like to share."

"Yes, I remember that about you rather distinctly," Allegra said seriously.

They broke into laughter. Nostalgia, memories, and all of the history between them was easier to talk about now. The past did not hurt as much as it had, and so long as they did not approach the sensitive areas, they could remain friends. She had never thought that possible but found herself relieved it had happened.

In a moment of honesty, Allegra admitted aloud what she'd never said before. "I would have married you if you had asked."

A sad smile crossed his face when he said, "What a disaster that would have been, for both of us."

"Indeed."

Then, a wicked grin crossed his face, and he said, "But what about the dear captain? What are your thoughts on marriage now?"

Allegra's stunned pause gave Walter all the arrows he needed, but he was kinder than he could have been. In fact, he was kinder than he would have been a year before. He just nodded his head, gave her a wink, and said, "I do worry that Rainier may be too polite to request your estate join his, so you might need to take the reins in hand for that one."

"My dear Walter, we were discussing you and the Bishop of Orsini, and not the handsome captain that openly shares my bed."

"Oh, I think I prefer to discuss the handsome captain right now," Walter said.

There was some teasing on that score before the conversation turned to demons, as was so often the case. "Now, tell me truthfully, for the cardinals will no doubt lob this question at me in our meeting, but why do you think there have been no demon markings in these last few days?"

"I truly do not know, though I have a theory," Walter said. At her prompting, he said, "It is rather suspicious, don't you think, that this person, or people I suppose, were at Borro Abbey and did what they did. Then, time passes, and the exact same scenario happens here. Now consider, what if the person doing this does not have control?"

"They, whoever *they* are, opened the portals near the gates, to attack Bonacieux's men. That shows control and purpose."

"True," Walter said, allowing her the point. "But what if they didn't know, or possess control, at Borro Abbey? Or, what if, depending upon their state of mind, they do not have complete and total control over their magical talents? Would that not explain the tiny portals we have seen, and also the large ones that were consciously placed?"

Allegra considered the questions, but remained dubious on the finer points. "I am aware, at all times, when I am adding magical properties to, let's suppose, a scarf or a pair of mittens. Would they not experience the same while walking about?"

"Have you ever added magical properties to your knitted items when you did not mean to do so?"

She recalled a terrible mishap. "I have added the incorrect properties, of course. That happens to everyone without personal control. But I confess I have never tried to knit or craft without adding magic. What about you?"

He shrugged. "I tried to help build a shed, and I caused the nails to sheer off. I cannot be trusted to build anything that is meant to protect people."

She was surprised by the sadness upon Walter's face when he said that. No, not sadness: vulnerability. She often forgot that Walter's bluster was an important cover for him, and his personality always went in that direction, but there was far more than just the showman in him. He must have seen great horrors in his life. No doubt he participated in several. She did not believe a man could see true horror, to put their eyes and ears to the sounds of evil and torture and pain, and not come out changed in some way by it.

After all, she had changed. She did not know a single person who had not.

"Don't look at me like that," Walter snapped. "I chose this life. I don't regret it. Not for a single day."

"You must have seen a great many horrors," Allegra said, ignoring his rebuke.

"Several were by my own hand," Walter said quietly. "And yet I have no regrets."

"Then I am happy for you," Allegra said. "For you are rare in that."

Walter scoffed. "Surely you have no regrets. All of your choices led you here, in that seat, and mine led me here, across your desk."

With that, the old friends fell into discussion that mixed the old and the new, the realities of now with the nostalgia of before. Allegra felt no attraction to him, beyond the memory of what she'd once felt. Recalling it always made her smile, both for the good memories—for, after all, she would not have stayed with him if there'd never have been any good moments—but also for how innocent she had been. Oh, life on the road with Walter would have been horrific and terrifying and, no doubt, would have led to amazing moments of the kind of frantic intimacy that only fear and survival could bring.

Allegra wanted to laugh at her young self, who thought Walter's passionate fire was the best kind of love. Perhaps for others, it would be. She grew out of that phase rather quickly and instead found herself wanting comfort and warmth above all else, and less of the passion and adventure of not knowing if one would be dead on the morrow.

And she had that right now.

But as most things went these last months, the spell of quiet reflection and thought ended with a door flying open and someone shouting, "Mr. Cram! Everyone is trying to find you! A portal has opened and we cannot find a mage to close it."

ALLEGRA SOON FOUND herself in a part of Orsini that she'd never stepped foot in before the demons followed her to the Cathedral. With each turn, the alleyway grew narrower and muddier, until eventually Allegra was forced to gather up her skirts to avoid ruining her hems in the mud and muck. In this part of Orsini, there were no children employed to keep the walks clean, for this was where those children lived. She frowned on that thought, and the stark inequalities of Orsini that she'd never noticed before.

They took a final turn and were confronted by a circle of men, armed with wooden planks, shovels, and other tools. Fear knotted her muscles, but she made a point to pull back her shoulders so far that even her mother would have been proud, raised her chin, and approached the gathered men.

She was in front, but she wasn't alone. She knew behind her was Dodd, Lex, Stanton, Walter, her guards Rahna and Martin, and a panting and gasping Imogen who'd rushed to catch up to them. She was in little danger, but fear did not care about facts. The part of her that knew she was an elemental mage would always fear a large group of armed men.

However, it was soon evident that the crowd had not armed themselves against her, but rather the small demons popping out of the hand-sized portal in the middle of the alleyway. Now closer, she could see splatters of gore on the men, their implements, and the ground around them. The memories hit her harder than the current scene, and she had to gulp down her tea and cake twice before she successfully kept her stomach's contents firmly in place.

Walter walked ahead to crouch next to the small portal. He eyed it, asked the men to not accidentally hit him, then put his hand down on the fissure, ignoring the rat-shaped demons crawling over his hand and forearm. A slight tremor shook the ground before Walter announced, "It's closed."

Allegra nodded, trying not to look at the ground and the mess about them. Even the mere thought caused her stomach to churn. She managed to ask, "Who found this?"

One of the men stepped forward to gesture for her attention. "That would be me, Your Ladyship. I was going about my business and I saw about a dozen or more of those little black mice with wings running along the street. I called out for help, and I grabbed a shovel."

"Are there no mages in this area that could have helped you?" Allegra asked.

"No one wants to say they're a mage nowadays," another man said. "They'll just be blamed for it. Except, I suppose, Her

Ladyship, and Mr. Cram there, who everyone knows saved our lives."

"If Mr. Cram says a mage is all right, then folks take his word for it," still another said. "He's the reason any of us are alive."

"A lot more than I helped protect this place," Walter said sheepishly.

"True enough, sir, but that's how folks see these things," said the man who found the portal originally. "So anyway, my wife sent our washing girl to fetch one of the Consorts, because we all figured that lot would know where to find a mage."

Allegra listened as Walter asked specific and pointed questions about the portal itself, whereas Stanton asked more general questions about the people who lived in the area and their occupations. Imogen sent Rahna to find a runner to get several of the mages who were with her soldiers outside the wall to come assist in sweeping for additional portals or markings in the area.

Lex and Dodd poked around, moving in and around a few of the nearby buildings to see if they could find anything, but the immediate area was declared clear. It took several more minutes to convince people to return to their homes and their jobs, and significantly more time to quell their worries. Finally, Allegra succeeded in getting people to break up the scene, and she asked her people to return to her office to speak in private.

They all held their emotions close right up until Stanton closed the door behind them. Tempers flared before Allegra had the opportunity to take her seat. She didn't interrupt them, allowing them to bombard one another with questions, accusations, demands, and general comments of despair. They all had worries and fears, and, like her, the memories of traumas of what they'd all endured only weeks before. A little spleen venting did a person good.

However, when the venting moved to arguing, she gathered their attention. They settled down enough for her to say, "I believe this answers Walter's first and foremost question."

Walter had been engaged with a heated argument with Dodd, but he managed to give Allegra a confused look. "What question?"

"This proves the mage is still here, in Orsini," Allegra said.

"It makes no sense!" Dodd insisted. "After everything, why start again? There's no army outside our gates. We're the safest we've been in months."

"I agree with Dodd," Lex said. "Why bother? There was no purpose in this."

Stanton frowned. "I believe the most important question right now is why would this person make such an insignificant portal, when we already know they are capable of destruction on an almost unimaginable scale."

When all heads turned in Stanton's direction, he continued. "I truly believe we need to know, without hesitation and with full certainty, that a mage, *any* mage, is fully aware of their magical actions. We need to know without any doubt that we are dealing with something that is conscious and planned."

Dodd snorted. "Does it matter at this stage?"

"I have been thinking on this point for some days now, and I believe it is important," Stanton said. "What if I did not know I was an elemental mage? What if seeing the portals open, attempting to close them, the entire frightening situation opened up a part of my abilities as an elemental mage that I am not even consciously aware is happening? What if so much as worrying or reliving the horrors of Borro Abbey causes me to create portals behind me as I walk, and I never know they are there because they are quite literally behind me?"

"Is that even possible?" Imogen asked.

All eyes turned to Walter, including Allegra's. She did not know the answer to that rather important question.

Walter, for his part, shrugged and said, "All the mages I know realized they were mages when puberty happened, but...Honestly, we know so little about magic, and what we do know is what the priests teach us. We all know how trustworthy they are."

"Well, you're sleeping with one, so they can't be all bad," Dodd shot back.

"So it's true?" Stanton asked. He looked at Allegra and asked, "Did you know about this?"

"He told me about two hours ago," she said just as Walter declared his love life was very much off-topic. She smiled and said,

"But, yes, Walter is right. His love life, as hypocritical as it is, is very much off-topic. Walter, how is your eyesight these days?"

Confusion spread across his face. "My eyesight has always been excellent."

"Good. Because I'm going to get you permission to go into the Cathedral archives. It's time we learn about the origins of magic."

CHAPTER THREE

IT TURNED OUT that most of the large, framed maps of Orsini were centuries-old originals that lowly Consorts weren't so much as allowed to breathe on, let alone destroy. However, Dodd turned on the roguish charm and successfully procured a damaged, decade-old map. It was missing a few buildings, but those were easy enough to draw in.

Taking this old one also meant it had already been framed and backed properly, allowing them to hang it on the Captain's wall. He'd had already left for his meeting with all of the big hats, but he'd finally relented and gave permission for his office to be turned into their little command center, as Cram did not want endless company in his suite.

After a fair amount of swearing, the map was successfully mounted on the wall.

"Now what?" Lex said.

Cram shrugged. "The map was your idea."

Dodd was too busy chewing a large mouthful of bread to do anything other than nod and point in Cram's direction.

Lex was tired of being the adult, but it was clear someone had to be. "The Captain suggested we indicate on a map all of the markings or portals we remembered, and add in notes and such from people. Like, maybe we could number them or something. Just so that the record is really clear if anyone wants to read it later."

"We're searching for trends? Today's portal was here." Cram put a finger on the location. He used the index finger of his other hand and drew an invisible line straight to the wall surrounding Orsini. "It's not on this map, but there's a guard tower right here. Now, if you follow the wall this way," Cram said as he moved his finger to the left, tracing the wall's edge. He stopped and tapped at a set of buildings. "Right there is a servant's entrance into the administrative building. That's where all of the deliveries come in. From there, a person with proper access and keys could snake their way inside the main Cathedral."

Dodd tipped his head to the side and stared. "Hey, see this? Just a couple alleys over. Isn't that where we found that barrel of dead rats?"

Cram shook his head, saying he didn't know for sure. Lex stared at the map for a moment before saying, "I think so? I don't remember if it was two alleys over, or three, but either way, what are you getting at?"

"I'm pretty sure that's the laundry right there," Dodd said.

Lex sucked in a sharp breath. The new laundry building hooked up to the administrative building so that the chambermaids didn't have to carry linens through the main corridors. "We need sewing pins and cloth right now."

Lex opened the door into the main barracks and called out to Calm Seas. She'd been working in the main barracks, sewing, so she had plenty of pins and cloth scraps in her repair kit to spare. She offered to pick them up some food, since she was under strict orders to walk as far as the outer wall twice a day for her health, and she'd not done either of her daily walks yet.

Lex's stomach gurgled at the thought of meat pies, but worried that it was too much for the injured girl. Her burns were still so raw. It was windy outside, and Lex didn't want the air to hurt her skin. Lex said so, as politely as possible.

Calm Seas offered a half smile. She pulled the gauzy scarf about her throat up over her head and tied it to cover her mouth and nose, providing a gentle protection from dust. "Honestly, Lieutenant Lex, it looks worse than it feels these days. The healers all say even the worst of the scars will fade, but that'll take a few years. It's just really important I don't scratch," she said. "The hair won't grow back, and my ear is messed up, but my face should heal well. Nadira insists I put lanolin on it before bed, and I have to use olive oil during the day whenever it itches, and that helps a lot. I'll be fine in the wind, I *promise.*"

Lex stared at the girl's hopeful expression and the desperate plea in her eyes to not be treated differently. Yeah, they sure as shit understood that desire. Lex let it be, handed over some coins, and instructed Calm Seas to purchase food for all of them, including herself. The girl handed over her sewing kit, grabbed one of the spare baskets in the corner, and rushed off.

Dodd waited until it was clear Calm Seas was out of hearing. "Should she even be working?"

Lex shrugged. "Didn't she have the fever, too?"

Cram nodded his head. "She wants to work, but no one will let her do regular duties, so Nadira has been trying to keep her busy without exhausting her. Otherwise, she'd be on her hands and knees scrubbing the floors, or so Nadira told Allegra."

"Poor thing has had a rough month," Dodd said. He glared at Lex. "At least her guts stayed inside her body."

"There's that," Lex muttered. The mention of guts made Lex's injuries burn and itch. That happened a lot. It was annoying.

Lex dug around in the sewing basket for scissors first, then separated various cloth on the Captain's desk to cut into little flags for the pins. While Dodd and Walter complained this was taking way too long, Lex said, "If we are going to have a map, then it's going to be a proper map."

"Lord God Almighty," Cram complained, "it's a map, not a children's school project."

Lex continued to make the tiny flags. "A map that will be done properly."

With a handful of miniature flags made, they all began marking the portals found before the main attack. Those were in yellow. Cram carefully pinned those into place. It was clear, even before Cram finished, that the portals were all within easy distance of the back alley servant entrances.

"As if someone was walking in and out, going about their business," Dodd said.

"And portals were appearing along that path," Cram finished the thought.

Lex did not like that conclusion, even if the evidence before their own eyes said otherwise.

Consort green was used for the day of the attack, and it took all three of them to pin the portals they remembered. It was soon a curious crisscross of the courtyard, as if someone was dropping portals as they walked. Then, Lex pinned a white flag for the latest portal. A different entrance than before, yes, but still near a back entrance.

The three of them stared at the map and all came to the same conclusion. It was just one person. One person going about their business, who could clearly blend into the background, unnoticed and unremarked. There were only two types of people in Orsini who could do that.

"I don't think it could be a cardinal. Folks would notice a cardinal walking around in the servant passages," Dodd mused.

Lex frowned. "What about a regular priest or one of the lower clergy? Or one of the clerical staff? No one would even notice them."

"I suppose, but I still think it's a servant," Walter said. "Otherwise, how did the pope's wine get poisoned? And why are they using a different alley now?"

"I don't have an answer to that," Lex admitted.

"Because everyone's been moved," Dodd said as he pointed at the map. "Think about it. The last small portals were all around the same entrance. Now, this one is near a new entrance, but same thing. I'd bet you real coin that we'll start seeing more of these tiny ones popping up in that area over the next few days."

"What if we got a map of the Cathedral, too? Like the entire floor plan, every level? That has got to exist, right? We might be able to follow where this person has stayed. Or works, or something," Lex said.

Cram crossed his arms and stared at the map for a moment before nodding, "We need to find the paths and routes, see who is able to move around in these areas. Then we'll find our mage."

"Assuming the mage knows they're a mage," Dodd said with extreme skepticism in his voice. "That can't be a real thing."

Lex nodded their agreement. "I don't know how you could go your whole life and not know. You'd think, eventually, a person would figure out everywhere they go, there be demons."

"I don't know," Cram admitted.

"Assuming this theory is right, and I'm not saying it is," Lex hastily added, "is it possible the person knew about the big portals and is aware they're making those, but, I don't know, their mind wanders or they're stressed or something and...Okay, Lex, think this one through. All of the small portals make no sense if done on purpose. They are crumbs leading us to the bread thief."

"Just like that barrel!" Dodd said. "The rats were dead because someone tried to hide the evidence of drugging the pope's wine. Why make portals next to the evidence?"

The silence said none of them liked the answer to that question.

IN ALLEGRA'S ESTIMATION, there were only minor differences between the old gathering of cardinals and this new one. They fit in Rupert's dining room, allowing them to be fed from his table. She was the Contessa of Marsina, so she was well acquainted with the comforts of a full stomach, but the meals at the Holy Father's table were well beyond even her usual fare. This was what Rupert declared to be a simple, working meal, as there was only one course. However, that one course had seventeen dishes, not counting the tea and wine service that would come afterward, nor the platters of small morsels that would arrive in two hours.

Allegra paced herself throughout the meal. There was rice in saffron with herbs and fruit, mushroom and spinach pie, sardines, beans in white sauce, smoked fish, gnocchi with smoked olives, roasted pork belly...she couldn't see the dishes on the other end of the table, which never made it up to her. Her curiosity was disappointed, but her stomach did not care, as she was stuffed within half an hour despite her best efforts.

Allegra had not yet informed anyone of her plans to allow Walter into the archives. However, she expected no opposition beyond the usual complaints about Walter, so she simply added that she had a request beyond the list in front of Rupert, and that was that. Hers would be near the end, as they first had to sift through the dull, but important, necessities of Orsini life.

They continued to work and eventually the dinner dishes were cleared away, and soon arrived silver platters piled with cheese, nuts, jams, pickles and preserves, twice-baked seedy flat breads, and fruit. Most of the fruit was dried, but there were some fresh strawberries on the platters as decoration. Allegra helped herself to a small plate of assorted goodness and accepted both a cup of tea and a glass of wine from the footman.

One of the most important issues on the agenda was the shortage of healing items. While that was no surprise, given the injuries as of late, the clergy who made the healing items were collectively exhausted. This, coupled with worries concerning their own members who'd been injured in the recent attack, resulted in new items of inconsistent quality.

Cardinal DeLancey spoke to the topic. "It is my opinion that we must stop the distribution of all magical items to any but the most grievously injured or sick. This will allow our people to rest and recover their wits, so that they can rebuild our stockpile of healing items."

It was Francois that spoke in reply. The voice of authority, and not the voice of the man she knew underneath the robes. She missed Rupert, her friend, but pushed personal feelings aside. For now, this was the business of saving lives. "Our stockpile was enough to sustain Orsini for years. Surely that is still accurate."

DeLancey shrugged. "That was true before the arrival of demons. Now, between Borro's destruction, our own attack, and the Cartossian refugees, our reserves are dangerously low."

"We should keep the supply for those of most importance," Cardinal Vittorio said.

"My troops are important, Your Grace," Imogen snapped.

That particular argument went on for twenty minutes before resolving. The group sided with common sense and not rank or birth, and Cardinal DeLancey was assigned the task of giving the entire Magical Crafters Guild ten days to do with as they will, be it quiet reflection and prayer, or even sleep.

The old cardinal sighed and said, "We should also make allowances for those who will celebrate their survival with drunkenness and debauchery. Captain?"

Stanton smiled at her and said, "Your Grace, I will let the Consorts know to keep an eye out for Brother Strozza."

"And warn them about Mother Isolde-Ysmaine," DeLancey instructed. "She has not been herself since she discovered demons were indeed real."

"Are any of us the same?" Francois asked.

Devonshire scoffed. "Some of us always knew demons were real."

"I confess I screamed the first time I saw one," Allegra said.

The wine and spirits making a second pass about the table, as demons were a topic that required extra fortifications to the spirit. This led to the ongoing argument concerning the lack of free access to the Cathedral's wine cellars. The clergy may have taken vows of poverty, with no wages drawn, but there was no vow of starvation and destitution, as Cardinal Giso pointed out thrice in as many days. A vow of poverty, he argued, was a philosophical vow not to use one's position in the church to enrich one's personal wealth.

It did not mean, Giso argued, cutting off the free supply of brandy.

Allegra took a sip of her excellent wine and said, "Come, now. We must all make sacrifices."

The undignified snorts and groans made her chuckle into her goblet, and she nearly spilled some of the precious and rare liquid. She pulled the glass away and covered her mouth as she laughed. "It is true, though!"

Cardinal Reinhold gave her a sour look. "Your Ladyship, please pardon this rebuke, but what sacrifices have you made? You are richer than any one person in this room, perhaps excepting Her Highness and Captain Rainier. You can afford whatever you wish, and the world will jump to make it appear before you."

"Oh, that is not true," Allegra said. "Or fresh strawberries would appear in January."

"As I understand, your estate has a heated greenhouse that produces strawberries in winter," Rupert said dryly. Definitely Rupert, and not the Holy Father, was speaking there.

"Hush," Allegra said. "I at least did not grow up royal."

Imogen scoffed, and the Ginny of their childhood antics came shining through. "Oh, *please*. I'm the youngest! I'd have to marry my own brother to be as rich as you."

"We do not approve of that in Serna," Devonshire said sternly, but Allegra could clearly see the twinkle in the old woman's eye.

"Why is everyone staring at me?" Stanton demanded. When no one answered beyond a few chuckles, he said, "I may outrank Allegra, and, true, I have both a job *and* an estate, but I know she is richer than I shall ever be."

"You'd have to marry her to be as rich as her," Ginny offered up in a rather sweet tone. The mischievous grin gave her away, however.

All heads turned so that the crowd gathered could observe the blushes upon her and Stanton's faces. They were rewarded when they turned to face Stanton, for his face grew flushed with a noticeable sheen on his forehead.

They were disappointed when they did the same to Allegra, however, for she did not even feel a slight change in warmth upon her skin. She was long hardened to such clumsy attempts at matchmaking, and she was never embarrassed by her wealth.

"My dear Ginny, surely you must know me well enough that I would never marry unless my wealth was protected against any husband. That is how I weed out the undeserving." Allegra popped a miniature pickled onion into her mouth while smiling at Stanton.

His only response was to roll his eyes, but the blush had most definitely progressed to his ears now.

Devonshire grumped and said, while looking directly at Stanton, "With your charms and estate, Your Ladyship, it is a wonder how you have remained unwed."

"Perhaps it's because the men have met her," Rupert said. Oh, not the Holy Father, but her childhood friend who knew her too well. When the laughter—and a few protests—died down, he said,

"Men are smart enough to know not to get involved with that one."

"Pish," Allegra said. "Walter Cram just told me today he had considered marrying me at one point."

No one bothered to hide their disapproving groans, but it was Vittorio who said, "Thank the Lord God Almighty that man used the sense he was born with and did not ask."

"You assume I'd have said yes," Allegra said.

"Be all that as it may," Giso said, raising his voice a little over the laugher, "we were discussing the wine cellar."

"Cardinal Giso," Allegra said, still smiling. "We have discussed the wine cellar every single for day for last two weeks. We require the wine, the brandy, and all of the decent spirits for medicinal purposes."

"The sick do not need the good wine," Cardinal Giso said. "They're sick! They can't tell the difference."

"Giso, the only wine we have is the good wine!" Francois said. "Buy yours from the merchants."

Giso harrumphed. "I went into the clergy as a blessed calling to do good for the Lord God Almighty. I did not do it to spend the precious little money I have on drinkable wine."

"Your father was a viscount," Vittorio exclaimed, rolling his eyes.

"A heavily indebted viscount!" Giso said, not bothering to regulate his tone.

"Gentlemen, this gets us nowhere," Cardinal Devonshire finally said. "Your Ladyship, I understand you had some business to present. Pray, do so in this brief moment of silence. Lord God knows there might not be another."

Allegra smiled, and did not turn it into a smirk at the muttering Giso. She detailed the demon portal from earlier that morning. She'd not had the opportunity to tell them before now, so was pleased to inform them no harm was done.

"Will we ever be rid of these cursed things?" Francois demanded.

"How is a man to sleep in his bed at night knowing at any moment demons may rip his face off?" Cardinal Tommo added helpfully, who'd been too busy eating to have spoken up before now.

This led Cardinal Neri, the newest member to the senior cardinal ranks, second only to Tommo, to speak. Cardinal Vanida's removal from all political influence within the cardinal's innermost circles had created a void, and someone was needed. Allegra would have preferred just about anyone instead of this rather young man, who happened to be the son of an influential earl who was friends with Vittorio's wife. She braced herself for the bravado that came every time the man opened his mouth. "Come now, my dear Tommo. We are not frightened women who cower in our beds. Brave up!"

Allegra and Ginny both stared at each other, eyes wide in shock that such a thing would be uttered. It was clear one of them needed to speak, but both had been stunned into silence by the inappropriateness of his statement.

Cardinal DeLancey smacked Neri's bare knuckles with her cane. He pulled his hand away, outraged that she would strike him.

"You are fortunate I did not hit your skull to rattle the common sense loose," DeLancey said. "How dare you speak of women as cowards? You were not even here when the Contessa limped into our courtyard, or when Her Highness arrived covered in blood. And where were you when mages fought and died in the courtyard? Cardinal Tommo saved the lives of eighteen children against the demons! Our own Contessa saved the life of Cardinal Rigi, and held ground against the demons while he and the healers moved the sick to safety. She saved the life of her own servant against a demon's attack with her own bare hands! Did you know that? Her bare hands!"

Cardinal Neri flinched. "No, ma'am, I did not."

"Of course, you did not, for you were too busy wailing in the ballroom about how the end was upon us! How dare you abuse the name of woman? How dare you, sir!" DeLancey swung her cane again, narrowly missing Neri's head. "You will apologize this instant!"

"I apologize!" Neri exclaimed. "Lord God, I apologize!"

"As you should," DeLancey said, finally setting her cane down.

Allegra and Ginny shared significant glances, while Stanton was very much trying to hide his laughter behind his hand.

Cardinal Devonshire cleared her throat. "Violence against one of our own is not tolerated, Cardinal DeLancey. However, neither are such disgusting comments, Cardinal Neri. Do I need to bring either of you before the censure board or shall I consider this resolved?"

DeLancey glared at the young man, and Allegra did not fault him for cowering. Neri, for his part, meekly said, "I spoke out of turn."

Devonshire stared at DeLancey, who sighed and finally said, "I did not mean to strike the young man so forcefully in my blind rage in the defense of my own sex."

It was Allegra's turn to join Ginny and Stanton to hide her smile behind her own hand.

Finally, the crowd settled down again, and Allegra got to the point, for fear that a full-fledged brawl would break out if she lingered much longer. She explained Walter's theories and then said, "I believe the best course of action is to investigate his theories. We know so little about the origins and history of magic. I wish to have Walter Cram granted special access to the entire Cathedral archive. I believe..."

Allegra did not get to finish her sentence. DeLancey, Devonshire, and Vittorio all shouted, "No!"

Not protested. *Shouted.*

Allegra had not expected it, and it took her a moment to recover enough amid the ensuing argument to even so much as raise a disapproving brow. She did not want to display her confusion, but she also could not help it. She'd expected some disagreement, but shouting?

"I apologize for raising my voice, Your Ladyship." It was Vittorio who finally spoke, though he glanced at Devonshire, who'd raised her own voice just as much, though his deep tone echoed the loudest through the room. "We cannot have someone like Walter Cram wandering around the archives."

Giso shrugged. "I can't stand the man, but what is he going to do down there? Steal a book?"

"He cannot be trusted. There are rare and sacred texts in the vault," Devonshire said.

Allegra was about to launch a defense of Walter's honor, when Rupert interjected, "Vault?"

A wall of silence fell over Vittorio, DeLancey, and Devonshire, while the rest of them exchanged confused utterances.

"Someone answer me, please." He used his pope voice, the one that made him Francois.

The three conspirators—for that was exactly what they appeared now to Allegra—exchanged significant glances. Entire conversations were had without a word spoken, of that Allegra was certain. Francois repeated his question, only not so politely, and Devonshire was forced to answer him.

"Not everything is necessary for the Holy Father's ears and eyes."

Allegra raised an eyebrow at Giso, who shook his head and offered a small shrug. He turned his attention back to his fellow cardinals.

Francois put his cup down and squared his shoulders. In a stern voice, he asked, "Excuse me, but did you just say to me that you keep secrets from the Holy Father?"

"Yes, a great many," Devonshire said with no shame. "I have kept many secrets from the previous two Holy Fathers and one Holy Mother. Some of us are the keepers of secrets, so that you can perform your duties without complications."

Cardinal Tommo said, "But they're just books?" When no one replied, he repeated, "They are only books, yes?"

"There are books in the archive vault that are not meant to be read," Vittorio said.

"All books are meant to be read," Allegra said.

Vittorio and DeLancey both turned to Devonshire, and then both nodded at her. Francois demanded to know what they were not sharing.

Devonshire inclined her head and said, "There are materials in the deepest archives, in the secret vault that only some of us even know exist, and fewer still know the contents. We three, and the senior archivist, are the only people in all of Serna who know what is in that vault. And, forgive me for what I am about to say, Your Ladyship," she said to Allegra, "but we all know your Mr. Cram. His curiosity would not be sated until he has gazed upon every speck of dust in that library. Then, the archives. And then, finally, he would discover the vault even without us telling him of its existence, and what he would discover there would do nothing but confuse an untrained mind."

"What is in there that's so worrisome?" Stanton asked. "Pardon me for dismissing your worries, but as Tommo just said, they are just books."

"No, Captain, they are not *just* books," Devonshire chided. When it was clear that was not good enough for the assembly, she blew out a frustrated breath. "The archives contain letters, items, and writing from the earliest days of our history."

"Walter will be careful, if that is your concern," Allegra said.

Vittorio scoffed and muttered, "That is not our worry."

The Holy Father had not heard Vittorio or had chosen to ignore him. "Setting aside for a moment the concerns expressed, I do not understand why he is not permitted there under special permission or circumstances. What are the rules for admission? For example, am I allowed in this vault?"

The silence that followed his question was rather telling.

"Well?" The longer the answer didn't come, the angrier Francois grew. Finally, he demanded, "I await an answer."

"It is complicated," Devonshire finally said.

Allegra had been watching the glances between the three senior cardinals. She interrupted Vittorio to say, "I find it very curious that the three of you did not ask why I requested Walter to have access. Cardinal Giso did. The Holy Father did. Cardinal Tommo asked what harm could come of it. But not you three. You clearly know what Walter might find, so what is it?"

"Things beyond his comprehension," Devonshire said.

Allegra turned to DeLancey, awaiting her justification, but the old woman merely ignored her. Allegra only found scowls and disgust reflected at her from Vittorio. "Well, Your Grace?"

After some stumbling, he clearly said the first lie that came to his mind. "I do not want Mr. Cram stealing something for his own profit."

She scoffed.

"That still does not answer my question," Francois said, his voice still raised, and his face still flushed. "Am. I. Allowed. There."

It was DeLancey's turn to smooth the argument. "Of course, Your Radiance. However, consider, with your many burdens, it would be an unnecessary waste of time for you to browse musty, dirty books when there are so many demands on your time."

Allegra knew Rupert well enough to recognize the look on his face. *Francois* did not argue the matter further, but that did not mean the man underneath all of those robes and titles had changed that much. She suspected she'd hear of the Holy Father's archive tour within the week.

Devonshire had begun to dismiss the assembly, when Francois raised a hand. Everyone stopped moving about in their seats. Finally, he spoke and Allegra worked hard to keep any expression of smugness off her face. "Walter Cram is granted full access to the archives. Please inform the archivist that an assistant is to be with our rebel mage at all times, to protect any vital documents."

To Allegra, he turned and said, "What do you hope to find there that will aid us? We can inform the archivist of any specifics to facilitate the search."

She contemplated lying, if only not to create more issues, but she decided for the truth. She spoke to Francois, not to the others. "I wish to learn about the origins of demons and elemental magic so that we—"

She did not get to finish her sentence.

The uproar was immediate. Allegra hoped her wince did not show on her face when DeLancey rapped her cane against the nearest table leg. She could not argue properly against the protests for she did not know what was truly happening.

"Granted," Francois shouted over the noise, which only caused more argument. He allowed it to go on for only a handful of seconds before he cut the air with his hand. "Enough. I will personally instruct the archivist to provide myself and Walter Cram a tour, and then I shall grant the necessary approvals for him to have full access as *my* representative."

"You cannot possibly suggest that we let a demon summoner like Walter Cram into our most sacred areas," Vittorio demanded.

"Walter is not a demon summoner!" Allegra snapped. She had not meant to raise her voice, but Vittorio's accusation could get a person killed, and she would not sit in silence.

"Do you have any evidence of Walter Cram summoning demons?" Stanton asked, cutting off all others who waded in to argue. At Vittorio's glare, he said, "Then, Your Grace, with all respect, I recommend not accusing an innocent man of murder."

"Enough," Francois said. "Good God Almighty, enough! Can anyone in this room tell me what Walter Cram will find that is so earth-shattering, so shocking, so rare that it warrants all this argument?" When no one replied, he said, "I see. So either there is nothing there, or it is something you do not want *me* to discover. In either case, I've heard your protestations and I have made my decision. I shall personally communicate that he has access, and I will be shown this mythical vault."

Devonshire sighed and said, "I suspect allowing Mr. Cram access to the general archives will do no harm."

"Allegra, please have Cram speak with my secretary to arrange this," Francois said. "Actually, I shall arrange it with Warin. Sent Cram to him. I do not want complications."

Allegra nodded. She didn't even speak, knowing that was the best course of action. Her oar was not needed in this river. Though she could not help but wonder what in the name of the Lord God Almighty was hidden away that had three of the most senior cardinals terrified of one rebellious mage who, most likely, wouldn't be able to read any of the aforementioned texts.

More protests arose and Francois made another cutting gesture with his hand. He was standing now, glaring down at the table's occupants. "Do not forget who holds ultimate power here. Do not push me on this."

CHAPTER FOUR

"I HAD NO idea you cared so much about the origins of magic," Stanton said.

The day had been hectic, and it was dark before Allegra and Stanton had the opportunity to sit down together. They were both reclining on the sofa in Allegra's drawing room, snacking on smoked olives and roasted nuts, washed down with a previously-opened bottle of good wine. Despite the heat outside, her suite was rather damp, so she had a small fire going. She was wrapped in her dressing gown, with her thin sleeping shift underneath, feet tucked up close to her so that they were covered in the folds of cloth. She contemplated a blanket.

"I didn't, until Vittorio turned the hue of beets," Allegra said.

"I thought he was going to drop dead on the spot," Stanton confided.

He'd already shed his trousers due to the "stifling heat" of the fire. His tunic strings hung loosely at his neck and the hem of the shirt struggled to cover his thighs. He balanced a book in one hand and his wine glass in the other. He'd said he wanted to forget the day and read, but he finally snapped the book shut and put it down on the end table.

"What do you hope Walter finds?"

She'd been reading a letter from her brother. No bad news, just the usual brotherly worries without him actually saying he worried about her. Because brothers didn't worry about their older sisters.

Never.

"I have no idea. Honestly, I had been grasping at all possibilities in hopes we would find something, *anything*, about this sort of mage. However, the more I consider their reaction, I find myself thinking there must be something in the archives that clearly someone like Walter should not know. And, now that my curiosity has been roused, I want to know it all the more."

Stanton offered up a grunt before asking, "Can Walter even read the old books? There must be documents centuries old."

"I doubt it. I'll speak with Nathan in the morning. I'm certain he will know someone who can read the language."

"Surely the archivists could."

Allegra let out a long sigh and tucked her feet in tighter. She should have risked another cup of tea, but she didn't want it to keep her up all night. It never used to, but now she was finding the tea stronger. Or, perhaps her system was growing weaker. "I do not trust anyone associated with the archives after today's spectacle."

"I hate to side with Cardinal Vittorio against you in anything, my love, but I would have some apprehension over Walter digging through my desk, let alone the most sacred texts of our age."

Allegra let out a good laugh at the thought, but the humor quickly faded. "There is something very odd happening that none of us truly understand. All I know is that they angered Rupert enough that he may order Walter to get to the bottom of whatever is happening there. Never mind my request. I can see him telling Walter to dig through every single scrap of paper in the entire archive."

Stanton tapped his fingers against his wine glass. "I cannot think of anything so shocking that the archivists or the cardinals would need to block the Holy Father, of all people, from that knowledge or...I cannot even fathom what could be so extreme or bothersome."

"What I know and have learned, and I believe this is the most important piece in this game, is that the position of the Holy Father, or Holy Mother in previous eras, is not the most powerful individual within the entire faith. They are the figurehead, and they are well pampered. But they do not hold total power. Devonshire does."

"And Francois outplayed her today. I suppose we need to watch for when she strikes back at him."

Allegra sighed. "Are you done with your wine yet? I have a chill I cannot break, and I wish to go to bed."

"Surely you do not need my permission to go to bed."

Allegra gave him a sly smile. "The sheets will be cold if I am the only person under the blankets."

Stanton downed the finger's worth of wine in his glass. "As my mistress demands. She who is richer than us all."

Allegra rolled her eyes as she waited for Stanton to adjust the fire screen and blow out the candles before they made their way to the bedroom. This was Allegra's second suite in as many weeks, but finally she was settled here. It was an L-shaped set of rooms, with its own personal bath off the bedroom, an incredible luxury only made possible because it shared a wall with the adjacent bathing rooms and the laundry below. She had not yet had the time to tour the water system, but Nadira had. She'd called it a marvel that must've ran on magic.

She considered taking advantage of her private bath, but decided to crawl under the blankets instead. The near-full moon allowed her to clearly see Stanton's outline when he pulled off his tunic to crawl naked into bed. She let out a little sigh of pleasure at the sight.

He extended his arm for her to snuggle in close. She did and pressed her cold feet against his warm calves. He cried out in protest and declared he would order Dodd to knit her thick stockings.

"Dodd can knit?"

"All of the Consorts can knit. Even me," Stanton said. "Lex made us all learn a couple years ago. He kept saying we needed to know how to sew and knit. I learned a valuable lesson that winter."

"How to knit?" Allegra asked.

"To never allow Lex to become bored."

Allegra laughed and moved her cold hands to press against his warm sides.

"Good Lord, woman! You are freezing. Here, cuddle in closer. If you die from a chill, Francois will burn me at the stake."

Her eyesight had adjusted to the dark and she glanced up at his handsome face. "I confess I eagerly welcome the change of life for perhaps I shall finally be warm."

Stanton's chest rose with his snort. "I am certainly no expert on the subject, but if the words of my mother, my aunts, and my eldest sisters are any help whatsoever, it appears you will still be cold during the change, only with humiliating bouts of searing heat and dripping sweat."

She sighed. She'd heard the same thing, but the idea of being warm was still intoxicating. "Don't take away my only hope to ever be truly warm."

Stanton kissed the top of her head. "I would be remiss in not mentioning the mood swings."

She soaked in his warmth and thought about the conversation at the cardinals' table. Not about the archives, though that nagged at the back of her mind. But rather about the conversations of marriage. She was proud she had not wilted under their gazes, but as she curled up against Stanton's naked body, basking in the heat he provided her cold hands and feet, she found herself wanting this for the rest of her life.

She could ask him what his own thoughts were on marriage. It was not a social taboo. Marriage was a business transaction for a woman of her rank. It wouldn't surprise him.

But she did not want this to be a note upon a ledger. She wanted this to be a love match, a choice to join hearts and not wealth. She wanted all of it. And it scared her that there was a remote possibility of rejection.

STANTON SUFFERED ALLEGRA'S cold feet between his knees until he was finally bereft of all personal heat and comfort. She insisted upon moving her freezing hands all over his torso until he pinned her hands in place against his chest and waited for them to warm up without them roving for any remaining warm spots on his flesh, sending his heart into shock with each new application of her icy fingers.

Of course, the close contact of his naked body against hers, with nothing but her thin sleeping gown between them, caused his heart to beat in other ways.

Then, he reflected on the morning meeting and his heart pounded for a completely different reason. She had not rejected the possibility of marriage. Specifically, marriage to *him*. She had been teasing, of course, in her own, protective manner concerning her estate. She was proud of her money, both what she'd inherited and what she'd earned herself. She was proud of her title, of her power, and of her independence.

He did not want a marriage of property. He wanted a marriage of equal minds. No matter how jokingly, no matter her grin, she'd laid out the path for her to accept him.

And he found her terms very agreeable indeed.

He did not care about her money. He had more than he'd ever need. He would sign marriage agreements that would allow her to keep control of her money, her estates, her title. Any and all of it. He would sign the papers to allow her to accept or refuse his title. If they were blessed with children at her age, he would accept whatever she wanted for them, be it titles or property.

He would give her everything for a lifetime with her cold feet.

He should just ask her. The worst that she could do would be reject him.

He had the gift already. Wrapped in brown paper and tied with a red ribbon.

He kissed the top of her head once more and she stared up at him, with her big, brown eyes and her sleepy smile. Her hair was already mussed from wriggling about in bed, contorting her body to ensure she stole every drop of his warmth.

"I love you," he whispered.

Indeed, the worst that she could do would be to reject him.

Her sleeping smile broadened, and she said, "You're just saying that because you want my money."

"My dear Contessa, no one woman should ever have as much money as you possess. You must learn to share."

She chuckled through a yawn and mumbled something but was already fading into sleep.

He should ask her, and soon. For only the Lord God Almighty knew what was to come yet, and he did not want regrets.

ALLEGRA PRETENDED TO drift off to sleep, for she did not wish to ruin this moment with discussions of wealth and property distribution. But she knew they would need to speak on the subject. She feared sooner rather than later, for she had no ability to see what was to come, but she worried for all of their lives.

She also wanted to be certain of him saying yes.

CHAPTER FIVE

EVENTUALLY, WALTER COLLAPSED gasping on his side of the bed. He'd sworn only a few hours prior that he was going to put a stop to this. Then the priest brushed up against him, and Walter discovered he lacked the willpower to turn down some fun. Heart pounding, he knew this was all a terrible mistake and one that he was absolutely going to look back on with regret. He also knew he'd roll over on top of the priest again if he were given the slightest encouragement.

Lord God Almighty knew that's how he'd ended up in this panting mess to begin with.

"You are uncharacteristically quiet," Michael said from his own pillow. While his breath was rapid, it did not have the wheezing nature of Walter's.

"I need to commit a crime or join the militia or something. I'm out of breath." Walter glanced over at Michael. "You're not even breathing hard!"

"I recommend a vigorous walk just before dawn. The fresh air does wonders for the constitution," Michael said. He reached over to intertwine his fingers with Walter's. "Are you still regretting opening your door to me?"

Walter let out a breathless laugh. "Give me an hour and I'm sure I will."

The priest laughed at that. Walter had no interest in leading anyone on. That was not his style, and he lived the kind of life that...he squinted at the stucco ceiling as the candlelight and firelight danced across it. What was he even saying? He currently lived the kind of life of the people whom he terrorized. He was in bed with the church, in all possible meanings of the word.

It was not shame he felt, that was for certain. Walter rarely felt shame, nor did he feel regret. He was not in love with the church nor the priest. He could not pinpoint the word that summed up the reason for his unease, but he knew there was one.

After a few moments with only Walter's pounding heart and gasping breath filling the silence, Michael finally asked, "So to the archives tomorrow? That is exciting."

The dizziness of exertion had faded, and Walter no longer had spots in his vision. All this sitting around in pomp with a full belly was not good for his stamina if there was to be another fight. Walter tipped his head and glanced at Michael. He couldn't help but smirk; it was affecting other areas of stamina, too. He should ask the princess if her troops could chase him through the woods as military practice. He was also going to ask Lex and Dodd to let him join in the sword practice.

"What are you grinning about?" the priest asked.

Walter took to staring up at the ceiling. "I have been sitting around this place for so long that regular meals and a priest in my bed seems normal."

"Do not concern yourself. Most still see you as the rebellious demon lover that you wish us to see."

Walter barked out a laugh and rolled over to kiss the priest on the mouth. It was easier to think of him as a priest, the Bishop of Orsini, one of *them* for it reminded Walter in every moment of the risks he was taking for sharing more of his life with this man. Complacency would get him killed. Walter knew that, with every breath he took, he knew that in his very soul.

That did not stop the heart and mind from growing comfortable. His joints enjoyed sleeping in a real bed, one filled with fresh hay and heather, with the ropes pulled tight underneath.

Part of him, the part that had been running for so long, ached to simply lay here until they came for him, to drag him away, to murder him in the courtyard.

He drew in a ragged breath, trying to ease his heart rate. None of this was real. If he grew attached to any of it, it would make running harder. He squeezed the priest's hand. He could not grow attached.

"I confess I am jealous of your tour with the Holy Father tomorrow," Michael said. "I miss my library at Borro Abbey. I had collected several original, banned manuscripts that I had not informed my superiors about. I suppose I do not have to worry about them being found now."

Walter recognized the sadness in Michael's voice all too well, but he did not know how to offer comfort. It was too close to caring, and he did not want to do that. "Are you saying that the holy and righteous Bishop of Orsini has kept secrets from the Holy Father? God Almighty, sir, do you not fear being struck down?"

Michael made a small, amused sound, but that was it. No laughter, no returning of the teasing. Instead, he spoke in a rather somber tone. "Oh, I fear my list of sins are such that the Lord God will see me severely punished long before he reaches the sin of secret books."

Walter turned on to his side and propped his head up on his elbow. There was enough moonlight, candlelight, and firelight to see the priest's features and the sadness in his eyes. "We have all committed sins, Father."

Michael groaned and rolled on his back. "I would greatly appreciate it if you did not call me that while we are naked together, *my child*."

Walter made a disgusted sound. "I hate it when you say that."

"And I hate it when you call me *father* when we are in bed."

Walter rolled his eyes and said, "Fine, fine. You win."

The good priest who wished to be called Michael when he was naked sighed and climbed out of bed in search of his dressing gown and the bottle of drinkable wine he'd purchased that morning. For a man who would not say on which side of fifty he walked, Michael turned out to be a rather trim man when the heavy robes finally came off. Perhaps the weight of faith kept the fat from forming around his middle.

Walter contemplated his own middle section and knew he'd soon have to face that Cathedral life was rather good for his digestion, but rather bad for his trouser measurements. Michael passed him a quarter-filled glass before searching around the room.

When asked, he said he was certain his dressing gown was on the floor, but could not find it now.

"Found it!" the priest declared. He wrapped himself up before stoking the fireplace's coals.

Walter sat up to sip at the wine. Far better than what was being served in the dining hall, which was nothing currently. "I should speak to Allegra and ask to draw a proper income. Serafina and Nathan keep giving me a little coin so I don't starve to death, but it's hardly fair that you are forced to purchase our wine with your own money."

The priest didn't look up from the fireplace when he spoke. He was busy getting the wood arranged. "Oh, I do not mind. I have a little money on hand and my vices are inexpensive."

Walter was grateful, for he had no money of his own and no legitimate means to earn any. The meager possessions he had were now somewhere in the abyss. Along with the body of a very young queen. Walter shivered with the thought and drank his remaining wine in one long gulp. He got out of bed, planning to pour himself a little more wine, when a knock came at the door. Michael waited for Walter's approval to open the door, being the most decent of the two of them. Previously, Walter had made Michael hide in the bed and once behind the curtains.

But there was no point now.

Michael did delay opening the door long enough for Walter to pull trousers over his private bits as a familiar voice echoed authoritative demands for the door to be opened immediately. Walter sighed, but gestured to let yet another annoying priest into his suite.

Walter managed to walk through to the main sitting room in time to say, as nonchalantly as possible, "Good evening, Rupert."

"Your Radiance will do."

"I like Rupert," Walter said.

"And I like you not living in my Cathedral, but we all have disappointments," the pope said.

They stared at each other with no further progression in the conversation. The pope was dressed in his full robes and glory, as opposed to a dressing gown appropriate for the time of night that it was. Walter was barefoot and bare-chested, shirt in hand, with the fucking Bishop of Orsini wearing nothing but a silk dressing gown.

Walter glanced in Michael's direction and asked, "Are you here to fire that one for fucking a demon lover?"

Choking coughs escaped Michael.

"What or *who* the Bishop of Orsini does in his own time is his business, no matter how ill-advised. No, Mr. Cram. I am here to escort you to the archives."

"What? It must be midnight by now."

"Later, in fact."

"And you want to go *now*?" Walter began hauling the shirt over his bare chest. He was all about pushing the limits, but even he was uncomfortable being half naked in front of the pope.

"My spies say there is a significant amount of activity in the archives, so I wish to get ahead of the mischief."

"Spies, Your Radiance?" Michael asked.

"Spies, secretaries, servants, whatever you wish to call them." The pope eyed Walter and said, "Put on your boots and let us go."

"Yes...yes, of course."

"Your Grace," Rupert said to Michael, "please remain here. Do not allow entry to anyone not of your immediate acquaintance into this room. Walter Cram, move your mage ass."

Walter was still struggling to get his suspenders over his shoulders as he shot Michael a worried glance. They were out the door in a few more steps, rushing down the mostly empty hallways, with Walter fastening the top buttons on his trousers. On their way to the archives, in the middle of the night.

Because that was completely normal.

THE SCENE IN his dining room had nagged at Rupert all day. There was something very wrong about the reaction to Allegra's innocuous request. The hesitation over his allowed presence bothered him, too. He was the Holy Father. If he was allowed into the lives and bedrooms of anyone in Serna, then surely he was allowed into a library within his own Cathedral. And, for all the protestations that he was a man of the Lord God and his vows of poverty and commitment, he did not fool himself: this was a position of power and authority. Anyone who blocked him from any space within his domain was challenging his orders and his power and his authority.

And if there was one thing Rupert hated, it was being told no.

He hadn't realized he'd not spoken to Walter Cram until the mage spoke up and interrupted his internal stirring of his own rage.

"Your Radiance? Listen. Don't penalize Michael for being with me."

It was too late in the night to bother with hiding one's emotions over something so trivial. He snorted. "Clearly, you are very new here if you think you are the first mage to be in bed with the clergy. You should ask Giso about the time troops dragged a wanted elemental mage from Mother Hunna's bed, when she was still a mere sister, and he was killed in the courtyard whilst resisting arrest. I fear you will not compete with that scandal, no matter what you and Michael do in private."

"Oh," Walter said.

"You sound disappointed."

"Well, perhaps a little. I used to have a reputation," Walter said.

Rupert smiled. "Oh, do not fret about that. Your reputation as a glory-hunting rabble-rouser is still very intact. If it helps sooth your worries, the current rumors are that you have enthralled the bishop using some form of magic, or that you are blackmailing him."

"Excellent," Walter said, sounding rather pleased that his reputation was not too badly hindered.

They turned the corner that would lead them toward the archives. The corridors were lit, and voices could be heard in the distance. Rupert turned to Walter and said, "Once inside, only I shall speak."

"I will attempt silence," Walter said. "Though, you should know the Lord God granted me many gifts. The ability to hold my tongue was not one of them."

"Indeed, I have heard the complaints from your neighbours," Rupert said sourly. Then, he paused his steps, just long enough to say, "I should not ask this, for it is none of my business, but how did that even happen? With Father Michael?"

Walter sighed and they continued their hurried pace. "We've known each other a long time and, well...you know how life is sometimes."

"Indeed, I do know about that," Rupert said. That satisfied his curiosity, and they continued the journey in silence.

When they arrived at the closed door to the archive, Rupert paused for just a moment. He squared his shoulders and shook out his robes to ensure his entrance was as regal as possible. He was trained to never think of himself as a monarch, and yet he was expected to project that aura of absolute power. This was his Cathedral. He would have his way.

He motioned for Walter to open the door for him. He'd expected a comment from the mage, but instead Cram merely inclined his head a fraction, and then swung open the door, stepped inside, and shouted, "The Holy Father, Francois. Bow."

It should not have surprised Rupert that the mage knew how to make an entrance. Items fell to the floor from startled hands. Others successfully held on to their possessions, all the while bowing low as he entered the room. Rupert did not wish to let his eyes roam about, but in his direct vision, he counted nine people gathering up items.

And, in the midst of them, he clearly saw a cardinal's robe.

"Vittorio," Rupert said with disgust. "What is happening here?"

"We are preparing the archive for Walter Cram's arrival," Vittorio said smoothly, without any hesitation. His face was flushed, though.

Rupert walked over to the nearest table to find a crate underneath it. He motioned to Walter, who pulled it out, ignoring the protests of several of the archives' highest-ranking clerical staff. It was mostly bundles of letters, the paper cracked with age and wrapped in ribbon. There were scrolls in the crate, too, clearly centuries old by the absence of true paper.

He pulled out a scroll at random and tugged off the ribbon, ignoring the gasps and cries that he could not touch the item with his bare, grubby hands. He unfurled the rather short roll and skimmed over it. He did not recognize the language at all.

"Please, Your Radiance! I beg you! Please, you cannot touch that without silk gloves!" one of the archivists said. He was an old man, with a shaggy, patchy beard and even more shaggy, patchy hair atop his head. "Please, I shall let you view the document, but only if you follow the protocols."

"Why are you packing these items?" Rupert demanded, still holding the unfurled scroll in both hands.

Vittorio spoke over the archivist's blathering. "As I said, Your Radiance, we were preparing for Mr. Cram's arrival. These items will have no value to Mr. Cram's research and we wished to move them to a secure location so they would not be damaged."

"Walter here says he has no intention of damaging anything," Rupert said.

"I assume neither do you, yet here you stand actively damaging that centuries-old document with your bare hands," Vittorio said. "Please, return it to the crate before poor Roul takes a chest pain and collapses."

Rupert considered ripping the sheet in half, but decided against it. A petty display of authority would not extend his control in this situation. Also, on a more practical level, he assumed the document was written on some form of fabric paper, and not modern paper, and tearing it would be akin to tearing at his own robes. The display of foolishness would indeed render him a fool.

He allowed the page to re-furl and placed it into the crate. He noticed Brother Roul's shoulders sink in relief.

"You will cease the removal of documents immediately. Walter Cram and his assistants will be allowed full and complete access to all items." He turned to the archivist and amended, "Using all necessary and established protocols to ensure the lasting life of our history, of course."

"Thank you, Your Radiance," the archivist said with a bow.

"Now, I wish to see the vault," Rupert said.

"Vault?" Vittorio stared at him for only a moment, but Rupert saw the glance of victory on his face. He'd known Vittorio a long time, and knew this was a move of power. "That crate before you is the vault. It is not a true place, merely a figure of speech."

Rupert knew Vittorio was lying to him. He knew it deep in his bones, even if he could not prove it. Vittorio had maneuvered himself into this position, waiting for his moment to strike. A rather simple request to have the mage investigate the history of demon portals had led to this moment. He did not know if this was merely a challenge of him as Holy Father, or if this was to protect some other form of power Vittorio held. Either way, it was a challenge, and he was not about to let it happen.

"Vittorio," Rupert said with full authority. "Send immediately for Rainier, the Contessa, and Devonshire. And I want some Consorts here, too."

"It is the middle of the night, Your Radiance," Vittorio said.

"Then I suggest you hurry," Rupert said.

Vittorio blinked. "Me?"

"Yes, or do you fear demons in the courtyard?" Vittorio glanced about the room, looking for someone of lower rank to send, but Rupert cut off the attempt. "Cardinal Vittorio, do as I have requested in the name of the Lord God Almighty. *Now*."

Vittorio left in a flourish of bows and fake smiles, leaving the confused archivists, Walter, and Rupert in the room.

Walter leaned toward Rupert and whispered, "What do we do now?"

"We wait," Rupert said, in a normal voice.

CHAPTER SIX

As A GENERAL rule, no one enjoyed being hauled from their beds in the middle of the night without a very good reason. From Allegra's perspective, there were precious few good reasons, and most of them involved fire or demons, or both. The pounding upon their door had startled them, and the poor servant was wide-eyed as she said Allegra and Stanton were both needed in the archives immediately.

Allegra could not find her heavy dressing gown, so wrapped herself in her thin one while draping an oversized shawl around her to protect against any embarrassing signs of a chill. She shoved her feet into knitted slippers, and waited for Stanton to dress. He'd been naked, so had to put on trousers, shirt, and boots.

Soon, they were overtaken by several Consorts, who all looked similarly dressed to Stanton. Interestingly, Lex and Dodd, who arrived a short time later, were suspiciously well-dressed in their best after-hours clothes and matching hats. Allegra had never seen these hats before: blue velvet that was so dark they looked black unless near candles, a wide band of red trim, with three brown feathers as decoration.

Allegra eyed them both and quirked an eyebrow. How did they even manage this? She was struggling to get gowns still, and they had an endless supply of fashionable hats.

Lex rolled his eyes and said, "We went to see the dancers."

"Why do you keep going?" They resumed walking as Stanton said, "You hate the dancers. You complain about them every time you go."

Lex sighed dramatically. "Work's been scarce for them since the entire demon thing, and I felt like I should support them or something. Ya know? Show of solidarity for the hard-working class."

"The drinks were on sale, weren't they?" Stanton asked.

Allegra covered her mouth to hide her laughter.

"All you could drink and eat for half a sovereign," Dodd said. "We'd not even gotten our money's worth before we got called."

"This better be important, is all I'm saying," Lex added. "No in-and-out, no refunds."

"We'd have to pay again to get back in," Dodd said. He was shaking his head. "Better be demons, and a lot of them."

They continued their trek through the Cathedral's mostly empty corridors toward the archive room. They had to pass through two sets of doors that were guarded. Allegra had never been in this part of the Cathedral at night and hadn't realized the doors were closed and locked at night. She'd always assumed they simply stayed open.

The guards commented on how busy the corridor had been that evening, and while Stanton asked who'd been by, an angry Giso joined them, complaining rather loudly that he'd been ripped from his bed for nothing but political nonsense. He'd not even bothered with any attempt to dress, marching down the hallway in his striped sleeping shirt, a nightcap, and a pair of slippers. Reinhold and Devonshire soon joined them from a side corridor, coming from the opposite direction. Reinhold made the effort to pull on trousers under his sleeping shirt and dressing gown, whereas the elderly Devonshire was wrapped similarly as Allegra, though in significantly thicker fabrics.

Allegra had no idea what they'd encounter when they arrived in the archives. Demons? Possible. Bonacieux's men? Unlikely. Assassins? Nothing would surprise her at this stage of the crisis.

Shouting echoed though the corridors long before they arrived at the archive doors. As they grew close, Stanton asked if that was Rupert's voice. Giso said he was certain Vittorio was shouting. Dodd swung open the double doors to the archive, though their arrival did nothing to dissipate the shouting.

Walter of all people was standing between Vittorio and Rupert. Around them were a group of archivists, if Allegra judged the robes correctly.

"Vittorio, for the love of God Almighty, shut up! You are not helping your cause here," Walter was saying. He caught sight of them and said, "There! There is everyone arriving now."

"Shut your mouth, you useless witch!" Vittorio shouted. "If I had my way, you'd be dead by now!"

"You will not utter that slur in the house of the Lord God Almighty!" Rupert shouted, and the nature of the library meant his voice boomed far louder than it ever should have.

"Do not raise your voice to me, you upstart, climbing, sorry excuse for a—"

"I will have your robes if you finish that sentence," Rupert shot back.

Walter turned to Allegra and said, "Someone stop this before I let them kill each other."

"Where is Devonshire?" Vittorio demanded.

The old woman stepped through the group, took one look about, and asked, "Is this why I was awakened from my sleep?"

"He brought that...thing...here to—"

Devonshire turned and walked away, motioning at Rahna to escort her back to her bedroom. Rahna glanced at Allegra, since she was her personal guard, but Allegra inclined her head by way of approval. She did not want to be responsible for the old cardinal falling and breaking a hip or her head.

"Where are you going?" Vittorio demanded.

"I shall speak to you on the morrow, at a decent time. Come, girl, give me your arm."

Vittorio blinked in confusion, before his face turned red with fury. "You're leaving? We have a situation here."

Devonshire did not so much as turn her head to look at him. Instead, she said to Rahna, "Come around. My left arm is stronger, and I don't want to fall. Giso has drank all of the good wine, and there'll be nothing left for me when they have to reset my bones."

Allegra could not make out Giso's exact words, but his mumbled backtalk was enough to announce he was not amused. She chose to smile inwardly only, for any display of humor was likely to set Vittorio off.

For his part, Rupert was happy to stoke the flames. "Is DeLancey not here? I summoned all of them."

Martin cleared his throat. "Cardinal DeLancey's maid said Her Grace was too old to be woken up in the middle of the night for...um...squabbling men, and the cardinal said she would speak to both of you when she was good and ready, and not a moment before." Martin glanced at Rupert and said, with a bow, "Your Radiance."

"Two-faced old bag," Vittorio mumbled.

"I'm sorry, Vittorio, what did I hear you just call the most prominent—"

"I called her a fucking old bag, Rupert!" Vittorio shouted. He lifted his hands. "Are you happy now? You are about to destroy everything!"

Allegra had nothing useful to offer to that proclamation, but she glanced at Walter, who honestly acted as confused as she did. Walter cleared his throat and said, "I have no intentions of destroying the library."

Vittorio made a disgusted sound. "You destroy everything you touch, you and that whore witch Rupert put in charge."

Allegra had already assumed she was the whore witch before everyone turned their heads to look at her. Stanton's expression turned hard, but she lightly touched his arm and shook her head. She did not need him to defend her. There would probably be a time when she'd need it, but not right now.

Walter and Rupert, however, joined forces to shout over each other at Vittorio, who now held a smug, satisfied expression that he'd finally struck a blow. Allegra contemplated a rebuttal, but Giso patted her arm gently before walking toward the warring priests. He yawned several times as he made his way to Walter's side.

"I shall take your place, my child. I must say, you showed extraordinary bravery here this night. Then again, anyone who has heard the tales of your heroism during the Borro Abbey attack, and again here upon our very soil, will know you are a man of great moral conviction, if a little too consumed by your own reputation."

Walter's mouth moved, but no sound came out. Finally, a smile flickered across his tired face and he gave the cardinal a quick nod of the head. He didn't leave Giso there, though. He just stood next to him, uncharacteristically silent.

Allegra had been in plenty of libraries in her time—her estate in Marsina boasted a large library of rare and historic texts—but this was different. This place held the accumulated work of centuries. It was not dusty, nor damp, nor dry. It had the exact perfect combination of temperature and humidity. She wondered if all of the ladders along the walls were used only by the archivists or if the servants were climbing up them to help control the dust.

Giso slowly surveyed the room and situation, ignoring Vittorio's protests for him to hurry up with it. Finally, on Giso's time and not Vittorio's, he said, "If I were to hazard a guess as to what has transpired here, I would say Vittorio snuck into this room with his flunkies. Oh, do not give me that look, Eunice. I know a flunky when I see one in the middle of the night when we should all be sleeping in our warm beds."

A woman about Allegra's age stepped from the shadows. She wore archivist robes, though she was not the head archivist, who was nowhere to be seen. Actually, as Allegra squinted to see the entire room, there were no high-members that she could see.

Giso was right; these were flunkies.

"Now, again, I will hazard the guess that His Radiance was up, dressed, and awaiting news from his spies. Yes, I did just call your servants spies and do not give me that sour expression, Rupert. It is too late in the night for me to care about dignity and court language. Then, Rupert here fetches Walter Cram because we all know he is no friend to the clergy nor the faith, with the exception of a certain bishop. Do not bother protesting, my child. He and I discussed it at supper earlier today."

Allegra had never seen Walter turn that shade of purple before.

Giso continued speaking into the stunned silence. "And now Walter Cram is here, backing up the pope, of all people, against Vittorio. Have I gotten the story correct so far, gentlemen?"

When neither priest made any movement to verify the facts, Walter nodded his head.

"I thought as much. So one of you thought waking the rest of us in the middle of the night would get themselves out of this mess, but clearly we've all been embroiled in Cathedral politics for so long that we can smell a dead rat in the middle of the night, when we could all be sleeping." Giso drew in a breath to continue speaking, when the boxes and crates caught his eye. "Why are all of these boxes out?"

"They were packing them when we arrived," Walter said. "It is what caused the argument."

Allegra saw all she needed to see. From the first argument in the meeting, she knew this was not about physical items, but all they kept talking about was the physical books and scrolls. However, staring now at this scene, in the middle of the night, with clandestine loyalists packing and hiding items, she had the sense that there was something in this room so shocking, so offensive, so revolutionary...

Allegra gasped audibly, enough to draw everyone's attention to her. Whatever was down here, somewhere in this organized mess, was the history of magic, mages, and demons. She was certain.

"I wish to clarify something," Allegra said, as all eyes were upon her. "To confirm the sequence of events, permission was granted by His Radiance earlier today to allow Walter into this room to read and research. And, upon your arrival this evening, you discover a small group of archivists and priests removing items out of Walter's reach. Is this correct?"

"That is exactly what has happened, Your Ladyship," Francois said, in his entire authority. His spine and shoulders were rigid, and he was genuinely enraged. "I am appalled that my order for Walter Cram to be given full access to the archives has resulted in the clandestine packing we see before us. Mr. Cram's research was an attempt to save us all from these horrific demon attacks. This is about our self-preservation, and I discover that there are those amongst us who will not, can not, it seems, follow the most basic of instructions to save themselves."

"I hate to interrupt, but where exactly were these crates to go?" Allegra asked.

No one spoke, either because they did not know, or they did not want anyone else to know.

"Someone answer the question," Francois demanded.

"The upper library," squeaked a young voice.

Everyone turned to find a small girl, still holding a scrub brush with a bucket next to her. She pushed herself to her feet. Allegra hadn't seen her until now, as she was in the far shadows of the archive room.

"Who are you?" Vittorio demanded.

"I'm the regular maid, Your Grace," she said without a trace of challenge or insult, and yet it sounded like both.

Allegra glanced about the room at the archivists, who did not seem overly concerned by the girl's presence. "What are you doing here? It's the middle of the night."

The girl did not raise her head. "The archivists do not wish me seen during the day, so I work at night."

"My child, step forward," Francois ordered. The girl glanced at the glaring Vittorio, and he said, "I am the Holy Father, my child. Obey me at once."

She did as she was told, her bucket and scrub brush still in her hands. She curtsied as best as possible.

"What have you seen?" Francois asked.

"I was already working when they showed up, but they did not tell me to leave, so I stayed to finish scrubbing the fireplaces. They said they were to move the items from the vault into crates and up to the upper library, where the witch would not find them."

"I assume I am the witch?" Walter asked.

"Actually, I think me," Allegra said.

Vittorio's smirk confirmed it.

"Child, is there a special vault here? Is it a real room?" Francois asked.

The little girl pointed to the bookshelf behind Vittorio. "Behind there."

Francois began walking and ordered the Consorts to watch the archivists to ensure nothing was touched. He pushed the shelf, and sure enough, it clicked and then the shelf revealed itself to be a door. Allegra followed the others into the small room with several candle lanterns, and two priests busy stuffing crates with items.

They froze.

"It appears I have found the limits of my own power," Francois said to the two priests. He raised a hand. "I have no patience for gibberish and lies. Tell me your orders at once."

The room was not quite the size of her suite, but it held so much more than just books. Floor-to-ceiling shelves wrapped around the room. Even the space above the doorway was not exempt. Wooden tubes were stacked alongside boxes of all sizes. Each had carefully painted messages on the front. Letters, names, historical events, eras, years, ages...all of it. On one full side, which had significant empty spaces, she saw the word "magic" written in various languages, ways, and words, but they all meant the same.

Her blood boiled and she interrupted Rupert's questions. "Why are you packing the sections on magic?"

All heads turned to her and she pointed to the gaps. "Everything else on this side here, from what I can see, is related to magic. Now, see the gaps? Am I supposed to believe these holes are just coincidence and not on purpose?"

"Mr. Cram is not capable of reading the language in any of these," Vittorio said from the doorway. "It would be too great of a risk to have him reading things he could not possibly understand."

"What language?" Allegra demanded.

"I'm sorry?" Vittorio asked, confused that she'd spoken to him.

Allegra did not hide the heat in her words. "What. Language."

She was beyond mere anger. This place held the historical record of her own kind, and it was already bad enough that it was hidden away from people. But to know they were hiding that record further, purposely and actively working to harm their investigations made her wish to scream insults at the top of her voice.

"What language, Vittorio? Answer the question," Francois shouted.

Vittorio sneered at them. "I wish you luck."

With that, Vittorio left.

Walter asked no one in particular, "So, what happens now?"

LEX WOULD NEVER say this aloud to anyone but Dodd, but the evening turned out to be far more exciting than the dancers. It took some time to depopulate the library of sneering toadies, but that still left a rather busy room of half-dressed important people, a few servants, a few more archivists, and the main archivist, who was an elderly man who was terrified someone would hurt his precious papers.

No one was speaking though, and someone had to ask the question. Finally, Lex spoke up. "What's our next step?"

No answer was forthcoming. Eventually, the pope asked Cram if he even knew what to look for in this floor-to-ceiling labyrinth of paper.

Cram shook his head. "Even if I knew, I can't say I'd be able to read it."

The pope rubbed his eyes and said, "So we just had that fight for nothing."

"Oh, absolutely not," said the Contessa. "There is something here that Walter is not supposed to see. Specifically, Walter, too. Otherwise, why would they hide it?"

"I didn't even know this room existed when I woke up this morning," Cram said. "I don't know why they'd think I had some devious plan here because...look at this? I can't even read the spine."

Lex leaned over to inspect the closest crate of books and picked one up from atop a protective pile of straw. One of the archivists who had stayed behind, a reedy man with wispy hair and an even wispier beard, let out a cry of horror when Lex touched the book's wooden cover.

The man pleaded and begged not to open the cover the entire way. Lex didn't; they didn't want to be responsible for this poor man's heart collapsing.

"Well?" The pope asked.

Lex skimmed, but shook their head. "I'm sorry, Your Radiance. I can't even read the entire title page. I know some of the words, but..."

Dodd walked over to lean over Lex's shoulder. They turned the book to make it easier for Dodd to read, but at the insistence of the archivist, Lex did not pass the book over.

Dodd made a thoughtful sound before saying, "That's not even Old Cartossian. This is a couple of centuries before then. I can only make out a bit. *Lord God Almighty be praised*, that's easy enough. Blessings, protectors? *Blessings upon our protectors*, maybe. I've not studied this stuff in years."

Lex snorted at everyone's shocked expressions. Dodd said defensively, "What? I had good tutors."

"Yes, and why did you have good tutors, Dodd?" Lex prompted.

Dodd made a few annoyed sounds before saying, "My parents had plans for me to go into the clergy, until it was clear, in the words of my mother, I was too much of a ragamuffin for the Cathedral."

"Maybe if you got a haircut, you'd appear more respectable," the Captain said. He glanced over Lex's shoulder and shook his head. "I can't read any of this, even though I had excellent tutors." He grinned when he said that last bit.

Soon, everyone was leaning over Lex's shoulder trying to read, all the while the archivist was slapping away outstretched hands who came too close to the opened page. The pope could read most of the page, and did so aloud.

"*The Lord God Almighty be praised for the blessings we have received in this age of*....something something...*Bring blessings upon our protectors and guardians, for we inherit*, I think it's inherit, *the joys of this world*." The pope shook his head and said, "I only know that because most of the older books I've seen all have something similar. I don't believe I could read a full book of this. Or, even a page."

The elderly archivist, a man Lex learned was named Roul, finally cleared his throat and gestured at Lex to hand it over. Lex considered accidentally dropping it, but knew that was just evil. They handed it over to the archivist, who returned the book to its crate and atop its straw bedding.

The archivist sighed and said, "I have been instructed by Cardinal Vittorio to provide no assistance to you lot. However, it is clear to me that, if I step aside you shall destroy all of the documents. I cannot allow that. Therefore, I shall render my assistance to protect what I have spent a lifetime guarding."

"I didn't hurt it," Lex protested. "I was quite careful."

"You touched it with your grubby hands."

Lex glanced down at their outstretched hands. Their fingernails were a little dirty, but "grubby" was rather harsh.

Several frustrated grunts escaped Roul the archivist before he said, "I am soon to retire in any case. I might as well be fired and sent away than live to see my books destroyed. Fine. Fine. I shall assist you, provided you do exactly as I say. No one is to touch a single thing in this room, not even the chamberpots, unless you ask my permission first. You must do exactly as I say at all times."

The archivist seemed pleased with his decision that no one actually agreed to, and he gave a stern nod of the head. He turned to the little servant girl, who was still scrubbing the fireplace as if nothing had just happened, and said, "Girl! Go tell Fiona and Fran to return the crates. We have work to do. But not tonight. We can work in the morning. Well? Why are you all standing about staring at me? What? Speak!"

The Contessa cleared her throat. "Pardon my bluntness, but how are we to trust your translations? You could lie to us."

He made a dismissive sound that was too close to Lex's childhood tutors' noises for comfort. "I assure you, there is no one else in all of Orsini, or indeed Amadore, who can read every single language in these texts. That includes all of my apprentices, too, who could not tell Lost Age Amadorian from Last Age Amadore script if their own lives depended upon it. No, you shall need my assistance. Gather your own group of translators, of course, so that I do not have to waste my time with the simple things." He made a dramatic sigh, as if he were about to thrust his own head into the mouth of a demon portal. "I shall gather up my translation books for your people to use if you promise upon the holy name of the Lord God Almighty that you will not damage them. They are my life's work and I do not want grubby hands upon them. You could smudge the ink."

"Captain, can you arrange a guard detail for in here? 'Round the clock," the pope ordered.

Captain Rainier nodded and said, "I shall speak with Her Highness. We are both stretched thin, but she is expecting reinforcements any day now, so I think we can manage this."

"Excellent. I'd have Lex and Dodd here, but our two best lieutenants are apparently on special assignment and cannot be put into active service," the pope said.

Lex's cheeks heated up at the idea of the pope calling both of them "best lieutenants." That needed to be included in Lex's next letter to their mother.

"Well, I am very willing to give up my guards for the short term," the Contessa offered up.

Everyone in the room, including the archivist, said "absolutely not" or some variation, Lex included. There had been enough attempts on her life, and no one had forgotten the poisoning episode yet. Or were likely to, so long as the Captain remembered it.

Which, knowing him, would be until the end of time. That man forgot nothing.

"My good Contessa," the pope said, and he said it in that smooth, condescending way priests always talk down to regular folks, "I could never live with myself if you were to come to harm."

"You seemed quite capable of it up until now," the Contessa said without missing a heartbeat

It was probably Lex's imagination that the room immediately got colder. The archivist glanced at Lex with a quizzical expression. Lex rolled their eyes and mouthed, "Later."

The previously grumpy elderly archivist made an "oo" sound before turning his full attention to watching the scene unfold. If Lex wasn't careful, they'd be stuck being the only grubby hands allowed to touch books, and Lex had a murdering mage to find.

The pope ended his little staring contest with the Contessa with a grunt and announced they should all return to their beds before something else happened. The Captain said he'd escort the Contessa to their room, while Martin would wait for Beatrix to take over at the door. The archivist apparently slept in the archives, so he shuffled off and pointedly latched his own door.

There was a lot of yawning chatter as they made their way out of the archives and toward their various rooms. Lex and Dodd, however, found themselves both wide awake given they'd drank enough tea to wake the dead. There was always food to be had in a place the size of Orsini, so they made their way outside, toward the back alleys, where a few vendors from beyond the north gates were inside selling their hot wares near the brothels.

They grabbed two hot sausage rolls each. They walked toward where they'd seen the demon portal earlier, but there was no sign of anything out of the usual. Though, it was so dark in this area that the demons would need to hit them in the face before either of them would notice.

Lex's stomach churned at the memories, and they struggled to swallow down the mouthful of food. They'd not even fully healed yet, and there were already demons. Again.

"Well, shit." When Lex didn't reply, Dodd pointed roughly in the direction of where the portal had been and said, "After this morning, no one is going to believe we're just wandering the streets helping you get back on your feet."

"Who the fuck cares what people think. There are fucking demons again. I can't deal with this shit, Dodd. I can't."

Lex was surprised by the lump that welled up in their throat at the thought of demons. Those little rat fuckers were tiny, but there would be more and more, until a massive demon, the size of a mountain, rose through the ground and...

"Hey, it's all right," Dodd said, giving their arm enough of a squeeze to pull Lex away from the past and into the now. "It's all right. We're all fucked up by the demons."

Lex tried to smile, but it failed to do more than a twitch. They leaned against a laundry post and tried to gather up the strength to speak. Finally, Lex whispered, "I see things. Like, when I'm awake and I scare myself. But they're not real."

Dodd was uncomfortably silent for so long that Lex started to worry. When Dodd finally spoke, his voice was strained. "I keep dreaming people are chasing me. People and demons. Sometimes, demon people. Sometimes, the people are ripped apart by the demons. Sometimes, I'm ripped apart. Sometimes, I wake up before any of that. Sometimes not. I hate sleeping in the barracks because I'm afraid...well...everyone's going to know if I start screaming. I've been sleeping in the brothel some nights, just renting a room alone, because no one there is going to notice one more man screaming. You're not the only one with bad dreams."

Lex's throat constricted and it was difficult to breathe. They didn't say anything because it was just going to get awkward. And this was in a back alley, which made this even more awkward. They hadn't known where Dodd had been sleeping. They'd not asked, and Dodd had not volunteered, but there were only so many places he could've been sleeping. Lex understood. Right now, Lex wasn't comfortable with strangers knowing about the nightmares, but also understood that Dodd preferred strangers hearing him scream. It all came from the same place.

Dodd drew in a deep breath and blew it out slowly. "I don't think anyone who was at Borro came out scarless. Like, scars in our minds and stuff. Then, we all come here, hurt and messed up, and then we go through it all again. And, I dunno, it's like folks here looked to us to how to deal with it, so we never got to be sick or weak or whatever you want to call it."

Lex swallowed hard.

"And now we have fucking demons again, and we just know it's going to be fucking awful, maybe the worst yet. This is hard on everyone right now."

"I don't care about everyone," Lex muttered.

Dodd turned to Lex and said, "Sure you do. If you didn't care, you'd have stayed inside the Cathedral where it was safe. You wouldn't have dragged your sorry ass outside to get your guts ripped open a second time."

Lex's eyes stung from all of the wood smoke in the air.

"See, you did that because you knew deep down you'd not be able to live with yourself if you didn't try to stop the demons. You were willing to take on even more scars for other people. Fuck, I don't even know what I'm saying here. Just...you're not the only one who feels like vomiting whenever they think about demons coming back through again."

"What are we going to do?" Lex whispered.

Dodd snorted. "We're going to kill the demons, and then we're going to kill the fucker whose keeps doing this to us."

"Can we get a nap in there somewhere?"

"That's a good enough reason to fight," Dodd said solemnly. He smiled, but it was soft and a little sad. "I would kill people right now if I thought it would help me sleep better."

Lex knew exactly what Dodd meant.

CHAPTER SEVEN

IT DID NOT come as a surprise to Allegra to discover her regular morning meeting had been canceled in favor of a closed-door meeting between the senior cardinals and Francois. If Nadira's news was accurate, and there was never any reason to doubt her intelligence gathering skills, the meeting was moments away from turning into a bare-knuckles brawl.

There was a benefit to the exclusion, as she gained a couple of hours to catch up on work. However, her first task was to find everyone trustworthy and skilled enough to assist in the archives. The archivist was correct; no one could read *all* of the languages. Allegra soon discovered that proficiency held a rather wide definition, too.

Thankfully, some in her circle had excellent tutors as children. When Allegra presented Serafina with the text the head archivist used to test apprentices, it was clear the young woman was proficient in reading two of the dead languages. Reluctantly, Allegra gave up her invaluable assistant and assigned her to work in the archives.

It took all of Allegra's strength not to laugh when the mere mention of Walter's name caused the pitch in Serafina's voice to rise and a dark flush to spread across her face. Allegra thought of herself as quite young, still, most days. And then she was confronted with the reminder that troublemaking mages no longer impressed her heart.

She smiled as gently as she could and did not mock the girl. Then, Allegra consoled herself that while she might not possess true youth any longer, it had been replaced with good sense and even better taste in men. And Stanton Rainier was indeed a fine and excellent man, who looked very good standing naked in front of a window, silhouetted in moonlight.

Allegra was quite pleased when Cardinal Rigi showed up at her door offering not just his assistance, but that of Sister Margarite and the more matronly Sister Bianca who said, and Rigi swore he was quoting the old woman, she would, "ensure no foolishness took place."

She immediately thought of Serafina's moon-sized eyes the other day in the courtyard. The wind had puffed out Walter's greatcoat, just enough to make him look like the kind of rebellious mage that young ladies loved, as opposed to the dusty, grumpy mage she knew he actually was.

Sister Bianca's maturity would go a long way in the archive room. Also, Allegra had quickly grown attached to the two priests, and also Cardinal Rigi, who was still enjoying Sister Margarite's company. Though the idlest of gossipers hinted that was why the sisters had not returned to their tiny farming village, most knew better. Reports from the refugees who managed to escape from that direction said it had been burned to the ground, along with most of the farming villages along the Cathedral highway. Most of their flock was now at Orsini, and Bianca had told her days before that she would stay there to administer comfort and protection to familiar faces.

The bigger surprise came when she'd opened the letter Cardinal Reinhold had written to her before his morning meetings to offer his assistance. Spite ached for her to reject him. She had not forgiven him for past wrongs, and the betrayal was still fresh and raw. Sitting on the council had been slowly easing it, but his letter that morning had picked at the scab.

My dear Contessa, I have prayed all this night, seeking guidance from the Almighty and my own judgement, and I write to you to confess that this business of the archives does not sit well upon my soul. The protection of those under our charge must be our most sacred duty, and I find myself fretting that there are those who are putting secrets above safety. If there is even a chance, no matter how small, that a letter or a book can assist Walter Cram with ending the demon threat than I, as a cardinal and a devotee to the Lord God Almighty, must offer my assistance. While it has been many years since I have sat with a tutor's harsh rule upon me, I shall remember my lessons well to protect those in our charge. I shall report to the archives with your permission.

Allegra was grateful this had come via note and not in person, for she feared she would not have had control over her face and its sneer. Thankfully, Stanton had stopped by her study before she'd penned a reply telling Reinhold she'd sooner seek assistance from the abyss than from him. Stanton said he had half of an hour's leisure before he was to meet with Imogen, and passed her an apple pork roll wrapped in cloth. She could smell the pepper and nutmeg on the steam as soon she exposed it to the air. While it cooled, she vented her spleen.

However, soon the aroma of the roll caused her stomach to protest its neglect, and she took several bites. Then, her heated thoughts having calmed, she wrote a reply far politer than Reinhold deserved. His guilty conscience was between him and the Almighty; she was allowed to maintain her grudge.

Nadira arrived with the morning tea things as Allegra wrote the letter. Nadira worked quietly and efficiently, with years of practice. The teapot went on the sideboard, and then Nadira poured both Allegra and Stanton a cup. Allegra's had honey stirred into hers, while Stanton's was plain. Even as Allegra wrote and ranted, she noticed Nadira scowling when Stanton placed his roll directly on the desk. Nadira pointedly, but silently, picked it up and put it on a small rosebud saucer.

It was difficult to maintain her ire after that.

Nadira fetched a silver platter from a waiting servant in the corridor, which she placed next to the tea service. Then she asked, "Your Ladyship, Captain, pardon the interruption, but might I make a request to the both of you?"

Nadira quickly outlined her concerns about Calm Sea's health, both the physical scars and the invisible ones. When Stanton pressed, Nadira said quietly, "She dreams when she is awake, and Serafina confided in me that Calm Seas will not sleep alone, and so has been crawling into bed with her, Ysabeau, Kia, or some of the other servants. No one has the heart to make her sleep alone."

Sadly, there was a lot of that going on. Allegra startled the ash girl who tended the study fireplaces. The poor girl screamed before bursting into tears and nervous giggles. There was a lot of suffering, and a number of invisible wounds that would take time to heal.

"I worry that removing her from all duties would only worsen her condition, for she'll think she's done something wrong. She insists upon working, and Kia told me that Calm Seas needs to keep her hands busy, for that eases the pain. I was hoping you could find her a quiet posting with people who'd understand her situation. People who would not judge her scars."

Allegra nodded in understanding. "Would you prefer her to be in the archives with Walter, or with the Consorts themselves? Lex and Dodd could probably use a hand."

"I would rather her not around someone like Walter Cram, Your Ladyship," Nadira said. "He's a bad influence."

"Oh, Nadira. Every young girl needs to have a harmless bad influence in her life. It's the only way she'll learn how to pick out the good ones later on," Allegra said, giving Stanton a grin.

"Am I one of the good ones?" Stanton asked innocently.

Nadira made a displeased sound that said the judge's supreme decision was still out on the matter. Stanton managed to stuff half of a roll into his mouth to avoid laughing out loud, but his eyes sparkled.

"I know Father Michael tried to speak to her about the importance of rest. She told him that she feels guilty sitting about while the other girls work cleaning up after the attack." Allegra smiled. "I suppose we would all feel the same way in her position."

"I fear her face will become infected," Stanton admitted. "It's not that the barracks are dirty; the maids do an excellent job there. But it's so easy to spread dirt to one's face, even when trying to be careful. Lex told me she keeps her face covered most of the time, though, so at least she is following the healers' instructions, but I'm worried all the same."

A disappointed expression crossed Nadira's face, one a younger Allegra knew all too well and was thankful she was not causing it this time. "I've tried my hardest to keep her out of the dirt, but it is difficult with such a stubborn, young girl."

"Oh, Nadira! If the injury was yours, we would have to tie you to a chair to keep you still and you know it," Allegra said.

"And, for the record, we *would* tie you to the chair if we had to," Stanton said solemnly.

Nadira gave one of her rare grins that said she'd been caught out and there was no true rebuttal. However, she did her best by saying, "Well, it is not my fault, Your Ladyship, that no one knows how to make a decent pot of tea in this place."

"Would you like me to speak to Lex and Dodd?" Stanton asked. "I'm certain we can find her some safe work that isn't taxing, with people who know her."

"I welcome any assistance, Captain." And, with that, Nadira gave a bow and left the room.

Stanton leaned back in his chair and attempted to puff out his chest. "Well, my dear, I believe Nadira likes me."

"The proof will be on the platter."

Stanton got up to survey the daily offerings. Nadira insisted that proper etiquette was followed for any guests who happened into Allegra's office, but also was simply too busy to stand about waiting to serve tea and a biscuit to the steady stream of arrivals. The tea service along with the platter of sweet and savory delights was the compromise, one that Allegra welcomed.

Stanton lifted the silver cover off the oval platter. "What am I looking for?"

"Caraway cakes," she said with a laugh. When Stanton confirmed his favorite treat was present, she said, "She has never brought Walter his favorite cake, not before nor now."

Stanton picked up a cake and offered Allegra one of the dried fig and honey squares. He sat across from her and said, before taking a bite, "Cram prefers a little hardship. Maybe Nadira fears he is growing soft and will soon have nothing to complain of."

"Walter will always find fault with something, including how there is nothing of fault to be found!"

A messenger arrived, one of the young boys who ran about the place at full speed. He was red-faced and panting, and announced Her Highness had fallen behind and could Stanton

KRISTA D. BALL

meet her for luncheon. He sent the boy off and poured himself a second cup of tea.

Father Michael arrived some time afterward to volunteer his assistance. Though he worried his duties as Bishop of Orsini would become all-consuming, he wished to help. Allegra happily granted him full permissions to the archives, providing him a letter for the guards.

From there, Stanton and Allegra managed to do an hour's worth of paperwork together to deal with the ongoing refugee situation outside their gates. Those with specific necessary skills had already been moved inside the walls to work, but that still left over a thousand beyond the walls with no support. The clergy had organized soup and bread twice daily in makeshift kitchens, and they all tried to hire temporary workers whenever possible. But there was only so much work and too many people. And the only available work right now was inconsistent, and sometimes dangerous.

Allegra authorized the hiring of twenty labourers, ten maids, and fifteen children from the refugees, all at standard Orsini daily wages for the term of one week. The children could work as street cleaners; there was still so much glass and debris everywhere. The maids were to start cleaning the mess from where demons had crashed through one of the smaller domes, collapsing it. The labourers were to assist them with basic repairs and removal of rubble. Giso was tasked with hiring the highly skilled craft workers to replace the stained glass, but he'd asked for her help getting it ready.

Lex and Dodd arrived, and both went straight for the platters first. They'd been interviewing several of Borro Abbey's former servants who were now at Orsini to track the movements of everyone in the moments before the appearance of the portal in Queen Portia's bedchamber. So far, they found nothing out of the ordinary. They planned to do the same with Orsini, leading up to the attack.

As Stanton peppered them with questions, Allegra's instincts tweaked that they were leading towards a request. Stanton must have, too, because he finally asked what was bothering Dodd.

"Well, Captain, it's tough for us right now to get any work done. We're using Cram's suite for all of our notes and stuff, and your office for the maps."

"Now that Cram is busy in the archives, he can't help us like he had been and now we're..."

"Oh, just ask whatever it is the two of you are dancing around," Stanton finally said.

Allegra chuckled. She was going to make them spit it out for themselves, but apparently Stanton lacked the patience for that.

"We need an office," Lex said.

"You're not getting mine," Stanton added helpfully.

Dodd and Lex exchanged an entire conversation in just eyebrow and neck movements. From what Allegra could understand, they were silently arguing over who was going to ask.

Lex lost the silent argument and answered. "Well, see, um, we were hoping that we could set up a small establishment in the old rectory building, out in the servants' area. See, no one wants to be there because it has windows."

"Or, used to have windows," Dodd added bitterly.

"Right, so we were thinking we could move in there. Calm Seas could help us, because she's on light duties still, but she's *really* bored and driving Nadira to wanting demons to return and fetch the girl," Lex said.

"It would be a way for us to be a little apart from the Consorts, just so that anyone with information could come forward and didn't need to walk through all of the barracks and everything and make a big scene," Dodd said. "Like, they could be pretending to deliver meat pies."

Lex nodded enthusiastically.

"So, you want an entire building to yourselves?" Allegra asked, pushing as much of a matronly tone into her voice as she could.

She must have pushed a little too much of her own mother because Lex and Dodd both winced a little before hurriedly talking over one another. She let them go on for a bit before interrupting. "I'll have to clear it with Father Michael first."

"He already agreed if you'd agree," Lex said.

"He'd like his suite back," Dodd added.

Allegra couldn't handle the straight face anymore and laughed. "Is he actually living with Walter now?"

Lex made a face and said, "You didn't hear it from us."

"But yeah, they're absolutely living together," Dodd added.

Allegra agreed to them setting up the old rectory, but Stanton had a few questions. "Imogen is sleeping in a tent outside the city, and she doesn't want to stay in the Cathedral proper. What if we turned the building into another set of barracks? She could rotate out her troops, so that they'd get some rest indoors, and it would free up some tents we desperately need."

"We'd need 'round the clock security on the building, since it is going to house all of the investigation notes for the demon portals," Allegra added. "With Imogen's men there..."

"There's plenty of room upstairs," Dodd said cautiously, "but there's no glass in the windows and it's still a mess inside."

Allegra tapped her thumb against her desk for a moment before picking up her quill to write. She spoke as she did. "I'm giving the authorization to use the arbiter's accounts to hire whatever help you need, but please keep repairs within reason. There's only so much wood and nails to go around."

"I understand," Lex said.

Dodd nodded enthusiastically. "We can make sure the building is sound, first off, and then get Her Highness' men moved in upstairs. So beds, windows, and the like."

"Don't bother requesting for glass. It's all going to repair the main Cathedral front-facing windows, so all you can hope for are storm shutters right now," Stanton added.

That pretty much represented most of her morning. There had been no real word out of the archives beyond there not being any news to report. Giso had been checking in on them hourly, from the notes she'd gotten from Walter asking her to either have the cardinal assigned to help or find him another job.

The afternoon turned out to be significantly more eventful.

IT HAD BEEN three full hours before Walter had the urge to run screaming from the archives that the end was upon them and every mage should save themselves.

Despite not having been raised in wealth or nobility, Walter had access to excellent tutors growing up. His father had seen the church as Walter's best chance at a stable and upward life. Walter had worked hard, first to please his father, and later to hide his magical abilities. He failed at both aims.

Years on the run meant Walter had not kept up his more esoteric skills, such as reading long-dead languages. While he occasionally enjoyed a challenge, his brain could not remember how to read the Third Era Northumberland alphabet no matter how much he stared at it.

"Are you well, Mr. Cram?"

Walter looked over at the matronly Sister Bianca, whom he had an immense amount of respect for, and not only because she'd saved his life. Though, as a general rule, he found respecting people who saved his life had never served him wrong.

"I seem to have forgotten all of my lessons," Walter said. He snorted before adding, "After all, what was the point to know how to read dead languages if you were being chased by farmers with pitchforks and torches?

"I believe the Lord God Almighty gave your parents the wisdom to teach you properly. If it is His will, those lessons will return, I am certain," Sister Bianca said.

Walter muttered something disparaging about the Almighty, but made no further reply. He wanted to be out there with Lex and Dodd searching for the culprit. Instead, he'd just endured a twenty-minute argument over if a word meant house or shit heap, since those were very different things, and yet spelled completely the same way to his eye. The issue was the additional tick. Was that a stain on the paper (meaning it was "house") or was it a real tick (meaning "shit heap")? Who knew! He surely didn't.

Thankfully, Nadira arrived with a trail of footmen and food as they finally decided it was an ink stain. Probably accurate, as calling the house of the Lord God Almighty a "shit heap" did not seem appropriate for a cardinal to have written in his journals. Then again, Walter had met a few cardinals in his time who would have absolutely written that.

Nadira announced that she'd brought footmen to set up a small dining area for the researchers, which sent Roul the archivist into a snit.

"These people cannot be expected to sit here all day without tea or cake," Nadira finally said, and Walter assumed the concern was not for him. Nadira wouldn't even pass him an empty glass when he was with Ally; she'd certainly not bring him...did he smell nutmeg? Surely not.

"It is not safe to have food here!" Roul cried.

"There is a perfectly acceptable empty space right here beside this door. I shall place a table there and that can be where tea and food can be eaten," Nadira said, pointing at the empty space near the entrance.

"That tapestry is eight hundred years old!" the archivist shouted, pointing at the wall decoration.

"Which can be rolled up!" Nadira shouted.

Shouted.

Walter wisely knew when to keep his damned mage mouth shut, and so watched poor Roul lose a fight with the most powerful servant in Orsini. Crossing Nadira didn't just mean crossing Ally. It meant crossing the pope and the captain of the Consorts. God Almighty help anyone stupid enough to make Nadira their enemy. Except himself, of course. Though, in his defense, he'd not tried to make her his enemy. She just didn't like him. Something about him being a ragamuffin and a bad influence.

"Well?" Roul demanded. "Are you just going to stand there and allow this insult to continue?"

That was directed at Walter. He sighed, thought of his own neck, and asked, "Where is the safest place to store the tapestry and also that carpet? It looks old."

"No one cares about the carpet!" Roul complained about the dingy floor covering.

With the war won, Nadira summoned forth her army of footmen. It took over an hour to deal with the ancient artwork. First, the tapestry had to be carefully removed from the wall. Then it was placed on bedsheets, covered with more bedsheets, and finally rolled up. Then, it was wrapped in blankets and then, as the final step, the old carpet from the floor was wrapped around it as a protective layer. This was placed on the floor of the vault, in the back, where Roul begrudgingly said it would only *sometimes* be in his way.

Walter pretended to supervise the arrival of the snacks table, though it was clear where the true power in the room lay, and it was nowhere near any of their feet. For which he was relived. There had already been too much of "Mr. Cram, what is your opinion?" as of late.

Mr. Cram. When in the name of the Lord God did he become *Mister* Cram? Some of them had begun calling him Walter, for the love of the Almighty, and that was just unacceptable. Yes, Allegra was allowed to call him Walter. And Michael, too. In fact, he'd even allow Rainier to call him that, only because of Allegra. Lex and Dodd had started calling him by his name sometimes now, too. Those two kids were also including him into their plans and inviting him to do things with them.

Why didn't people fear him anymore? They were supposed to run screaming at the very sight of him. Now, they were inviting him over for tea cakes. Tea cakes! What was happening? Was this a trick? Had he fallen into the abyss and discovered it was nothing more than a warped version of this existence? He'd never become a rebel for the power or decision making. He'd certainly never become one for the friendships.

A small voice, deep within his mind, whispered he'd become a rebel to be remembered forever as a martyr.

He drew in a deep breath, enough so to fetch the attention of those around him, inquiring if the snack arrangements were not to his liking. He made a dismissive wave, saying he had no preference and just wanted to get back to work or eat or both, and allowed the servants and important people to finish their work.

Walter watched and listened to the servants detailing the food on offer, as if he could not tell most of it by its appearance or smell. Sage pudding, various pickled vegetables, rolls and buns, smoked pork, and three trays of cakes and sweets of all kinds. There was a curiosity that caught both his and Roul's eye, and Nadira said it was butter, shaped into various types of fruit. The pope himself had directed the leftovers from his breakfast table to them, and they should all be honored. Or so the others said.

Walter found himself staring at the fruit-shaped butter. It was artistry on its own, with ivy leaves wrapping around strawberries, apples, and what he believed was a pineapple, though he'd only ever seen drawings of the fruit. It was all made of butter, though. A commodity that was in short supply now, and yet there was enough to turn it into fruit for the most important people in all of Serna.

He was included in that, he realized with a shock. It was a castoff, yes, but he was still high enough in Orsini society now to be adjacent to power. No one was chasing him. No one was trying to murder him in is bed. No, he was getting fat off the pope's own table, while his own kind languished beyond these walls, in Cartossa, across all of Serna, in pits and kitchens and running from those with power.

This place was rotting his soul. He did not belong here. He didn't belong anywhere, not truly. Not so long as people wished his kind dead.

"Mr. Cram, you have gone quite pale," Sister Margarite said. "Are you ill?"

"He doesn't eat properly," Nadira announced loudly before Walter could shake himself from his introspection in time to reply. She turned to Sister Bianca, giving her strict instructions to ensure Walter eat frequently, lest he become "sullen and moody."

Those were her exact words: sullen and moody. He was many things, but he did not consider himself sullen nor moody.

With that declaration, Nadira ordered her army out the doors and left him to be fussed over. They would not stop offering him food, which annoyed him greatly at the start, until Rigi began listing the sweets on the trays. A full quarter of the largest platter was some form of spiced sweet. Molasses cookies and buns, the same taste but with different textures. Nutmeg-sprinkled sweet rolls. King Yves biscuits with cinnamon and pepper. Lady Clara cakes with nutmeg, honey, and cardamom.

"Why are you smiling?" Rigi asked as he handed him a cup of tea.

"I do believe Nadira has warmed up to me," Walter said.

Serafina was stuffing a Lady Clara cake into her mouth when she said, "I heard Nadira call you an unkempt guttersnipe who needs both a shave and a haircut."

Nadira knew how much he loved spiced sweets, as she'd previously made a point to never serve them whenever he was around. He took a cautious bite of a molasses cookie, ensuring it wasn't some form of trick. It wasn't. It was simply divine.

"It appears the Lord God still performs miracles," Walter announced and took another cookie. He managed to get two more into him before the afternoon crisis hit Orsini.

THE OLD RECTORY was deemed safe by the Cathedral's master builder, and she'd said as long as no one wanted the windows replaced or any of her masons or carpenters to work on the building, Lex and Dodd were welcome to do whatever they wanted with it. However, when Her Highness stepped inside, she made a cursory survey from the entrance and asked if Lex was dipping into the pain tinctures.

"Your Highness, it's not that bad," Lex argued.

She pointedly stared up at gore splatters on the ceiling, and then back at Lex.

"It just needs soap and water," Lex said with less enthusiasm. "Folks need the work, so we'll be helping them out. It's a win for everyone, Your Highness."

Her Highness made a sound that an ungrateful lieutenant would've called dubious. Lex was not an ungrateful lieutenant, however. "Let me know when the guts are off the chandeliers."

With that, Lex left for the treasury while Dodd went to the camps. The assistant treasurer's clerk advised Lex that they were running out of the smallest coins, and asked if Lex could take whatever they had on hand. Lex nodded in agreement and passed them a pouch and the clerk filled it up with a mixture of coinage. The clerk first got Lex to sign on the main ledger, detailing the various coins they'd put into the pouch.

Lex chatted with the clerk for a bit, while they dug around underneath the counter for another ledger. This one was for the arbiter's accounts, and Lex signed that one, too. Then, with a pouch full of coins, Lex made their way back to the old rectory. Over the course of the afternoon, twenty-seven workers arrived. Most were family units—parents, children, cousins, and the like— and Lex sat down to do the maths necessary to pay fairly, but also work with the coins on hand. The Contessa insisted everyone be paid fair Orsini rates, which Lex didn't have a problem with; it was having to work out the sums with everyone watching that bothered Lex.

Lex got the maths all worked out and helped Dodd gather up the necessary buckets, brushes, and brooms. While they were getting all that set up, Her Highness sent over three of her own who were on report, with instructions to make them do the worst jobs.

It was soon discovered that there was a rotting demon corpse in the attic—that explained the smell, at least—so before Her Highness's men dragged out the demon body parts, Lex marched the children outside and around the back to pick up debris there. They didn't need to see what was festering upstairs.

They'd spent the morning like that, until Her Highness returned, this time with a full quarter of her troops carrying planks, nails, and hammers. Lex didn't ask where they'd managed to get building materials, and Her Highness didn't say. But by mid-afternoon, the rundown building was cleared of gore, debris, and glass shards, and smelled more like fresh air and less like rotting flesh.

The building wasn't ready for anyone to sleep in it yet; there was almost no furniture, and the chimneys were still being cleaned. They'd all planned to look around the north encampment to see what personal belongings people were selling, to use up some of the coin Lex had gotten from the clerk. Lex was uncomfortable with buying *stuff* from fleeing, desperate people. Dodd had argued it was helping them resettle elsewhere.

"We gotta make sure we offer Orsini prices, though," Dodd had said. "That is what's fair."

Lex tried to remember that, as Orsini was notoriously expensive, but it still crawled under their skin.

Lex mentioned it to Her Highness, who'd said in a perfect world they'd envelop all these fleeing souls into Orsini. However, there were simply too many to take in. Lex had glanced at a gleaming dome when she'd said that, the one that wasn't smashed, and Her Highness sighed and said she wasn't completely convinced of her own words, either.

"All we can do is be as reasonable as possible," she'd said. "Fair wages and fair prices will go a long way, Lex. Sometimes, that's all we can do."

She wasn't wrong. No one was hurting these people, and the militia, the Consorts, and Her Highness's men were taking turns providing protection within the two encampments, especially the southern one that was moved through Orsini every evening to the significantly safer northern encampment. Some did not want to move, but every evening several people, along with Father Michael or one of the younger cardinals, went to explain how dangerous it would be if Bonacieux returned.

Still. They didn't like buying furniture from those fleeing civil war and there was no changing Lex's mind. They'd do it, but they didn't have to like it.

With the cleaning done, Lex paid the workers that had small children with them and sent them on their way. The Amadore soldiers on report carried over the large, framed map, wrapped in a sheet to preserve the flags. While they worked to nail it to the wall, all the workers and soldiers without an assigned task were sent with Calm Seas with a list of items to buy and carry back; Calm Seas had control of the purse for that. Dodd also told the girl to pick up enough food for everyone.

"Something easy to hold," Lex said, motioning at the empty room. "There's no where to sit and eat."

Calm Seas was only gone moments before Her Highness complained, "You forgot a tea pot for the fireplace."

Lex pointed at the sheet of paper that rested on a wooden chair, the only piece of furniture in the room. There was a short pencil on top of the paper. "I started a list over there, Your

KRISTA D. BALL

Highness. I've already added the pot, but you're welcome to add anything else."

Her Highness wrote down a few things on the paper before turning her attention to the map on the wall. There was only her, Lex, and Dodd in the building now; the soldiers who'd mounted the map had rushed off to join Calm Seas.

"What am I looking at?" Her Highness asked, staring at the map. "Orsini, obviously, but what are the pins for?"

"Yellow flags are for the portals we found before the main attack. Green is the portals Dodd and I could remember from the day of attack. White will be for all of those we find now. Each is numbered, by who added them. Most are me, Dodd, the Captain, Cram, Father Michael, the other Consorts, and a few of the servants. The numbers with who added what is all in Cram's ledger, over there." Lex gestured at several books in a neat stack next to the chair. "If you see some missing, we'll add them."

She nodded and made several thoughtful sounds. "Without any context, those green flags appear to be someone walking about dropping breadcrumbs."

Dodd whistled. "Shit."

"What's wrong?" Her Highness asked.

Dodd glanced at Lex with his "I'm not telling her" look. Lex sighed and said, "We were hoping we were wrong about that."

"You're not. Look here, though. The person changed their pattern. That white flag isn't anywhere near the others. I don't know the Cathedral all that well, honestly, but that says to me someone either moved living quarters or jobs. They're going back and forth through a different door than before."

"Double shit," Dodd muttered.

Lex nodded. "Yeah, we thought the same thing."

"It narrows down who it could be," Her Highness said.

"Someone from Borro Abbey, living inside the Cathedral both before and after the attack, moved apartments inside." Dodd shook his head. "That's still a lot of people."

"Good work, both of you. I can see why Allegra put you in charge of this."

Lex successfully did not puff out their chest. Dodd failed and visibly grew a little taller.

"Do you think it's one mage doing it?" Her Highness asked.

Lex nodded. "They might have help, but we think it's one person. The thing is, none of us know if that mage knows they're doing it. That's why Walter is digging around in the archives. In the meantime, I've ordered floor plan maps of the Cathedral itself, and whatever outlying buildings we have. That's going to take some time to dig up, and some will need to be copied. I was able to get two old floor plans, though. They're fifty years old, and covered in mold, but it's a start. And I'm allowed to draw on them. So Dodd was planning to interview a few more servants from Borro, and I was going to follow the maps and see if I can find the servant passages that lead into those alleyways."

"Remember that some of the doors are locked. I don't know who has keys, though." Her Highness made an approving sound. "Well, let me know how to help since all I do these days is break up religious arguments between the mages and my soldiers. How bad would it be if I banned religious discussion all together?"

Lex made a thoughtful sound as they looked out the front hole of the building where a window used to be. "Well, it might be considered a little eccentric, Your Highness."

"I'd like to get everyone moved in here by tomorrow night, so advise me if you need my help progressing that." With that, Her Highness left for a meeting with the important people.

Lex and Dodd continued making a list of people to interview that day. Mostly servants and the like, but Lex wanted to get the Contessa's statement on record, too. She'd need to be booked ahead of time, though, which Lex had forgotten to do when they were there earlier that morning. Lex decided to simply send a note asking for a good time, since they didn't want to make the trek back over there, and Lex highly doubted Dodd would do it.

"Hey Dodd, I forgot to ask the Contessa for her statement. You want to run over and ask her when she's free?"

Dodd made a rude gesture. "I have my own shit to do."

Lex figured as much, but a person had to ask. All in all, Lex was pretty proud of their new barracks and office. An office! They were definitely moving up in the world.

"Think there's anything good to eat right now in the dining hall?" Dodd asked.

Lex doubted it, but with the grumbling sounds their stomach made, thought it was best to go in search of it. After all, Lex thought grimly, with the way things were going, every meal could be their last.

CHAPTER EIGHT

EVENTUALLY, ALLEGRA WAS summoned to Rupert's drawing room for a leisurely, if late, luncheon. The meal was informal, though that did not prevent the servants from bringing out the gold dinnerware. Allegra had not eaten much all day, so her rather dainty plate was piled higher than usual. Stanton and Imogen didn't even bother with the petite plates, and instead combined the assorted rolls together in a near-empty basket so that they could each take a serving plate. That got a rise out of Vittorio, which only encouraged Imogen more.

All gathered made valiant efforts not to delve into politics or policy while food was to be had. There was a small detour when Giso brought up Vanida, and Rupert twice attempted at redirection before finally saying he wanted the pleasure of eating his spinach pastry in peace.

After that, they managed to enjoy several bites of food and light conversation before the Lord God Almighty decided they had enough food in their bellies to ward off fainting spells.

An out-of-breath soldier flung open the double doors, looked frantically about until she laid eyes on Imogen. "Lord Renouf just arrived with prisoners. Cardinal Vanida is assisting."

Imogen swore under her breath, then hammered the soldier for details. The rest of them set down their wine glasses and rose, excepting DeLancey and Devonshire, who waved them off, stating their rushing days were long behind them. Allegra fell in beside Imogen and the soldier, listening to the details. At first, this seemed to be the promised reinforcements from Amadore's king, and there were expressions of relief at the additional support that just arrived at their door.

However, Allegra's own relief soon faded when the soldier said "mage prisoners" and she realized this would not be a happy occasion after all. In fact, the closer to the exit, the louder the commotion beyond became. They rounded the final turn at a now-hurried pace towards the partially opened main doors, which explained some of the noise filtering through the corridors.

The guards pulled the doors back completely, allowed the party to exit in a large grouping, and the people gathered on the stairs themselves quickly moved to allow them to make their way down to the courtyard and Lord Renouf. All the while, Imogen peppered her soldier with questions, most of which she could not answer. She had taken one look at Imogen's cousin—the horrible one—and came running for help.

"You did well to fetch me," Imogen said finally.

"We shall know what he wants soon enough," Stanton said.

"Nothing good," Imogen muttered darkly.

For her part, Allegra had only met the man a handful of times and only when they were children. Even in her youth, she could not stand to be near him. She tried to remind herself that people grow up, and that they cannot be judged based on their behaviours as children, but Imogen's grim expression did nothing to help quell the worry.

As they approached, Allegra saw Renouf arguing with Lex and Dodd. Dodd was gesturing wildly, and Lex was pointing emphatically behind them at a set of carts. It took several more steps before Allegra realized the carts Lex pointed at were filled with prostrate people. More steps, and it was clear they were bound and gagged people.

Imogen must've seen it, too, because she swore again.

"That is why I fetched you, Your Highness," the soldier said. "I worried Walter Cram would see it."

Allegra made a pained sound because, for all her fury about the sight of bound people, Walter's reaction would not be as checked as her own if a single person in those carts was even hinted at being a mage.

She looked at the carts, though, and found her own anger rising dangerously. After all they had been through, and all of the dead they'd had to drag away, this scene was undignified, horrific, and poured salt water into raw wounds.

Renouf glanced over his shoulder. He turned completely, ignoring the shouting and gesturing lieutenants behind him. He began to walk toward Allegra and the others, with no great urgency in his step, though Lex and Dodd were hot on his heels.

Allegra was surprised by how much Renouf reminded her of Stanton. Both were dark, tall, broad-shouldered men who held themselves in that way only soldiers did. But as he stood in front of them, bowing deeply to Francois, she realized that was where the similarities ended.

He straightened to reach into an inner pocket to produce a sealed letter, which he handed to Francois. "Greetings, Your Radiance. Here are my orders."

There was no kindness in his face. That was what Allegra immediately noticed. Stanton's face always exuded compassion. Renouf's eyes did not reflect anything but hard determination.

As Francois read the letter, Renouf gave Imogen a slight incline of his head. "Your Highness."

"Lord Renouf," she said with the exact same nod and the exact same tone. "I doubt you remember Allegra, Contessa of Marsina."

"No, I would not have recognized her. It is an honor to renew our childhood acquaintance."

Allegra gave a miniscule inclination of the head. It was all she could muster as her gaze continued to flick to the carts of human beings, who clearly were alive and suffering.

Renouf's face brightened a little when he recognized Stanton. He offered a hand to him and said, "Barrington! Good to see you, man."

Stanton accepted the gesture. He glanced at the carts pointedly and asked, "What's this all about?"

Renouf rolled his eyes. "Oh, troublemakers, escaped slaves, mages without the proper paperwork. The usual riffraff. Some of them had the nerve to carry forged documents signed by yourself! I knew you'd not be out here freeing slaves like that, so we rounded them all up. Pardon me, Your Radiance, I know it's a hanging offense. I would have carried it out myself, but there was too many of them. I dealt with the ringleaders, of course and..."

"Oh Reny," Imogen said. She swore under her breath. "What have you done now?"

Francois raised a hand, just a little to soften the argument that was about to come. "Thank you, Lord Renouf. We are in desperate need of assistance, and we appreciate your arrival. Lieutenants Lex and Dodd?"

"Your Radiance," they said in unison.

"Please arrange with Her Highness to have the prisoners released." He turned to Allegra and asked, "Shall I assume you wish to correct the papers issue?"

"Indeed," Allegra said, still glaring at Renouf.

Francois nodded. "Very good. Lex? Dodd? May I put the two of you in charge of this? The Contessa is very busy, so if you could..."

"Are you planning to release these people?" Renouf demanded. "Forgive me, Your Radiance, perhaps I have not made myself clear. All of these people are criminals. They were carrying forged documents and some did not have documents at all. Some were clearly branded as elementals and were out, free in the air, to summon demons and destroy us all in our—"

"Oh, enough," Imogen said. "Reny, enough. No one wants to hear the lecture."

"I'd have hanged them all if I had enough rope," Renouf said. "Since when did you grow soft?"

"You hanged people?" Giso shouted. They all turned to the older cardinal, whose face was red with fury. "Are you saying you hanged innocent people?"

"Those documents were legitimate," Allegra managed to say without raising her voice. It took all of her self-control, though. The shock and horrors of the last weeks had shaved her refinement down to the raw skin underneath. The very idea of all they'd been through bubbled close to the surface of her emotions, and she was shaking from the repressed rage within her.

At first, Renouf snorted, but his expression quickly faded to confusion when Lex and Dodd began ordering the Amadore guards to untie the captives. Renouf watched the scene for a moment, his own soldiers all looking to him for orders, before turning back to them to speak. He tried to keep his attention on Francois, but kept glancing at Stanton. "Are you telling me, seriously, that you have given safe passage to elemental mages who should be, by the holy name of the Lord God Almighty, swinging in the wind if they so much as step out of a mine?"

A shoving match broke out near the carts. An Amadore soldier pushed Lex, who stumbled. Dodd dove in swinging, and nine Consorts jumped any Amadore soldiers who tried to assist their fellow. Several bystanders pitched into the fray, and soon, Amadore soldiers, Orsini militia, and other Consorts all jumped in. Imogen and Stanton rushed toward the fight, both shouting orders for it to stop.

"This is why you cannot side with mages," Renouf said to Francois. "It always becomes violent."

"How many people did you kill?" Allegra demanded.

Renouf held his hands behind him and stood straight. To Francois, not to her she noticed, he said, "I did not kill a single innocent."

That was when Walter pushed her aside from behind, slammed Renouf to the ground, and began beating the man with his bare fists.

TO CALL WHAT happened next a riot would have been an exaggeration, but only slightly. Walter's knuckles were bleeding from where they'd scraped Renouf's teeth. He'd only gotten a few punches in before Allegra and the pope had pulled him off.

The mob itself took longer to break apart, as Renouf's men had no true sense of what had taken place at Orsini. Lex was no delicate pastry, but the kid had been grievously injured protecting elemental mages. While the words had never been spoken aloud, all mages knew Lex was off limits. No one pushed Lex and got to stay on their feet for long.

It took Walter shaking the earth, just a slight tremor, to announce an end to things. Renouf was shocked and started his protests, but was told to shut up by Vittorio, of all people.

Imogen had an oozing rash on her arm, where she'd fallen on gravel, and Stanton a limp from where he'd been kicked in the knee. The pope ordered the bloody to the healers and surgeons, the angry to their jobs, and everyone else to their homes.

"Come, let us go inside," Francois said. "Giso, are you injured? Why are you limping?"

Somewhere in the mess, Cardinal Giso had apparently twisted an ankle. Walter had a few bloody cuts and several red spots that would soon be nasty bruises where Renouf had gotten a few lucky hits in. Renouf was significantly bloodier than Walter, though he'd at least managed to get away with only a swollen nose, as opposed to a broken one.

Francois ordered all of them into his suites, including Walter. He followed, for no other reason than his stomach was grumbling and there was always food at any meeting with the pope. Devonshire and DeLancey were still seated in the large drawing room, each with a cup of tea, and judgmental raised eyebrows faced them when they walked into the room.

"My dear Contessa, you look as though you were rolling around in the dirt," DeLancey said. "Mr. Cram! Are you bleeding? What happened?"

"I need wine," Allegra announced. She walked straight to the corner table that held the spirits and poured herself a generous glass of red wine. She drank it all. Then she tugged her shoulders back and straightened her spine, and then realized there were several holes in her dress, along with her torn hem and sleeve.

"Nadira is going to murder me," Allegra said with a sigh. She'd had this blue brocade gown for less than a week.

The elderly cardinals did not hide their disdain as the others took their positions one by one: a bloody Renouf who stood off to the side, a slightly less bloody Walter who sat down, two very scruffy lieutenants with angry expressions and bloody knuckles who collapsed on a settee together, and a limping, cursing Giso who was helped to a chair.

"Why is he allowed here?" Renouf demanded. He said it while speaking at Imogen, but everyone knew it was about Walter.

"Lord Renouf, silence is the will of the Lord God right now," Francois snapped.

"I will not share a seat with a dangerous criminal," Renouf said. He stood erect, like a soldier ready for inspection. "I shall stand."

"Then stand in silence," Francois said. He held up a hand, emphasizing the need for that silence.

Walter glanced about the room. His gaze fell on Rainier, who gave him a shake of the head. Rainier stood behind Allegra despite the protestations that his knee needed to rest. Rainier stubbornly said sitting would cause it to lock up, and he'd rather that embarrassment in the privacy of his own office. The room was a mixture of angry and red faces, along with frustrated sounds and a pervasive silence that said there were still a great amount of shouting in their immediate futures.

Then, he heard it from beyond the doors: Vanida demanding entry. He protested that he was to be let into the meeting. Reminded the guards who he was, and of the power he held. That went on for a bit before DeLancey stood to go silence the disgraced cardinal.

In the awkward silence of the elderly priest's departure, Walter announced, "Well, I need a drink. Anyone want something? I'm pouring. Your popeness? Do you want some wine? Hopefully it's not poisoned this time."

Francois glared at Walter, but then motioned for him to start serving. Renouf stared at them all in a mixture of revulsion and horror, as Walter Cram, demon lover, served drinks to the senior cardinals.

"Cardinal Devonshire? Wine, Your Grace?" Walter asked. "There is also sherry and, I think, gin. There's tea, too, though the pot feels cool to the touch."

"Thank you, Mr. Cram," Devonshire said, and there was not even a hint of sarcasm or challenge in her voice. She smiled at him and said, "I will take half a glass of the sherry, please."

Walter played drinks servant until the actual servants arrived, with platters of rolls, cold meats, pastries, and a northern delight that was slowly being accepted within Orsini's walls with the arrival of Imogen and her men: sandwiches.

No one spoke about the scene that had just happened outside, nor how Walter's face was swollen and how Renouf's still had caked blood all over it. Lex had the good sense to clean his knuckles against his jacket, though the scabs and caked blood where still there, and Dodd was developing a nasty black eye. Renouf glared at anyone who offered him a sausage roll or a pickled sardine paste sandwich, even when Giso pointed out they were of exceptional quality because, "they have a touch of pickled horseradish."

Allegra accepted a sliver of the sardine sandwich and, after taking a bite, declared to Giso that it really was excellent. Walter grabbed one and loudly confirmed that the horseradish made all the difference.

"My dear Lord Renouf, you should eat something," Allegra said. "There is no guarantee when General Bonacieux will return and besiege our front door once more. Lex? Dodd? Please, eat. That is not enough, Lieutenant Lex. I have it direct from the surgeon that you need to eat frequently."

"Indeed," Cardinal DeLancey scolded. The woman had not even returned to her seat yet from yelling at Vanida and was already scolding people. "I will report you to the healers this very day if I think for even a moment you are not eating enough."

"You must keep your strength up," Giso said. He took a second sandwich. "These are trying times. We do not wish to starve on top of it all."

Vittorio snorted. "You are weeks away from starvation."

Giso patted his middle. "Protection against famine. This stored food cannot be stolen from me."

"Enough!" Renouf finally roared. Honestly, Walter was surprised it took him that long. "What is happening here?"

"Whatever do you mean?" Her Highness asked.

Renouf's astonished face sent a cold chill of realization through Walter's body. So much had changed.

It was Allegra who spoke. "I believe Lord Renouf is correct. Look at us. Mages. Cardinals. Abolitionists. Conservatives." She inclined her head in Vittorio's direction. "It must be difficult for someone from the outside to understand the bond that exists between us all now."

Vittorio snorted. "I hate to disagree with you, my child."

"But don't worry, he will," Giso interrupted with a sour expression.

"As I recall the scene," Walter said with a laugh, "Vittorio caught Giso when he tripped, preventing him from taking a tumble."

Vittorio stuttered before saying, "The man annoys me, but I do not wish him ill."

"I do not care about any of that," Francois said. "What I want to know is how our promised assistance arrived and started a riot."

"Would we call it a riot, Your Radiance?" Allegra asked.

Francois snorted. "Take a glimpse at Lord Renouf's face and tell me it wasn't anything but a riot."

"So tell us, Lord Renouf," Allegra said, and the smile was gone from her face, "why did you kill innocent mages?"

Walter was one of the few people in the room who did not choke on their wine when Ally asked her question. She was damned good at disarming people, only to stab them with words when their guard had dropped. He had loved that about her at one time, and he'd hated her for it at another time in his life. Now? He saw it for what it was: dangerous. It was easy to forget how much power she held, by rank, by birth, by wealth, by her friends and connections. She was a dangerous woman, and Lord Renouf was about to learn a very important lesson.

"Well?" Allegra demanded.

Renouf made the mistake of turning to the pope when he answered Allegra's question. "Your Radiance, I do not think—"

"No one asked you to think, sir," Allegra interrupted. "Why did you kill innocent mages and arrest others? Do not turn your gaze away from me. I am the one who is asking the question, and you will answer me, sir. Or I shall write to the king and demand he send someone more competent."

Walter was tempted to bring out another round of drinks for this display. Ally could be as determined as a scent hound, and he almost felt sorry for this Renouf prick.

Renouf sputtered. "I protest! I have done nothing wrong."

"You killed innocent mages!" Giso shouted. He slapped his hand against his chair's arm for emphasis. "You, sir, should be hauled before the magistrate and tried for your crimes."

Renouf laughed. A short, barking sound escaped him before he realized it was said in earnest. "Your Grace, you forget to whom you speak."

"Reny, shut up," Her Highness said. "You have undone so much work."

Now came the boring part, where Lord Renouf decided to close his mouth and open his ears, something he should have done from the very start. Men like Renouf never learned that lesson as children, it seemed, and the sight of being corrected in public made them all the worse for it.

He protested and defended himself against their accusations, but he did listen all the same. Walter caught the pope's eye, who motioned at the wine, and Walter nodded and poured a glass for him. DeLancey asked if he wouldn't mind splashing a little port in her glass, and then Vittorio asked if he would also pour him half a glass of port.

"Thank you," Vittorio whispered as he accepted the glass from Walter.

"You're welcome," Walter said in the easy habit of manners.

They stared at each other. Walter hated this man. He'd hated Cardinal Vittorio all his adult life, either the symbol of him or the actual man himself. In Vittorio's eyes, Walter saw the same thing. They hated each other. This hobnobbing would never change the fact. Walter could, and would, bring this building down on Vittorio's head if he thought it would end mage mistreatment.

Vittorio's mouth quirked upward. He made a point of looking down at his glass before tipping the entire thing back and drinking without pause. Walter smiled at him and wished he'd poisoned the port. There had been a time he would have, too. That time was not all that long ago.

How could Giso be friends with someone like Vittorio? The old ladies he, at least, understood. Giso, though. They were opposites on all points.

But then he reflected on who warmed his own bed these days, and a sick, sinking feeling filled him. These people were like an infectious cough. It seemed harmless enough when one person had it, but it could—and would—spread until it infected everyone. Until it consumed their lives. This place was a contagious complacency.

"Well? What's going on?" Francois asked, and the irritation in his voice said this wasn't his first time asking.

"Nothing," Vittorio said. "Mr. Cram was fetching me a drink."

Walter let just a drop of his control slip and the porcelain in Allegra's teacup clattered on the saucer. Ally gave him a disapproving glance. He rolled his eyes, for her benefit, not anyone else's, and stopped the tremor. He wordlessly walked toward the door, where Renouf was standing.

"Cram, where are you going?" the pope asked.

Walter turned, just long enough to look at the collection of cardinals, military, and Amadore's royalty all staring at him, glasses in hand. He did not belong here. What's more, he didn't want to belong here. It was instantly easier to breathe once he was in the corridor, away from people who'd never be his own kind.

He had to keep that in mind at all times: no matter his connections, these people were not his friends. He was using them. He could never forget that.

CHAPTER NINE

ALLEGRA'S MOOD DID not improve, not even after Renouf had been thoroughly scolded. There was no punishment that would bring back the nine mages he'd murdered. There was no reversing the trauma for the other mages, all forty-six of them, whom he'd captured, bound, and gagged, before dragging them back to Orsini.

The only comfort she could find, and it was a pitiful one at that, was in the actions of the captured elemental mages. Those handful of people decided not to burn the Amadore soldiers alive, nor cause the river to surge and drown them all. True, she'd known all along that a piece of paper mattered little to those who believed mages were sent from the abyss, but she found a little comfort in knowing they believed there was help for them at the Cathedral.

Allegra reissued papers to the mages at the encampment, where they were recovering in body and spirit. She offered a few small coins of compensation, knowing that too much would only tempt others into violence and crime against them, and these people had suffered enough. Imogen, who outranked Renouf in all forms of the word, ordered eight soldiers from the militia to stand guard around the released mages, and forced Renouf to replace those soldiers with his own men.

Renouf protested his men being assigned to basic tasks, such as keeping the peace in the back alleys, but he was swiftly reminded of his place. He was someone important at his previous assignment. Here, however, he was under the authority of the temporary Colonel of the Orsini Militia, namely Imogen. And, as the letters Renouf had carried stated Imogen was to remain in the post for as long as her assistance was needed by the Holy Father, Renouf was to obey her. There was no other option.

Predictably, Renouf stormed off to write his letters protesting this injustice. Allegra found herself unmoved by his thorough humiliation. It had been self-inflicted, and mages were dead because of it.

That was where her mind was when she left the encampment, with her two guards in tow a polite distance behind her. She did not know them, being from Renouf's band of soldiers, but the Consorts were exhausted. The militia fared no better. She instructed these to stay a respectful distance behind her; she did not know them, so she did not trust them.

"Allegra!" Walter called out. He was coming from the small cluster of food carts that were still allowed to operate inside the walls, to take the pressure off the dining hall and to reduce the distances the laborers needed to walk to get a meal.

Allegra waited for him to join her. In between bites of his sausage roll, Walter asked, "Where's Rainier?"

"Stanton and Ginny are meeting with Rupert and DeLancey to go over security concerns about the north gate." She sighed. "I'll have the follow up meeting tomorrow morning. Apparently, they wanted to argue out the big issues before presenting the issues to the rest of us."

"How thoughtful," Walter said dryly.

"Isn't it just?" Allegra said, matching his tone. They shared a glance and laughed.

As they weaved their way through the narrow alleyways—Walter knew them better than Allegra—he made a comment about Dodd and Lex. It was innocent, Allegra was sure, but she knew it was time for her to say something.

"Walter, I do not know how to say this without offense, but please, stop interfering with Dodd and Lex." He began to deny it, but she interrupted him. "Lex has been through enough. And, for all of his brashness, Dodd is clearly struggling. I can see it, and I know you can. Leave them alone."

"I want them both to be happy," Walter said with a little sulk.

"They are happy being friends. If they want more, let them figure it out for themselves without you filling their heads. Besides, they're both still so young. They don't know what they want anyway beyond having a good time. Let them be."

Walter complained for a few steps before he finally agreed he'd stop interfering in the love lives of children. "I was never that young."

"Yes, you were," Allegra said. "That's why you thought you could run off to save all of the mages. Your knees hadn't started cracking in the morning."

Walter made a disgusted noise. "Every time Michael gets out of bed, he has to spend a minute cracking all of his joints so that he can move, and honestly, I hope someone burns me at the stake before then. It's bad enough my knees and ankles are always popping now."

Allegra laughed. "Oh please. You've been wanting someone to burn you at the stake for years now."

Walter grinned at her, but it faded from his eyes. He looked around at the dirty, muddy alleyway and sighed. "Less so lately. I forgot what it was like to be in one place all the time."

"You were at the abbey with us," Allegra countered.

Walter shook his head. "It wasn't the same. There, I was moving back and forth between the refugee camp, the town, and the abbey. I was in the tunnels, up the hills, down the hills. Here?" He sighed. "I poured Vittorio a glass of wine and handed it to him."

"What's wrong with that?"

He didn't answer, and she didn't push. Instead, she turned her questions to the archives. Roul had pulled out a number of banned texts. Serafina, Rigi, and Reinhold had been tasked with reading those. So far, most were merely banned for political reasons and nothing to do with the faith or magic.

"The rest of us are going through the texts on magic, but progress is slow. When a word can mean pork or garbage, it takes an hour to research the meaning of a sentence."

Walter motioned for them to take a side alley. At her silent question, he said, "This way is faster and has less stairs. According to Roul, everything Vittorio removed was related to either the history of the Guardians and what happened with Tasmin's supposed disappearance into the abyss, and general stuff about the origins of magic. But not the modern things. All of the old stories about it. Roul said he's never opened any of those books, but there are journal notes that senior archivists have written about the items in the vault, so he's been consulting that first. Most of the books we're reading aren't even real paper, that's how old they are. It's rather extraordinary, when you think about what is hidden in this place and no one knows."

Allegra waited for Walter to open the door for her, and they nodded at a couple of servants carrying laundry. "If I didn't know you better, I'd say you were enjoying yourself."

Walter laughed. "I'm surprised by how quickly I've adapted to not running for my life, I'll say that for myself. But," he suddenly grew grave, "do not think for a moment that I wouldn't level this place to the ground if I had cause."

She knew very little of what Walter had done in the years when they were apart, but she'd heard the rumors, the accusations, and she'd heard a few of his own stories. Moreover, she knew Walter. So, she gave him a soft smile and said, "But only if you had to."

Because, for all of his bluster, there were mages in these buildings. There was no where in all of Serna that did not have mages hiding within their midst. Some were branded, some were like her. Others lied, like her, too. Walter would never hurt another mage unless he was forced to in defense of himself or others.

For him to destroy Orsini would be for him to destroy himself.

Allegra turned her attention to Walter, and so did not notice someone had stepped in front of her. Allegra slammed against a warm body, and a startled sound escaped her. "Lex!"

Lex looked like he'd seen demons when he stared at them. Lex blurted, "What are you doing here?"

Walter assumed the question was for him and said, "I stopped to get a sausage roll. Paid for with my brand-new earnings, I might add."

"By who?" Allegra asked.

"By you," Walter said with a grin. He let Allegra sputter for a moment before he amended, "Well, Nathan, to be specific. He said the pope instructed him to give me a clerk's wages, since they could not have me running around stealing from mage oppressors."

"No, I mean," Lex said, regaining his composure, "what are you both doing here, in this specific corridor, right this very moment?"

"Walter said it's a short cut," Allegra said. "Lex, what's wrong?"

"When did you learn about this?" Lex asked. "I...I only found out about this today."

"Rigi showed me," Walter said. "Apparently, everyone working on the east side of the Cathedral proper comes down this way if they're heading outside the gates for food, because it saves them having to come down the main steps."

"Lex, what's wrong?" Allegra asked.

"I'm...there's just so many paths and hidden rooms and passages...No one knows them all. Not even the servants, and half of them are all locked," Lex said. He motioned around them. "This passage has doors, but they're never locked, according to everyone I've asked. It's on the plans I was given, but there's apparently a connection further up that isn't even on any building plans that any of the archivists could find."

"You mean the one that goes to the back alley, where the waste goes?" At Lex's surprised expression, if it was possible for him to look more surprised, Walter said, "I ended up there by accident when Rigi first told me to come this way. Nearly got splashed in chamberpot piss. A man remembers that."

Lex gave them both the strangest expression. "I bet. I...have to go. I'm trying to add on all of the passages on this map. Do...do you know of any others?"

Walter shrugged. "Just a few. Mostly, people tell me where they are. It's not like I ever spent time here before all this."

"Right," Lex said. "Hey, are you able to show me around tomorrow after we do some sword practice? Maybe take a few hours and we can get out all of the maps? If the archives can spare you?"

Walter shrugged. "Sure. I'll see if Rigi can help. He knows more of these than I do."

Lex did not seem visibly relaxed by that. "All right. Well, I better get back at it. Contessa. Walter."

They waited until Lex was well beyond hearing before Allegra said, "What just happened?"

"I don't know, but Lex just called me Walter. That's never a good sign."

LEX'S SWEATY PALMS were clenching the maps too tightly, and they tried to ease their worried grip. Lex hurried as quickly as possible back to the old rectory without running.

They burst into the building and announced, "I just found the Contessa and Cram there!"

Dodd and Her Highness were both leaning over a table that was pushed up near the large wall map. They both talked over each other, but basically their questions were of a similar thought path.

Lex waved them off. "I didn't tell them exactly what I was doing, only that I was trying to map servant passages for Her Highness. Cram said it was Cardinal Rigi who told him about that passageway, and that everyone working in the east side of the Cathedral uses that path if they're looking for a shortcut to the carts outside. Then, Cram knew about one of the hidden passages, and said it's where the chamberpots are dumped, but I couldn't find that room."

"There must be four thousand people on that side. We cannot investigate that many people."

"But most of them were not at Borro Abbey," Dodd said.

"Both of you have lived here for years," Her Highness said. "Why don't the two of you know all of these routes, but Rigi and Cram do?"

Lex shrugged. "Orsini is a big place. Like, it's not just the distance across, but Orsini is built up both high, and underground. Until recently, I'd never even been past the inner barricade, where all of the cardinals live. This place isn't a grid out in a field. Pardon my frankness, Your Highness."

"Call me Imogen," she said.

"Sorry, Your Highness," Lex said. "If I did that, my grandmother would find me and box my ears for being so disrespectful to my betters."

"Perhaps we have the same grandmother." Her Highness was thoughtful for a moment. "I find it very suspicious that each and every step you take in this investigation always leads back to Walter Cram, and yet, something about that path to him always feels off. I don't like the man, and I've spent a good portion of my career hunting him down, but every time he ends up where he should not be, it makes the back of my neck itch."

"Listen, I hate to ask this question, but I'm going to say it," Dodd said. "Are we sure Cram isn't the person? I know, I like him well enough, too, when he's not preaching at me about mages, but..."

"I believe there's a demon in the room that no one wants to talk about," Her Highness said. "Allegra."

"Are you accusing the Contessa of being the demon summoner?" Lex was not about to stand there and listen to anyone bring false allegations like that against anyone, not even Cram, but certainly not the Contessa.

"I'm only saying that you need to completely rule out, beyond all doubt, that it is *not* her," Her Highness said. "And then, you need to do the same for Walter Cram."

Lex shook their head. "Dodd and I have already gotten her statement and Nadira's, all of her servants, and as many of the Borro servants as we could find. It isn't her."

"Then, I believe we should consider Walter Cram our main suspect until we can find the evidence to the contrary. Then, by going at it that way, his name will be cleared and clean."

"His name will never be clean," Lex shouted. They didn't mean to, but once it was out of Lex's mouth, there it was. They sucked in a breath, trying to control their temper. They were only partially successful. "You're falling into the same trap everyone does. Walter Cram is a loudmouth jackass, who puts on this big, bad show about being the biggest, baddest, bravest mage in all of the world, but...Your Highness, if someone told me Walter burned down Cardinal Vittorio's estate for fun? I'd believe it. But you're saying that he is trying to endanger mages for his power-hungry need to...I can't even come up with something to finish that thought. It's a joke, that's what it is. Your Highness."

"Lex, why are you taking this so personally?" Her Highness asked.

"Personally?" Lex's throat was constricting, and they could not push out enough air from their lungs. "I nearly died trying to protect Walter. I nearly died. I saw what he did at the end. None of you saw it. I did, though. I saw him. And accusing him...and..."

Lex leaned forward, gasping for air now. Tears were streaming down their face, and Lex slapped at them, trying to gain control of their vision and self. All the senses of that day —the smell, the shouting, the fears, the pain—came rushing back. Lex's vision blurred as memory took over sense, and their heart pounded painfully.

"Lex." That was Dodd, and Lex grabbed for his offered hand. Just to be rooted to what was real.

It took what felt like an eternity for Lex to regain control over their body and mind, to force away the bad memories and to confront the reality of the present, which was bad enough without the unwelcomed and unwanted memories.

"Sorry," Lex whispered. They didn't know what else to say.

"Don't apologize," Her Highness said. Her tone had softened, but not into pity territory.

"Listen, you can keep mapping the routes, because we need that," Dodd said. "But I don't mind being the one to look closer at Cram. This isn't the first time we've found demon portals and him in the same spot. I think it's best to make sure we can say, confidently, it's not him."

Lex didn't like it, but nodded their head. It was the best way to find out who was doing it. And, if it was Walter Cram, Lex would kick the stool out from under his feet. But likewise, Lex wasn't going to let someone like Renouf or Vanida hang someone, *anyone*, just because they smelled dead rat. Lex was going to insist on seeing the dead rat first.

CHAPTER TEN

ALLEGRA RETIRED TO her suite to finish up the last of her paperwork while she waited for Stanton to return. She had dismissed Nadira and the chambermaids for the evening, and told them not to get into any trouble with renegade mages. That made Nadira scoff and mutter about ragamuffins.

She was finishing a letter to her brother when Stanton returned home. He seemed exhausted, but offered her a wide smile when their eyes met. He walked over to her desk, and leaned down to kiss her mouth. He tasted of wine and cake, and she guessed he'd had a healthy helping of both. He'd been carrying a small basket and put it down on the corner of her table. She lifted the cloth, as Stanton sat down to pull off his boots. Stanton had robbed the Holy Father's table again, bringing back several slices of cake, a few muffins, several types of bread rolls, and miniature spinach pies. Allegra grabbed one of the spinach pies. Even cold, the crust was still flaky and not soggy underneath. Two bites and it was gone.

"I'm desperate for a bath. Do you mind?"

"I will call one of the footmen to work the pump," she said.

She rose to fetch a footman. It wasn't that Stanton could not work a couple of pumps, but it turned out that it was rather tricky mixing hot and cold water, and after three failed attempts, the head laundress came to speak with her, begging that they fetch a servant next time for Stanton was wasting too much of the hot water.

The footman came in, bowed, and disappeared around the corner of Allegra's bedroom to work the pumps. It would take some time to fill up the indulgent tub, so the couple shared the details of their day and drank the rest of the wine bottle they'd opened the previous night. Stanton declared himself full, so Allegra ate freely from the basket, while Stanton told her about the meeting.

"We'll go over all of the details tomorrow, and make a decision then, but the refugees are flooding from everywhere now," Stanton said. "It's only going to get worse, as long as Cartossa is fighting itself."

On they chatted, and Allegra eventually covered up the basket to protect the rolls. The footman declared the tub full, asked if Stanton knew how to work the drain plug (he did), and they were left in privacy once more. Stanton was peeling out of his clothes before the footman had left the suites, and Allegra heard the splash of water and his initial hiss. Finally, the sigh.

He beckoned for her to join him. She came across the corner and eyed the copper tub dubiously. "Is there even room?"

He reached out his arms, and she rolled her eyes. She removed her dressing gown and the thin shift underneath and eyed the tub suspiciously. Stanton moved one of his legs over the edge so that she could put a foot in. Tentatively, she stepped inside, with Stanton guiding her by the thighs in case she slipped. She crouched, not wanting to accidentally step on any of his delicate bits. Carefully, she eased herself in, water sloshing dangerously close to the lower edge of the tub, until she was finally leaning her back against his chest.

Water splashed over the lower edge, but that was why the marble platform had a drain, bringing the water back into the laundry system for reuse.

She reached over the edge to grab one of the woven linen towels from the basket the maids kept well-stocked and rolled it up so that Stanton could comfortably dangle a long leg over the edge. As it was, she had to bend her knees to make room and rested them against the side where Stanton dangled his leg.

There, they sat and soaked, talking gently about the little nothings of life. For a brief time, demons did not exist. A rogue

131

mage did not exist. Magic was forgotten. Elementals were imaginary. It was just them, alone and naked, enjoying the sweet comfort of the special kind of intimacy that could only come with familiarity.

Finally, after the water's temperature began to cool their rising arousal, they carefully climbed out of the tub, water going everywhere. Allegra began drying herself off, skin all bumpy and shriveled from the chilled air hitting her skin. She pulled on her shift, but Stanton stopped her when she went to put on her dressing gown.

"Wait," he said. "I have something for you. Let me put on clothes first."

"Don't on my account," she said.

He laughed, but the look he gave her was one of embarrassment, like he didn't want to be naked in front of her in this moment. She didn't say anything when he picked up his own dressing gown from his side of the bed, neatly draped over the blankets. Once he wrapped it around himself, he reached under the bed. Out came a bundle wrapped in brown paper and tied with a red ribbon.

He handed it to her across the bed. She smiled and scolded herself for reading too much into the red ribbon. "Oo, did you get me a gift?"

He pulled himself across the bed to be near her. He kissed her neck, just under her ear, and whispered, "Just open it."

She did and pulled out a dressing gown. Only, it wasn't just a dressing gown. She had to stand to inspect it properly. It was embroidered with elements of her family heraldry, wrapped around aspects of Stanton's family emblem. Not his new rank, but that of his family. His parentage. His roots.

And it was in red silk.

Wedding clothes red silk.

She knew she was supposed to say something, anything, but words failed her. This was an incredibly intimate gift, meant for her quiet moments alone with him or with Nadira, or one of the chambermaids. This was not meant for the public. The stitching was of the highest quality, and there was plenty of gold and silver thread throughout the garment. It would have taken a dozen women, day and night, to finish this.

"Don't you like it?" Stanton asked, in a vulnerable, soft voice. Wedding red silk.

"It's beautiful," she managed to whisper.

"I had to bribe Nadira with saffron cake before she'd agree to give me your measurements. That cost almost as much as the gold thread she insisted be used."

"She knew about this?" Allegra whispered. "She didn't say anything."

"I asked her not to. Aren't you going to put it on?"

Wedding red.

The garment fit her perfectly. But of course it would. She looked at him. Really looked at him. The man she wanted to spend her life with.

Wedding.

"Ask me properly," she blurted.

Confusion spread across his face for a moment, until realization dawned. This was not the kind of gift one gave without expectation on some level. This was an offer, a request, a proposal.

He drew in a breath and let it out, controlled and steady. Then, he pulled himself across the remaining distance of the bed to stand next to her. He took her hand. "Allegra, Contessa of Marsina, Arbiter of Justice, Constable of Orsini, richest woman in Serna," he laughed when he said that line, "and love of my life. I offer you my reputation, my title, my lands, my wealth, my heart, and my life for as long as the sun rises in the morning."

Her eyes filled with tears. She could say no. She probably should say no. And yet, in her heart, she was always a bit of the romantic.

"Lord Barrington, Captain Stanton Rainier of the Holy Father's Own Consorts, war hero, defender of Borro Abbey, and love of my life. I offer you my reputation, my title, my lands, and my extensive wealth," they both chuckled when she said that, "my heart, and my life as long as the sun rises in the morning."

"Marry me, Allegra," Stanton said as he cupped her face.

She'd said no to that many times in her life, especially when she was young and men saw her for her lands and wealth. It had always been the right answer. And now, she knew in her heart that she could finally answer differently, and it would still be the correct answer for her heart.

"Yes. I will marry you."

What followed was not the love making of innocent youths, who did not understand the cruelties of life yet, but of equals, of adults who knew the trials ahead of them and decided that those challenges were best faced with a companion by their side. They laughed and kissed and moaned in pleasure, and then laughed some more.

And throughout it all, Allegra knew she had found her home.

CHAPTER ELEVEN

STANTON WOKE TO the soft footfalls of the first chambermaid of the morning. She was exceptionally quiet while lighting the fire, but the sound of water pouring into the fireplace kettle stirred Stanton's bladder. Once she left, he had only enough time to crawl out from their curtained bed to deal with the necessities and tug a tunic over his head, before the door creaked open again.

Crawling back into bed caused Allegra to stir, but she settled back into the steady breathing of slumber. He pushed the curtain out a little, hoping to locate his trousers, but he didn't see them. Nor could he remember where and when he'd discarded them the previous night.

Another maid entered. This would've been the laundry maid, who took care of his and Allegra's wash. They'd both lost all of their clothes in the collapse of Borro Abbey, and had been struggling to replace their outfits since. That meant more work for the maids, who couldn't let the clothes pile up for weeks on end before tackling it over the span of a week.

Nadira was working her hardest to have Allegra's outfits expanded, but so far she'd only been able to find ready-made clothes and had those tailored. Stanton chuckled at poor Nadira, who clucked and complained about her mistress's poor attire, but as Allegra was fond of saying, the servants needed clothes more than she did.

That included Nadira, who scoffed at the idea, but dutifully found a seamstress to have four new gowns made for herself.

He really needed new shirts, though. He only had the three, and it was a burden on the maids to have his clothes constantly at the laundry.

Stanton's heart picked up its beat and he was grateful for the privacy curtains. Another maid entered just as he took several deep breaths to wash away the images of demonic fire and ash. This would be the maid who delivered the mail. That meant Nadira was soon to arrive with her small army of maids, who'd rouse them from bed to clean and dress Allegra.

Stanton had not grown up poor by any definition of the word. Yes, he chose to live simply as a captain, but that was not for lack of funds. But Allegra's morning rituals were very different from his own. He'd watched one morning in stunned fascination as three maids cleaned and dressed her, all under Nadira's stern gaze. Then, her hair was combed and plaited and pinned, all the while Allegra ate and read her letters aloud, asking Nadira for various tasks to be dealt with during the day. For her, the quiet acceptance of never being alone, even for the most basic of tasks, was a part of life as a contessa. She knew nothing else.

Mercifully, the poor chambermaid who lit the fires stopped pulling back the curtains upon her arrival. It took her a week before she could make eye contact with him without blushing.

All of the bustle in the room beyond finally stirred Allegra. She blinked and yawned. "Was that the maid?"

He bent down and kissed her gently. "Nadira's invasion force shall arrive at any moment."

Allegra groaned protests and wriggled to get closer to him. Her naked bottom rubbed against him. He sighed. "We don't have time for that, love."

She looked over her shoulder in that sultry way half-asleep women always did, and said, "You're not my husband yet, so you don't get to boss me around."

He snorted. "I doubt that will change, even when I am your husband."

He reached down to stroke the most intimate parts of her when the inevitable hard knock came at the door. That would be Nadira.

He rolled on his back. "I need my trousers to cover up what you've done to me."

"Me?" Allegra was laughing as she leaned over the edge of the bed to pick up her shift off the floor. He cupped her bottom, and she jumped, losing her balance, and half fell out of bed.

He shouted out of instinct, and she was partially outside the curtain when Nadira and her army walked into the room. Allegra was laughing as Stanton hauled her back into bed, her bare legs dangling in the air, moving the curtain. A giggle escaped Allegra.

Nadira clapped her hands severely and said, "Girls! Have some decorum. We do not giggle in the presence of our betters."

Allegra put her hand over her mouth, trying to hold in the laughter. Stanton was less successful and a snort escaped him.

"Decorum!" Nadira snapped.

That sent Allegra into full giggles and she collapsed back on her pillow. Stanton couldn't hold in his laughter anymore and he laughed alongside her. Nadira's sighs and tuts did not help in the slightest, though when Stanton peeked out beyond the curtains to find his trousers, he saw Nadira grinning as she picked up Allegra's new dressing gown from the floor.

She caught his gaze and glanced at the robe still in her arms, already being expertly shook out for her mistress to wear. She raised an eyebrow.

He smiled and mouthed "yes." Nadira's features brightened. She allowed herself just a small moment of that, before wiping the expression from her face. She nodded sharply. "Your Ladyship? I have your robe ready." In her left hand, she picked up his trousers, which were haphazardly hanging off a nearby chair. She shoved those at him through the curtains with such a severe look of disapproval that he was transported back in time, to when he was caught naked at fourteen in front of his old nanny.

Allegra gave him a final kiss, whispered, "Duty calls," and tugged open the curtain on her side of the bed. She climbed out, fully naked, and ducked her head for Nadira to put a clean shift over her head. From there, he knew how the morning would go. He struggled and panted as he attempted to climb into his trousers while laying prostrate on a soft bed.

That was it. He was having someone find him a privacy screen for his side of the bed. If Allegra insisted he sleep here—instead of the comfortable privacy of his small barrack's room—then he needed a privacy screen.

Good God Almighty, no wonder his father had his own bedchamber.

Three heartbeats after he got the flap buttons of his trousers done up, the curtains at the foot of the bed flung open. The noise and the sudden sunlight startled him. Nadira stared at him for a moment, with deepening disapproval, though he had no idea why, before she began her task of straightening up the curtains and tying them back into place around each bedpost.

He crawled out of bed and pulled up his suspenders. This particular shirt he wore had four buttons at the neck, and he did all up for modesty's sake. Two of the maids were stripping the bed behind him, all to shake out the linens before re-making the bed. Allegra was in her new dressing gown, and she was stunning in the red. He stared at her, longer than was proper in this company, but she was radiant. She stopped reading her letter to give him a wide smile. But then she turned back to her letter, allowing the maid standing behind her to continue brushing out the tangles from their night of lovemaking.

He had to move twice because he was in the way of the maids. Allegra's suite was large by Orsini's standards, but was not meant for this many maids and a suitor standing in the corner. His father was right: separate bedchambers was the key to a successful marriage.

But when he walked over to the breakfast platter, there were all of his favorite foods. He smiled. Nadira still liked him.

LEX FELT IMMEASURABLY improved with a good night's sleep. Their knuckles hurt more than their ever-healing stomach wound, and Lex discovered a rather impressive bruise upon their jawline that must've come from falling during the brawl, though they had no memory of hitting their face.

138

Wanting to get an early start on the day, Lex headed to the old rectory. Hopefully, the bedrooms would be set up soon, and Lex could sleep there and save the morning walk. Lex probably didn't need the lantern they carried, as the sun was slowly making its way above the horizon, but it was nice to have in case of any demon portals.

Lex sucked in a breath, held it, and slowly exhaled. There was no shame in having a hard time. That's what the healers, surgeons, apothecaries, everyone said. The Captain said it, too. Lord Almighty, even the pope had said it, in a sad, knowing tone. And, if Lex was going to be honest, they'd also say it to other people. Everyone was right. It just somehow still did not help with the isolation and fear.

Motion caught Lex's eye. After an initial heart-pounding moment where memory and fear gripped the heart, thinking finally took over, and Lex's shoulders dropped in relief. It was only Father Michael. He was in his robes and walking with purpose. Lex was about to call out, but the priest seemed busy, determined, out for a long, brisk walk. They didn't want to disturb him, especially given that anyone who had to share Walter Cram's bed would need moments to vent the smoke that rose in their hearts.

Lex glanced back at the direction the priest could have come, calculating. It seemed everyone was using that alleyway to skirt around having to use the Cathedral's main entrance. They'd talk to Her Highness and see if any of those still on light duties could help map the corridors and servant passages. The map archivist said many of the oldest passages were lost generations ago. Not the passages themselves, but the knowledge to find them. In fact, they'd learned that even the Cathedral's Grand Housekeeper had keys in her study to passages that no one could find, even though they were all labeled. She'd even offered them to Lex, in case they discovered a hidden locked door in their search.

Lex pondered on that as they approached the old rectory. They opened the door to two of the Amadore soldiers on duty. The soldiers said how they'd been on the second shift, and thought getting ready for the day would make Calm Seas' burdens easier. Even though there were the wood boys who handled that, Lex also knew Calm Seas well enough to know the girl would be doing it herself at four in the morning if there was no one to stop her.

"Thanks for doing that," Lex said. "I'm sure Nadira will appreciate anything that helps make less work for Calm Seas, too."

The fire was lit, and the kettle was already on its hook, ready to steep strong tea as needed. Lex realized that they didn't have any cups with which to drink the tea, nor did they have any tea leaves. In fact, surveying the room, they were still missing several items. Lex made a passing comment about that, and the soldiers, eager for something to keep them busy, offered to go to the camp market. At this time of the morning, they'd already be setting up, so they'd get first crack at anything new.

Lex scribbled out a quick list of odds and ends, and the soldiers added a few more. Simple things, like soap and linens, tea and sugar, more kettles for upstairs, and all of the typical luxuries and comforts. Lex also added items for their and Dodd's room; the beds had apparently arrived late the previous evening, but the mattresses weren't ready. Lex added a few smaller furniture items, just in case anything was seen at the market.

Lex unlocked their desk and pulled out a small wooden box that contained several promissory notes from the Contessa, as well as some from Rainier, and explained to the soldiers how they worked. Lex would have to get Her Highness to write up a few, too, for things to come out of the militia's budget. But for now, most of the spending could come from the Arbiter account. Lex also handed over eighteen silver sovereigns, since individuals selling might not want to wait for the Cathedral coffers to pay out the monthly accounts. And finally, Lex handed over the few precious small coins they possessed; the treasury was struggling with small coinage with all the refugees and interruptions in trade and...

Lex snorted. Maybe the family was right after all: Lex would have made an excellent administrator for the Cathedral. Lex resisting touching the sword that hung at their hip. Less dangerous, too. Looking back up at the soldiers, Lex decided that no, they were where the Lord God Almighty wanted them. They had to believe that, for there was no room right now in Lex's soul for theological debate.

There was enough shit going on already.

The sleeping soldiers upstairs had not stirred, so Lex sat down at one of the desks to do some paperwork: lists, letters, the usual. Lex had no idea when the morning mail delivery would arrive, or if someone had to be sent for it. They might have to simply wait and see.

A few vague details about Borro Abbey had come to Lex the previous night while talking with the others, so they pulled out the folded paper filled with scribbles and carefully wrote them out, using concise language and a careful hand with the ink. On the bottom, Lex printed the names of all involved in the conversation; they'd get them to read and sign it later.

No one could hide forever.

The front door opened. Lex was about to ask if the soldiers had forgotten anything. However, it was Dodd, and not the Amadore soldiers. "Oh! What are you doing up so early?"

Dodd scuffed his boots on the provided mat. Lex added *outdoor boot scraper* to a new list of needed items, before shuffling back to the original sheet they'd been working on.

Dodd put his lantern down on his desk, which was directly opposite and facing Lex, adding significantly more light to the windowless room. He looked around and declared, "We need a window. Shutters keep out the bugs and the rain, but also the sun."

"No argument from me, but I suspect we'll be way down on the important things list," Lex said. They didn't mean for it to come out bitter, but it did.

Dodd scoffed. "Because finding the murderous asshole doing all this shit isn't nearly as important as repairing the upper ballroom windows, be reasonable, Lieutenant Lex."

They both let out bitter sounds that weren't quite laughs. The conversation died in that way when someone has to say something that's pressing on them. Finally, Dodd sighed, and said, "Listen, I've not had a chance to talk to you..."

Lex got that sinking feeling that they were heading down awkward lane. Then, their mouth blurted, "I can't do this!" before their brain had a chance to filter if that was what needed to be spoken.

Dodd's shocked expression made Lex's heart pound and they were certain this was the end of their relationship, of a life's long friendship of support and comfort. Lex's brain began a litany of measured words and phrases, things that needed to be said, things that should be said, things that...

"Oh, thank the Lord God," Dodd said. The relief was evident.

Lex stared at him, now completely confused. "Huh?"

Dodd sighed. He came over to lean against Lex's desk. "That's what I've been wanting to talk to you about, but I've been too much of a coward. I hadn't realized how close we'd come to all losing each other until I saw you lying in that bed. I can't begin to tell you what I was feeling, because I don't even know. But then Cram goes and fills my head with all of this stuff that I should've known better to keep inside."

"But I'm glad you told me," Lex said.

"I just told you too soon," Dodd said. He tried to laugh, but it was an awkward, gasp of air more than anything. "You were nearly dead, I was starving, and...I need time, Lex." His voice quivered. "And you need it, too, and I was selfish because I thought..."

"You thought this would fix it," Lex said gently and without malice. When Dodd's breath hitched in his throat, that was enough answer. They were both silent for a few moments before Lex decided it was time to open up a little, too. There were things on Lex's heart.

"I thought you were dead. The healers gave me these drugs and I couldn't always tell what was real. I must've been reunited with you a hundred times. And I saw you die at least a hundred times more." Lex sniffed. "It's not that I'm against any of it or whatever. I just need time to accept all of this is actually real. I need to figure out how I feel, and I can't do that while," Lex sucked in a breath, "my nightmares rule me."

Dodd grew quiet and he looked down at his boots. Lex didn't want to hurt him; that was the last thing they ever wanted to do. They opened their mouth, ready to explain, to apologize, to try again, when Dodd said, without looking up, "Since I told you, all I've had are nightmares now of you dying."

"Oh, Dodd," Lex said, and suddenly understood all of it. They pushed their chair back to stand and wrap their arms around him. They both hugged and cried. Then, they laughed a little at themselves, then hugged and cried some more about how cruel life had become.

Love came in many forms. It changed. It evolved. Lex didn't know what the future held for the two of them, if it would morph into something predictable or be rooted in the heart of friendship. But whatever it would become, it would be eternal. They could wait. They should wait. Just be honest and open, even if that was the hardest thing in the world.

The scars needed to heal, and they'd heal them together. Lex smiled and honestly felt better and more hopeful than they'd felt in days.

"*Anyway*," Dodd said, his big grin returning, even if his eyes were puffy. "Just wanted to get that out in the air."

"Same," Lex said, wiping at their own eyes. "So what do we do now?"

"Breakfast first, and then conquer the world?"

Lex made a show of thinking hard before saying, "In that order. I'm starving."

They laughed, then shushed each other as footsteps sounded on the upper floor. The soldiers were finally waking up. Lex put their hands on Dodd's shoulder blades and pushed him toward the door, and it felt natural again, the way it had been, the way it should always be.

Dodd whined and complained about being manhandled, and that Lex's fingers were bony as shit and hurt. Once outside, the sun had risen enough to see without lanterns. In case of demons, Lex thought. There were always going to be demons.

But first, meat patties.

At least, that was the plan until Cardinal Vanida came huffing and puffing in their direction to ruin everything.

CHAPTER TWELVE

ALLEGRA FOUND HERSELF in a giddy mood, which was both distracting and completely inappropriate for the topic of discussion. Renouf and Ginny were detailing the growing refugee situation. The geography of Orsini itself made it a picturesque location for contemplation when in one of the Cathedral upper rooms, high enough to see over the walls and rooftops, to overlook the river or to stand on one's balcony and gaze out at the woodland to the west, and pretend one was all alone in the world.

Of course, Orsini was not just the home of the faithful. It was a city state, a great monument to neutrality and strength, uniting all of the nations of Serna under one God, under one faith, under one man: Francois.

No wonder the people fled to the Cathedral; all roads led to their door.

However, the southern road was completely congested now. Petty crime was rampant, as was pockets of unrest between mages, free slaves, and all of the farmers and merchants. Then there was the issue of the fleeing aristocrats, who did not stay to defend their estates against Bonacieux's advancing army, and who thought the Cathedral would offer them sanctuary.

"Francois and the cardinals give their permission to move people through Orsini, to get them to the north and allow them to travel onwards," Allegra said, holding up a letter that had come in the first delivery of the morning. "They leave the planning to Imogen and Stanton."

Ginny accepted the offered letter and read it. She passed it over to Renouf. "I'll speak with Rainier when we're done here. It's going to take all our soldiers to do this without causing a riot."

Renouf passed the letter back to Allegra. She placed it in her Read basket, where Nathan would eventually gather up all of these items for filing and safe keeping. He was a twitchy kid, but he was obsessed with knowing everything and having the right piece of information at hand to legally slap another down when they stepped out of their place. She rather liked him for it, though that was admittedly because he used his skills for her cause, and never against her.

"We should first move the quality inside the walls," Renouf suggested.

Imogen and Allegra both stared at him in dismayed shock. It was Imogen who said what they were both clearly thinking, "I just said I wished to avoid a riot, not start one."

"We cannot expect noble personages to languish with the scum," Renouf said.

"Reny!" Imogen said, and Allegra exercised the wisdom of rank by letting relations work out their own squabbles whenever possible. "First, there is no room for them! Parts of the main Cathedral building are completely uninhabitable until the repairs are finished. The last report I read said that twenty percent of all of Orsini's buildings had damage, and forty percent of the main administrative block is still unusable. I've been sleeping in a tent for weeks. Me! I'm a fucking princess and I sleep on the fucking ground, Reny."

"I did offer to let you stay with me, and Stanton would go sleep in the barracks," Allegra said quietly.

"That's not the point, Allegra," Ginny said. "We have all had to make sacrifices. There is so little space left inside of our walls right now, and it is not right that many of Orsini's servants can't return to their homes yet."

"We cannot ask people of rank to sleep in tents!" Renouf scoffed.

"We asked you to do it!" Ginny shot back.

"That is different! I am with my men!"

Unfortunately, as most family discussions went, this one soon turned to bickering. Allegra had to step into those dangerous rapids. "If I could, I would house every single person within our walls. However, we simply do not have the space. The last count I have as of yesterday stated there are now over four thousand people encamped. Where are we to put them all? How do we fairly distribute space? What's more, how do we feed them? The only reason we have not had a food riot yet is because the Sisters and Brothers of Mercy are out there every morning serving soup. We cannot even serve them bread now because there are not enough ovens!"

"But those are just mages," Renouf said with a scoff.

Allegra's voice turned hard. "Have you forgotten I am a mage, Lord Renouf?"

He made a dismissive wave of his hand. "You are a woman of the blood, not some rabble from the mines."

"It is only by the grace of the Lord God Almighty that none of us are one of them," Allegra said. "Ginny, how soon can we begin moving people through the city to the north wall?"

"Days, if not weeks, at the rate people are arriving. However, any release of pressure would be helpful, I'm certain."

"Renouf, can your men assist?" When he nodded begrudgingly, she said, "We should do it in waves, though. Send riders down the path, letting people know we'll start moving. We'll need guards all along, too, and mounted, to help keep order. We cannot have a panic. Some will claim they have relations here. I shall send a note to Nathan to see how best to vet those people." Allegra tapped her fingers against her desk, thinking. "For now, ask any of those people to hang back, just until we can get Nathan's assistance. Unless, of course, someone from Orsini can vouch for them? I do not know how to do that properly."

"Perhaps have a couple of the servants and Consorts, those who are still on light duties who might recognize people?" Ginny suggested. "They could act as an easy verification."

"Orsini is too large for anyone to know everyone," Allegra cautioned.

"True, but perhaps that might save some of Nathan's time," Ginny countered.

Allegra thought about it and found she liked the plan the more she mulled it over. "Renouf, we will need a strong military escort for this, but gentle. Please, only assign your most patient and experienced soldiers. This isn't a task for hot heads. We should also have tables and chairs, and paper. And ink and quill. That way, everything can be done properly and fairly. If people are willing to take on their relations and share their space with them, that is completely different."

"You could give up your room," Renouf said.

"My suite has windows and a small balcony that demons can perch upon while they throw one's screaming body to the ground below." Allegra knew he said it to start a fight, but she smiled sweetly and added, "No one is brave enough to take it."

Ginny shivered. "After seeing a demon fly off with the main portcullis, I have to say that I, too, do not look upon windows with the same friendly eye that I once did. That is why I told them to give Cram that suite of his. I'd thought we could set up a makeshift barracks there, but my men took one look at the windows and said to give to the mage. We'll sleep in tents until the old rectory has enough beds for all of us."

Renouf did not say much to that. What was there for him to say? He'd missed Borro Abbey, and he missed the partial destruction of Orsini. The majority of the bodies had been cleaned up by the time he'd arrived. He could not be faulted in his lack of understanding, no matter how much she wished she could blame him for his ignorance.

"Shall we head out then, Your Highness?" Renouf asked as he stood.

Allegra motioned for Ginny to stay. "Renouf, may I steal her for a little longer? There's a letter from home that I wished to discuss with her. It will only take a moment, I promise, and then I'll release her."

"As you wish, Your Ladyship, Your Highness," Renouf said as he bowed with each of their names.

After he closed the door, Allegra turned to a curious Imogen and said, "Stanton asked to merge his estate with mine."

Ginny's expression made the delivery worthwhile. "And your answer was?"

"I believe I shall," Allegra said with a grin.

"Well, it's about time! Tell me everything."

She told Ginny about the dressing gown, their proposal in bed, leaving out the details of the bath. It wasn't that she was ashamed, but wished to save Stanton's pride in case he told the story differently to save her modesty. They'd not discussed how widely known they wanted this, just that they both wanted to keep it fairly quiet. Stanton did say he wanted to be the one to tell the Consorts, and once that happened, all of Orsini would know. Likewise, she wanted to be the one to tell Rupert and Walter and, again, all of Orsini would know after she told those two.

"Duchess has such a pleasing feeling on the lips when you say it," Ginny said. "Duchess. Duchess. *Duchess.*"

Allegra laughed. "I believe one of your titles is Grand Duchess Imogen of Amadore."

Ginny made a face. "That doesn't count. I was born royal! My parents had to make up a title for me because they'd ran out of them. As it is, I got no land with mine. I have to work for a living, unlike some people in this room."

"Oh please," Allegra said. "You never wanted for a single thing in your life, except a little more discipline from your father."

"I was always his favorite, wasn't I?"

"Unbearably so," Allegra said gravely.

They were laughing and talking about wedding plans, and how, if Imogen had her way, it would be the wedding by which all weddings would be judged. They continued in that way for a few more minutes, until bad news arrived with the full brightness of dawn.

The hard rap at the door was the first indication that it wasn't one of the servants, for theirs was a polite, almost timid tap to announce their arrival without being intrusive. This knock was to signal purpose. The door opened and in walked Lieutenants Lex and Dodd, both wearing somber expressions. She invited them in, and when Ginny offered to go, they requested she stay since they'd need her assistance.

"Contessa, we have a problem," Lex began.

"Only one?" Allegra asked. She had meant it to be funny, to ease the tension, but it came out flat.

"It's a big one," Dodd said.

She pressed them to begin, and when the name *Vanida* finally made its way into the story, she knew her day of happiness and bliss was over. "I shall stop you both there. You know that I am going to question any intelligence gained from Cardinal Vanida, yes?"

"We know, Contessa," Lex said. He pulled out several folded pieces of paper from the satchel on his belt, where Lex had taken to carrying paper, pencil, and a ledger for the investigation. "We took down his statement. I apologize for my handwriting; he was speaking so quickly and you know what he's like."

"We tried to tell him to slow down, but he just got angry," Dodd said. He rolled his eyes by way of emphasis.

"I'll re-write it properly later," Lex promised. "But what's important is that he said he has proof that Walter Cram is creating full, open portals."

Allegra muttered, "I've heard that one already," as she reached out her hand for the papers. When Ginny asked what she'd said, she repeated it, only louder.

"Oh, everyone's been saying that for some time now," Ginny mused. "Reny won't shut up about it."

"I'd be lying if I said it never crossed my mind, too, Your Ladyship. I've talked to Her Highness and Lex about it," Dodd said.

"You have?" Allegra said.

"Well," Lex said, clearing his throat. "We have decided that proving Walter didn't do it would help us stop the rumors."

"Walter now, is it?" Allegra skimmed the notes. "You two realize he's not just a lost puppy, but a grown man?"

"He is really pathetic, though," Dodd said. Then, he shrugged and added, "I don't want to admit it, but I'd be properly hurt if it were Cram. After all we've been through lately, and all."

"And how he saved our lives," Allegra said with a small smile.

Dodd grunted. "It seems wrong to accuse the man, but facts are facts."

"What about you, Lieutenant Lex?" Ginny asked. "Are you supportive of this?"

"Well," Lex began. He stopped to think and then rolled his eyes. "I just don't believe any of this."

Lex's handwriting was atrocious in sections, especially where it was clear Vanida was speaking too swiftly. Entire sentences were merely a few words, missing all of the refinement and clarity Lex normally wrote with.

Nevertheless, it was clear Vanida's complaint had a purpose: why was Walter so often seen in the back alleys that had nothing to do with his tasks, and why had open portals or demon markings been found in those areas? Vanida was quoted as saying, "However ill advised it is to task him with anything, his duties do not require him access to certain passages in the outer halls of the Cathedral itself, and yet has been found there at all hours of the night."

The statement went on to accuse Walter of using Father Michael as a shield against scrutiny, and to use their "shocking, ill-advised, lacking in any sense" budding relationship as a distraction from investigators. Allegra read that part aloud, and the others, again, all shrugged and said they'd all heard that theory, too.

Vanida did not seem to offer much in the way of proof, though he did provide all of the passageways where he'd personally spotted Walter. His use of time was rather frustrating, being as it was organized by which bells were tolling, if he could hear the choir practicing, and who else he was with at the time.

"Did he give any indication he knew what was in the archives, or that he was attempting to remove Walter from that task?" Allegra asked.

Lex and Dodd shared a look, both shaking their heads in silent conversation. It was Dodd who answered. "I asked him why Cardinal Vittorio made such a fuss about Cram being in the archives, and he brushed it off."

"It was a normal, usual reaction," Lex added. "You know? Walter Cram should not have his dirty mage hands anywhere that priceless artifacts exist for he'll steal them, or sell them, or sully them with his mage ways."

"The usual," Allegra said sourly.

"We tried to press him, just a little," Lex added, "I didn't want to come across as being suspicious, so I tried to make it sound like I wanted to gossip. But if I'm going to be honest, he seemed to think it was just because no one likes Cram, not because there was a real reason he shouldn't be there."

Ginny took the hastily-drawn map that Dodd had made, where several entrances, buildings, and servant passages were drawn. It was difficult to follow, with lines going in all directions and labels everywhere. At her confused expression, he said, "Yeah, sorry, Your Highness. It was hard getting him to draw breath long enough for me to get this done properly. The scribes are still making us some tracings, and I'm waiting for onion paper so that I can pin it all together. Once I have that, I'll go back to the cardinal and see if we can tidy this up."

Ginny pointed out to a section of servant passages. "Have you ever found markings or any evidence at all in this area?"

Lex shook his head. "Not as far as we know, though not everyone was reporting those types of things, especially early on."

"It might be Cram is closing portals we don't know about," Dodd added.

"If he is, we need to know that," Allegra said. "Shall I assume you are hoping I will speak to him?"

"No, it's fine. We have to talk to him anyway about some of the servant statements," Lex said. "We were planning to drop by the archives to talk to him and we'll bring this up."

"All right, but don't tell him Vanida said all this, or Lord God help us all," Allegra said.

"We should tell him," Lex said.

Ginny scoffed. "He's being investigated for a crime."

Allegra handed the papers back to Lex. "I have to talk to him about something else, so I'll find a way to do it gently. The last thing we need is him strangling Vanida in the middle of the courtyard."

"That's a bit of an exaggeration, Contessa," Dodd said. "If anything, he'd just collapse a building on top of him."

"How comforting," Allegra muttered.

CHAPTER THIRTEEN

WALTER'S ENDLESS YAWNING made his jaw ache and his eyes water as he made the trek to the archives. Behind him, keeping a respectful distance, followed two of Princess Imogen's soldiers. Apparently, they were for his protection, but mostly they just made the back of his neck itch. They'd said a servant arrived with a note that he was needed in the archives for some reason or another, when all he wanted was to sleep the morning away.

He had planned a quiet and peaceful evening the night before. The priest had vacated to his own room for a change—something about wanting to get some work done without distractions—so Walter had intended to laze about his over-decorated suite and perhaps make a visit to the bathing room and enjoy an indulgent soak in steaming hot water. Perhaps drink some wine.

What had happened was that he spent most of the evening either crawling on all fours trying to reach a set of demon markings or laying in bed unable to sleep because he kept dreaming about demons.

The first portal was found by night girls; the maids who worked at night cleaning various public rooms. It turned out to be a fake—someone had thought it funny to splatter some dark paint in a corner and hang black cloth from the chandelier so that it looked like those small bat demons were in the room. The poor maid screamed so hard that she fainted. Her companions in the hallway, brave things they were, rushed into the room with the supposed demons, grabbed the feet of their unconscious friend, and dragged her out before shutting the door and calling for help.

Walter did not find the prank amusing, nor did the poor girls who were only doing their jobs.

The second, however, was real. Found beyond the north gate, along the road, in plain sight of guards, merchants, and the Lord God Almighty, and yet no one had seen who'd sprinkled the earth with demon markings. Then, the markings were all set off when the Amadore soldiers and the mages training with them walked by, causing tiny fissures all over the place. None of those mages knew how to close the fissures, and Lord God Almighty, two accidentally made the opened portals bigger, something Walter didn't even know how to do.

The soldiers stomped on the miniature crawlers while waiting for Walter, because apparently no one knew who else to call upon. By the time he'd finished his work, folks had begun to emerge for the day, and he just simply said it was a false alarm, and let them not worry.

Was it a lie? Of course, it was.

Would he do it again? Absolutely.

He'd written notes for Allegra, Her Highness, and Rainier, and sent the footman to drop them in the deliveries before collapsing into bed. He'd write one for Lex and Dodd when he woke up. That had been his plan, at least, until he was dragged from his bed seemingly minutes after his head hit the pillow.

Walter arrived at the archives sleep-deprived, grumpy, hungry, and still wearing the same clothes he'd been wearing when on his belly trying to close what was a winding trail of tea-cup portals to the abyss. His forearm burned, and he rolled up his sleeve as he walked in the door to reveal a nasty swollen welt, with a circle of tiny pin-prick teeth marks. That must've been when one of the little fuckers bit him. He was going to have more nightmares about those teeth marks than the massive, winged creature that had flown away with the front gate.

He scratched at the welt. It didn't help.

"Good morning to you, Mr. Cram!" Roul cheerfully greeted him. The old fuss was in a good mood.

Walter greeted everyone through a yawn. "Why are you lot looking so *happy*?"

Roul waved Walter over to the special desk, where only the very special books were permitted. It had a raised wooden block built into the desk's top, and on that block was a fragile book. Roul was holding his special book tongs, with the thinnest metal ends Walter had ever seen. Roul was also wearing his special silk gloves.

That meant the book was indeed priceless.

"I believe we have found what Cardinal Vittorio was hiding," Rigi said.

Walter tried to summon excitement, but he was exhausted. He hated all of the reading Allegra had him doing, and Roul's fussiness over the books wore on him in the best of moods. The archivist did not notice Walter's bad mood, though, and used his tongs to carefully turn over the cover to rest it on the wooden spine protector. He turned a few pages of intricate, if faded, artwork. Then he read aloud:

"Remembrances of the Great Battle Against the Demons from the Abyss, by Abbot Burgi, in my own hand, faithful and true to the Lord God Almighty, may He shine bright upon us."

Walter frowned at the book and back at Roul. "I'm not religious these days, but I distinctly remember being told there were only paintings and the traditions, no writings whatsoever."

Margarite was frowning. "The same with all of us, but it appears we have the evidence to the contrary before us."

The exchange, and subsequent discussion, sounded like they'd had it several times before he'd been dragged from his warm bed. Roul turned the page. Walter struggled to read it. He would never tell feminine plural from masculine singular in Old Amadore no matter if his very life depended upon knowing.

He yawned again. "How old is this book? Do we even know who this abbot is?"

"That's what we've been doing all morning," Cardinal Rigi said with a smile. He pointed at a stack of books on another table, with one opened haphazardly on the table. That one clearly did not require special measures. "This Abbot Burgi became Bishop of Orsini, shortly after the guardians stopped the demons. He is contemporary to the events, and future records list this book right here as having been written by him, but with all copies lost."

"Clearly not *lost*," Roul amended. "Purposely removed from the records. I checked the register list. This book was listed as lost four hundred years ago. I believe I shall summon the juniors to go through every single scrap of paper in this building to ensure everything is registered properly."

Chills gripped Walter's spine as he stared at the simple book with its tattered cover, so old that it could not be touched with bare hands. Could it hold the true history of mages? What caused the abyss to open? Were the details of the final battle true? Were there any mages who fought in that final battle against the darkness? Did Tasmin herself allow mages in her army?

Were the Guardians real? Did Tasmin truly lead an army to their deaths through a portal in what is now Orsini's main courtyard? What had they done to cause them? What had they done to stop them for all of these centuries?

Would this book exonerate mages and finally condemn those who enslave them? Did the enslavement and branding of mages even exist in that time? Or would it be more of the same hypocrisy, the torture of those who sacrificed all for the safety of those who would make the laws and live comfortable lives? Whose robes would never be tainted with the blood, soot, and gore of a hard life?

Why did the priests hide this book? Why did Vittorio want to keep it from him? And Devonshire? And DeLancey? Why? Why? *Why?* What were they hiding? They were hiding something, and specifically from *him*. Something they were terrified of his eyes seeing it. And now, this mythical book from a time when no writing survived of any kind, appears in the collection of things Vittorio tried to hide. There was something in these pages.

As sure as the Lord God Almighty had turned his back on mages, he knew this book was the key to everything.

They'd come for it, too. Vittorio, DeLancey, Devonshire, Francois, all of them. Even Rigi, he could not be trusted. He'd steal this book or dump tea on it or find a way to burn this room to ground. He had to hide this book. No one could be trusted with it. They would steal it from him, and steal the...

Pain suddenly seared in Walter's forearm and his knees buckled. It wasn't until he hit the floor that he blinked and discovered Rigi's thumbnail digging deep into the welt on his forearm. Blood and pus ran down his upraised arm and dripped off his elbow. He tugged against the cardinal's grip, an automatic response, and Rigi let go immediately.

"What...why did you do that?" Walter asked. He rubbed his arm. It stung more now than it had when the demon grub had bitten him. He was panting, struggling to catch his breath. Several piles of books had toppled over. Three books were near where he knelt. "What happened?"

Cardinal Rigi crouched down beside him, handing him a handkerchief. "I apologize for hurting you. I could not think of a better way to stop you."

"Stop me?"

"We feared you would bring down the building," Margarite said.

Shame shook him to his core. He had lost control. He could not remember the last time this had happened to him. He had frequently made the earth shake and used it to destroy evil people. But that was a choice. That was him commanding the elements to obey him.

This? There were children in this building. He had no idea who or what was above them. What if it was a sick room? Or a nursery? What if there were mages working above him, fighting the good fight in their own way, all the while scrubbing the floors to a perfect shine?

"Please forgive me," Rigi said. "You appeared lost in a dark, lonely place. I did not know what else I should do."

The pressure of the handkerchief had stopped the bleeding, and was already easing the pain of the welt and cut. Walter glanced up at Rigi, who smiled, and said, "My last healing item. I kept it for emergencies."

"I shall replace it," Walter muttered.

Rigi put a hand on Walter's shoulder and gripped it. In a tender voice that men too seldom used around him, he said, "You must ease yourself. You are amongst friends here."

Walter stared into Rigi's concerned face and it struck him that he had friends in this place filled with his enemies. Allegra, for all that happened between them, he had thought of her as a friend, someone he trusted with his secrets and life. Rainier, too. Something had passed between them, when Walter had returned with Allegra, and when they'd fought side-by-side. Lex? Dodd? They were kids, and kids were sometimes annoying, but he'd take an arrow for either of them, even if he never wanted them to know.

Tears welled in Walter's eyes. Being on the run, preparing his life to be a martyr meant he should leave whenever his heart grew comfortable. Now, in this moment, here, with people who called themselves friends, he knew he had rooted. This was everything he tried to avoid in his life: attachment. It would destroy him, and he knew it. He'd always known it.

He should walk away, right now. Steal whatever portable gold he could get his hands on. Walk out beyond the gate, and always keep his back to Orsini.

Vittorio still had estates that needed torching. He could do that.

He could go to Allegra's brother and ask for assistance. Provided he didn't kill Walter on sight, he might let him sleep in the stables. Well, perhaps not with the horses, but the pig stables would be fine. He'd allowed it twice before, for Ally's sake.

"I'm sorry," Walter whispered. Sobs overcame him and he gasped and struggled for air. There was no air in this room. "I can't breathe."

"Take a deep breath, my child," Sister Bianca said. "Steady now. Hold it. Now, let it out. Come now, you know how to do this. Take another. Slowly, my child. Slowly. Be easy in your heart."

It took several more tries before Walter's lungs remembered how to breathe. He accepted Rigi's outstretched hand and stood. "I don't know what has come over me. Please forgive me."

Sister Bianca glanced at the book, mercifully not injured in his lapse in control. "I believe you have more cause than most to feel betrayed."

There was nothing more to say to that.

"Can we read the syntax at all?" Walter asked, trying to move the conversation away from him. His skin was hot, and waves of dizziness washed over him.

That seemed to lighten the mood of the room. Roul nodded and said, "Yes, indeed. Myself, Cardinal Rigi, and Sister Bianca all know the language well enough to translate. I propose you and Sister Margarite investigate some of the other texts, and the three of us will take turns at this book. We have sent Cardinal Reinhold with Miss Serafina to the upper archive."

At Walter's confusion, Rigi said, "Sister Bianca was concerned about the delicate nature of the book. Serafina we trust. However, the good cardinal..."

"It is possible he wouldn't have kept the discovery quiet," Rigi interjected. "Serafina is leading him on a hunting expedition."

"It is work that needs to be done," Roul insisted. "There are several texts missing that my predecessors state exist on these shelves somewhere. There are also two missing reference books, that have notes and commentary written about this original that we cannot find down here. If we can find those two books, it might help us with translations."

Walter knew they were talking in that soothing, easy manner to help him. However, his feet itched to run. His lungs cried out for fresh air. To fill his nostrils with the smells of the morning. But Nadira walked in at that moment, just as he was losing the battle with his feet. Her army of footmen blocked the door. He could not bolt in front of Nadira, for Allegra would hear of it. It would worry her, and then he'd have to deal with her, Rainier, Lex, Dodd, and Michael all fluttering about him like he was a precious vase.

His shirt sleeve was still rolled up, and he whispered to Margarite if she could tie the ends of the healing handkerchief in place. Nadira heard him and stared right into his eyes. He hoped his face wasn't swollen so much as to be obvious he'd been crying only moments prior. He did not want that to get out; the great demon lover sobbing in the archives. Her piercing eyes dropped to his forearm injury, watching the cloth tied into place. He tried not to flinch. Then, finally, she looked at the fallen books upon the floor. He had nearly brought this place down. He could have crushed someone by accident. That had not been his intention

So much shame filled him. He was always in control. What was wrong with him? What was happening?

"Walter Cram," Nadira announced sharply.

He snapped his attention to her. He prepared to accept her scorn, her disappointment, anything except what she offered: kindness.

"For reasons that first escaped me, my mistress tasked me with the duty of seeing you properly attended. Now, I see the reason behind her commands, for it is abundantly clear to me that you will not look after yourself. Look at the state of you! You are shaking." Nadira made a very disappointed sound and gave him a once over with a critical eye. Her frown deepened as she found fault with his entire being.

"A butter roll and two pieces of cheese before he passes out." She snapped her fingers. A footman immediately turned to comply with her order. "Don't give me that look, Walter Cram. I will tell Her Ladyship you have not been looking after yourself, I will. Do not tempt me. You? Get him cider. The good stuff that the cardinals' apothecary is hoarding, not that cheap swill they are serving in the dining room. Tell him I sent you."

"It's not necessary, Nadira," Walter said. Perhaps it was, but he did not want anyone to know about today.

"Best you do as she bids," Roul said as a footman bowed and handed Walter a napkin with a shiny, knotted roll and two generous pieces of cheese, one a soft yellow and the other well-speckled with blue.

"Eat!" Nadira ordered.

Walter dutifully put the blue cheese to his mouth and took a nibble. It was smoked, and the scent filled his nostrils. It wasn't the outdoors, but it was close enough. His stomach grumbled with the first bite. Maybe she was right; he hadn't been taking care of himself as well as he should.

Rigi walked beside him, turning his back to Nadira slightly. In a low voice, the cardinal said, "I once saw her guilt the Holy Father into putting back a third dessert just with a glance. I've heard she is the most powerful servant in Orsini."

Rigi probably didn't know Walter had once warmed Allegra's bed, a lifetime ago. He didn't want to embarrass Allegra by saying

159

that, and he certainly didn't want Nadira knowing he appreciated her fussing. So instead, he said, loudly, "Nadira has always been bossy."

The old servant gave him a look of smug satisfaction before turning around to berate the footmen for not setting up the table properly. She had read him easier than they would read the abbot's book. Damn her to the abyss. Damn them all for being kind to him. And damn the cheese for being so delicious.

RUPERT WAS ALREADY awake before his valet arrived, but he made no effort to move from his lonely bed until the last possible moment. Since donning the robes of power—for that was what they were, no matter how they tried to pretty it up—his days were all the same. Every morning, his valet would wake him before dawn. He'd dress, read his letters, have a private breakfast with Pero while his secretaries went over the business of the day. Morning prayers. Return to the drawing room or dining room for meetings all morning. Dinner. Meetings all afternoon. Supper. Lead evening prayers once a week. Otherwise, more meetings and letters. Spend an hour arguing with Pero about mages, or gossiping with Pero about the cardinals, or making love to Pero.

For years now, an hour every night was all the time he had to offer his husband.

The valet—this morning, it was Vic—entered, bowed, and announced it was time to begin the day. His clothes were placed in their usual location, on the gold chair off in the corner. Rupert nodded and said he'd be right out. He crawled out of bed, glancing over at the closed door, the simple barrier between his and Pero's adjoined bedchambers. They had often slept apart with no ill-will; Pero loved to stay up late and Rupert was up with the birds. Neither wished to disturb the other crawling in and out of bed. Both rooms entered each other through the adjoining door, and both had another door each that exited into their private breakfast room, where only servants and staff gathered. The proper breakfast room was just beyond, where he normally hosted Rainier, Allegra, and Giso.

Twenty-seven guest rooms. That was what he had in this place of poverty and austerity. Four breakfast rooms. No, five. That one was being refurbished with new frescos. That's why he kept forgetting about it. Even more drawing rooms. Several prayer closets. Even more storage closets.

But no matter how many rooms there were, no matter how many he forgot he even had, the door between him and his husband had never used to be closed.

Rupert pulled on his dressing gown and pushed his feet into slippers. He wondered if the door was locked. Guilt tugged at him then. In all of these weeks, he'd not even thought to check.

Why would he? He was a spineless coward.

He regretted so much of what they'd said to each other, of his handling of what happened with Allegra. Words had spewed from his mouth that he did not even recognize now that they were filtered through the passage of time and the return of good sense. He felt so much shame whenever he pondered his words and actions, and his memory ensured an endless loop of those words to let him know how wrong he was.

He could already hear the bustle on the other side of the door, leading into the breakfast room. There was a similar door on Pero's side, too. Would Pero join them this morning? No, he didn't do that anymore. Rupert rarely saw him in the mornings now.

He rarely saw him ever now.

He had never checked to see if the door was locked.

He had turned into the thing he swore he would never become: complacent.

And for what? It didn't stop people from dying.

He ruined everything for nothing.

But he did not open Pero's door. He went about his normal routine, washing, dressing, hating himself. When presentable, Rupert drew in a deep breath, squared his shoulders, and opened the door leading into his private breakfast room. It was already aflutter with servants and clerks, as it was every morning. The food was already laid out. Tea, hot chocolate, cold boiled eggs, leftover cold meats, several types of rolls and buns, sweet nut pastries, fruits, cheese, oat cakes, jams, bread...enough to feed himself, Pero, and all of the servants that would be in and out of the room that morning.

He had insisted on that, when he'd first been elevated. Graciously, he allowed them to eat his cold leavings while he was at prayers. Now? He just looked at the food and felt dirty.

His morning secretary, Warin, waited patiently at the door, waiting for Rupert to acknowledge him and begin the morning ritual. Letters would be read to him. He'd dictate replies. Five servants would help dress him into his vestments and various accessories of power.

He had never taken a morning off. He had done this every single morning for...how long now? Too long.

"I am ill."

Rupert had not meant to say that, not even just a moment before when he was staring at the food. But Warin had taken a step toward him, itinerary in hand, and Rupert's ability to think collapsed.

"I shall call the healer," his secretary said.

"That will not be necessary," Rupert said.

"I shall anyway..."

"I said no," Rupert said, raising his voice. He never raised his voice. All of the servants stopped. He took a deep breath and said, "Cancel all of my meetings. No one is allowed in this room for the rest of the day, just me and Pero. No one else, I don't care if Tasmin herself returns from the abyss with news. She can bloody well wait her turn."

His secretary sputtered something about the cardinals, but then said, "Of course, Your Radiance."

From there, Warin clapped his hands and ushered the servants and clerks from the room. Rupert stood there, watching them leave. No doubt, they were thinking he was not remotely ill, but he was, deep in his soul. His heart was sick. His spirit was covered in tar.

Warin was the last to leave, and offered a short, sharp bow before turning and closing the double doors beyond.

Rupert let out a long breath. He was so lonely, in that bone-deep way that made a man feel alone even in a crowded room. He had been disconnected for too long.

He walked back into his bedchamber, not interested in the food or hot beverages. He could always order more. He was the Holy Father. What would they say? No?

He had gotten used to people saying yes to him. And when Pero had pushed back, what had happened? He'd lashed out at the man he loved. The man he married. The man he vowed to stand beside for as long as the sun rose in the morning.

He stared at the closed door. Then, decided to walk over to it. He couldn't bring himself to try the door knob.

Pero had demanded Rupert support the full emancipation of mages or he'd leave, and leave for good. Of course, he supported it. He just didn't know how to do it. Get past the demons. Get past him leaving. Put it off. Always put it off.

Rupert had said enough to convince Pero to stay, but it had not been the same. They did not share a bed. They did not share meals. They did not share a moment alone together. He saw Rainier now more than he saw his own husband.

He rested his head against the door as tears flowed from his eyes. There was wrong, and then there was the kind of wrong that ruined a man's life.

He should try the door knob.

He should knock first. He should...

"Roo, is that you?"

The coward in him said he should be silent, but he summoned the strength to say, "Yes."

There was a pause before Pero said, "The door is unlocked."

Arriving teary-eyed in his husband's bed did not immediately lead to intimacy, but eventually, the barriers between them eased. They were tender together, trying to find their way back, until finally heat and need took over and crashed down the remaining walls between them.

When they finally had exhausted themselves, Rupert put his head on Pero's bare chest and stared up at the ceiling fresco. Tasmin was fighting the demons, sword held aloft, hair escaping her helmet, bodies all around her. He found himself wondering if any of it was true. The stories, the myths, the legends, even. What had happened on that fateful day?

Had it ever happened?

"Roo, love?" Pero whispered.

"Hmm?"

His chest rose as he took in a long breath. "This doesn't change anything."

"I know," Rupert whispered back. The weight on his chest was already returning. "I'm so ashamed of myself."

Pero sighed. "Then why haven't you just said that?"

"I'm a fool," Rupert said. He reached until he found Pero's hand. He draped it across his own chest, fingers entwined.

"Yes, you are," Pero said. He chuckled. "But you're my fool."

They were quiet for some time, quiet except for their breathing and the occasional cough that sounded so loud in the room. He couldn't remember the last time this room was so silent. There were always servants, and clerics, and clerks and guards, the constant opening and closing of doors.

Not today. Today, he could pretend they were just two men who loved each other, who did not have the world pounding at their doors.

"I saw all of those demon bodies," Rupert whispered. He'd been avoiding this. It had been eating at him. He knew he could tell Pero anything, and had many times. And yet, this time was different because his faith was tied up into it.

"It was terrible," Pero said back. He squeezed Rupert's hand.

Then, he said what no pope should ever say aloud. "I realized, when I saw them, that I had never truly believed in my heart. I do not even know what I believe anymore. The things I've found while searching in the parts of me where only the Lord God sees. Do you know what I found? I never wanted to be the pope that freed the mages because I have never had the full conviction of my own faith. I do not know what I believe anymore."

"Everyone doubts sometimes."

"Not when you are the head of the faith," Rupert said. He lifted Pero's hand to kiss it. "I should have tried the door a lot sooner."

"Yes, you should have," Pero said.

"It opened both ways, you know," Rupert said.

"I'm still angry with you."

Rupert let go of Pero's hand and rolled over. He pulled himself up to prop his elbows up on his pillow. He stretched his neck, and then glanced over. "You're still mad at me? After what I just did to you?"

"Well," Pero said, rolling his eyes. "Maybe a little less angry now."

"High praise indeed," Rupert said. Then, after a pause, he let the humor fade from his voice. "I am, truly, so sorry for what I said that night."

"We both said a lot of things," Pero said. "I apologize for all of mine."

"Do you still believe I am a mage oppressor?"

"I don't want to start," Pero said.

Rupert rolled over once more, collapsing back down on his pillow to stare up at Tasmin on the ceiling. "I need to know."

Pero sighed and said, "I said it in anger, nothing more. Am I frustrated by how slowly things are moving? Of course I am. Am I angry that we sit here and dine with slave owners? Absolutely. Do I think you could do more? Always. Do I want you to do more? Every day. Do I think you're sliding into complacency?"

Pero paused when he said that, and Rupert gulped hard. He knew what was coming, but he needed to hear the words.

"Honestly? Some days, I worry that, yes, you are. I'm sorry if that hurts you, Rupert, but you asked."

A lump formed in Rupert's throat. The truth was rarely an easy thing to endure. "I've fallen so far from my ideals that I don't recognize myself anymore."

"Oh, Roo."

Rupert broke into hiccupping sobs. He turned his back on Pero. He was so ashamed of himself. Between his gasps of agony, he said, "I destroyed my friendship with Allegra. I've known her my entire life and she's trusted me and what did I do to her? I was ready to feed her to wolves. I destroyed my marriage with the only man I've ever truly loved."

"You've not destroyed our marriage," Pero said. Warm arms picked him up and wrapped him close. "Rupert, I'm right here."

"We don't even talk anymore."

"We're talking right now."

"I don't know how to come back from this. I have ruined everything I love."

Very gently, Pero asked, "Do you still love me?"

"Of course, I do."

"And I still love you. We will figure this out, together. That was the vow we took."

"I love you so much," Rupert whispered. "I don't want to lose you."

It was Pero's turn to grab for Rupert's hand. He squeezed hard. "I am not lost yet."

They stayed like that for some time, just talking gently about the hard things still in the air. It hurt. It all hurt. But Rupert had been so lonely, and here in bed with Pero, the love of his life, he did not feel so lonely anymore.

There was some bustling and slamming of doors, followed by someone calling out his name. Rupert sighed and said, "They have found me."

He heard his bedroom door open. "Rupert! Are you in bed?"

"Best cover up before Giso sees more than he planned," Pero said, pulling the blanket over his nakedness.

Rupert groaned in protest, but grabbed the offered edge of the blanket and pulled it over himself. "In here, Giso."

The door opened and Giso bowed. "Good morning, Pero. I apologize for barging in like this."

"What's wrong?" Rupert asked as he accepted his dressing gown from Pero.

Giso sucked in a long breath and said, "Bonacieux broke through the siege. The Grand Duchess is dead."

"God almighty," Pero said.

Rupert stared at Giso, only one arm in his gown. "Dead? Are they certain?"

Giso passed a letter to Pero, who handed it immediately to Rupert. He jumped from the bed and wrapped the dressing gown about him, tying it into place. He took the offered letter and opened it.

"Go on," Pero said.

Rupert stopped, torn between his duty and his heart. Giso stepped quietly out of the room, declaring he needed to eat something, and to shoo the guards away. Rupert bent down and kissed Pero on the mouth. "I have to go."

"Of course, you do," Pero said, and he gave him the smile he fell in love with so many years ago. "I'll be here when you get back."

"I love you," Rupert said.

"And I love you. Now go," Pero said, making a shooing gesture.

When Rupert exited Pero's bedchamber, he was no longer a husband. He was the Holy Father.

Because someone had to be.

CHAPTER FOURTEEN

LITTLE GOPHER TRIED very hard to stand still while Allegra skimmed the various notes he'd delivered that required her immediate reply. He'd brought eleven with him this time, plus a personal invitation from Walter to rescue him from the archives before he ran screaming through the Cathedral stark naked and raving that the end was upon them.

She didn't bother replying to that one.

For the rest, she scribbled short, concise replies on the various notes. Some were a simple yes or no, while others just required a direction or authorizing signature for someone to proceed. Once she finished, she commented that she thought the boy had grown, and she made him stand tall and straight and declared that, yes, he had most definitely grown.

"The Consorts mark my height in the barracks because they keep arguing how tall I'm going to get. Lieutenant Lex says I'm going to be taller than Captain Rainier if I don't stop growing!" Little Gopher said proudly.

"Then you better tell Nathan I said you need new trousers. We can't have your ankles showing by next week, now can we?"

"No, Your Ladyship!" He bowed and rushed off.

The boy was always running, but it's what he liked to do. He had to be told a few times not to run in the hallways and servant passages, unless the note was of life and death, but it was impossible to get that through his head. He was a runner for the Holy Father's Own Consorts; he was paid to run.

She picked up her shawl and wrapped it about her shoulders to walk to the archives to fetch Walter and stretch her legs. It was Stanton's turn to train with the mages and soldiers beyond the wall, and he'd warned her he would not be back until after dark, so she did not even have his very fine form to distract her during the day.

She'd have to settle for poor Walter's company.

She switched shawls to the thicker one, recalling that Little Ferret had said everyone was complaining about how it might rain. She corrected her thoughts: Little Gopher. She must be careful with his name, even now after so many of the offended parties were dead. She could not—would not—risk anyone harming this child.

She left just as her guards were changing, so she asked Martin and Beatrix to walk with her, while Renouf's two men took over the position. She smiled at them, though they barely acknowledged her presence. She tried to remind herself that this was due to her rank; a year of unique circumstances and cramped quarters and all of the stress of demons had made many of them far closer than she'd ever allowed previously.

It was not even that she felt the distinction of rank needed to be preserved, but rather they had all been through the darkest parts of the abyss, whereas Renouf's men arrived to a fist pounding and then a scolding.

As they walked, Allegra turned around and asked Martin about Rahna, who'd been suffering headaches since the previous morning, or so Kia and Calm Seas had said. There was no news from the barracks yet, he said, but he'd check with Lex at the old rectory once they went in that direction.

Poor Rahna. She wasn't sleeping. There was a lot of that going around, now that the terror of the attack had faded enough for the trauma to settle in. An entire healing team was called, Martin said, but they all said there was little they could do for her in this stage of the process. Now, it was hot soup and soothing tea, and the quiet company of friends. She had to sleep, but they did not wish to risk reliance upon the mixtures. This was the hard part now.

Allegra worried her moment would come soon. Until then, she would continue forward, knowing the collapse would come. It was hitting everyone else around her. She was not so arrogant as to believe she would be spared.

Mercifully, she caught sight of Walter further down the increasingly busy corridor, as she neared one of the main junctions. There were clerks and sisters, brothers and servants, all rushing to and fro, and it was becoming difficult with her there holding up the flow of bodies. Many stopped to bow, some attempted to trade greetings, and others tipped their head, but the end result was the same: it slowed the movement.

Walter had an easier time getting through, as the crowd parted for him. She wondered how much was those in awe of his bravery and sacrifices, and how many because they were absolutely terrified of the demon lover, Walter Cram.

She'd put it even odds, personally.

"I'm starving. Would you like to walk down to the cardinal's dining hall to see if there is anything edible on offer?"

Walter did not smile when they turned to walk in the same direction. He simply said, "Let's walk."

"The carts, then," she said. "Is everything well?"

"Not even remotely. I need air."

From there, they barely spoke as they made their way through the busy corridors. Walter knew the servant passages and shortcuts better than she did, and they soon found themselves beyond the main bustle, and through to where the day-to-day administration all happened. There, people did not stop to bother her, for they were in as much of a hurry as she. She got occasional greetings and inclined heads, but they were not accosted.

She ached to tell Walter about her and Stanton, and knew he would be genuinely pleased. He would no doubt take some of the credit for it, as it was him who kept putting the idea in her head in the first place. She prided herself in knowing her own mind enough to not give Walter all the credit; eventually, she'd have figured out that she wanted to sleep with the captain of her own guard. But, as annoying as Walter had been about the entire thing, it was him who helped her give herself permission to want Stanton.

Finally outside, Walter's guards resumed a more respectful distance behind them, and Martin veered off to the old rectory to see if there was any news about Rahna, saying he'd return. Beatrix stayed in tow; the Consorts did not completely trust Renouf's men.

"So," Allegra asked, itching for whatever it was that was eating at Walter, "what is bothering you?"

He glanced around him. The courtyard was busy, of course; there was a steady line of refugees and merchants queued from one gate straight across Orsini to the other gate. As it was, the majority of the carts they relied on were all outside now, forcing them all to walk upwards of three quarters of an hour to get something decent to eat.

Finally, he leaned toward her and said, "We found a book this morning."

"I should hope so. You are working in a library," she said, chuckling.

"Ally," Walter said, and the desperation in his voice struck her. She stopped walking and stared at him. He looked about again and leaned close whisper, "We have found a book from the time of Tasmin."

It was her turn to glance about to ensure they could not be overheard. "There are no writings from that period. Not even copies of the writings."

"Roul verified it is authentic," Walter said. "It's real."

"What does it say?"

He motioned for her to start walking again. "I can only read a word or two out of every paragraph. Roul and Sister Bianca can read it quite well, and Serafina has a passable ability, but she's in charge of distracting Reinhold. Translation has been a slow process. Serafina and Reinhold are looking for another book to assist, but Reinhold doesn't know the reason why they're looking. Thing is, though, we have a book the Cathedral teachings have always said didn't exist, and we are already finding theories and beliefs we have never been taught."

"What do you mean?"

"Roul said there have been banned theories over the centuries about the nature of demons. Apparently, that had been a huge area of study for the clergy," Walter shrugged. "Theories about time in the abyss being different than time in our world. How the abyss is not a reflection of this world, but rather just another part of it.

171

How the abyss is made of cheese, I've not really been paying attention to all of that. The truth of it is that Vittorio tried to stop me from being there, and now we have found a book the priests have always said didn't exist."

"Do you think Rupert knew?" she asked.

Walter was quiet for a moment before he said, "I think it's time you and the pope sat down over a good bottle of brandy and talked. Don't roll your eyes at me, Allegra, Contessa of Marsina. You know I'm right."

Walter was right, in that she missed Rupert's friendship. He would've been the first person, outside of Nadira, she would've normally told about her and Stanton. She had not, and got a sick feeling in the pit of her stomach whenever she thought about it. She even missed arguing with him and Pero over grand suppers, well past when Rupert should've been in bed. She missed him so much.

"I can never forgive him," she whispered.

"Why not?"

She was so shocked by the question that she sputtered over her words before finally saying, "He was going to have me killed."

"Do you honestly believe he'd have allowed it? Or was he playing politics?"

"He was playing politics with my life," she said. "He slapped me! In the courtyard, in front of everyone."

"And he embarrassed you and betrayed your trust. No one likes being the rabbit, hunted through the warrens. Everyone wants to be the ferret, doing the hunting. I know that he hurt you, and I'm not forcing you to like him or be nice to him. He's not my friend, so I don't care. But he's been in your life for a long time, Ally, and you need to talk to him. If for no other reason than to tell him you and our dashing captain have decided to unite your estates."

"How did you find out?" she blurted. Walter's grin said it all and she immediately flushed. "You were fishing, weren't you?"

"I'm always fishing for the latest news. How do you think I've stayed alive all this time?" His smile faded, and when pressed, he said, "Listen, if Nadira says she is worried about me, would you please tell her I'm fine and to stop fussing?"

"What is the matter?" Allegra demanded. Nadira would never worry about Walter unless it was serious. "Are you ill? What is wrong?"

"I just said I was fine," Walter said, and he didn't bother to hide the annoyance in this voice.

She did not care in the slightest. "Actually, you said Nadira would be worried about you, which means you are not fine, Walter Cram, demon lover. Answer the question. Tell me right now."

"You are no longer my lover, my dear Contessa. You do not get to demand anything of me."

Allegra was slightly offended, until she realized that, indeed, she could not demand anything of Walter, and it had been some time she could not. Nevertheless, she smiled and said in her best court voice, "My dear sir, I am one of the powerful women in Orsini right now. I recommend you obey me at once."

Walter laughed at that, though the humor quickly faded from his face. Finally, he told her about losing control of himself in the archives that morning. How the others calmed him, and called themselves friends. About when Nadira had laid eyes on him and threatened to alert Allegra to the sorry state she'd found him in, still trembling and sweating from the shock. He told her how scared he was, that there could have been children nearby, fellow mages, innocent servants who were only doing their jobs.

And, finally, he told her what was the hardest truth for him to even admit to her: he had grown attached.

"To whom? Father Michael?"

"It's far worse than that. I've been here too long, and experience says I am no longer safe and should run. And yet, when I try to plan my escape? When I try to picture all of the silverware that I can easily steal, I find my feet are rooted to the carpet. Worse even still, I have to admit I do not want to leave." He was trying to force a smile, but he looked miserable.

She reached out and touched his arm, to get him to stop walking. She wanted to look him in the eye when she spoke. "You are welcome here."

He shook his head and turned back to walking. "This is all your fault. I have never overstayed a welcome, except when you are involved. Borro Abbey, not once, but twice. I even went to

Marsina and your brother hid me, and I overstayed my welcome there. Twice. Now I am here, once again in a place for far too long. I am not a tree. I do not root."

"Caring does not make you vulnerable," she said quietly.

He shook his head. "Oh, Ally. That is how they will get me, in the end."

She had always suspected that about him, though he rarely talked about it. He'd told her before he rarely travelled with the same people twice in a row and had gone so far as to never share his bed with the same person for too long. She had been the last real commitment and attachment he'd made.

She did not flatter herself that it was a testament to her charms; she was too old and too sensible to think that. But she knew he purposely kept himself apart for all of these years because he must've seen how dangerous it would have been, if he had been on the run with a family, friends, responsibilities. They would find those he loved. They would use them to hurt him.

It was what he'd said when she asked about him and Father Michael: he was lonely. That had been his words. She had asked him to set aside the rebel mage, just until the crisis ended, and to be a human being first. It must've stirred something inside him, reminding him that life could be comfortable and warm, knowing where one's next meal came from.

"Don't look at me like that," he said. He glanced at her and said, "Seriously, Ally, stop with the pity eyes."

"It's concern, not pity," she said.

He made a sound that said he didn't believe her, but would let the argument drop. Then he laughed, and asked, "So, when will you and Rainier merge your estates?"

She decided to let him change the conversation; she knew it had been difficult for him to say the little he'd confessed. She could switch to a happier topic for now. "We've been too distracted to come up with a date."

"Ah, it is good to know the good captain has stamina alongside his good looks," Walter said.

"Walter!" Allegra could feel the heat rising in her face.

"You are blushing!" Walter declared in triumph.

"You cannot just talk about such things in public! People might overhear us!"

Walter grinned, and it only made her face warm more. "If it were in private, I'd expect to watch a demonstration."

She made a disgusted sound and slapped his arm, and called him a filthy heathen who should be ashamed of himself. He complained about how everyone kept attacking him in the same place, and that she probably made a cut bleed, of which she did not have a drop of sympathy for him.

"Why must you say things like this? Oh, I just pictured it. Oh, Walter, no."

Walter let out a pleased sound. "And now we are even."

"What have I ever done to you to deserve *that* in my head?"

They bickered for the rest of the way, and he told her about the demon attack with the small grubs that had bitten him. She would've normally felt sorry for smacking the wound, especially since Rigi had dug his thumbnail into it, but she was still too angry at him for embarrassing her to have any mercy in her heart.

Renouf had done an excellent job organizing the people outside of the north gate, even in the short time he'd been working on it. The Orsini merchants were positioned nearest the gate, as they all had their seals which allowed them to conduct local commerce. There were guards posted throughout that area, plus along the path, allowing the continued flow of refugees.

She tried, whenever possible, to purchase both from the displaced Orsini merchants, and those who were selling all they had on offer, even if it was merely their time and own hands. Today, they visited the Orsini merchants, and were pleased to discover stuffed rolls were the popular choice of the day, as three different carts had them.

Allegra decided that she could not return to the Cathedral without bringing rolls for everyone, including Lex and Dodd, who they'd pass by on their way back to the study. Her escort, and Walter's, would need rolls, as would all of the archive workers, and her Amadore guards, and the guards outside the archive.

That turned out to be a lot of rolls.

She made Walter carry the basket, since he required a little oppression in his life to be content. Unfortunately, they'd not thought to bring a basket, so one had to be purchased, as did the cloth to line the basket and to cover the food. She'd also not brought her purse, for she rarely carried coin with her; that was what Nathan and Ysabeau were for. So Walter had to write down all of the merchants and what she owed, only neither had pencil nor paper.

"I am not your secretary," Walter said firmly, as he was forced to also purchase a pencil and a small piece of paper, to write down that she now owed someone for a pencil and one sheet of pressed paper. She smiled sweetly, and he sighed and moaned and complained, but then also wrote down everything.

That's what he got for saying she had no power to demand anything of him.

She could have simply sent someone to fetch Little Gopher to run back with the coins, but this was significantly more entertaining. They visited several stalls and carts. Many did not allow credit, but being Her Ladyship had perks, and one was not needing ready coin. They ended up purchasing a second basket, and filled both baskets with various types of rolls, along with some fruit tarts, cheese wedges, and smoked kippers. Also, Allegra purchased two miniature gammon pies, since Lex needed to keep up his strength, and a third so that Dodd wouldn't end up eating Lex's pie.

With the conclusion to shopping, Allegra took the list from Walter and carefully folded it. She carried that and the pencil. The two baskets laden with food were for him to carry. They first stopped to deliver pies, rolls, and kippers to a grateful Dodd and several Amadore soldiers. Dodd solemnly promised to wrap Lex's pies and not let anyone touch them, including himself. Imogen was off with some of her soldiers, and Allegra put aside tarts and rolls in case the dining hall had closed by the time they returned.

Dodd had mentioned Lex was off interviewing Father Michael, so when Allegra and Walter began their trek to her study, she inquired about the bishop. Walter confessed he'd not seen the priest in over a day. Martin returned to join them, and they continued on their way. Allegra tried pressing for more details about Father Michael, but Walter mostly shrugged or grunted his answers. When she asked whose idea that had been, he sighed.

"I suppose his?" Walter said. He thought for a moment before adding, "It might have something to do with how much I complain about his presence."

"But I thought you liked him."

"Not really."

"Surely there is someone out there you *like* who could keep you company."

"I didn't say I hated him!" Walter said, rather defensively. "I'm simply saying I should not be sharing my bed with a priest. And not just a regular country parish priest, but the fucking Bishop of Orsini."

"Surely you are not saying you feel...coerced?" She lowered her voice when she asked the question.

He waved her off. "Oh, it's nothing like that. I do not feel obligation or that my life would be inconvenienced if I said no. It's simply that me, Walter Cram, demon lover, should not be fucking the Bishop of Orsini at all hours of the day and night."

"Fair enough," Allegra said. She quirked a smile. "After all, you're supposed to be fucking demons, not priests."

"That's the Contessa I know," Walter said with a smug grin.

The two friends were laughing and carrying on in the manner that old friends so often do, and so much so that they quite literally bumped into Rupert when they rounded the corner. Her laughter immediately died away when she saw how drawn and worried he looked. Walter must've noticed, too, because he went silent and did not offer his usual disrespect of authority.

When she asked what had happened, he said they'd come in search for her. That's when she noticed Giso just behind him, face equally drawn.

"Is Stanton injured? My brother? My estate?" she blurted. "Rupert, what has happened?"

"They are all safe," he assured her. "Please, we must speak in private."

Knowing that, at least, Stanton was not dead in a gutter somewhere and Marsina was not in ruins from a fire allowed her heart to slow its pounding pace. She could not handle much more bad news. They all turned as one and began the trek to her study.

Behind the priests were guards and Warin, the secretary, who seemed more stressed than usual.

Idly, she said, "I was planning to write to you as soon as I returned from getting food. Walter found more portals last night."

"Were they serious?" Giso asked.

"One set were a series of tiny portals, none larger than the palm of my hand," Walter said. "The other was a fake portal meant to scare the night girls."

"Fake portals," Rupert said it like a curse. "Do we not have enough problems without people being needlessly frightened? What did those poor night girls do to deserve such an attack? This should be a crime."

It was difficult to hear what passed between them, but Allegra distinctly heard Giso say, "You are the Holy Father, Rupert."

Rupert stopped walking so abruptly that it nearly caused a collision behind them. She could not recall Giso ever calling him by his given name, and it dawned on her that they may have been closer friends than she'd ever realized. Pero and Giso were good friends; it would make sense that Giso and Rupert would be friends, too.

And something passed between the two men. Whispers, a look. It was hard to tell with all the bustle around them.

Then, Rupert said as if he were speaking to himself, "Yes, I am the Holy Father."

Giso inclined his head rather deeply.

Walter gave her a questioning look, but she was honestly as confused as him.

Then, in a commanding voice, Rupert said, "Warin."

"Yes, Your Radiance?" The rather harried secretary stepped forward from the unusually large gaggle following Rupert this morning.

"Write this down and inform the printers and criers, as well as Her Highness, Captain Rainier, Lord Renouf, and all members of the council. Fake portals are hereby illegal as of this moment. Anyone caught attempting to sow the seeds of fear and discord will be punished severely. My statement is thus: mages have stood beside us, have fought beside us, and have given the ultimate sacrifice to protect the people of Orsini, without consideration of rank, wealth, or power. We must stand against any and all of those who oppose the peace within our walls."

"Your Radiance?" Warin seemed baffled.

Francois stared back hard. No, she was wrong: it was her oldest and dearest friend, Rupert. That look said he had finally picked a side. She'd known Pero had threatened to leave if Rupert did not choose. But he'd stayed, and the rumor had been there was still much tension in the Holy Father's grand suites.

But this was not the voice of compromise. This had the ring of conviction.

"Yes, Your Radiance. I shall...do you wish me to soften the message?"

They were standing in a busy administrative corridor, and the stream of attendants and clerks behind Rupert was such that they were holding up the flow of others. No one would push past the Holy Father, of course; no one would dare be so rude.

Rupert physically turned around and gave his secretary a hard glare. He held it until Warin dropped his eyes. Then, and only then, did he speak. "No. I want you to convey that the Holy Father, His Radiance, appointed by the Lord God Almighty, is personally offended by the concept of fake demon portals. It is a sin in the eyes of the Lord God Almighty. Anyone caught committing such a grievous offense will be evicted from Orsini and immediately excommunicated. I do not care who their parents are, or how much property in Serna they own. Do you require more clarity, or shall that be sufficient for you to complete your task?"

"No, Your Radiance. I shall speak to the printers immediately."

Rupert stood there, waiting for Warin to get the message that immediately meant immediately. The secretary figured it out, bowed, and pushed back behind him, as another scribe stepped forward, ready to ensure the Holy Father's will be done.

Finally, Rupert motioned for them to walk on, and they continued their journey toward Allegra's study. She was debating if she should say something, ask anything, when Giso said, "I see we are taking the hardline this morning."

"Not now, Giso," Rupert said, and he sounded weary again, as if the mere standing up to Warin had exhausted him. Perhaps it had.

At first, Allegra thought she had the wrong room, for her guards weren't there. Even Giso commented on it, and Walter suggested maybe they were inside for some reason. When she opened the door, however, Allegra screamed until her throat turned raw.

CHAPTER FIFTEEN

ALLEGRA'S REASONING SHUT down as Walter rushed into the room, with Martin and Beatrix in tow, swords drawn. Rupert grabbed Allegra and wrapped his arms around her, as if he could protect her and not be a victim himself. Heavy footsteps sounded, doors slammed, trays and platters hit the floor. A wall of bodies enveloped her and Rupert, all to protect the Holy Father from imminent attack.

A moment later, Walter shouted out, "Fake! Allegra, they are fake!"

She heard Martin called out, "Your Ladyship! Your Radiance! It is safe!"

Allegra's heart was pounding so hard spots appeared in her vision and it was difficult to hear the conversations about her. Walter shouted out once more for her to come in, that what she'd seen was fake.

She struggled to control her breathing, and her hands shook from terror. She put one foot in front of the other, struggling to catch her breath. She dimly heard Rupert telling the guards to stay in the corridor. Her teeth chattered as she looked at the entrance to her study.

"It's paint," Walter said. He was sniffing his hands. "Just tarry paint."

Her guards, Renouf's men, were missing. They were not outside guarding the place, and nor were they dead, ripped apart by demons. Instead, her room was full of splatters. Walter, Martin, and Beatrix were smeared with the black paint, as they touched each and every splatter to ensure they were fake. Walter walked over to her and said, "You both should see what's in the next room."

Allegra carefully stepped through her study, the main room where she worked, gathered her colleagues and friends, and where she spent most of her days. The room was ruined. The servants would never get the carpets clean now. Her wooden floorboards were splattered and sticky. Her walls were ruined, as the tar was already eating away at the bright paper. A painting was ruined, one of her sideboards was ruined. Her desk, all of her work, had not been spared. Neither had her chair.

The bucket was still on her desk, dripping down its sides. The brush that committed the crime had been thrown on her desk, as if the criminals had feared being caught, and all of her letters, papers, and ledgers were covered in splatters. That morning's letters bore the worst of it, and she doubted the top few letters would even be readable now, soaked as they were.

"Allegra, this way," Walter said, motioning for her to come into the sitting room, where she took tea with Stanton or one of her friends whenever there was a free moment to spare. Those had been so rare as of late.

Painted on the wall, wet drips all down the rosebud papered walls, were the words DIE DEMON WHORE.

Rupert swore when he saw it.

She sucked in a breath and said, "They must've thought Walter lived here."

No one laughed, but then again, she'd not meant it as a joke. It had been a long time since she'd been called this, and she'd gotten rather used to it as mages and normals and everyone worked together not to die. It was clear to her now that Renouf's men had either done this, or allowed it. This was a threat. No, it was more than that. This was a message, a promise of future action.

"Where were her guards?" Rupert shouted.

"Renouf's men were supposed to be here," she heard Martin say. "They were here when we left."

"Find Lord Renouf this instant!" Rupert ordered. There was some rustling in the main study; one of his guards must've gone, for Martin and Beatrix did not move.

She was still staring at the wall when her attention was turned to more commotion beyond. Soon, Vittorio and Imogen entered, escorted by Giso. She turned to stare at the wall again. Die demon whore. She was no demon whore; she'd never even shared a bed with one, though facts did not seem to matter to mage haters.

Those were the thoughts upon her mind when Vittorio gasped. Imogen was demanding to know if anyone had been injured or if the culprits had been apprehended. No to both questions.

"This is an outrage!" Vittorio was saying. "If they've done this to her, they could do it to any of us! Look at the carpets! They are ruined. Your Radiance, the servants will never get the paint of out the furniture. Everything is ruined. Look at the carpets!"

"I do not care about the carpets! This is a matter of safety!" Rupert shouted back.

Rupert was angry. Giso was swearing and praying, in an odd combination of evoking both the Lord God and the darkness of the abyss. Imogen shouted for more people to fetch Renouf, and that she wanted his noble ass dragged here immediately and may the Lord God Almighty protect him if she had to find him herself. Walter told Martin someone needed to get Stanton, and Imogen passed on his location. It would be a couple of hours before he arrived; that she knew. He was training with mages well beyond the northern encampment. Cooperation. Friendship. Cohesion.

This was going to upset Stanton. She tried to remind herself, coldly, with the facts and no emotion, that this was not the first time she had heard the phrase, or been called it. For all of her wealth, her rank, and her privilege, she knew this would not be the last time she'd see or hear the phrase. Her rank could protect her from branding, enslavement, and torture. Still, it could not shield her from everything. She'd heard such sentiments so often in her life that she sometimes automatically corrected them without even noticing she'd spoken. It had become an expectation of life; just something she did and would have to do for the rest of her life.

This was different. It shouldn't be, and yet it was. The words stung. They hurt her, and she could not look away until she figured out why.

"Allegra, come," Rupert was saying. "You should not see this."

"No," she muttered. She wanted to see this. She wanted to know why it hurt.

Then she puzzled it out: this was her home. She had been working to save this place, a place she hated. She hated so many of the people who lived here, who controlled the power in this place. And the more she learned of them, the more she hated them.

And yet, she worked to protect them all. Those who would have abandoned her. Those who didn't know her from Tasmin herself. She had not just worked for mages. She'd worked for everyone. She had risked so much and for what?

"Demon whore," she read aloud. "That is all I shall ever be to them, isn't it? A thing, and not a person."

"Come away, Allegra." That was Ginny with a warm hand on her arm.

She looked about at the gathered people, their faces full of pity and anger, and even a little fear, and asked, "Why? I was meant to see this, was I not?"

And *that* was why it hurt so much.

With further coaxing, she finally turned away from the scene. She did not leave her study, though. She walked over to her desk and sat down, knowing she would ruin her dress in the process. No one spoke to her, instead only issuing orders as necessary, demands for someone to find Nadira, and for tea. Distressed people needed tea.

The vandals hadn't even respected her enough to leave their bucket on the floor. No, they'd dropped it on her papers and letters. She had not opened the latest letter from her brother yet, and now she wondered if she'd even be able to without ripping the paper. Her jaw clenched. This would have news about her nephews and nieces, of her estate, of the servants, her cows and chickens, and the orchard. She kept those letters to read at the end of her day, for the joy and comfort of family.

"Why did you come to see me?" she blurted out, suddenly remembering the entire purpose of why they'd all arrived together.

"It can wait," Rupert said. "Right now, we need to ensure your safety."

"No, what happened? You both looked so grave. It must've been important." She glanced at the stained letter in her brother's hand. "Are you certain it wasn't news from Marsina?"

Rupert looked about the room, frowning. Giso seemed to understand that and nodded to himself. "Please, everyone out. The Holy Father must speak to the Contessa. Please, everyone outside."

Walter was painstakingly checking all of the splatters on one wall when Giso said for him to leave, too. "I'm not going anywhere, not until Rainier gets back."

"She can be trusted with me," Rupert said.

"No, she can't," Walter said flatly.

Rupert didn't seem to have the energy to argue. Giso tried, but Allegra told him it was fine; there was no point keeping secrets from Walter. He'd only find them out later. When the door finally shut, Allegra lifted herself up, having to peel away her dress. She accepted the letter Rupert produced from a hidden pocket within his robes.

"Prepare yourself. Only Giso and I know so far."

She opened the letter and read in horror the final details of the siege. She paced as she read of Bonacieux's final push, and the inevitable breaking of the castle's defenses. Of how he had hauled Katherine—a grand duchess—out into the square and lopped off her head in front of his entire army and God Almighty. How his men were sent to murder everyone inside, no matter their rank or station: everyone from the servants straight to aunt of the king, it did not matter. The only ones to escape were the scouts, for they knew the escape tunnels and holes, and ran for their lives.

Katherine, for all her faults, for all of her pompous needling over the years, did not deserve such an end.

Bloody images flooded her mind, of her friends and all those she loved, in the future that Bonacieux wanted for them. So much blood flowing the ground could not soak it up fast enough to hide the crimes of men. Of screaming when Stanton's head would be eventually relieved from his shoulders. Of Rupert's headless body, robes soaked in blood. Of Nadira. Of Serafina. Of Walter being beaten to death and his head bashed in, to stop him from killing them all. Of Nathan. Of Imogen fighting to the bitter end. Of Giso, Devonshire, Dodd, Lex...

Bonacieux would come for her. He'd kill all of them to get to her. They would all die as sure as the Lord God Almighty sat wherever he sat and did nothing for the plight of the powerless. He would do nothing to stop this. He would not protect her. They were coming. The paint on the wall said they were close.

She collapsed to her knees, wailing in despair.

"Allegra!" Walter whispered, warning and danger in her voice.

She was losing control of herself. She knew that. She could feel the warmth and anger and the emotions and the anxiety all stirring within her. She grabbed Rupert's hand, trying to find some grounding for herself, to stop the rivers of blood in her mind.

Rupert jerked away from her touch, but then grabbed her hand in a crushing grip. She leaned against Walter, desperately wishing Stanton was here, and yet thankful he was not to witness this. She sobbed and sobbed, and even that release and the need for comfort made her anger grow deeper.

Then, and only then, did Walter said in pain-filled voice, "Allegra, you're hurting me."

And when she pulled herself together, enough to move away from him to see what he was talking about, she saw the hot, red handprint on his neck, where she'd grasped him close.

"I'm sorry," she whispered. "I'm so sorry."

She balled her hands into fists, and, refusing help, got to her feet. She was dizzy, weak, enraged, desperately afraid. She turned to the fireplace and screamed, pushing out all of her anger and rage into the only place that could handle her grief. Fire exploded, so hot that the hook for the tea kettle turned red hot from her anger.

Then, she mentally grabbed her self-control, her sense, her fire, and stuffed it all back into place. What she had just done was so dangerous. It would get her killed. It would get Nadira killed. It would get everyone killed. What was wrong with her?

She didn't even like Katherine.

Guilt struck her, and she berated herself for the monster she was for such a terrible thought. Only a terrible person would think such things. Perhaps she deserved to die, more than Katherine, for only evil would have such thoughts.

A pained sound escaped her, but she calmly walked through the grief, or as much as one could. For grief attacked a person's mind from all angles, without mercy and without sense. It was irrational at its core and did not see reason nor follow the rules of logic. It had no purpose. It was nothing more than random attacks of the mind.

Finally, she whispered, "I have control over it."

Rupert let out a sigh, and Walter finally got to his feet. She examined the mark on his neck. Thankfully, it was not blistered, just dark and angry. Rupert moved to look at the damage and frowned at the inspection.

"It looks like you scratched your neck with the tar on your hands. That stuff can peel the skin right off your body if you aren't careful." Rupert wasn't smiling when he added, "And no one will expect *you* to be careful."

Walter rolled his eyes. He touched his neck but pulled his fingers away with a wince. "Feels like a bad sunburn."

"Stop touching it, or you'll draw attention to it," Rupert ordered.

"It's hard not to with my neck stinging," Walter snapped back.

She wanted to cry some more, but she'd finally used up all of her tears. Just heaviness now. She waited and braced herself for Rupert's lecture on her carelessness, on how she was going to destroy everything he'd worked for. Instead, he said, "I'm so sorry, Allegra."

She did not get to ask him if he'd meant the letter, the paint, or anything else, for Nadira burst into the room then. She took one look at Walter's neck and then glared daggers at Rupert. She shouted for servants to pour into the room, and they did at her command.

"Walter Cram! How many times have you been told to look after yourself?" she demanded. "Look at you! You burned yourself with that abyss-forsaken paint. Look at your face! It's all over you.

That paint has tar in it, I would bet my wages. And you know what tar is like! What were you thinking!"

Allegra wanted to correct her, to tell her dearest servant and protector that it had been her fault. But Rupert said, "I told him, Miss Nadira, but you know how stubborn he is."

Nadira tutted. "Your Radiance, you try to talk some sense into him. I wash my hands of him, I do! Look at the state of him. Oh, Your Ladyship! Come, let me fix that dress. Monsters."

Then, in a bluster of blankets, tea, and cakes, Allegra was bundled up by the servants and escorted away from her study, from her work, and to safety.

She let them.

CHAPTER SIXTEEN

LEX'S MISSION FOR the morning was supposed to be simple: interview Father Michael. This seemingly straightforward task morphed into an hour of walking about Cathedral administration looking for the Bishop of Orsini. When it was determined he'd not shown up yet in his study that morning—his secretary grumbled something about mage lovers and warm beds—Lex dropped by the archives, thinking the priest had headed there to assist. No luck there; they'd not seen him. Cram had left to find the Contessa, and Serafina had reported breathlessly that, apparently, Father Michael did not spend the night with Cram and it was the talk of the archives...when Cram had left, of course. They had manners, after all.

Lex backtracked up to the inner barricade, where the Contessa, Captain, and Cram all had apartments inside. They knocked on Cram's door, just in case. Kia answered the door and said he wasn't home; she was delivering messages and a parcel from Nadira.

"She insisted he have new tunics," Kia said breathlessly. What was it with Walter Cram that made all of these young women struggling to breathe around him? He wasn't that handsome.

Well, Lex amended. All right, he was decent to look at after he bathed and put on a clean tunic that didn't have gravy stains down the front, but still not handsome enough to risk fainting from lack of air.

At that juncture, Lex realized they didn't know which of the doors was Father Michael's, so Kia took Lex into the corridor to point the way. Lex muttered that the doors needed name plates, the way the administrative building had directions carved into wood.

"I was told it is for security of the residents," Kia said.

Lex did know that on an intellectual level, and it made complete sense. Except when someone was trying to run a murder investigation. Then, it was seriously annoying.

Kia pointed at the correct door and headed back to Walter's room, saying she was going to tidy a little before the ash maids showed up. Lex successfully hid their grin; the ash girls wouldn't care in the least about the level of tidiness of Walter Cram's room, as it wasn't their job anyway. But, of course, Kia's lingering might catch her a sight of the rebel mage.

"I was never that young," Lex muttered. They knocked and were relieved to hear the reply from within to enter. Lex tried the door, only to find it locked.

"Oh, sorry! I'll be right there!" Father Michael called out. There was some rustling about on the other side of the door before the latch gave way and the door opened. The priest's face brightened at the sight of Lex. "Oh! Come in, come in. What can I do you for today, my child?"

Lex stepped into a war zone. To call the room trashed would have been a grave underestimation. It would require Nadira and her army of footmen an entire day, if not more, to bring order to the chaos. Father Michael looked about for an open chair, finally upending one. A stack of books and all sizes of paper fell to join its fallen companions on the floor.

"If I had known how much work it would be becoming the Bishop of Orsini, I'd have declined the position!" He motioned for Lex to sit down on the offered chair, and then leaned against his cluttered desk.

Lex chuckled as they sat, saying they absolutely understood. "The Captain keeps saying I'm after his job, but I've seen the number of letters he gets in the run of a day, and he looks absolutely miserable every time he has to answer them."

Father Michael tried to laugh, but instead let out a long yawn. He crossed his arms and leaned back. Lex distinctly heard the muffled crack of several joints. "What brings you to my messy room today? Do not misunderstand me. I've been working in this disaster for two days now, and I welcome any distraction you might offer."

Lex had previously sent a letter with a list of information they'd hope Father Michael would clarify. It was simple details, mostly all from their time in Borro Abbey. Lex had hoped the bishop could fill in the missing holes in everyone's memories and confirm some conflicting information. Father Michael said he'd received the letter, and had been working on notes the previous night. He went off to the back of the long room to fetch them from his bedside table.

Now alone in the mess, Lex took the opportunity to look about. This room was significantly smaller than Cram's. The main room had no fireplace or balcony, though the stream of natural light further down the long suite said there was at least a window in the bedroom. Lex was struck by how narrow this room was; at least two-thirds narrower than Cram's. The ceiling was low, and the walls were bare. There was no carpet underneath all of the mess, either. He had almost no furniture in this room. Just the desk, and a couple of chairs. He did not even have a dining table here.

Lex frowned. They supposed it was possible the room angled off the bedroom, and there was a dining room beyond. However, the Contessa and Cram both had similar style rooms, where they combined dining and sitting all in the same area. This room was awkwardly narrow, true, but Father Michael had made no attempt to organize this to be welcoming to anyone.

Father Michael's Borro Abbey rooms had looked nothing like this. He'd always had piles of books, and plenty of papers and letters laying about, but they were neat and tidy. This placed looked like he barred the servants.

What a strange place for a bishop to be placed. Perhaps the stress had finally gotten to Father Michael, too. It was going around.

Father Michael called out that he knew his notes were there "somewhere," and to just give him a moment to find them. Lex idly read the titles of the books scattered directly in front of them on the floor. Most were about magic; history, translations, why mages were evil. The usual stuff.

One book's cover was flipped open to the title page: *Development and Practice of the Elemental Arts; a translation by Brother Theodore of Northumberland, by the Grace of the Lord God Almighty.* The spine was broken, and many sheets of paper were sticking out of it, and several had mostly fallen out, as if the book had tumbled from a higher location. Lex glanced around. There were no wall shelves. The book must've already been in bad shape when it tumbled from the desk to the floor.

Curiosity nudged at Lex and they moved the books around with their boot. The pile underneath had more about elemental mages. The majority were all translations of the same title. Not all by Brother Theodore, but all the same title.

Father Michael walked in just as Lex was bending over, head cocked to the side, trying to read one of the far titles. Lex froze in embarrassment; they'd been caught snooping.

But Father Michael cocked his own head to stare at the book and said, "What are we doing beyond hurting ourselves?" Then, before Lex could answer, he added, "I do not believe I will be able to straighten my neck now, my child. Oh, do not get old for it is a cruel mistress."

"You aren't even that old, Father! You're just balding, and you like to pretend you're sixty and I know you are not." Lex laughed and stood to take the necessary one step to bend over to pick up the book in question. "Why do you have a dozen copies of the same book? Are you a book seller on the side?"

"Ha!" was all the reply Father Michael gave, but he motioned for Lex to flip through the copy they held. They did, expecting to find a readable book in the way that all books were readable. Instead, what Lex found inside was nothing like any book they'd read before. The book was composed of only parts of a sheet of paper, as if the book was printed on sheets too large for the binding, and the pages were cut to fit the binding.

They turned the page, assuming to see the next continuation of the first line, but no, it was completely different. "What is this?"

Father Michael smiled and held out his hand. Lex passed the book back. Then, he bent over and picked up a stray piece of paper that fell from the book. While he did that, he said, "It's a puzzle. I used to own the original copies, and three historic fakes." His smile vanished. "I was very proud of my book collection. Serves me right."

Lex decided not to argue that point and instead asked, "How is it a puzzle?"

"There are sixteen books in total. You'd put them all together, in a square, and then you'd think you'd be able to read it then, correct? No! Each individual square is randomized within each book. You have to put it all together like a puzzle. I'd had all of the first editions at the abbey, but all I keep finding here are fakes." He angrily tossed the book on the desk, scattering several more books in the process. "I lost an entire life's work."

"Oh, I'm so sorry," Lex said.

Father Michael's smile returned, though it was not genuine this time. "Well, I believe this was a message from the Lord God Almighty that my life's work was to bring peace to the people of Serna, and not to solve silly puzzles. Now, enough of that. You did not come here to listen to an old man complain."

"Father Michael, seriously, you cannot be much older than the Holy Father," Lex said.

"Pish," he said, "I feel old and that is all that matters. Now, here are my notes. As you can see, they are almost legible. That is what I get for writing them by candlelight well after I should've been in bed."

Lex squinted at the papers and declared the handwriting better than Dodd's. "Do you mind if I ask some questions as I read?"

"Not at all, provided I have your permission to clean this disaster. Now that I see it through the eyes of another, I am humiliated to ever let it get to this state." In that moment, he let his mask fall, and he was just a man, not a bishop, not a priest. Just a man who seemed tired beyond words. "I do not even know where to start."

"Well, if my mother was sitting here, and Lord God help you if she was, let me tell you that, she would advise you to start with the furniture first. Then, the floor." Lex smiled. "The schoolroom looked like this in our house every time our tutors went away for a few days. Me and Dodd were small, but we could destroy a room faster than demons."

"Who am I to argue with the wisdom of your mother?" Father Michael said. He turned to organize his desk and Lex began reading the letter.

Lex found it difficult to pay attention to the letter, as Father Michael's cleaning bordered on obsessive. There were various pieces of paper, from large, full sheets normally reserved for music, to the tiniest scraps. He carefully looked at each one, before deciding if they went on his desk, into a drawer, or into the waste basket that now rested on his chair.

In the end, Lex knew there was a question they had to ask, and were only stalling for time as they mustered their courage. Finally, when Father Michael seemed at ease, and somewhat distracted, Lex asked the question that needed to be said aloud. "Does Cram take the servant passage through the administrative building to get outside in the early mornings?"

Father Michael froze.

Oh, he covered it up well, trying to pretend he'd been caught stretching his back. He asked Lex to repeat the question, as if he'd not heard. Lex did so, trying to keep their voice calm and easy, just another inquiry into getting to the bottom of things. It was clear both of them realized it was not *just* another inquiry.

"Walter prefers to stay up late with the bats, whereas I prefer to be out walking just before the birds begin singing for their breakfast."

Lex asked about Walter's mage acquaintances, trying to determine if he knew anyone along the paths where Vanida had said he'd been seen skulking about.

"You will have to ask Walter, my child." A dark expression came over his face, and he turned his back on Lex and went back to sorting his papers. He was more careless now, not paying nearly as much attention.

He didn't speak and Lex wasn't certain if they'd been dismissed or not. Then, Father Michael turned back abruptly to face Lex. There was no smile now, nor an attempt at one. "I realize all of Serna knows about how Walter and I spent some of our evenings together, but I do not know every single moment of his day, nor he of mine. We are both rather busy men and neither of us are the other's keeper."

Lex had angered Father Michael, more than the question should have. But there was one question that Lex desperately wanted to ask, and it had nothing to do with the investigation, with demons, with...

"It is none of your business, child," Father Michael said with a smile.

"I didn't even ask anything!" Lex hadn't meant to sound defensive, but that was the end result.

"I could guess by how your eyebrows were drawing together as you gathered your courage."

"Well," Lex said, "what was I going to ask?"

"You wanted to know why me, a bishop, would share a bed with not just a mage or even an elemental, but rather one of the leaders of the mage rebellion."

Lex's face heated up. "Well, yes. That was what I was going to ask, only nicer."

"And that, my child, is none of your business." He smiled, but as before, it was no longer touching his eyes. Lex made note of that; even priests could get angry. "After all, I have never put my oar into the waters of you and Lieutenant Dodd, unlike others of our acquaintance."

Lex rolled their eyes in hopes of brushing off that conversation. "We're good friends, and that's what we decided to be."

Father Michael tapped his nose. "And the demon lover and I are long acquaintances, and we decided between ourselves what we wished to do in our free time. Oh, did you hear? The Holy Father called in sick this morning. It's caused quite the scandal."

"Surely the man is allowed to be ill," Lex said. They knew Father Michael was trying to get them off course, and yet it felt impossible to steer the cart back on the path now.

"Apparently, His Radiance is as healthy as a young draft horse." He leaned forward and made a show of checking to make sure there was no one eavesdropping. Of course, there wasn't, being that they were alone in his suite. "The rumor is he and Pero have patched things up."

"Oh, good for them," Lex said, still unable to figure out how to veer the conversation back. "I hate how they've been fighting."

"It is never good when the head of the faith lives in turmoil at home. Now, was there anything else? I do have to do some work today, or I fear my clerk will quit in protest."

"No, but, um, if I think of anything, can I come by and ask? Or, drop you a note?" Lex asked.

His real smile returned, even if it was tinged with sadness. "Of course, my child. I love to see you up and about. You are my daily proof that the Lord God can choose to listen and answer prayers."

Lex didn't know how to respond to that, nor to the evident sadness in the priest's voice. But these last months had been hard on all of them, and Father Michael would not be the first to have a crisis of faith.

So instead of prodding where one's fork did not belong, Lex looked about the disaster and said, "I shall leave you to it."

Father Michael escorted them to the door and said, "I feel utterly ashamed that I let it get to this state. I shall blame Walter for this. It is the easiest path, is it not?"

Lex made their farewells and stepped out of the room. They were in front of Cram's door in the now-busy corridor before Father Michael's words really struck at what bothered Lex so much: it was always easier to blame Walter Cram.

Lex looked back down the corridor at Father Michael's room, debating to go back and tell him about the direction of the investigation. But something tugged at Lex, stopped them from taking that first step. Something was wrong with Father Michael.

That was when Lex saw him come out of his room. There were enough servants, couriers, and footmen in the corridor to easily obscure Lex from view, though Lex did see him looking about. Lex tugged their hat down, and lowered their head, enough to avoid eye contact in case he looked in this direction. He looked at Lex, they noticed that, so Lex raised a fist to pretend to knock on Walter Cram's door.

Lex stood there, pretending to look for Cram. Father Michael disappeared out of view, having taken one of the side corridors. Lex lowered their hand, no longer needing to pretend they were knocking. They walked back and tried the doorknob. Locked. Rarely did anyone lock their doors during the daytime in this part of the Cathedral. After all, how would the maids get in to deal with the laundry, the chamberpot...

Something about his room was off. His desk at Cram's did not look like that; his desk there was neat, tidy, ready for work and writing. His room looked nothing like how Father Michael's study at Borro Abbey looked, either.

Lex kept walking, and took a different route than their original plan. It was probably nothing, but Lex felt like they'd been lied to for that entire visit, and they were going to get to the bottom of it. Because all of this time, for all of the debates and arguments, Father Michael had summed up what bothered Lex the most.

It *was* easier to blame Walter Cram.

CHAPTER SEVENTEEN

LEX DECIDED TO make their way back down to the archives. Cram hadn't returned, allowing Lex a private moment with the archivist. They both stepped into Roul's over-stuffed study to speak. The room smelled of dust, mildew, and oiled leather, and there were stacks of books as tall as Lex in every corner. There were baskets and boxes everywhere, all with books and scrolls, letters, and ledgers, piled up. And yet, the man's desk was bare, except for one book on a special display mount, and a single sheet of paper in front of it. There wasn't even ink on the desk; a pencil was behind the archivist's ear.

Lex explained about the book in Father Michael's room, leaving out the details about where they'd found it and only saying that they'd heard rumors about its existence and was curious. And Lex *was* curious, because that was a large number of books about magic for a man who wasn't a mage.

They'd forgotten the book's title, but had remembered it had been written by *Brother Theodore of Northumberland.* Roul beckoned Lex to follow, and led them back into the main archive area, where curious eyes watched them, but said nothing beyond polite greetings. Lex followed Roul to the back corner, through a door, and stepped into a vaulted room. Hundreds, if not thousands, of books lined each of three walls. The back wall, floor to ceiling, was a cabinet of various sized drawers.

Lex whistled. "Young me would have opened every single one of those drawers."

"Young you would have gotten his hands slapped as soon as those grubby fingers touched the first drawer handle," Roul said absently. He gestured at a shelf high above and asked if Lex would climb up to get it. Not afraid of heights, Lex didn't mind. They ensured the ladder was latched into place first before climbing, so that the ladder didn't go sliding down the length of the room.

Which, Young Lex would have loved to do, and would have absolutely done.

As Significantly More Mature Lex climbed the ladder with care, they reflected that Young Lex was only an impulsive troublemaker because that was Dodd's influence. Young Lex was a good kid in their heart, who never wanted to cause any mischief.

Lex kept repeating that every time they fought against the urge to hurl that ladder the entire length of the room like it was a racehorse trying to hit the finish line.

Being a responsible adult sucked pickled eggs.

The book Roul needed was as thick as Lex's forearm was long, and they struggled to get a grip on it and not fall off the ladder. However, once braced against their chest, Lex was able to use their other arm to grip the ladder and climb down carefully and slowly. Then, Lex carried the massive tome over to the desk Roul pointed at.

Finally, when the book was placed on the book reader, Roul carefully opened it. He flipped through the book, muttering to himself and paying no heed to Lex's questions. It was pages and pages of names and book titles. In some cases, scraps of vellum were sewn into the original page, with additional titles. In other spots, there were scraps of paper attached to the margins with skinny sewing pins, again with more writing upon them.

Eventually, Lex realized all of the names were that of clergy members, and that their writings were all listed, be it in the original book or attached with additional papers.

Lex looked about the room. "Do you keep a record of every book ever written?"

"My predecessors have strived to keep a record of all writings by members of the clergy, and any Orsini residents."

"That's a lot of books," Lex said with awe.

Roul found Brother Theodore and announced, "He's banned. Let's check his spot."

Apparently, that was what the back wall of shelves was for: the good stuff.

Lex ascended a different ladder, climbing nearly to the top of the vaulted ceiling to pull open the small drawer. Inside was a wrapped packet that smelled like the cedar the entire wall was made of. Lex put the bundle into the basket that hung off the side of the ladder and lowered that down to Roul, before descending.

Roul donned white gloves and told Lex not to touch anything. He cut the thick thread that held the bundle's protective wrap in place with a tiny pair of scissors he pulled out of his jacket pocket. Roul carefully peeled off the outer fabric layer. Then, he meticulously opened the oiled leather pouch within. Inside that was a protective vellum sheet. And finally, inside *that* were several pieces of fragile vellum that were covered with writing. Lex couldn't read most of the words, so it was clearly old enough to make Roul's motions justified.

Roul read the top letter. "Ah, so all of Brother Theodore's books were banned five hundred years ago or thereabouts because they taught the basics of elemental magic. That does not explain the design you heard about." He turned the page to a drawing. "Ah! It was made like that to avoid the inspectors."

"Inspectors?" Lex asked.

"In those days, the Cathedral had inspectors who went house to house, building to building, to find banned texts."

"I never learned about that," Lex said.

Roul nodded. "Very few have, including those who live and work and serve in this building. Back then, they soon realized that it was better to gather all of the dark secrets of our past into one place and attempt to bury the rest. That is why this place exists, even now, and why I have had employment since I was seventeen years of age. This is the room of centuries of our secrets."

"I wonder how many secrets are here," Lex said.

Roul chuckled as he carefully turned the page over to the next. "So many that I do not know them all."

The next lot of vellum squares were numbered in the corner with a directional arrow, and he laid them out according to the grid pattern. He read from a sheet of paper, written in significantly more modern language.

"It says the Cathedral was unsuccessful in suppressing this set of books, so they published several fakes and had lower level clergy travel Serna pretending to be booksellers and then to sell these fakes. Ah, there are no surviving originals at the Cathedral now, according to this entry written by the main archivist ninety years ago. A note has been added to that, here, by Cardinal Vittorio dated nine years ago. 'All attempts to locate the originals have failed, and the knowledge is now considered officially lost.'"

The archivist frowned. "Nine years ago. Hmm. His Grace must've done this while I was away for two months to attend my brother's funeral. That is upsetting." Roul looked about the room, a worried expression on his face, no doubt wondering what else had been tampered with.

Lex pondered on Father Michael's words, that he had originals at Borro Abbey. He was clearly aware of fakes, that was obvious because he'd said as much. Which meant, somehow, he knew of the originals and had been able to identify them and keep them out of Vittorio's hunt.

Lex searched their memories; they were pretty sure Father Michael had been the Bishop of Borro for longer than nine years. The priest had been keeping secrets for a very long time, and from his superiors. "What was so bad about these books? Does it explain that?"

Roul flipped over a few more pages, some were paper, some were vellum. "Banned for knowledge of demonic rites, but that doesn't necessarily mean the actual summoning of demons. When this was written, the very existence of a mage meant they engaged in demonic rites. Of course, most of us know that is not the case."

"Some people still think that," Lex said.

Roul shrugged. "True enough, though I do not believe anyone of sense or education who has lived in this world believes Her Ladyship is out there dancing naked with the demons." He paused. "Though, I don't think anyone would put it past Mr. Cram, but that's because he likes to be the center of attention. Does this help you?"

"There's a puzzle that's bothering me, but I don't know why, or even what the puzzle is about."

"Collecting banned books is a pastime," Roul said. "It is human nature: if you ban something, we all turn into children and want it even more. That's how you know mages were born the way they were."

"What do you mean?"

"If you could study and become a mage, well, we would have many more, for no other reason than the spite of thumbing one's nose at holy orders."

Lex chuckled. "Do you want me to put this back?"

"I'll make Cardinal Rigi do it. The man loves to be useful. I wouldn't want to deprive him of the opportunity."

Lex thanked the archivist for his time and left, pausing only for pleasantries with the researchers. As they made their way back to the rectory, the gnawing sensation in Lex's stomach grew.

It was easier to blame Walter, wasn't it?

ALLEGRA KNEW, EVENTUALLY, she'd have to return to her study, but for now, she did not have the strength. Serafina had been summoned from the archives to assist, and Nathan and Ysabeau carefully peeled apart Allegra's letters, ledgers, and all of the papers that had been on her tar-splattered desk.

The servants had provided an old table for the middle of Allegra's drawing room, and it was covered in a stained cloth; one that no one would miss once thrown out. Nadira was organizing servants and runners; she should have stayed at the study, but would not leave Allegra's side until Stanton could arrive. Allegra did not have the strength to tell her to go; she was not too proud to admit she needed Nadira.

Her three assistants wore gloves, which were thoroughly ruined, as were the several discarded pairs on the table. However, that was better than the alternative.

Nathan had several red sores where he'd touched his face or neck, and his skin reacted far worse than the others. Nadira scolded him every time he did it, and Serafina once had to grab his hand to stop him from rubbing his eyes with the tarry paint all over his gloves.

Finally, Nadira put her foot down and Nathan was instructed to read aloud letters of business and to write Allegra's responses. The letters not covered in tar or paint. Most of her replies were short, simple requests that required little thinking on her part.

She needed to be busy, but her mind did not know how to focus.

Somewhere in all of that, Calm Seas arrived with a large bottle of gin. Nadira sat down at one end of the table with Allegra's dress spread across it to see if she could get the stains out. After several minutes of scrubbing one spot with no real improvement, Nadira declared it would be easier and cheaper to just have a new dress made.

Stains at the hem were one thing; stains all over the front and back were a completely different issue. She thought they could salvage the bodice at least, but upon inspection, no; the damage was too thorough.

Stanton finally arrived, smelling of horse and sweat. He flung the door open to her suite, looked about the room for her, and then hurried to her side. She was already standing by the time he reached her, and he wrapped her tightly in his arms. He declared he'd come as soon as he'd heard. He asked how she fared, declared himself having been worried sick as he galloped back to Orsini, asked again how she was, hugged her tighter, and only gave her enough time for a timid, "I'm fine now," before launching into the details about the hunt for Renouf's missing men.

"I'm glad you came," Allegra said, tears welling up in her eyes. His greatcoat was splattered with mud, and she could feel it rubbing off on her hands from the embrace; it was going to dirty the carpets and make the maids' jobs harder. She pulled away and said, "Does Imogen need you?"

He nodded and said, "She said for me to see you first."

"I am unharmed, I promise."

"The shock was the worst of it, I fear," Nadira had said when Stanton asked her for details. "Especially as the news of the Grand Duchess came upon her at the same time."

"There is news of the siege?" Stanton asked.

"Oh, love," Allegra said. "Rupert got word today. Bonacieux broke the siege, and executed everyone inside, including my cousin."

"Lord God Almighty," Stanton whispered. "Tell me everything."

There was not much to tell, and soon a hard knock came at the door; Little Gopher had been sent to find him, as Imogen needed him immediately. Allegra told him to go on, that she was safe, and Nadira assured him she'd not leave her mistress's side until his return.

She had dozed off in bed by the time Stanton returned. She awoke blurrily as he climbed into bed, but he shushed her. He said the others were still all asleep in her drawing room, and he did not want to wake them. He pulled the bed curtains about them for privacy, leaving a small opening on his side for moonlight to filter in.

Stanton whispered they'd captured the Amadore soldiers. Renouf was interrogating them now. They were his men, Stanton said, so it was only fair and right that he ask the questions. Though, soon they would all get their pound of flesh. Not him, though, he said to her and rather bitterly Allegra thought. The Holy Father had ordered Stanton to stay home, to avoid the taint of a mistrial.

"Mistrial," Stanton said with a snort. "If they did it, Renouf and Imogen will string them up and that'll be that."

"You don't think they'll hang them, will they?" Allegra asked.

"They are soldiers accused of not just disobeying orders and destruction of property, they deserted their posts to avoid capture. Renouf's reputation will not survive if he doesn't do it, and, if he does not, Imogen has the authority in a dozen ways. And I know her well enough to know she'll do it herself if Renouf pushes her hand. But he won't."

"I do not want anyone hanged for me," Allegra whispered.

It was a moment before Stanton spoke. "Then pray they are innocent."

Stanton was asleep moments later, and she found herself reflecting on the day's revelations. She had lost control of herself. Walter had lost control of himself, too, and he never did. She worried that something was affecting them. Walter had such fine control over his abilities, far more than she ever had.

Maybe they were being affected by something.

Or maybe, just maybe the stress was finally taking a hold of them, which scared her more, for there was no way to stop that.

CHAPTER EIGHTEEN

LEX WAS FUCKING exhausted and decided, in the end, that they'd rather sleep in the half-furnished old rectory building for the simple fact that it had less stairs to climb than the barracks. The Consorts had assisted the militia and Her Highness's troops with the search for Renouf's men. Five were eventually apprehended and arrested. Two of the assholes were charged with destroying the Contessa's study. Two more for abandoning their posts and not stopping the first two. And one more for purposefully hiding the previous four from the hunt. And, of course, all of them were further charged with desertion.

Renouf had been so enraged that he'd threatened to hang all five from the northern wall himself, and it took both Captain Rainier and Her Highness to control him. Then, just as they'd managed to calm him enough to stop demanding rope, some of Renouf's men started bitching and whining that they'd not been allowed to assist in the search themselves. That provoked some shouting and shoving, until Renouf threatened to hang everyone who so much as looked at him the wrong way.

Now, with the five idiots in the drunk lock-up awaiting their fate, the Consorts, including the Captain, were banned from any involvement by order of the pope himself to ensure the trial was completely fair. It had annoyed the Consorts a fair bit, since they'd done all of the fucking work, but the Captain had been wildly offended and took it as a slight against his honor and reputation.

And that pissed off Lex and Dodd, who didn't tolerate anyone talking shit about the Captain, which was only proper and just.

However, Her Highness threatened everyone with Cardinal DeLancey's cane if they did not go to bed and get some rest. She was looking straight at Lex when she'd said it, which pissed Lex off, since they were not a fragile teacup and they were tired of everyone treating them like one. But that, at least, deflected Captain Rainier's anger, and, finally, a plan was hatched all could tolerate: Her Highness's men, supplemented with the Orsini militia, would take charge of the prisoners. Everyone else was to get some sleep.

It surprised Lex to find a crackling fire in what would later be their bedroom. And it surprised them again to see a fully-clothed Dodd on the floor on a mattress. Without the ropes and ties of a bed frame, the hay-stuffed edges had rolled up around Dodd. He probably could've fixed that by laying diagonally, but that might've been too much effort.

"Too tired to walk back to the barracks?" Dodd asked. His eyes were still closed.

"Sorry to wake you. I didn't know you were in here." Lex's bed was set up, but they had no linens or blankets. They tugged off their boots when they sat down on the edge of the bed and were convinced their feet immediately swelled. The stench of old cheese filled the room.

"Don't worry about it," Dodd said. "I climbed into bed about half a minute before you walked in. Calm Seas just left to sleep upstairs. She's been keeping the fires going for everyone. The barracks were too far away for her, too."

Lex took off their jacket to use as a pillow, wincing from the agonized torso muscles that had been pushed to their limits. Though, it could've been worse, and would've been if Lex hadn't been insisting on so much training.

"I've not really seen you all day. How did things go with Father Michael?"

Lex had completely forgotten. No wonder their shoulders ached so much; today had been unnecessarily long. They didn't mean to sigh, but they did, prompting Dodd to ask what had happened. "It's hard to explain. Father Michael was acting strange, and he said something to me that's been gnawing at me."

"What did he say?"

"He said it was easier to just blame Walter."

"For what?"

Exhaustion and time had already faded some of the memories. "I don't even exactly remember. He kept changing the subject. I'm certain he lied right to my face, too. I would wager real gold on it. I know this sounds paranoid, but something was off in his room, and how he was acting. Then he said something about how it's easier to just blame Walter, and that's been on my mind all day."

"It *is* easier to blame Walter Cram," Dodd conceded.

"And I'm not saying that Cardinal Vanida is lying to us, or that Father Michael is part of some kind of grand conspiracy, or that Cram is some kind of innocent bunny, but I'm telling you that my guts say something is off."

Dodd was silent long enough that Lex thought he'd fallen asleep. Eventually, though, Dodd asked, "What are you going to do?"

"I don't know. For the love of the Lord God, he's helped us with the investigation. Do we have to interview all of the servants again? What have we done?"

"I think you're just overtired."

Then, Lex said out loud what had been nagging at them all day. "What if...Dodd, what if we assume everyone is a mage? How would that change our investigation?"

Dodd blew out a breath. "That would mean me, you, Cram, and Rainier are probably the most likely suspects. We've been around most of the markings or full portals. We're the ones investigating them. So, no, I don't really like the idea of thinking about everyone being a mage."

"Dodd..."

"I hear you, I do." Dodd sighed. "Look, I like Father Michael, and I like Walter. Just don't tell him I said that. But if it is either of them who did this, who killed all of those people? Lex, I'll be the first to get out the rope and to light the fires under their feet."

"I know," Lex said. "I know. I just...don't want it to be them. I don't want it to be anyone we know. I want it to be Vanida or

Vittorio or a complete stranger. Or Bonacieux. I really, really want it to be Bonacieux."

"Do you remember when we first found out about Cram and Father Michael?"

"Yeah, we were pretty surprised," Lex said with a half-hearted laugh.

Dodd didn't laugh. "No, we both thought he was using Walter and we wanted to warn our friend. Don't get me wrong. I'd throw myself in front of a crossbow to protect Father Michael, and I'd do it right the fuck now. I'm just saying for someone who spent all winter saying he never wanted power, he sure as shit took the Bishop of Orsini post rather quickly." Dodd was quiet for a moment, but when it was clear Lex had nothing to offer, he continued. "And he never seemed to care about us finding out about him and Walter. Calm Seas and Kia both told me Nadira was talking about it, too, and she never gossips, not like that."

"Maybe being here is making us all a little crazy," Lex said. When Dodd asked what they should do, Lex said, "I can't think right now. I'm too tired."

"I think we need to follow up on what Vanida said. Maybe a discreet patrol through the back alleys, but we can't have anyone who served at Borro do it, though. And, if we're watching Father Michael, we need to watch Walter, too. You know that."

"I know," Lex said.

"For what it's worth, I hope it's no one we know."

"Same," Lex whispered.

"I hope it's not the Contessa," Dodd whispered. "That would kill me."

"Don't even think it," Lex said. "If someone like Vanida hears that..."

"You know I don't just believe everything he's telling us, right?"

"I know," Lex said.

"But we have to follow it up, just in case."

"I know, Dodd."

"I just didn't want you to think I was picking on Cram."

Lex's eyes grew heavy. "I think I like Walter. He grows on a person, like mold on bread in the heat. But after everything we've gone through? If it is him," Lex's voice cracked, and they couldn't finish.

Lex was certain they'd only just closed their eyes moments before when the sound of pounding, shouting, and flashes of light underneath the door startled them awake. Lex bolted upright in bed, gasping and listening, waiting for the silence of the real world to pull them from their waking nightmares.

"What the fuck was that?" Dodd asked.

Lex jumped out of bed to rush for the door, as someone hammered on it. The sounds of fighting were clearly evident when they opened the door. Light from lanterns and torches hurt Lex's eyes, and they had to squint and turn away, unable to see who was pounding at the door.

"Demons?" Dodd asked from behind them before Lex or the Amadore soldier at the door could ask.

"The mob is after Renouf's men. Get your swords," the soldier said.

WHEN THE RUNNER had woken him, shouting and pounding on his door, Stanton had assumed demons. After all they had been through, demons were always the most likely scenario when awakened in the middle of the night and told to bring his sword. However, after pulling three men, feral from drink and rage, off an unconscious Amadore soldier with a gushing head wound, he had to remind himself that demons were not the only terror in the world.

The bulk of the mob gathered about the drunk lock-up. It had taken all night for the full details of the day to circulate through the city and refugees; the attack on Allegra's study, the hunt for Renouf's men, the location of their incarceration. It was impossible to hide a coordinated hunt for soldiers, nor that they had painted a death threat on Allegra's wall.

Stanton ducked a rock and pivoted to punch a man hard in the kidney, stopping him from kicking a downed Amadore soldier.

The attacker fell to his knees, gasping for each breath, and Stanton held out a hand to assist the soldier back to his feet.

On it went, with Stanton cutting a path to the center of the mob. Ducking, punching, and trying not to hurt anyone too badly. However, that did not work perfectly, and he ran his sword through one of Renouf's men who was beating a woman's skull in with a rock. He checked her breathing, in case his healing buttons would be of use, but the woman was beyond needing a healer now. He sighed, flicked the blood from his sword, and continued his journey forward, pushing and shouting, ever trying to stop the stampede.

The air rushed from Stanton's lungs as something struck him from behind. He kept his footing, at least, and whirled about, successfully avoiding a plank-welding woman. Even as he struggled to catch his breath, he still had to dodge her unpracticed swings. She cursed at him, screaming about Allegra and mages, and she would not listen that he was a Consort. Finally, he grabbed the plank, his skin stinging from the slap of the wood against bare flesh. He gripped tightly and wrestled it from her.

He shouted, "No!" with such force she stumbled backward, seeing him for the first time. She spat in his direction before dashing off.

His shoulders slumped as flames enveloped the roof of the lock-up. There would be no saving the building, or the people inside. Nearby scaffolding burst into flames moments later. They were going to lose the entire quarter now. Most of these buildings hadn't been repaired from the demon attacks yet; and...yes, there went the building materials.

Stanton turned his focus to controlling the beatings and small fights in the midst of the chaos. He could not make it to the lock-up now, not with a riotous crowd in the middle. He worked to temper the actions of the soldiers around him, pulling them alongside to form a line.

"Try not to kill anyone," Stanton continuously instructed, knowing that it was an impossible task. He knew accidents happened, even during the best intentions.

They marched forward, dealing with the pockets of mayhem. Most of the mob fled when Stanton's line reached them, and they let them go. A few did lash out, and Stanton did his best to avoid seriously harming anyone. He had to repeat his order twice before threatening to put his own sword through one of the Amadore soldiers if they didn't heed him. These were unarmed rabble. Let them flee.

Soon, it was clear Imogen was leading her own circle of soldiers. As he grew closer, he recognized the silhouettes of Lex and Dodd, along with several others he did not know, all going toward the fires.

Water came from nowhere with his own group. A horizontal waterfall gushed through the air, hitting the burning rooftops, hitting the scaffold, drowning the burning building materials.

Stanton let out a relieved breath. He would never tire of mages saving the day, though he was sick of how many days needed to be saved as of late.

CHAPTER NINETEEN

"SEVENTEEN DEAD!" FRANCOIS roared. "Forty-nine grievously injured and might not survive because we do not have enough healing items in storage! Two hundred, at least, requiring the aid of the healers and menders. Buildings and materials damaged! Is this your notion of peace?"

Stanton and Renouf flanked Imogen as they stood in front of the Holy Father and took their scolding. The three of them had not so much as changed into clean attire, let alone bathed and scrubbed the blood and mud off themselves. Stanton found himself caught between utter exhaustion and the rush of the fight, though even that was now starting to ebb. What he wanted most was a bath, a good meal, and a warm bed.

"What in the name of the Lord God Almighty happened out there?" Francois demanded finally.

"I take full responsibility, Your Radiance," Renouf began.

"No one was speaking to you, Renouf!" Francois shouted. "We never had this trouble before you arrived, and we've had demons attack us! Your Highness, what in the name of the Lord God Almighty happened out there?"

Imogen's voice was hoarse. She'd been closer to the flames and smoke than Stanton had been, and it had clearly done some damage. She paused frequently to cough. "I was with my men in the old rectory, so I arrived with seven of my own soldiers, three militia, two of Renouf's, and three Consorts, including Lieutenants Lex and Dodd. I sent a runner to find Mr. Cram or any other mage to assist us. Together, we formed a barrier against the door of the drunk lock-up, hoping to prevent the mob from breaking in. Regrettably, I must report we killed at least six people in that struggle, and injured many others, who attempted to rush us. I assure you, Your Radiance, it was in our personal defense only."

That did not feed the Holy Father's ire, so he turned it on Stanton. "And where were you located in all of this, Captain?"

"I approached from the main Cathedral stairs, so emerged at the rear of the mob. I mustered all available guards and soldiers to me, and we formed a protective line in an attempt to disperse the crowd and reach Her Highness. Regrettably, several were already dead, and we were slow to reach Her Highness as we were required to assist...members of the mob."

Francois raked his gaze over Stanton's bloody self and said, "Did any of them survive that help?"

Stanton blew out a hard breath through his nose so that he would not curse out the Holy Father, who knew him well enough to never say such a thing. When it was clear Stanton was not going to offer a reply, Francois continued his pacing and shouting.

"And yet, in the midst of all this organized assistance, we still have two soldiers who somehow escaped the burning building and who were not ripped limb from limb by the mob, which is rather suspicious given they were the entire reason the mob was there!"

"With regret, Your Radiance, my arrival has not gone as smoothly as any of us anticipated," Renouf began.

"I have a mind to banish your entire army back to Amadore!" Francois shouted, by way of reply.

Renouf cleared his throat and said, because the man never did possess much sense, "Your Radiance, if I might be so bold as to suggest—"

"Shut your mouth, Renouf! No one has asked you to speak."

Stanton rarely had seen Francois lose his temper and had never seen him lose it this fully in front of others. He was enraged deep in his soul. Stanton knew that anger well enough to know there was no reasoning with it, no words that could calm it, so all they should do was allow him to vent the chimney until the fire was exhausted.

Francois whirled about to bring his full attention on them. "Your Highness, you are Renouf's superior in this. What will you do with the two remaining scoundrels?" He pointed a finger in the air. "In such a manner that preserves the peace."

"Once we are discharged, Your Radiance, I will escort the two remaining offenders to Renouf's encampment and I will personally see them hanged."

That did not come as a surprise to Stanton, but Francois's reaction did.

"So you plan to solve this issue by killing more people?" he demanded.

Stanton cleared his throat to get the Holy Father's attention. "Your Radiance, as distasteful as this is, Her Highness is correct. There is no other path forward now for her and Lord Renouf. They are dealing with desertion, along with all of the other charges. This will be a stain upon their honor so long as those soldiers remain alive. Forgive me for speaking so plainly, but—"

"Oh, I expect that of anyone who's spending as much time with Allegra as you have been!"

Stanton gave Francois a stern look, but did not take the bait dangling before him. He knew the words were in anger, and not real, and he would not be deterred from the topic at hand. "When you appointed me to this role, you told me I was not only to protect you, but to advise you and the senior cardinals when necessary. It is my advice that this is a military matter. Let them handle it, in their own fashion."

"I will not have people hanging in my courtyard!" Francois shouted. Again. His voice had grown noticeably hoarse over the conversation, and he had to clear his throat to finish his thoughts. "I am opposed to such barbarity."

"Why?" Renouf shrugged when all heads turned to him. "If they were mages, it would've been done by now and no one would care. Simply think of them as mages and be done with your conscience."

An expression of such absolute fury washed over Francois's face that Stanton took a step forward to calm the man. "Rupert..."

Silence hung over them, as the Holy Father seethed. That comment had cut him deeply, of that Stanton knew. Allegra and

Rupert had still not healed the wound between them. Theirs was not an argument based in avoidance—that was an impossible task given the natures of their positions—but rather one of snide remarks, snippy retorts, and frosty receptions.

And Renouf had decided to pick at that scab so hard he'd made it bleed.

"Your Radiance," Imogen said, trying to draw his attention back to her. "Listen to your captain. It is what must be done."

Francois turned back to Stanton, who gave him a small nod. The fury drained from his shoulders, and he visibly shrank. Anger was exhausting, and it had been a long night and morning already.

Finally, he waved a hand and said, in the cold voice of authority, "I have no control over the Amadore army, only so much as the King has lent us assistance. Deal with your issues as you see fit, but know that I want none of it within my walls. Orsini has seen enough bloodshed."

"It will be clear it is a private, disciplinary matter, and by my order, Your Radiance," Imogen said.

That seemed to appease the Holy Father, at least.

Stanton could have kept his mouth shut at that moment, but he opened it anyway. "I should attend, to show that we are one force, united."

A part of Stanton desperately hoped someone would argue; he hated hangings. He'd seen enough death, and he knew Allegra would hate that he had volunteered to attend. He also knew there would be those who'd blame him for the hangings, because his lover had been humiliated. He could not deny that had been his motivation during the original hunt, but this was different. Before becoming a Consort, he'd been in Amadore's army.

What Renouf's men had done, and caused, was well beyond excommunication or banishment. They had eroded trust. They had endangered persons. Their actions caused the deaths of others. Imogen could not let that stand, not as a major in the king's army, not as Colonel of the Orsini Militia, and certainly not as the sister of the King of Amadore.

And, so, he must attend and witness.

His stomach rolled and he was glad he'd not eaten in hours. He knew he'd fail to explain this to Allegra properly. Perhaps Pero, who had his own military career in his youth, could shed better light on the situation. Either way, the killing wasn't over yet.

ALLEGRA STOOD ALONE as she surveyed her study. The servants must've scrubbed non-stop since the unfortunate event, for there was no obvious sign unless one knew where to look. Her desk's top and side has been sanded down past the stains, as was her chair. New carpets, smaller than the last, were strategically spread across the floor, with occasional patches of sanded floors where the carpets failed to cover the evidence.

Her papered walls were beyond easy repair. They'd need to be stripped and sanded, and repapered, a task that would've taken far too long. Now, large tapestries covered her walls, along with various strategic paintings. She pulled back one such from the wall, expecting to see the hurtful words still scrawled there. She sighed in relief; the servants had scrapped off as much of the paper as possible in the limited time they'd had. She would have to ask Nadira for the names of those who'd done the work and send a small token of thanks. This was well beyond the normal daily tasks.

She glanced about her sitting room. Overall, the redecoration was pleasing. The paper was fading in spots, in any case. Perhaps when they finally succeeded at killing her, the servants could take their time to re-paper the room for the next scapegoat. She'd choose green paper, though. It would match the new rugs wonderfully.

Allegra turned to look out her windows. Thankfully, they did not face toward the north, where Stanton would be. They had fought, and fought hard. She was against hangings. No matter the crime. Lock them away. Banish them. Make them work the mines instead of mages. It did not matter to her. She was against the action.

Still, her words had been harsh and she'd insulted his personal honor. And he had been harsh and called her unfortunate words.

Neither had slept much. Stanton had arrived covered in blood, and she had not been prepared for that.

She should not have fought with him. Upon reflection, she realized she had barely inquired if the blood was even his before tempers flared. Who was to know what might happen once the rope was set? They should not have parted in such a manner.

The door opening interrupted her dark thoughts. She pushed against the intrusive voice, whispering they had come to tell her Stanton had died, died angry at her, died with her yelling at him as the last words she'd ever say to him. Her eyes were already glistening when a familiar voice asked, "Am I interrupting?"

"Yes," she said. Then forced a smile and turned to face her oldest friend in the world. "However, sometimes interruptions are very welcome."

Rupert's face was drawn, and the redness of his eyes said he'd not gotten much sleep either. He turned to motion for someone to come forward, and a few footsteps later, Martin came into the sitting area with a covered basket, which he placed on one of her small end tables. He inclined his head to both before heading back out to the other room. They were both silent until the door closed.

"The maids brought too much food, and I have no one to share my luncheon with today." He shrugged awkwardly. "I thought you might be in the same predicament."

She ignored the clumsiness of his attempt and motioned for him to sit. She missed how it was, and she longed to have her old friend with her. He filled up the teapot, and she fetched the teacups and the canister of tea from the other room. They sat and waited for the tea to steep.

Finally, she decided to break the silence. "Did Pero go?"

Rupert let out a weary sigh. "He left with Stanton. Did the two of you fight over it?"

It was her turn to sigh. "Yes. You and Pero?"

"I'm surprised the servants didn't announce it when they delivered the mail." He didn't bother hiding the bitterness.

Silence settled as the tea was poured and tea cakes pulled from the basket. He'd brought a marvelous assortment, but his table was always excellent. It would be a great insult if the Holy Father was fed second best anything. Still, he'd brought the things he knew she'd like. She nibbled on the tea cake, not asking from where its sugar originated. It would cause a needless fight, and it was not likely he'd even know.

He put his teacup down so hard on the saucer that it rattled. "I am so sorry, Allegra. I cannot apologize enough."

She did not reply. She could not, for she worried she would break into tears. More than anything, she wanted to be angry with him, the kind of anger that seeped into one's bones and never left. But that took so much energy, especially when all she wanted was her friend back.

"There are no words for what I did. I wish I could justify, or explain, but I feel neither are important, for no matter what I tell myself, in the end, I cannot look in the mirror now without hating what I see, and what I have become."

Allegra's jaw trembled.

"I have spent so much energy aimed at reaching a consensus that I forgot what it meant to have conviction. I lost the passion, the principles, all of it. I used to feel a fire in my soul, and Pero and I would stay up all night, arguing, and fighting, and making love, and doing it all over again." He sucked in a breath, calming his speech's tempo. "Trust is funny. It takes forever to build, and a moment to destroy."

"Yes, it does," was all she could whisper.

Silence fell once more. He did not pick his teacup back up. She put hers down. She wanted to hate him for as long as the sun rose in the east. She wanted him to suffer. But, when she examined the truth, she found herself suffering alongside him. What he had done, what he had allowed to happen, what he had put her through was wrong. There was no excusing it. And he had not.

What was more, she had not gone to the gallows. She had not been handed over. She had not been burned. Yes, he had slapped her, and that had hurt more than her face. She also did not know of his plans, and she had never cared enough to ask. They had all done and said things they regretted.

"I wouldn't mind trying to rebuild the trust between us," she whispered. "I've missed you."

Rupert's voice cracked. "I've missed you, too."

She reached across the immeasurable gulf between them, and he grabbed her hand. She squeezed as she thought about Rupert in the corridor. How he'd banned Vanida from his presence, no matter how much he shouted on the other side of the doors. How he'd come to her, to tell her the news about the Grand Duchess, and then stayed with her until Nadira could be found when the insults were upon her walls.

She mustered her courage and forced the words out. "I forgive you. Together, we shall move forward."

Rupert covered his face with his hand, the one not gripping hers. He wept hard, and she finally felt true compassion for his suffering. Life was nothing if not a series of choices. He had made his and had lived to regret.

She drew in a deep breath. "I know all too well the balance of compromise. I know I am a hypocrite, Rupert. Every day, I lie to so many people. Every single day, I sit in this study, in your dining room, in the courtyard, and I declare that I fight for mages, that it is absolutely acceptable to be an elemental mage. And yet, I have told less than a dozen people in this world. My brother does not even know. Nadira does not know, and she practically raised me."

"Nadira is a smart woman, Allegra," Rupert said. He wiped his eyes on the back of his free hand. He'd not let go of hers yet. "I am certain she knows."

"Yet, she does not know from my own mouth. Nathan and Serafina work for me, and yet, they do not know. Of the Consorts, who bled to protect me all winter, only two know. Giso does not know. Pero does not know, unless you told him."

"It is the only secret I have ever kept from him," Rupert whispered. "For it is your secret to tell, and not mine. Though, Pero would support you, which I am certain you know in your heart."

"You. Walter. Stanton. Lex. Dodd. A few of the girls from my school days. A handful of mages who fought the demon at Borro Abbey. I believe they are all dead now. I cannot articulate to you the guilt I feel when I think upon the relief in my heart when I realized most of those mages did not make it. And if someone managed to live? Who would believe them that the great Contessa of Marsina, friend of the Holy Father, lover of the gallant Captain

Rainier, was nothing but a sad, little elemental mage, like all of the rest of the rabble?"

She let go of Rupert's hand and stood. She walked over to the windows and stared out at the sunny spring day. What a fine day to be one's last before the hangman's noose did its duty. She hoped it rained the day they tried putting her to the flame.

"And yet, Bonacieux knows what I am. No matter all the lies we have told, he saw me. And soon, I shall face my choices, and every good deed I have tried to do in this world will have been for nothing. They shall kill everyone I love to get to me."

Rupert jumped from the chair and came to stand by her. "I promise you, Allegra, it will be over my dead body."

She sniffed. "Oh, Rupert. That is the problem. I believe it shall be over a number of dead bodies. Some days, I wonder if I should simply walk out of the south gate, and not stop until I find Bonacieux, for I wonder if that is how we find true peace."

"No," he said harshly. "Compromise does not bring peace. There will never be peace, not so long as some of us remain subjugated. Either we are all free, or none of us are."

Chills went through her. A younger Rupert had said those things, when they sat about her sitting rooms at home, when they were young and foolish and saw the world in binary.

"You have changed," Allegra said.

"No. I merely remembered what I had always believed."

"Then I hope you are prepared to die for it, for I fear one way or another, someone will be giving their life for their beliefs."

"Then, I shall pray you are wrong," he said, "for I am tired of death."

STANTON HAD NOT known where to go when it was over. Allegra's suite was supposed to be their suite; she had repeatedly insisted. His room in the barracks did not even have a bed now, as Lex and Dodd stole it for the old rectory. Even his pillow was upon Allegra's bed. He considered it his home, every single day, until now. They had fought too hard, fueled by exhaustion and worry

221

on both sides. But he was raw, and felt naked and alone. He just wanted to be home.

So he went back there, and found the apartment empty. Uncharitable, horrible thoughts filled his mind of where she could be. He ignored them, knowing it was the hurt taunting him. He poured himself some of the good brandy Nadira stored in the tiny closet off the sitting room. He'd taken the bottle, and one of the glasses, and had only meant to drink enough to ease the edge off the repeating scene in his mind, of men dangling by broken necks. Of the soldier he'd killed in cold, methodical choice during the riot.

One glass did not prove helpful, and he poured another. By the time Allegra finally returned home, he had lost count of how many glasses he'd poured. Only it had been enough to reduce him to the floor, leaning against one of the chairs, unable to stand. Or, maybe he was merely unwilling to stand. He did not know if the difference mattered. All that mattered was that he hurt, and continued to hurt, and not even the brandy could chase that away.

Allegra stared at him for a moment before looking at the bottle. She sighed. He realized he did not think he'd ever been drunk around her. Not like this. Not in the desperation of escape. He watched her remove her pelisse, a garment worth a servant's monthly salary, he suspected. Not a stitch of dirt on it. He did not deserve her. He loved her and wanted to be the best man in the world for her, but how could he be when he was sitting here on the floor, running away from the consequences of duty.

She gathered up her skirts and lowered herself to the floor. It always amazed him she could do that, wrapped in so many layers. She smiled at him, and said, "I am so sorry we fought."

He had thought of a hundred things to say in this moment, to try to explain why he'd made the choice he had. He had practiced it, running it over in his mind until he'd memorized both his lines, her retorts, and his rebuttals. Yet, at the sound of her voice, he broke into heavy sobs. He did not know why. Exhaustion? The drink? Moral agony? All possible. Or maybe it was simpler than that: the calm, loving balm she had upon his spirit.

She wrapped arms around him that said she would fight every single demon in the abyss for him. He hated this kind of death so much, the kind that left smears upon one's soul. The voice in his head, the one who whispered that he had not seen nearly as much of it as Imogen and Renouf, and that his pain was not as worthy as theirs, mocked him as he cried, and it only made her squeeze him tighter.

She knew of his nightmares, for those were impossible to hide, and she had a share of her own. He rarely talked about what it was like, being a mere Lieutenant Stanton, the eager, dutiful young man protecting priests against bandits. Even now, when the woman he loved held him, he struggled to tell her the secrets of his heart.

Then, as if her magic allowed her to read minds, she said, "You do not need to say anything. Just breathe for me."

So he did. Leaning against her, breathing. Listening to her voice, calling him back from wherever his mind had taken him. Long, deep breaths. He did as she instructed, to focus on the room, his body, her body, the present. Two people trying, and failing, to time their breathing together. The tricks his mind played, of gallows, of demons, of blood and bandits, all faded. It was just her.

"I'm sorry," he whispered, not even knowing what needed the apology, but he knew he was truly sorry for it all the same.

She pulled out of the hug and smiled at him. "Have you eaten?"

He shook his head.

"When did you last eat?" she asked.

"A tea cake or two, I think, yesterday evening? I can't remember what day it is."

"Then it is no wonder you are in such a state." She got to her feet and held out her hand. "At your age, you cannot drink as if you are Lex and Dodd out having a good time."

He slapped his hand into hers, even as he laughed. "We're practically the same age, woman!"

"Yes, and I cannot drink brandy, port, or any spirits on an empty stomach, or after the sun goes down, lest I be up all night ill. Now, come, let me help you to the bed. I shall fetch you water and whatever Nadira left for us." She sighed. "And I shall find something for you to waste all of that good brandy into later tonight, no doubt."

He stumbled along with her guidance and found the bed, even as he protested that he was not as drunk as she was making him out to be, and that he would not be vomiting, nor would he have more than a headache in the morning.

She did not believe him in the slightest. He loved her for it.

CHAPTER TWENTY

WALTER HAD SPENT hours wanting nothing more than to be in his bed. Now atop the bed, naked and scrubbed clean of the night's filth, he found himself unable to sleep. His mind refused to stop to catch its breath. He'd not helped with the hunt for Renouf's men; he had enough of his own problems, though he did gather a few mages in case things got very bad.

He didn't give a shit about Renouf and his problems maintaining control over his soldiers, except for how it impacted himself and the other mages. Even then, it did not really affect Walter, for his guard was generally staffed by the Consorts' junior members, or occasionally the local militia. Slowly, a few of the princess's soldiers even took turns, though that was usually the women. And the younger ones.

Walter tried to smile at that. He wanted to, and most days he would have, but instead he only sighed.

Dodd had ruined the fun of it all by explaining it to him. They'd all known the devastation mages could bring, but it had changed when they saw how Walter could use his power for their protection. They knew his importance now, his role in keeping them all alive, so the younger members had an easier time with that change. And, as it happened, most of Her Highness's younger members right now were giggling girls. They trusted him and wished to protect him.

Walter sighed audibly as he stared up at his ornate ceiling. Never in his wildest dreams did he imagine Amadore soldiers would trust him. Worse, never did he imagine he would trust them enough to let them follow him about.

That realization sent a shiver of cold through his body and he twitched. He trusted soldiers, the very people who had hunted him and his kind.

Most of the decorations in this room were valuable. The pewter was easy to sell, and real silver cutlery was easy to both carry and sell. He'd seen Allegra served with real gold utensils. He could steal those off her plate and she'd never notice. He should plan his escape. Grab what he could carry and run. Go burn Vittorio's estates to the ground. Sometimes, it took fire to kill the roots.

He puffed out a breath. What Walter needed was a distraction. He glanced at what had been Michael's side of the bed. The priest had not been by for three days now. Granted, Walter had not made any effort to seek him out, either. He was too busy, and too old now, to play silly games. They'd been keeping different hours as of late, so they'd not so much as bumped into one another in the corridors, let alone naked up against the desks.

Walter tried to chase that memory from his mind…and sighed when his body reacted to the pleasant recollection.

He could not think of anything he'd done to scare the priest away, beyond the usual issue of him being a demon-loving elemental mage who'd as soon murder them all in their beds as fuck them. Excepting that, of course.

A knock came at his door, and he had enough time to cover himself before one of his guards swung the door open. She inclined her head, apologized for waking him, and said his presence was needed at the old rectory immediately. Once she left to give him the privacy to dress, he collapsed back on his pillow, berating himself for hoping it was the priest.

Walter crawled out of bed and dressed in clean clothes the laundry maid had left for him sometime in the middle of the night. She must've been a mage because that woman could break into his suite at any hour and he never heard so much as the door creak.

He went outside and greeted the guards. He didn't usually have them at night, since there simply weren't enough people to go around, and, in theory, he was supposed to be in bed, protected by the Orsini militia that guarded all of the corridors. One said she'd escort him, while the other stayed behind to ensure no one wrote Die Demon Whore on his walls. His guard kept a respectful distance behind him, and despite the temptation, he did not veer to knock on Michael's door.

"Good morning, Mr. Cram," someone said in passing.

"And a good day to you, Mr. Cram," another said.

"Shall we see you in the dining hall this evening, Mr. Cram?" asked a cardinal. A junior one, sure, but a cardinal nonetheless.

His shoulder blades itched the entire trek through the corridors. He knew the guard was there to protect his back, to ensure no one plunged a knife into his spine. Walter had to keep telling his instincts that the guards had no interest in killing him. They wanted to keep him safe.

Him.

He could feel vines wrapping around his feet as he walked. Entangled did not encompass the mess he was in.

He did not stop at the security barricade, which were always swung wide open during the day. Those thick, heavy doors saved the lives of so many children during the attack. And the lives of important, foppish people. And the lives of people like Vittorio, while good people fought and died. Walter tried not to imagine the scene at those doors during the attack, but he'd heard the stories, and many from Rigi. So many stories, in fact, that he was having the nightmares of others. As if his mind felt his own traumas were not enough torture.

A familiar figure in the distance caught Walter's attention. He did not call out to Michael, nor veer toward him. The priest had to have seen him, as he was walking toward Walter. But, when their eyes met, the priest pretended to not notice him, looking past Walter's shoulder, and then took a hard turn down an alley.

So that answered the question of why his bed had been empty. Apparently, they were fighting. He'd have preferred if someone had alerted him to this fact. Walter stewed on that for the remainder of his escorted walk, and, by the time he reached the gaggle outside the rectory, he found himself desperate for demons.

Rainier and Her Highness were there, as were about twenty soldiers. Walter's heart pounded, and he struggled to draw breath.

Inside was a rope. He knew it. Everything in his being said he was about to swing from the banisters. Or out a broken window for all to see.

Rainier, however, did not look grim-faced. He looked confused. "They're waiting for you inside," he said.

Walter stopped and asked, "Will it be rope or fire?" Rainier seemed completely at a loss over his meaning. "How are they planning to kill me inside?"

"As far as I know, they're not," Rainier said.

"Would you tell me if they were?" Walter asked.

"I wouldn't," Her Highness said flatly.

"I would," Rainier said.

That did not instill calm in Walter's heart. He turned to look at his guard. She moved her hand to the sword at her hip and raised a questioning eyebrow. He told her to follow, and to watch his back. He did not like where this was going.

He stepped inside, ready to fight for his life. Instead, what he found was a bright, warm room. Several lanterns were lit, as well as candles, and there was a sizeable flame flickering in the fireplace. Inside stood Bianca, Rigi, Roul, and the Holy Fucking Father.

Walter didn't approach them. He stayed near the door in case he needed an escape. And he was going to need an escape, of that he was certain. He knew betrayal when it was written in guilt across someone's face.

Walter did not try to pretend this was not suspicious. He wasn't Allegra; he didn't play the social games. "What's going on?"

"Mr. Cram," Roul said, "thank you for coming."

"Are you gathered for my funeral?" He laughed, thinking that would dispel their somber faces. Only, it did not at all. If anything, their expressions grew more concerned. "Should I run now, or wait until you're done your speeches?"

"My child, this is not a betrayal," Sister Bianca said, in a mildly annoyed tone. "We simply felt this conversation would be best had elsewhere. Now, please, come join us."

"Allow me to be perfectly clear, Sister," he said, his temper rising, "I will not be going anywhere, not even the distance to that chair, until you tell me what is happening."

"Walter," Rigi said, in that tone Allegra used. In that tone Lex and Dodd used. In that tone even Rainier sometimes used. Nadira. Serafina. Nathan. The fucking Holy Father. Lately, they all used that tone with him.

"My name is Cram," Walter snapped. "I am not your friend. I am not anyone's friend."

Walter felt a twinge of guilt when Rigi's shoulders slumped. Then, the young cardinal squared his shoulders and said, "Be that as it may, we wanted you to be safe when we informed you of what we have discovered. And, since we are *not* friends, I desire to say none of us wish to have unnecessary victims if you lose control of yourself."

Walter released a touch of magic and the table between them danced a little. The others jumped in fright, and then all scowled at him. They all looked so fucking terrified of him, and that hurt deep within his soul. "What in the name of the Lord God Almighty is going on? I can control myself."

"Just like the other morning?" Rigi asked.

He wanted to lash out, but shame overtook him.

"Forgive us, Walter. *Cram,*" Rigi said. "We needed to bring you somewhere safe. I was only included as, well, I thought you considered me a friend, and we wanted you to have a friendly face."

It was then that Walter noticed the reading block was on Lex's desk. The one they used in the archives for the old, fragile books. Roul pulled out his white gloves.

"Leave us at once," Rupert ordered the guard.

She hesitated, but Walter nodded for her to go. If they'd been planning to kill him, they'd have done it by now. When the door closed, he asked, "All right. It's just us now. What is this about?"

"We discovered this last night," Roul said as he pulled a book from a small box. "It was referenced in Brother Theodore's book. Apparently, it was with the banned books, the ones from centuries ago. Of heretic teachings."

"And?" Walter asked. It was hard to keep up the tension when they were dragging it out so much.

"Well," Roul began, "it covers the usual theories, now banned of course, all concerning the passage of time in the abyss—"

"Oh, is that all?" Walter rolled his eyes. Everyone had heard the theories that said the descendants of Tasmin lived in the abyss. As if there would be air and sky and food to sustain a population of people in the place of demons. "You were scaring me."

Roul's expression did not change. Nor did the others for that matter. "Sister Bianca and I worked through the night, and Cardinal Reinhold and Miss Serafina have verified what they can. Before I read this aloud, I want to assure you both, the Holy Father and Mr. Cram, that I personally had no knowledge of this." He looked straight at Walter, worry and fear etched in every single wrinkle on the old man's face. "I swear to you on the graves of my parents, and before the Lord God Almighty, Walter Cram, I did not know."

"What on earth does it say?" Walter whispered, now frightened. What could the book say that would make this man so terrified of him?

Roul first read in the original tongue. Walter only understood every tenth word or so, but he recognized Rupert's expression of confused concentration. He recognized more of the words, Walter was certain, and looked as though he questioned his own understanding of the text.

"And now, for the translation." Roul closed his eyes and gulped hard. The old man was terrified. Even his hands were shaking now. "And then Tasmin, she who was the appointed of our Lord God Creator, the very essence in all of our hearts, brought forth fire from her soul that cut a path through the demon army. She held them back, the glory of the Lord God Creator flowing from her outstretched hands, and the holy army of the faithful were not harmed. Inspired by her example, wanting to exalt the name of our Creator, in who all things be praised, others took up the challenge. Their hearts formed a shield wall of fire. The demons could not harm them, though they screamed in rage and disgust that the Creator who made them came to our side in the final battle."

Walter stared at Roul, his mouth gaping open. He had to have misunderstood what he was hearing.

"Tasmin, our defender, the guardian of truth and life, pushed toward the great fissure, and no demon could stop her. The army plunged ahead of her, even as she directed the fire of her heart away from them, for this was their plan, the plan to save our world, the plan to exalt the name of the Lord God Creator. Then, and only then, when the army had fulfilled their purpose, rushing into the abyss itself to bring the final battle, was Tasmin left alone upon the field of battle. The demons fled both her heart and the army that marched into the fissure, the trap sprung perfectly. With the calmness of the Lord God Creator's grace upon her, our defender Tasmin walked to the edge of the fissure, even then needing the fire of her heart to purge the demons that wished to drag her to the end. She fell into the rift, the tear between us and the demonic home, and she pulled the fissure shut as she fell from view. When the fire and smoke receded, we could not count the thousands of demons felled by holy fire. Mercy and grace, praised be the name of the Creator, our Lord God who gave us such saviours."

Walter could not speak, as his thoughts could not stay still long enough for them to exit his mouth. There was silence in the room.

"There is more, of course," Roul said. He blew out a breath. "However, I feel that was the most important part of the history."

"Is this genuine?" the pope asked. "Can we be certain these are not the ravings of a madman?"

Roul bowed in Rigi's direction, who answered the question. "Your Radiance, myself and Sister Margarite and Serafina have been working most of the night to answer that very question. From what we can gather, it is legitimate. Further, it appears that some senior cardinals are currently aware of the information in this book, and are part of a centuries-old conspiracy to hide this information, and all links to it."

"In fact, Your Radiance, we have found adjacent writings by well known, and well-respected historians amongst the clergy who reference these events, but by other contemporary authors. Those writings were all banned," Roul said. "Some are lost to history, but it appears some were merely misplaced within our own library."

Walter watched as the lanterns danced on the desks and ledges. Chairs jumped on the floor, shifting and moving. Tables joined them. People became unsteady, putting out their arms for balance. This explained why Allegra was not here. They would trick

231

him, scare him, force him to bring down this building and hide the information that could free his people. Those whose robes were stained with generations of blood would make him a murderer, all to allow the continued subjugation of his kind, to be tortured, to be enslaved, to be murdered, to be...

Fine. If it was a fight they wanted, he would give them one to ensure his name was a whisper for the rest of eternity. He stretched his hands out to his sides and gathered the will in his soul. He knew this day would come. He had prepared himself for it. "I will not let you bury me, not without taking all of you with me. This will be your only warning, in respect for the moments we have shared."

Sister Bianca stepped forward. "Be calm, Walter Cram. We are not here to trick you."

"I swear to you, Cram, on whatever you need me to swear upon, I did not know any of this," the pope said.

"Then why bring me here," Walter demanded. "Why not simply tell me in the archives?"

"So that if you had a repeat of the incident previously, you would only kill us and not others," Rigi said. "We felt it was the best compromise."

"Why are you here then?" Walter demanded of the Holy Father. "You don't even like me."

"I don't like most of the people I work with," Rupert said. "What difference does one more man make in that?"

Walter's hands trembled as the magic ceased flowing. He lowered his arms, now weary from the gesture and tension he'd been holding. He stepped to the side, giving him a better view of the door without taking his eye off the others. No one had stepped inside behind him, ready with the dagger. He continued backward until he bumped against a table. He skirted around it, his back finally against the firm surface of the wall. He took a deep breath. They could not sneak up on him now.

"Why am I here? Why are you telling me all this?" Walter demanded.

The world had stopped shaking, but Walter could—and would—bring this building down upon them if necessary.

"We decided this needed to be entrusted with someone, beyond politics and the faith," Roul said.

Bianca and Rigi nodded in agreement. The Holy Fucking Father just stared at him.

Sweat beaded and dribbled down Walter's spine, down the side of his face, dripping off his nose. He did not wipe at it, for fear taking his full attention off them could trigger an attack. His hands were shaking now, his teeth were chattering, his heart pounding, and he struggled against the urge to run.

Finally, gulping for air, pushing past the lump in his throat, Walter managed to ask, "What do you expect me to do with this?"

"You tell us, Walter Cram," Rupert said. Why was the fucking pope asking him for help? "Will this help you find the creator of the demon markings?"

"We don't even have markings anymore! We have fully realized portals!" Walter shouted. He gasped, trying to find enough air to fill his lungs. He put a shaky hand through his sweat-soaked hair. His head was pounding now, and stars floated in his vision. "Is that honestly saying that Tasmin, fucking Tasmin, was a mage?"

"Yes," Roul said. "And I believe it is the truth."

The wooden boards across the blown-out windows clattered, and nails creaked. He shouted, shouted loud enough that the entire world should have heard him, loud enough that maybe even the Lord God would finally pay attention. "Are you saying everything I have suffered has been for nothing?"

Sister Bianca stepped forward, an elderly woman with full confidence that he would not murder her where she stood. "Archivist Roul and I, and Cardinal Reinhold, and Cardinal Rigi, and Miss Serafina, we all spoke, and decided that we needed a mage here, with us, brought into this knowledge."

Walter looked over at Rupert. "When did you find out?"

"After they had already dispatched the guards to fetch you," Rupert said, "and thereby preventing me from ordering them to stop."

"You'd have stopped them?" Walter demanded.

"Probably," Rupert said. "I'd have rather Allegra be the mage to know, not you."

"But I insisted," Sister Bianca said. "For all of your bluster, you know mages have received many a hot meal from my own table. And, the Lord God willing, many more meals to come. Have faith, my child."

"Don't call me that," Walter said, though without heat. He could not keep up the anger, the shock. Exhaustion was overtaking him now. They were wearing him down, depleting his energy, to make it easier for Rainier to strike the killing blow.

"Then, pray, what do I call you? Brother? Friend?" The sister's voice softened. "Or would you prefer if I pretended you were still the outcast mage, friendless and alone?"

Tears stung Walter's eyes. Damn her words. Damn her into the abyss. "If Tasmin could do that, if she did that, why did they sacrifice themselves?"

"We don't know the full story," Roul said. His voice turned tender and full of pity. "We only know that an entire generation of mages sacrificed themselves."

A sob escaped Walter. Tasmin was not *just* a mage. She led an army of mages, to save whatever stood at this very spot so many ages ago. An elemental mage practicing her art in public, with so much control...he had never seen anyone remotely on her level or ability. As strong and practiced as he was, he could never exercise that level of control. At best, he could make a lantern dance upon a still table. He would've killed every single person, and most likely himself, to hold back that army of demons.

And then, with all of her sacrifice, with the sacrifice of her soldiers, she was turned into a goddess-on-earth, but at what cost? They erased the one thing that made her special, that allowed her to do the very thing she was venerated for.

The people who lived within these protective walls, who continued to exist because of a choice made long ago.

"Vittorio knew," Walter said. He did not ask, for he knew in his heart this was what the mage-hating cardinal wished to hide from them all.

"We cannot be certain of that yet," Rupert said. "Regardless, the decision was made to alert you before I make my own decision on what must be done next."

"What is there to decide? We must tell people!" Walter exclaimed. He laughed, a bitter, mocking sound even to his own ears. "Or did you think I would keep this to myself?"

"And what, my dear mage, do we tell them? Hmm? A book, one book, was found, that almost no one can read. It takes three people most of a night to translate a few pages. Would people even believe you?"

"You could tell them Tasmin was indeed a mage," Walter said.

"Ah, yes, I am certain the mages of Orsini would be all too happy to stone Vittorio to death, but I suspect both you and I would soon follow. After all, my dear Walter Cram, you are more of my circle than the rebels now."

Walter glared at the pope, even if he knew in his heart that he spoke the truth. "I will not keep it secret."

"No one expects you to," the pope said. "However, the problem we have is that we need more evidence to convince those who matter. Roul, who else in Orsini can translate this?"

"Cardinal Vanida," Roul said.

Rupert scoffed. "I wouldn't trust that man to translate my breakfast menu. I shall shake the tree, then, and see what falls out."

"Roul," Walter said, in a small voice. He regretted opening his mouth. But, now that he had, he had to keep speaking. "Does Michael know?"

The archivist shook his head. "No. We purposely did not invite him. We did not wish...entanglements."

"Thank you," Walter whispered. He slumped against the wall. He had no fight left in him. All he wanted to do now was weep for the life he could have had. The rising despair in his soul shocked him. He had not realized how much it hurt, the life he was forced to live. He did well to shove so much of it into tiny, individual crates on the shelf of his mind, the contents hidden from view. This news knocked all those boxes to the floor, and the memories poured and jumbled together.

He would never be the same now.

"Walter, Cram, whatever you wish me to call you, come with me."

Walter stared at the pope. He did not move. "Where?"

Rupert turned to face him and, after a moment's silence, asked, "Is your problem specifically with me, or authority in general?"

"Both," Walter said.

"That I believe," the pope said. He drew in a breath and asked, "Can you control your temper around Vittorio? I need to know this, truthfully and plainly. No matter what is said, no matter what is revealed, can you control your temper?"

"I don't know anymore," Walter said. It hurt him to say that, but it was true. He didn't know if he could.

Rupert nodded. He walked to the door and opened it. Walter made note that he turned his back fully to him, daring him with the tempting target. Outside the door was the pope's usual hangers on, plus his guard, plus Consorts and militia.

"Warin! Summon the entire council to my drawing room, immediately. Give them no reason. It is an emergency. Walter Cram, come with me."

"Why?" Walter asked.

"I need you to witness, assuming you can control that temper of yours."

CHAPTER TWENTY-ONE

THE INNER CATHEDRAL corridors were abuzz with rumor. Walter Cram had been arrested. The Holy Father was enraged. The archivist had been arrested. So on, and so on. No one seemed to know what was actually happening, only that the entire senior council had been summoned to the Holy Father's suites for an emergency meeting.

And that Walter was already there.

Allegra walked in with Stanton and Imogen, the last three to arrive. Devonshire still had her prayer stole wrapped about her shoulders; she'd been pulled from mid-morning prayers. She took a seat. There were no servants in the room. Not even their guards. They were completely alone, a rarity for Rupert's drawing room.

"Does anyone wish to make a confession before the Lord God Almighty and unburden their hearts?" Rupert demanded as soon as Allegra sat down.

The anger in Rupert's voice, the tight, restraining effort to not lash out was palpable. She glanced at Walter; he was faring better.

"Vittorio? Devonshire? What about you, DeLancey? Nothing to say? No confession to make?"

After several awkward moments of silence, Giso asked, "What is going on here?"

"That is an excellent question, my dear Giso," Rupert said. He was still staring at the others, rage bubbling in his voice. He pulled folded paper from one of his robes many hidden pockets. "I wish to read something very enlightening. From the time of Tasmin. Ah, yes, Vittorio, the book *has* been found."

"What book?" Allegra asked.

"Did you say the time of Tasmin?" Giso asked. "There are no books from that time."

"Oh, there are," Rupert said. "Aren't there, Vittorio? Do not lie before your God's anointed, sir, for I may send the mages with torches toward your estates."

"I only await your command, Your Radiance," Walter said.

Allegra managed not to turn to stare in utter amazement. The others failed miserably, so much so that Giso put one arm over the sofa he sat upon to get a better view of Walter. Vittorio only scoffed in feigned amusement.

Then, Rupert read to them a translation from a book found in the archives, from the time of Tasmin, of fire and demons. Of the sacrifice of elemental mages. Of lies told generation after generation. Of the deceit of the powerful.

Allegra covered her mouth with her hand, anything to help her collect her emotions in front of these people. The lessons of her youth failed her now, as she whispered, "Tasmin was an elemental mage?"

It was Giso who lost his temper first. "Is this real?" He'd asked first in a calm, collected, measured tone. When Rupert and Walter nodded, it became clear they had only both now found out, and clear that there had been a conspiracy somewhere in this building, Giso turned on the three senior cardinals, his friends, his allies, his sparring partners. "Is. This. Real."

Devonshire stood. She was elderly and needed the assistance of both arms of the chair to lift herself up. She removed her prayer stole, dropping it to the floor. Silence filled the room as the old woman made her choice. She nodded to herself before squaring her shoulders and speaking.

"At the election of a new pope, we speak to any new senior cardinals that are brought into our circles, along with the new pope. However, our previous Holy Father, in consideration of Giso's blatant leanings, and then Cardinal Rupert's inclinations, as well his husband's anti-establishment activities, decided that the information not be shared beyond myself, Vittorio, and DeLancey."

Allegra was too stunned to speak. She tried to move her mouth, but nothing but tiny gasps escaped her. All she could do was stare in shock. She could not even muster outrage, for that required her to ferment the information in front of her, of which she could not.

Devonshire was not done, however. "When Cardinal Rupert was elected pope, and took the name Francois, we three decided not to share this information and to finally allow it to die with us. Considering that a notorious criminal now stands in our midst while having this conversation, I believe we made the correct choice."

Every teacup in the room rattled against its saucer, even though Walter's expression did not change in the slightest. Allegra pushed down her jealousy about his control.

Admittedly, Allegra did not expect Giso would be the one to start shouting first. And that man could shout when he put his mind to it, as they all discovered that day. His age melted off him, and he morphed into a robust, passionate man half his age, the one of stories and reputation she'd heard but had never seen.

Vittorio jumped to his feet, pointing an accusatory finger at Giso, calling him a good for nothing witch lover. Giso slapped Vittorio's hand away, shouting for him to get out of his face. That only made Vittorio point harder, emphasizing each and every insult until, finally, kindly old Giso snapped. He slammed his hands against Vittorio's chest, his palms hitting him so hard that Allegra could hear the air leaving the cardinal's lungs. Vittorio fell backward and crashed against an end table, which toppled with him. Stanton and Imogen managed to separate the old schoolmates before they hurt each other.

However, even with Stanton in front of Giso, the man continued shouting, incoherent rage bubbling from his soul. Walter stepped closer to her, putting his hand out, as if to shield her. It took her a moment to realize she'd been bracing for the same thing as Walter: the unleashing of elemental magic.

But that did not happen. Giso's defense of mages, all of this time, was not because he was secretly a mage. He was simply, truly, a good and decent man. Her eyes moistened at the thought, and tears dropped down her face as she realized his pain, in this moment, was as great as hers. She had been betrayed as a mage, and Giso had now discovered his life had been unwittingly dedicated to the oppression of mages.

"Will you not stop this?" DeLancey shouted at Rupert, as much as the old woman could shout with her thin, raspy voice.

"Let him rage. Someone should," Rupert snapped back at her.

Allegra went to Giso's side, asking him to calm himself. Giso had begun weeping, his face red with pain and fury. He grabbed her arms and apologized, then he grasped for Walter until he managed to make contact, all the while apologizing. His shouts morphed into hiccupping sobs as he begged their forgiveness. Allegra had to swallow hard against the lump in her throat. Walter's eyes were damp as he told Giso he did not blame him. Giso did not listen, repeating his apologies over and over.

"Decorum!" DeLancey shouted. "We must have decorum!"

"I have a mind to put all of you on the censure board," Devonshire announced.

Rupert laughed, an angry, mocking sound, that lasted too long for the severity of the situation. "After all that we have just heard, what bothers you the most is that Giso lost his temper."

"We must have decorum in this place," Devonshire said.

"Or what?" Rupert challenged her. "If we do not control ourselves, what then? You will keep lying, keep protecting and perpetuating the lies we tell so that Vittorio and his ilk can keep owning human beings?"

"How dare you," Vittorio growled. "My father was..."

"I do not give a shit who your father was!"

Allegra gasped at the venom that came from Rupert. She took a step back, in fact, simply from the force of his fury. Her instincts told her to prepare for an attack, to seek out the exits, to start running.

"This place is full of rot," Rupert said. She didn't know if the disgust in his voice was aimed at Vittorio or himself, but with each word, his volume grew. "Look at us! We are covered in imported silks! We live in gilded rooms. There are starving children beyond these walls and here we are drinking Cartossian wine!"

Rupert grabbed a nearby wine carafe, the object of his rage, and threw it against a mirror on the wall. Shards of glass flew through the air as everyone flinched to protect themselves. As Devonshire shouted for Rupert to gain control of himself, he picked up another bottle and threw it at her feet, all the while screaming if the Lord God did not want glass to break, he should have made it sturdier.

Decorum be damned, apparently.

EVERYONE WAS SHOUTING at him now, and the more they shouted, the more Rupert hurled glass bottles through the air. He grabbed a crystal bottle of port and smashed it against a painting upon his wall. DeLancey was shrieking he'd ruined a thousand-year-old painting. Who cared? Certainly not the Almighty. If the Lord God cared, he'd have intervened by now. He had not, so Rupert hurled another bottle at the painting. He missed and hit a figurine upon the shelf. The priceless work of art fell to the floor and cracked into several pieces.

"Why should I stop? It's only money! It's only things! Why does it matter? It is all a lie!"

For the love of all that was holy and just in the world, he had upheld the status quo all this time, and it had all been a lie indeed. He had not even mustered the courage to go against the smallest injustices, for he'd wanted this power. He'd always wanted it; from the day he'd stepped foot into the inner sanctum.

Not satisfied with just the drinks upon it, he grabbed the table's edge. Even as the others shouted for him to stop, to think of the carpets, to just think for a moment, he flipped the table over with such force that it sent glass and alcohol everywhere when it hit the floor. Liquid enough to pay the wages for dozens of labourers for a decade each, spilling all over the floor and ruining priceless, historic rugs.

He was screaming now, screaming incoherently, screaming as he tried to rip his robes off his body. He was suffocating. He had to get them off.

Somewhere in all of that, Pero, several Consorts, some lower ranking cardinals, and several servants came rushing into the room, all from various doors and directions, all assuming they'd find the Holy Father murdered in his drawing room.

"Rupert!" Pero shouted, a familiar voice cutting through the noise inside his mind.

When Rupert stopped, he discovered he was streaked with blood. Some of the glass must've cut him. His throat itched, and he touched the skin; it stung. He flinched, pulling back his fingers, startled to see them wet with blood.

"Rupert, you've made yourself bleed." That was Allegra, standing next to him. He had no memory of her approach. Her hand was extended, reaching out for him. Tears streamed down her face.

"Rupert, my old friend," Stanton said from off to his side. He'd been next to Giso. He never saw him move. "You must calm yourself."

Pero approached him, but Rupert held up his hands to stop him, unwilling to accept comfort yet. He did not deserve it.

"What happened?" Pero asked.

"You cannot tell him," DeLancey said. "You cannot tell anyone."

"Everyone out!" Stanton shouted, a booming voice that echoed in the room. "All of you! Out!"

"What is happening?" Pero demanded again.

Allegra said, "Just wait."

Even as Stanton was ushering the others out, Devonshire said, "If you tell him, we will lose everything."

Rupert pointed at the rather silent mage in the corner. "He already knows! Do you honestly think Walter Cram is going to keep this secret after all that we have done to him?"

"I have done nothing to him personally," Devonshire said sharply.

"Inaction is harm, priest," Cram said. Out of all of them, the mage was the calmest.

"Allegra, what is happening?" Pero asked, in a low whisper.

"Do not tell him," Devonshire ordered.

Allegra glared at Devonshire for a moment before turning to Pero. "They found a book in the archives, written during the time of Tasmin. It says she was an elemental mage, and that she led an army of mages against a demon army, and then they sacrificed themselves to seal the rift."

"What?" Pero demanded. "Rupert, you knew this?"

"No," Rupert said. "No, I never knew."

Walter pointed at the guilty. "Those three, right there, hid it from Rupert, Giso, everyone. They knew."

Pero unleashed decades of anger upon Vittorio. Now that his own anger had physically exhausted him, Rupert could watch dispassionately. Vittorio had been taking the brunt of the anger, when the two women had their own share in the lie. But even he felt Vittorio was different. For all of their faults—faults he would never forget—Devonshire and DeLancey sat upon the fence, where they urged calm, and never sided for mages, except in minute increments of change.

Vittorio, however, was always openly hostile. He still held all of his estates, from his wife's inheritance and from his own, and used his position to further his purse. He kept enslaved mages on his properties, even now. Even when he was ordered to free his slaves. Rupert pushed it aside, every single day, so that he could work with Vittorio.

And the man had been lying to his face.

He had been such a fool, blinded by power.

At some point in the argument, Giso collapsed to the floor, weeping. He cried out to the Lord God Almighty to forgive him of his sins, for not fighting harder for the mages. He begged the Lord God to forgive him for every single step he'd taken that had allowed this atrocity to linger.

Walter walked over to the priest and put a hand on his shoulder. Giso gripped it and begged the mage to forgive him. The man was well over sixty, and had dedicated his entire adult life to the faith, to the goodness of the Lord God Almighty, to hope, peace, and kindness. Giso had fought for mages for as long as he'd known the man, and if Vittorio were to be believed, Giso had been fighting since they were children.

Tears welled up in Rupert's eyes at that; he'd not even realized he had any tears left to offer, but he did at that sight. Walter whispered something, well beyond Rupert's ability to hear, but whatever it was made Giso sob harder, declaring he did not deserve such mercy.

Giso had always pushed Rupert. He had pushed him, guided him, molded him. Giso would never be voted pope, so he saw the ambitious centrist as the compromise. He'd put a fence sitter, a man who would compromise everything, into the robes of power, all to protect mages as best as possible.

And now, Giso cried out for forgiveness for that very choice.

Now calmer, Rupert found it easier to unbutton his robes. He'd managed to strip some of the buttons off in the fray. He'd torn some of his clothes in the process. Now, he carefully folded his robes and placed them on the chair. He removed his rings and dropped them on top of the robes. He sucked in a deep breath and pulled off his necklace, the pendant of power, the acknowledgement of his greatness, and an amulet imbued with so much power that he could survive a stab wound straight through the heart. At least, until the healers could get to him.

He wanted none of it. He couldn't do this anymore. He would not be the kind of man who used up good men like Giso for his own power. No more.

He walked over to the painting, the one he'd soaked in wine. He carefully pulled it off the wall mounts and turned it over across the arms of a ruined chair, allowing the wine to drop off its surface. He felt so much guilt about the work he'd made for the servants. They'd be scrubbing day and night now, to return this room to how it had been. All for his temper, for his guilt. He could not even offer to help the servants; they'd never allow it. Besides, what did he know about getting port out of carpets?

He turned to Giso and offered him a hand. "Come. Enough. The Almighty does not want you upon the floor, not with your bad hip. Come."

Rupert and Walter, together, helped Giso to his feet and escorted the exhausted man to a nearby chair. Rupert put a hand on his shoulder, and Giso squeezed it hard. It was then Rupert discovered his heart wished to weep once more, but found no tears left.

Devonshire finally said, in that commanding voice of hers, "We have been under a great deal of pressure lately. I suggest we take two days to ourselves, for quiet prayer and reflection. Then, we gather together, as one, for a day of prayer and healing. We have many hurts between us, and—"

"Prayer will not fix this," Giso said.

"Your Radiance, please speak sense to him," DeLancey said. "He will listen to you."

"Do not call me that." The weight on his chest pressed until finally he whispered the words, "I no longer wish to be Holy Father."

He had finally uttered the words. He had worked so hard, for so long, to get to this suite, to wear the robes, to have the world call him Your Radiance. He'd been unhappy for some time now, knowing in his heart he did not follow the path of righteousness.

"This is a calling, not a job," Devonshire said. "You do not quit being the Holy Father, not until the Lord God decides."

Pero put a hand on Rupert's back, and he leaned against the love of his life. Strong and lean, ready to catch him whenever he faltered.

"I do not even know if I believe the Lord God exists," Rupert whispered. "And, even if he did, he would not recognize me as one of his own."

"Francois...Rupert, Rupert my friend," Giso said. "I beg you. You were our best option, our best hope. Without you, think of how horrible the winter at Borro Abbey could have been?"

"We all have crises of faith, my friend," Stanton said. "I have had many in this very room. It is only natural, especially after the shock of this news."

Rupert shook his head. This was not the same thing. "I do not know what I believe anymore, only that I cannot, no, I will not uphold an institution that has purposely and willfully had at its fingertips the very means to end the civil war, and yet it did nothing."

"Oh please," Devonshire said. "Use the sense the good Almighty gave you. Imagine what would have happened if we'd told that foolish and impulsive Cardinal Rupert? He'd have told Pero. And then what would have happened to us?"

"Walter Cram and his ilk would have burned us alive in our beds," Vittorio said.

"I'd have let him," Allegra snarled.

"I wouldn't have," Imogen said.

"And does anyone in this room think our valiant captain would have ended up with our delightful contessa? Or that she'd have lived long enough to so much as make it here to become the Arbiter of Justice? No, of course. We'd have all been killed by elemental mages bent on destruction," Vittorio said.

"They wouldn't have killed me," Allegra said.

That truth silenced the room. They would have elected her their leader before riding to Cartossa to burn the place to the ground, and she'd have lit their torches one by one, with Walter Cram by her side the entire time.

Not him, though. He'd have always ended up here, comfortable and safe, until that mob finally came for them. And the captain would have died fighting that mob. And Allegra, perhaps by Rainier's own hand. And Walter, too, God Almighty even that caused cold glumness to seep into his bones.

"If he wants to go, let him go," Vittorio said. "We can rule the cardinals without him. We don't need him. We don't need her, either."

The her was clearly Allegra.

"Careful," Her Highness said. "My sword can cut through anything."

"Are you threatening me?"

"Yes," Imogen said. She quirked a smile. "Absolutely."

"Enough!" It was Allegra who finally decided to be the adult in the room. It did not surprise him. "A lot has happened today, and it will take us time to sort through our reasoning and our feelings. We should not be so hasty as to say the things that we might regret in the morning's light."

But then she turned to face Vittorio, and with a cold smirk said, "They'd have never burned me in my bed, Your Grace. They'd have risked their very lives to save me. Never forget that, and never forget who and what I am to the people you despise so much."

Rupert smiled. And for the first time in a very long time, it touched his eyes and his soul.

CHAPTER TWENTY-TWO

AS A GENERAL rule, misery loves being inconvenient, so it did not
surprise anyone that General Bonacieux decided to arrive while the
senior-most officials still suffered from the shock of recent
revelations. Allegra and Stanton sat together in her study, a pot of
tea between them and a lovely platter of warm, sesame flat bread
still wrapped in cloth, and an array of seasonal spreads. She
commented on how she loved the smell of sesame, and how it
never seemed to make its way to Borro Abbey. They shared the
memories of food, family events of one cousin or another acting
ridiculous or causing a scene, with sesame flat bread featuring
somewhere in the tale.

Allegra spooned a little garlic paste on a torn piece of bread
when the annoying knock came at her door. It was one of Renouf's
soldiers, surprisingly, who came to fetch Stanton. Runners had
arrived from the south gate. Refugees were desperately pushing
inside the city, all running for safety. Her Highness had requested
Stanton's assistance, and that of the Consorts.

Stanton kissed her, told her he'd be careful, which she knew
was a lie, but she appreciated it all the same. She only took one
more bite of her bread before the next runner arrived. This time,
announcing the heraldry had been confirmed: the King of Cartossa
had arrived.

Of course, there was no king. Just an upstart butcher who
murdered innocents. She would never call him *Majesty*.

She abandoned all hope of finishing her meal when Warin arrived, the Holy Father's secretary. Her assistance was requested immediately in the Holy Father's residence, for there was a problem that she might help solve. Warin did not offer further instruction or detail, only that he was off to the tailors, and something about damage to a historic wardrobe.

The journey to the papal residence took longer than normal, for people stopped to ask her about Bonacieux's arrival. Others stopped to provide her updates. At least Bonacieux seemed to have no present plans to bring his army inside yet to murder them all in their beds. He'd even stopped his approach to allow frightened merchants and poverty-stricken farmers to run from the harbinger of death.

Allegra had assumed she was being summoned to a meeting, or perhaps to serve as a moderating force between Vittorio and Giso. Or, Lord God save them, Vanida had managed to get inside.

What she had not imagined was Rupert to be the center of a heated argument, and nowhere to be found.

"Ah! Finally!" Giso said, beckoning her over to the door where they all stood. "You're his oldest friend. Perhaps you can talk some sense into the fool."

"What has happened?"

"As like a child, he refuses to exit his room," Vittorio said. He had a visible bruise on his jaw, where he'd previously made contact with the furniture, and then the floor. Allegra held no pity for his discomfort.

Allegra considered making a snide remark, but decided against it. With Bonacieux at their doorstep, decorum was the order of the day. She knocked and then called out, asking if she could come in.

Pero came out a moment later, and said, "He's in my room."

Pero joined the others and she stepped inside the bedroom. She found Rupert fully dressed in papal robes, though he was missing his regular stole. That one had been soaked in wine. She wondered if that was Warin's mission after coming to see her.

"How bad is it if they've sent for you?" he asked.

"Oh, I suspect it's worse than we know," she said. She smiled at him. "But we need you to play your role."

"How can I, when I've lost my faith," he whispered. He motioned down at his clothes, the symbol of his office and authority. "How do I come back from this?"

She let out a long breath. Finally, she said, "In the long term? I do not know. That will be something you must work out between you and the Almighty. For the present? I suggest you do the job you were given."

"I know what they're all saying, that I'm acting like a child."

Allegra made a dismissive wave. "Only Vittorio is saying that."

"I have never hated anyone as much as I hate Vittorio at this moment," he said. "I know that I should have the same ire for Devonshire and DeLancey, but Vittorio is more personal. I barely got along with the man in the best of times. Pero and I have had so many arguments over him, and for all of my defense of him, I discovered he was even more of a lying bastard than I had ever imagined."

"Nevertheless, you are needed, and needed still," Allegra said. "Giso was right. A centrist is better than Vittorio, or one of his lackeys. Later, when this is over, you can put down the job if that is what you truly wish. For now, though, we do need you."

"I am so sorry for what I have done to you," Rupert whispered.

She took his hand in hers and squeezed. "I believe you. What's more, you apologized before you even knew all of this. I appreciate that, and I forgive you. We have all been manipulated, and it is time we end it. But first, we need to deal with the monster outside of our door."

"I do not know what I should do," he said. "What is right? I truly do not know anymore."

"You go out there and tell Bonacieux that he can die in the abyss for all you care."

Rupert chuckled. "I believe you meant to say, for all *you* care. After all, I am the Holy Father, Pope Francois, the calm voice of reason. The man who cannot make a single decision without a committee voting upon it."

"That is not what they say about you behind your back."

He grunted. "No, they say I have domestic troubles."

Allegra smiled. Yes, they did say that. "They say you were voted pope because you were young and malleable. No doubt they think I am in here, right now, influencing you."

"You *are* influencing me."

"Always, and without shame nor remorse," she said. She gave his hand a final squeeze before pushing herself off the bed. "Now, gather your wits and courage. Be the Holy Father you wish to be, for what does compromise matter now? You have attempted to quit the position, and Devonshire will not let you."

"It's probably too much paperwork," Rupert grumbled.

"Then make her regret that decision."

He blew out a long, controlled breath. He nodded and pushed himself up from the bed. Then, he slowly morphed before her from Rupert, her dear old friend, to Francois, the Holy Father. He straightened his shoulders, pulling his spine straight and tall. His chin lifted with the posture adjustment. Another deep breath and all evidence of his emotional turmoil disappeared. Another breath, and calm politeness, with a slight smile, washed over his face. She had forgotten how much practice that took, but they'd all had those lessons whacked into them as children.

"Ready?" she asked.

He nodded, and Francois said, "Let us meet the general."

ALLEGRA, VITTORIO, AND Giso escorted Francois through the Cathedral before sending word to Bonacieux that they wished to meet him and a dozen of his men in the public ballroom. Runners were sent to fetch Renouf, Stanton, and Imogen, as well as other members of the senior council.

And Walter. Apparently, Francois wished to have an elemental mage representative at all meetings now. Allegra quirked a smile at that; they both knew she had secretly been that mage, but it was important to keep Walter busy. And it would annoy Bonacieux.

The public ballroom was missing all of its windows still, as were most of the rooms in Orsini. Glass took time to create. Servants rushed about getting the required number of chairs at the table, while moving scrolls, ledgers, and notes, all carefully placed on a back table exactly how they were found on the main table, as per Francois's order. This room has been used by various builders and tradesmen, and the pope had no wish to see their work disrupted needlessly.

However, there existed no justification in any of their minds to give Bonacieux admittance to the upper ballroom, inside the inner sanctum. The less the man knew about the building itself, the better.

As they waited for the rest of the cardinals to arrive, as well as the general himself, word was passed to the kitchens to send up food, wine, and anything easily portable for the meeting, but not to put themselves out. Francois did not want to offer anything beyond the most basic standard of politeness.

For her own part, Allegra wore a clean gown, and found she held no desire to go change it. The dress did fit well enough, even though it was far lower in quality than her usual standards. However, with no time, no supplies, and no wardrobe, Allegra had made the choice that decent clothes were more important than perfect gowns, and Nadira worked to find ready-made gowns that could be quickly tailored.

Allegra's first set of bespoke gowns should be ready for a fitting any day now, or so Nadira said, but today, Allegra would happily greet Bonacieux, the murderer of her cousin, in a hand-me-down, purchased ready-made, that anyone might have worn before. The more she thought on it, the more he did not deserve the dignity of her wearing her best.

Stanton soon arrived, in his regular green Consort's uniform. She noticed his boots did not shine like usual. All of the soldiers had been complaining they'd run out of boot polish, and they'd lose their weather proofing when the spring rains decided to finally show up. They were also running out of spices, sugar, honey, and wheat.

War turned out to be terrible for one's digestion.

When Stanton smiled at her, she suddenly realized she had still not told Rupert or Pero about her acceptance of his proposal of marriage. She considered announcing it at the table, right then and there, but it was not appropriate. No, that was happy news, and they all needed their attention on the butcher about to arrive.

Allegra's stomach knotted with the hard cadence of approaching soldiers in the corridors. Dodd, Lex, Martin, Beatrix, Rahna, Renouf, and Imogen all arrived, and took positions near the table. Francois nodded, and Renouf stepped back into the corridor beyond. A commotion began, arguing and raised voices. Renouf reappeared.

"Your Radiance? The general insists Cardinal Vanida be admitted. He's with them now."

Francois cut the arguments short and gave his consent. Though, when Renouf left them, he said, "I will no doubt regret that decision within the hour."

The doors opened, and Francois rose from his seat. The rest of them followed his example. Bonacieux did not wear a crown, which honestly surprised Allegra. She'd have thought he'd have done it out of spite. He walked in with the same number of advisors, and the same number of guards.

Except Vanida. He made things unequal.

"Greetings, General Bonacieux," Francois said in a cool voice. He held out his hand, the one with his ring. He rarely did that, for he hated people kissing his hand. He'd told Allegra he found the entire thing rather disgusting and degrading.

Bonacieux smiled, and then smiled wider. He walked over to Francois, giving a deep bow, and then kissed the ring. "Thank you for inviting me inside."

Francois waved for Bonacieux to stand up. "We await refreshment to arrive. Please, take a seat."

The seat was at the opposite end of the table. The only open seat. They did not bother the servants with adding a second table for the rest of his entourage.

"Forgive the lack of seating," Francois said as he sat down. The others followed his lead. "We lost a great amount of furniture lately."

Bonacieux made a point of looking at all of the chairs off in the corner.

"Those, of course, are already spoken for and it would be rude to take what belongs to someone else," Francois said.

Bonacieux's smile continued, not bothered in the slightest by the lack of good manners. He turned to Allegra and said, "Contessa, I offer my deepest condolences on the loss of your cousin. I assume you've not heard?"

"We are all very aware of recent events," Allegra said.

"Then, I find myself surprised you are not in mourning clothes. But perhaps she was not that dear to you, and you wish to make a statement."

The statement she wished to make was burning him alive right there in his chair. However, since that would be awkward and inappropriate for all involved, she instead removed all emotion and expression from her face. Not a twitch. Not an uneven breath or a raised eyebrow. Nothing but haughty disinterest.

"And I see you brought the demon lover, of course," he said, not even bothering to look at Walter.

Walter snorted, but that was all. He did not even make the chairs in the corner dance, which seemed to disappoint Bonacieux. They were all too old for games.

"General, we are all very busy, yourself included no doubt. What brings you to the Cathedral? Surely not the weather. We're overdue for the spring rain."

Bonacieux, unable to get anyone to fall for his baiting, said, "Since we are dispensing with pleasantries, I am here to arrange the details of my coronation."

No one spoke. Silence. A few coughs from the soldiers echoed.

Bonacieux did not flinch. "I have defeated the Grand Duchess's army. I have broken her siege, and I have taken control of the Cartossian crown. And while rule had never been my purpose, the people asked for my sword to guide them, and now so I shall."

And no one spoke. Allegra did not want to look about; it would've been rude. However, she did make eye contact with Giso, who did not seem to know the plan either. However, soon she noticed other heads turning to look at Francois, to see if he'd fallen asleep.

Finally, after the silence dragged on for far too long, Francois said, "I confess my Cartossian line of succession is rusty. I shall consult the archives tomorrow and provide you with a list of those with the best claim."

Bonacieux's false smile faded. "I sit on the throne now, Your Radiance."

"Hmmmm," Francois said, making a show of searching his memories. "I do not recall ever seeing your name as part of the lines of succession, but I would be happy to add it to the list, at your request. Though, I anticipate it will be quickly dismissed by the people. After all, our own Contessa here has more of a claim to the crown than you ever will."

Terror unlike anything Allegra had felt in her entire life struck her. She absolutely did not want the crown of anywhere, and especially not in Cartossa, the center of mage oppression.

"She *is* the cousin of the former heir of Cartossa."

Allegra's mind turned into a blubbering, hysterical mess, but she successfully kept her face neutral.

"Contested heir," Bonacieux said. "Now, if the dear witch—"

"Mage," several people at the table immediately corrected him. Allegra's mouth quirked.

Bonacieux's smile returned; it did not reach his eyes. He'd not touched his wine, not even to make the show of it. He did not trust them. If she were him, she'd have downed that glass and stared right into Walter's eyes while doing it, but she was raised differently than an upstart.

"Witch bitch," Bonacieux said, thinking that would hurt her feelings.

"My dear general," Allegra said, and she allowed the smile to overtake her face. And hers did reach her eyes when she said, "I have no inclination or thought toward Cartossa's throne. Your upcoming civil war to claim the throne from a dozen others shall be safe from my influence, I assure you."

"Why is she here?" Vanida demanded. "I do not understand why we must have a witch—"

"Mage," several of them said at once.

Vanida slammed his palms down on the table, hard enough that the wine in Allegra's goblet sloshed about. So did the wine of those around him. "This is what I mean! She has contaminated all of you. She has rotted your brains, and we cannot speak our minds."

"Indeed, from what I understand," Bonacieux said, "you are punished for speaking your mind."

Devonshire, who'd been quiet throughout all of this, finally spoke. "Words, like actions, have consequences. If Cardinal Vanida will not follow the rules, he will endure censure. It is as simple as that."

Vanida pushed himself from his chair, which tipped precariously until one the Cartossian soldiers behind Vanida pushed it back on all four legs. He pointed an accusatory finger at Devonshire. "I am a cardinal! I was appointed to be the voice of the Lord God Almighty. It is my Lord God ordained right to be heard!"

"Cardinal Vanida," DeLancey said in a clipped, crisp voice. "There is no requirement for anyone to listen to your rambles."

"Why is he even here?" Allegra asked, just as Vanida sucked in a deep breath.

Before Vanida could speak, Bonacieux answered. "I requested the good cardinal's presence, as I do not agree with his removal from this council."

"I do not recall voting to grant you the authority to alter the censure of Cardinal Vanida. In fact, I believe the only person in all of Serna who can even call that vote, or overturn the ruling, is Cardinal Devonshire." Then, Francois stood. Abruptly, and without any signal that had been his plan. He waited for the rest of the table's occupants to rise. "Now, if you will kindly take your army back to wherever it came from last, I shall return to morning prayers. I find myself rather late with my daily appointment with the Lord God."

"Are you refusing to acknowledge me as the rightful ruler of Cartossa?"

Francois turned back to the table, to face the general. "I will consider your claim, when the succession crisis has ended, and you stop the persecution of mages."

Bonacieux laughed, complete shock in his voice. "That will never happen in Cartossa so long as I draw breath. I plan to root them out until nothing remains but a smoldering heap where their bones once were."

Francois stared, coldly, and Allegra got a sick feeling in the pit of her stomach. She noticed several of the Consorts, and Renouf, carefully move their hands to their swords. The Cartossian soldiers, seeing that, matched the gesture.

Then, when they all seemed to expect an order for violence, Rupert spoke. Rupert. The young man who had been Allegra's closest friend, who used to speak passionately about all the changes he would bring if he could only become a bishop. She had not seen that man in a very long time.

"Are you refusing a direct edict from the Lord God Almighty?" Rupert asked.

Everyone in the room gasped. Bonacieux looked as though he'd been slapped across the face. Even Devonshire was whispering for him to control his words. In fact, the only person in that room who was not wide-eyed was Vittorio. He simply looked resigned.

Bonacieux straightened his shoulders and lifted his chin. "My calling here was a courtesy, nothing more. I am not required to recognize the authority of this...over-indulgent place, nor a pampered mage lover in silk robes."

"So be it," Rupert said. His expression turned hard. There was no mirth now, no games, no politics. "General Bonacieux, Pretender to the Throne of Cartossa, murderer of Queen Portia, murderer of the rightful heir to Cartossa, you are banished from this place."

"We cannot handle the refugees," Vittorio muttered, even as Rupert continued speaking. Allegra shot a look at Vittorio, who gave her a shrug.

"As long as you sit upon the throne, no trade is to come to you. No aid is to be offered to you. All cries for protection or assistance will be unheard. You are a pox on the land and shall be treated like one."

"No one has done this for two hundred years," DeLancey muttered.

"You do not have the authority!" Bonacieux shouted at him.

"Then why did you come here?" Rupert did not shout. His tone was hard, and heartless. "Since you clearly do not need us. So go, be gone from our sight."

Bonacieux put his hand on his sword, and snarled, "Do not order me, priest."

The distinct sound of swords leaving their sheaths echoed in the room. For that terrifying moment, no one spoke. No one coughed. Allegra would have bet gold coin that no one breathed. Then, Rupert did something that hadn't been seen in generations: He turned his back on Bonacieux.

Giso marched to Rupert's side, made a pointed look at the general, and then turned his back. Devonshire sighed, but she stood and turned her back. DeLancey asked Renouf for assistance standing, and then she turned her back. Vittorio looked at Allegra, shook his head, and turned his back. One by one, they all did, except the guards, of course.

They stood like that for longer than it should have taken the man to get the hint, but finally he said, "Be it upon your heads."

CHAPTER TWENTY-THREE

WALTER HAD BEEN sprawled on his sofa for long enough that his lower back ached. He decided pacing would help, only to find his knees cracking upon standing. He rotated his knees slightly and was rewarded with more sounds of the hardships of life. Then, his toes suddenly felt stiff, so he bent them under his foot. Then, because why not at that stage, he arched his back and deep pops vibrated from his spine.

He bitterly lamented that no one warned him he'd feel old before ever hitting forty.

The entire Cathedral had been tense after the excommunication of Bonacieux, who was not just a man, but a leader. An entire nation had just been abandoned. Walter had never seen one before, only the stylized paintings, which always presented the romanticism of it. He had never considered how humiliating it would be, not until he watched. He didn't turn his back, of course. First, he held no power in the clergy, and second, he loved watching Bonacieux's face contort.

But now, popping and cracking his various joints, the rush of the day had ended, and all Walter felt was loneliness. The sadness of having no one to talk through the events. He'd not even had the opportunity to talk to Allegra or Stanton about their upcoming nuptials. In fact, he'd not even told Michael.

Michael hadn't been around.

In fact, Michael had been avoiding him.

Walter was out his door before he'd even realized he'd made the decision. He had no guards again. And, honestly, it was for the best tonight as he didn't want anyone witness him slinking across the hallway. No, he never stood outside anyone's door, knocking pathetically. He purposely walked into the darkness, into the light, into the flames, into the hazards. They came knocking at his door, begging for his attention.

Except tonight, apparently, as he stood outside of Michael's door, knocking. Ear against the door. Silence. He rapped again. He said Michael's name, in a low voice as to not attract unwanted attention, but probably meant anyone inside could not hear him anyway.

Two sisters and a brother walked by, all with prayer stoles about their necks. The three inclined their head at him and wished him a good evening. One of the sisters—the youngest of the three—looked over her shoulder at him and smiled.

A year ago, they'd all have tried to kill him. Now, they all wanted him between their—

"Mr. Cram?" He turned sheepishly to find Kia, Allegra's servant who'd been helping him out. Who smiled and blushed a lot. "If you're looking for Father Michael, I saw him leaving through the back way, about twenty minutes ago."

"Ah, thank you, Kia," he said.

She smiled in that way young girls did, with the slight giggle in her voice. God Almighty, he had gotten old and hadn't noticed it. "Is it all right if I collect your laundry? I am about to get Her Ladyship's and Captain Rainier's, too, for the maids."

"Um, oh, sure. It's unlocked."

"Thank you," she said, and gave him a little curtsey. Another giggle, and she rushed off across the corridor and went into his room.

Walter sighed and lifted himself from Michael's doorway. Notorious mage rebels should not be seen pathetically knocking in the hallways. He went in the direction Kia had signaled. He passed through checkpoints of guards, who all were very friendly. It bothered him; no one in this place should be polite, let alone act like they trusted him.

But, since they were trusting him, he asked at several stops if anyone had seen the annoying bishop who was absolutely avoiding him, and he was directed accordingly. Eventually, Walter emerged from an administrative building and into a back alley. He'd never come this way before; in fact, when the door closed, he realized there was no way to get back in.

That was strange. Why have a one-way door? No wonder Lex had been stressing so much about the passageways and maps. This entire complex of buildings, interior paths, and tunnels was a labyrinth. It had saved many lives during the demon attack, since doors were locked, servant passages taken, and clerics hid in their own secret areas. This place had been built in the time of great wars, years-long sieges, and constant upheaval. Not recording every single escape route was probably a choice, not an oversight.

A familiar figure caught Walter's attention, and he veered in that direction. When it was clear who it was, Walter called out. The priest turned and waited for Walter to catch up. It was dark out, but there was enough ambient light and starlight for Walter to see the priest's smile did not touch his eyes. At Walter's quizzical expression, the priest smoothed his expression, relaxed his features, and said, "Ah, good evening, my child. Out for a nighttime stroll, too?"

Walter rolled his eyes. "You know I hate it when you call me that."

The priest's face did not change. It was becoming eerie. "What are we, but all children in the eyes of the Lord God?"

Walter bristled at the tone, that hint of condescension that so many priests used. He glanced about, to see if anyone was listening or watching. There were people out, even at this hour, but no one lingered. Still, Walter leaned closer and said, "I've not seen you lately."

The smile faltered. The tone hardened. "I have been very busy, my child. Was there something specific you required of me?"

"I..." Walter was rarely lost for words, but he'd expected excuses, insults, attitude, even. Not whatever this was. "You've not been by the apartment."

"Oh, was I expected? I had assumed Lieutenant Lex had acquired all his information. I apologize for not assisting further."

"Lex? Michael, what is the matter?" Walter lowered his voice. "Did someone say something to you about us?"

The priest laughed, and it was a cold sound he had never heard from Michael. "Us? My dear mage, there is no *us.*"

He'd known the man for a long time now, and never had Walter seen him be cruel. Something stung in Walter's heart, but he managed to keep his temper in check. "My mistake."

"Clearly," Father Michael said. He bowed and said, "Have a good walk, my child, and may the Lord God walk beside you."

"Go fuck your god," Walter muttered as he walked off.

"YOU ACTUALLY SAID that to a bishop?" Lex was incredulous. "No joking around now, you said the words to a priest, go fuck your god?"

"Yup," Walter said. He lifted his mug, and Dodd poured more beer into it.

They all drank in silence. Walter hadn't known what to do, after the encounter in the alleyway. He'd wandered about for a bit, saw lantern light flickering between the planks that covered the windows of the old rectory. Before he knew it, he was inside, in front of a needlessly roaring fire, being served beer—from where it came from Walter decided it was best not to ask.

"Where did you get Northumberland beer?" Lex asked.

"Best you don't ask," Dodd said.

Walter smirked. Lord God help him, but he loved these two idiots.

"Well, we all learned something important today, I think," Lex said.

Dodd nodded. "Do not piss off Father Michael, and do not sleep with him."

Walter sighed. Perhaps he was too hasty with his prior thought. "I'm not upset."

"Really? Because you sure as shit look upset," Dodd said.

Lex nodded, pointing and drinking with the same hand, like he'd done it a million times before. "There's nothing wrong with being upset."

"I'd be upset if a priest used my body and then tossed me out when he got bored of me," Dodd said.

Lex nodded supportively.

Walter laughed. He couldn't help it. "What am I even doing here right now?"

"Well, you see, we *were* working," Lex started.

As ever, Dodd finished, "And then a moody mage showed up."

They all laughed together and enjoyed their beer. Walter turned down a third mug, saying he didn't wish to be greedy. Dodd proudly announced he had seven jugs under his desk, which only stirred Lex to interrogate how in the name of the Almighty did Dodd manage to even find that much beer, how he got it back to the building himself, and why hadn't he been sharing?

With a couple mugs of warm beer in him, Walter started talking. He regretted it, but the words were desperate to come out. "You know what bothers me the most about all of this? I cannot tell you if I liked him, in that way, or if I'd even had plans for him in my life. But there's something about this place that eats at you, or at least me. My feet have grown heavy, and it's hard to leave. I worry this place is making me feel things I've never felt before, because I've always needed to be ready to run."

After a sip from his mug, Lex said, "Feeling isn't a bad thing."

"Eventually everyone makes friends," Dodd added helpfully.

Walter didn't want friends. He didn't want roots, or connections, or a home. As soon as he thought that, a sad, empty feeling washed over him, knowing the lie for what it was: self-preservation. He didn't want the kids to see it in his expression, so he said, "Do either of you know if there's been spies following me about lately? I've been noticing it in the evenings, when my guard leaves me."

Dodd and Lex exchanged looks before Lex spoke. "So, us."

"You're spying on me?"

"Well..."

"See, Vanida came to talk to us," Dodd said. Then he sighed. "And now just saying his name, after everything that happened, I suddenly feel very stupid for having listened to him."

"Vanida came to us with some information," Lex said, rolling his eyes. "Mostly, he thought you were up to no good. It's just that, so I asked Father Michael about it, and he...I guess we all know why he was acting so strange. Say, Walter? You might know this. Did you know there's a magic book that's been banned?"

"Nearly all of them are banned," Walter said.

"This one is like a puzzle. You—"

"Oh, yeah, I know that one," Walter interrupted. Then, he eyed them both. "You shouldn't know about that book, though."

There was silence for a few sips of beer, until Dodd finally said, "You should tell him."

"Tell me what?" Walter asked.

Lex put down his drink, so Walter knew he wasn't going to like this.

"The other morning, I visited Father Michael in his room. I wanted to go over some of the statements from Borro Abbey servants, see if he had anything to add. His room was trashed. I'm not talking a bit messy, either. I'm talking the aftermath of ..." Lex stared wide-eyed. "Blessed Lord God Almighty."

Dodd turned his head to stare at Lex. "Tell me you don't think what I know you're thinking."

Lex was breathing hard now, physically struggling for breath. "Anyway, he had a book on the floor. He said he collects magical books."

"Yeah, a lot of priests collect banned books. What's upsetting you?" Walter demanded.

Lex was shaking his head, like trying to rattle out his words or thoughts, or maybe even memories. "He was so angry about how he'd lost his old books, and he got so angry with me when I asked about you. Like, he didn't say anything, but the look on his face. But what he said to me has been crawling under my skin. 'It's easier to blame Walter.'"

"You lot thought it was me all along, didn't you? And that's why there's fucking spies everywhere." Temper flared inside Walter's heart. He slammed his mug down. "Thanks for the drink."

He was barely out of his chair before Lex was shouting for him to wait, and Dodd was blocking his way. Dodd was a short man, or, at least shorter than Walter, but Dodd was built for blocking doorways and stopping people, not running away from soldiers.

"Walter! Walter Cram, wait," Lex ordered. "Just wait your mage ass one minute."

Walter turned around to face Lex. He knew plenty of people blamed him for the demon markings, all of the destruction and death, but he'd saved peoples' lives. He'd risked his own to stop the demons. And, yet, they still suspected him. Even people he considered friends.

Still, he felt compelled to listen to Lex's weak excuses, to allow the rejection and hurt to cut his roots completely. Allegra would understand him fleeing, and if she didn't, Stanton would.

"We don't know who has done what. What I do know, though? What I know more than anything? We all have secrets. You. Me. The Contessa. The fucking pope. This...place has secrets. For most of us, though, our secrets don't get people killed, but someone's out there killing our people. And if I thought for a moment that Dodd might've been that mage? Dodd, my oldest friend in the entire fucking world? I'd have sent a thousand people to spy on him, for no other reason then to make damned sure it wasn't him. It isn't personal."

"It feels personal," Walter said.

"Would you have preferred if Dodd and I brushed Vanida off? Hmm? He'd have spread his rumors and neither of us would have any evidence to refute him."

Dodd stepped around him. "Look, we couldn't tell you. Think about how that would've looked? We were trying to protect you in the best way we knew how."

A hot reply was on Walter's lips, and it nearly came out. But then a curious sensation spread over him: shame. The kids had been trying to protect him, all this time. His mouth moved a few times before he managed to say, "Thanks."

"For what it's worth, I am really sorry about Father Michael," Lex said.

"Me, too, man. Me, too," Dodd said. "Come back and sit down with us. Screw the priest."

"That's what got him into the mess he's in," Lex muttered.

"I heard that," Walter said, but a smile was back on his face when he said it. He collapsed back into the chair. "Between this, Bonacieux, and Tasmin, I can't even remember what day it is."

"Tasmin? The ash girl down in the brothels?" Dodd asked. "She all right?"

"No, not her. The one we're all supposed to worship with awe-filled voices," Walter said. He had no idea if the high and mighty actually expected him to keep this to himself. He had planned to tell Michael, to vent his anger to someone who'd understand more than most. Allegra had been pointless for this; she was still in shock. He didn't want to tell his mage acquaintances yet, those from the rebellion, as there was no telling what they would do. Devonshire was right on that one.

He started to tell them what had happened. Somewhere in the back of his mind itched, saying that Lex had dropped a thread, and a rather important one, before Walter had lost his temper. Something about Michael being off. He'd gotten so used to Michael's presence that...Lex was right. Something was off.

So not even a quarter of the way though his story, Walter asked, "What book did you see in Michael's room?"

"Um...I don't remember. I wrote it down when I went to talk to Roul," Lex said. He pulled out his notebook, the one he scribbled down everything, including his meals so that he'd not forget to eat three meals a day. He said the name and title, and the year it had been written.

Walter stopped breathing. He stared at Lex, certain this was all a terrible mistake. The kids asked him twice what was the matter, and then Walter jumped to his feet. "Which one of you knows how to pick locks?"

"Um, me," Dodd said. "Why?"

WALTER DID NOT ask Lex and Dodd to break into Michael's suite; that would have been wrong, and illegal, and would've been completely expected. Instead, he brought them to his own suite to unlock the priest's desk that was still there, piled with papers, and several locked drawers. That was his property, in Walter's eyes. As Dodd fiddled with the lock, Lex said they were all being pedantic, but Dodd said location was nine tenths of not getting hanged.

As far as he'd known, Michael had not been back to the suite to pick up his items. Not even his secretary from his office. Not even Kia, who had full access to Walter's room. Yet, the drawers were full of letters. Walter frowned. He picked up a couple at random, but they were all normal business for a bishop. Nothing extraordinary. He sifted through the papers on his desk. More nothing.

"Check for a ledger or a journal," Walter said.

Dodd shrugged and got under the desk for a better view; Lex helpfully angled the candle so that it only sometimes dripped on Dodd's hands. After some fiddling and rattling about, Dodd crawled back out, stood, and then removed the drawer with the letters. He dumped the letters on the desk, and—like he knew what he was doing, of which Walter took note for the future—carefully slid the bottom off the drawer. Inside were two leather-bound books.

Dodd unwrapped one at random, untying the layers of leather thread. He opened to a random page. He passed it to Walter. "It's a journal. I don't feel right reading that." When Dodd checked the second one, he said, "This one is dated more recently."

Walter put down the first book, taking up the second. He flipped to the last entry, dated...Walter let out a long breath. It was dated the last night Michael had stayed. He'd left the books. But why?

And as I watch him, asleep and peaceful, full of trust that I will not murder him in his own bed, I realize now, in the darkness of night, how wrong I have been. I have not heard the voice of the Lord God Almighty. I have heard my own ambition, mine own sins, mine own mistakes. The sins we seek are mine, and mine alone. In my blindness, in my ambition, in my stupidity, I have endangered the world.

"What's wrong?" Dodd asked.

Walter's eyes filled with tears. He struggled to gulp past the lump in his throat. "Oh Lord, no."

"Walter?" Lex said, full of concern. "What is the matter?"

He held up a hand, hoping for silence. Hoping to keep reading, hoping that this had been a misunderstanding.

I have been using him, and he I, though his actions are not offensive to my soul. I can no longer look in the mirror. It is too painful to shave, for I spend too long with this monster looking back at me. I can no longer pretend I am whole. For I am but broken glass upon the floor. Even if I found Tasmin now, even if my theories are sound, I have breached the barrier too many times. I have destroyed centuries of her world. I am what they fear in the shadows.

And still, they come to me, and ask my assistance. The guilt consumes me.

The part of my soul that cries I was once a just man, a good man, screams inside my heart, inside my mind even right now as I write this, to walk out this door, to find Captain Rainier, the most just man in all of Serna, and allow myself to be taken to the place of execution, and to be hanged by the neck until I am dead, and may the Lord God Almighty turn his back upon my soul for it is all I deserve.

There is no salvation for me now. And, worse, the longer I tarry in the arms of that man, the longer I endanger him. For they shall come for him. And I fear that I will not be brave enough to speak the truth, and I will watch him burn, screaming for his life, ripping the earth apart, and I will have allowed it to happen.

Walter's hands were shaking. His jaw was chattering. His heart was pounding. And yet, he managed to gulp down as much air as possible, for he did not wish to demolish this room, right now, and kill the two wide-eyed people in front of him who had no idea the man they had all trusted with all their secrets had been lying to their faces all of this time.

"Leave. Right now. Go." Walter managed to force out the words. "You have to go."

"What does it say?" Dodd asked as he made a rather simple movement to take the book.

Walter pushed him, far harder than he'd meant. Dodd hit the desk, bounced, and tripped, and only managed to stay upright because he'd grabbed Michael's chair back.

A sound, far too anguished to be called merely a sob, escaped Walter. "Oh, Lord God. I'm sorry, I'm so sorry. I didn't mean it. Oh God. You have to go."

"We're not going anywhere," Lex said. "What is in the book?"

He couldn't move. He could not put the book down because they'd read it. They'd know. Lord God, Michael had used them all. He'd used Walter as protection. He'd used the kids to...

"How was I so stupid?" Walter whispered.

"Was he in love with someone else? Let me see it," Lex said as he reached out his hand. But then Walter looked up at Lex, letting all of the emotion into his face, and Lex stumbled backward. "You're scaring me now. Does it say...if Father Michael is...Walter, you need to tell us."

Walter scoffed at that. He shook his head, even as his throat swelled and his vision blurred. "It's Walter all the time now, is it? You're just like him, like everyone. Using me."

"Walter Cram," Lex said, in a strong, even voice, "I took a sword protecting you."

"I never asked you to!" Walter roared. He'd not meant it, but it took so much focus to control his magic right now. He could not control that and his emotions at the same time.

"Friends don't need to ask!" Lex shouted back.

"I am not your friend!"

Dodd interrupted whatever angry retort Lex had building. "You are our friend, no matter how much you shout at us. And, as your friends, you know you need to show us what is in that book. We cannot help you, Walter, if you do not let us in."

"Help? Help!" A mocking sound escaped Walter. "I'm going to hang for this. They're going to kill me, and it'll be for something I did not even do. This is not how I wanted to die!"

Lex held out his hand. "Let me read it. I promise I will not kill you."

LEX'S HEALING GUTS already knew the book's contents. Betrayal always wore the same expression in the end. Nevertheless, Walter had to let go of the book, so Lex held out their hand and urged him to trust them. He struggled, as anyone would, but he passed the book over.

Lex flipped back a few pages and read it aloud.

I never should have knocked on his door that first night, and yet it was what I'd wanted. I should have told him what I'd done. He would have helped me, but I am now beyond even his reach to save. I cannot even go back to my room. One attempt, one small, meager attempt to open and close a portal, with no markings, no assistance, nothing, and I even failed at that. And now am I to explain the demon corpses in the room, or the stench as I slowly smuggle out the rags I use to clean up the guts.

Then, I simply walked back across the hallway, and knocked on his door once more. Because, for all that I have done, sitting here, even now, I can forget what I have done. I can believe the lie I tell myself. By his side, I can fool myself into thinking I am still on the side of righteousness.

Lex flipped back a couple more pages.

Listening to Lieutenant Lex screaming in his sleep for all of those days broke something within my soul. The demon that reached out was acting his nature. But me? I caused it. I did that. I did it, and listened, and stood by him, and the others who I saw in pieces, burned and maimed, and what did I do? I offered my blessings.

I am the monster. I am the demon. I can no longer fix the mistakes I have made. I see him, and my burdens are too much to bear, and they weigh down my soul, and I was stupid and reckless and I convinced myself of the lie.

Still, I will knock upon his door yet again, I know that in my soul.

"Lex, I need you to stop reading right now or I swear I will pull this building apart looking for him," Walter said. Gone was the anguish in his voice. Now, it was the wronged man.

Lex obliged and closed the book. They picked up the other, from the desk, and handed both to Dodd. Then, turning back to Walter, asked, "Where is the safest place in Orsini for those?"

Walter stared at Lex with such anger in his eyes that Lex did not flinch when the furniture scraped against the floor. He had never been quite that good with the fine control, from what Lex remembered. It seemed openly practicing with the princess, openly fighting demons, practicing with them in the mornings had done a lot for the mage. Good for him.

"Walter Cram, I need you to tell me the safest, most secure place in Orsini for those two books." Lex actually knew several secure locations, including the Captain's hidden safe that only they and Dodd knew about. Still, Lex knew in their heart the importance of Walter making the decision himself.

"I'm such a fool," Walter whispered.

Dodd reached out his hand, ready to offer comfort, but Walter stepped back. He raised his hands, forming a barrier between them. "No. Do not touch me. Not right now."

Lex wanted to fall apart, wanted to scream, wanting to run through the corridors shouting Father Michael's name while brandishing a sword. They did none of those things. Instead, they asked Walter the question once more.

Walter closed his eyes, and a few more tears escaped. Then, he heaved a deep breath, and visibly shook himself. "Lex, I need you to get Rainier this instant. Tell him to meet me and Dodd in the archives. Dodd? I need you to carry the books. Hide them in your jacket, if you have to. I cannot see them right now."

"You don't have to come," Dodd said. He unbuttoned his jacket as he spoke. "We can both lie, say we broke in here on Vanida's information. I don't mind lying. At this stage, it doesn't matter how we even found this, only that it's been found."

It hurt Lex to see the struggle on Walter's face. "No. I must do it. But thank you. Both of you. You are good friends."

Lex wanted to make a joke, but found they could not muster the mirth for one. They turned to Dodd, but even he could only offer a small, sad smile. Dodd couldn't get all of his buttons done back up, not with the books pressed against him, but he pushed them far enough away from the buttons that they were not visible, beyond the shape, of course. At least their uniform belts should keep them from falling down and on the floor.

"This is going to be really bad," Dodd said into the silence.

"I know," Walter whispered.

"We'll be here for you, both of us," Lex said.

"No jokes now," Dodd said, "We'll stand by you."

Walter tried to speak, but his voice cracked.

It was Lex who finally said, "Let's do this before *I* change my mind."

CHAPTER TWENTY-FOUR

MICHAEL SAT IN the small, quiet chapel; one of the many that filled the Cathedral proper. He has never been allowed in here, as Bishop of Borro. However, the Bishop of Orsini, considered by most to be a holding position for future cardinals, was given a key to the room, to use at any time, day or night, to lock himself in with the Lord God Almighty.

This evening, he had no great urge for prayer. Instead, his greatest desire was to take in the sights and smells around him. He knew his time was coming to an end. Due to their altercation, Walter would lose his temper and destroy his desk. Then, he could discover the journals. Then, the soldiers would come. Then, Michael, traitor to the true purpose of the Lord God, would die.

So, he leaned back in the pew and stared up at the ceiling's fresco. It amazed him that such a minor, insignificant room still had such elaborate artwork. Every step taken in this place filled a man's eyes with wonder. He wished to fill his final hours on this earth with quiet beauty. He knew Walter. The desk would be destroyed soon, just as he had destroyed so many things in this world in his blundering attempts to save it.

He loved this life. This world. The people in it. All he had done, all he had destroyed, it had all been to save it. To stop the madness. He had let ambition, foolhardy though it was, to guide him. Of course, he had not heard the voice of the Lord God. Anyone who claimed they had was only hearing their own. He'd learned that early in his career, when he was still studying to become part of the low ranks of the clergy, having had no idea to the paths and career he wished to take.

Yet, it was the first lesson he abandoned. He had allowed the thoughts in his head, the worries, the anger, the helplessness, to trick him. He never heard the Lord God's will. He only heard his own.

Worse, they would never even understand the truth. Not even Walter. They would say Father Michael had always been a mage, lying as part of his oath ceremonies, lying every time he led prayer, lying every time he spoke to the plight of mages.

He did not know he was a mage, until it was far too late.

He had tried so hard to assist mages. In his stupidity, he had thought bringing back Tasmin would have solved their misfortunes. Imagine being the man who brought back the Guardian who sacrificed herself to save humanity? He would be the first to talk to her, and he could explain why he pulled her back through time and the abyss.

Unfortunately, he never found Tasmin. The theories were false, just as his own beliefs. Time did not move differently in the abyss. She was long dead and gone, having died the moment she plunged into the tear with her army. There would be no Tasmin. There would be no Lord God. There was no one to save them. The mages would suffer and die, and there was truly nothing he could do.

He should have told Walter, that winter at Borro. To this day, Michael did not know if he had caused the cave-in that nearly had killed both Walter and Allegra. If he had, it had not been on purpose. Though, that mattered little, for he had no control over his actions.

Still, he could have told Walter. He'd have understood. Walter would have helped him, or have found someone to assist. Or, just have been a comfort. In the end, they would have probably still ended up in bed together, only it would not have been based on a lie. If only he'd had the courage to say he did not know he was a mage, that he did not understand the power to open portals was a form of elemental magic. That he was only studying the theory of demonic rifts...

His thirst for knowledge brought him to this place.

That first time, that first accident that caused all of this, he had been so certain—so certain in his soul even now—that he had looked upon the face of Tasmin through the abyss. Now, he knew it had been imagined, or, at least, a trick of light and shadows.

Now, all Michael could do was hope Walter killed him in a moment of rage, if only so that he died by the hand of a friend. Or, whatever Walter was to him.

No, not a friend. Friends did not use each other.

He really should have told Walter last winter.

Boots sounded in the corridor. The heavy footsteps of soldiers. They were coming for him. His heart pounded and his vision blurred from fear. He gulped and focused on breathing. In. Out. Calm. He did not want to open a portal now, not in this place of holiness. He did not even create marks most of the time now. Just rifts into the abyss.

"Oh, Lord God, make it swift. Let their rage take them, for I wish not to linger."

Then his prayer was cut short by the screams of the dying, and Michael realized it was far, far worse than Walter's wrath.

STANTON STRETCHED OUT his legs in front of him and tried to push away the desire to pull off his boots. Even though he was in the Holy Father's suites, and Rupert—the pope insisted everyone call him that now, and Stanton did not have the heart to argue with a man amid a crisis of faith—insisted he feel at home, Stanton believed keeping one's boots on in the pope's residence was basic, but important, manners.

Allegra would be along later, where both couples would enjoy a late meal and some subpar wine. Stanton's role before Allegra's arrival? Ensure Rupert did nothing "dramatic," according to, well, everyone's advice.

Stanton couldn't help but laugh at that order. The man had excommunicated the self-declared King of Cartossa in front of dozens of witnesses. What in the name of the Lord God were they afraid he'd do *without* an audience?

However, Allegra had sent a runner with a note that her work not yet complete, and she would be along when she could. For now, she wished them to go ahead, and to save her something to eat. Pero informed the staff, and platters of cold snacks appeared within minutes. As ever, Rupert's table offered enough food for ten hungry men...or Lex and Dodd after they'd been doing some light duties.

Stanton craned his neck to see what was on offer as a trail of servants brought in dishes. One tray from what he could see contained several small porcelain bowls of various pickles. A variety of rolls. A platter of cold, sliced meat. A smaller platter of various hothouse fruits, as well as some seasonal fare, along with the usual cheese, flat breads, and spreads common to Orsini springtime.

When the servants left them, Rupert motioned for Stanton to come raid the food. He said he would, as soon as he finished his wine, and left the man to pace about the food, full of nervous energy. Stanton recognized a man needing to stretch out his mind through his body, so he decided to swirl about his wine in its glass and see if some food could settle the man.

Rupert complained about the size of the plates, and Pero joined in to agree. Pero held one up for Stanton, who agreed they weren't much larger than a teacup saucer. Stanton stood at that to inspect the table, and the men chatted, the usual small talk of life mixed in with the big issues of the past days, all a jumbled mess.

"I've realized as of late that I have not inquired how life fares with Allegra," Rupert said abruptly. "I trust all is well."

Allegra had told Stanton she could not seem to find the proper opportunity to tell her friend. He had not mentioned it, not even to Lex and Dodd, because so much had been happening. However, he'd been hearing rumors himself, no doubt all started by Walter Cram, who gossiped more than any village crier in Serna.

Pero put on a mischievous grin. "I recently heard the most delicious news about a gallant captain and a certain contessa."

"I have not heard," Rupert said. "Why didn't you tell me?"

"You've been rather busy as of late," Pero said.

Stanton smiled when both men turned their attention to him, expecting an answer. Of course, Walter was already out there trying to spread gossip. He'd put real coin down on the table that Walter had probably known he was going to propose to Allegra before he'd known himself. Walter was that kind of man.

"Well?" Rupert demanded, the imperious Holy Father voice creeping into his voice.

This time, a small laugh escaped Stanton. "Yes, I did quite recently ask Allegra to join her property with mine."

Stanton had prepared himself for excitement, perhaps, or at least intrigue over her reply. However, Rupert's expression turned downcast. He stopped his pacing to put a hand on Stanton's shoulder, giving it a solid grip. "I'm so sorry, my friend. Do not take her refusal to heart. She still loves you, of that I am certain, and marriage is not necessary for happiness in love these days."

"Her refusal?" Stanton blurted before realization struck him. He laughed, a big, joyous sound. "My dear Rupert! She has said yes!"

Rupert stared, while Pero made giddy sounds of joy. Finally, Rupert seemed to rouse himself and his face lit up like a thousand oil lamps at once. He grabbed Stanton into a tight embrace. "I never thought I'd see this day! Let me embrace my new brother!"

He laughed as Pero joined in, wrapping his arms around both of them. The well wishes flowed, as did the shock that someone finally convinced Allegra to legally join herself, and her property, to another's.

Stanton knew Allegra saw Rupert as one of her family, and the betrayal had cut the way only family could. It did him good to know that rift was healing now. What's more, he was glad Allegra and Rupert had started to mend themselves, as well. With all that had happened to them as of late, they all needed to begin the darning process, to knit back together their hearts, minds, and friendships.

He was happy to share this moment with his friends.

"We need something good to drink!" Rupert declared.

The three men decided to go on an expedition in search of the good spirits, laughing all the way through the maze of the Holy Father's suites that, surely, they could sneak into the storage areas without any issue. Rupert confessed he didn't even know where the spirits were located; that was the role of servants, after all.

"And your husband," Pero said sullenly. But he could not maintain the expression and laughed.

The sound of running caught Stanton's attention. He slowed his steps. The sound grew closer. He heard distant shouts to lock the doors and the pounding coming closer. His own heart picked up the pace, matching the thundering footfalls.

He put his hand on his sword and took one step forward.

Then the door flung open. It was Martin. He skidded to a stop, startled to see the three men walking toward him. He was splattered in blood.

His sword was still in his hand.

Blood dripped from it.

"Captain! Bonacieux is inside the inner sanctum!

WALTER'S HEART WOULD not stop pounding. He did not speak, not the entire trek from his suite to the archive, Dodd by his side. He did not trust himself. Not with the book. Not with leading the journey to the archives. Not with letting Dodd out of his sight, because he would absolutely go looking for that priest to wring his neck with his bare fucking hands.

At least Dodd did not ask him a single question, nor make a single observation. In fact, Dodd was unusually silent and grim, for which Walter was grateful. Right now, he could not articulate his emotions, for they were in constant flux. Hurt. Betrayal. Anger. Sadness. Grief. Disappointment. Disbelief. Rage.

So much rage.

Between the pounding heart and the rising tears, Walter's vision was blurred by the time they made it to the archive door. Despite the late hour, Roul was in his little office, enjoying a cup of tea and what he called a "good book," which could mean just about anything. Roul's smiling greetings faded at their grim expressions.

Dodd pulled both books from his jacket, still neatly tucked out of view. Walter's heart pounded even harder at the sight of them, the lump in his throat now threatening to cut off his breath.

"Sir, we need you to hide this," Dodd said, "and in the safest, more secure place you know."

Roul frowned as he accepted both books. He flipped open the one Walter had not read, though he assumed it contained the same ramblings of a deluded man who used people for his own means.

"What is this?" Roul muttered, flipping through pages now. He shuffled the books and started flipping through the other.

Neither Dodd nor Walter spoke. Walter merely closed his eyes, listening for when Roul's gasp came. It did, and then Walter said, "Do not read it aloud. Please."

Walter opened his eyes and saw pity reflected back at him. He hated that look more than any other. He deserved it now, though, because he'd been that much of a fool.

"Listen, we need that put somewhere safe that no one except you will know how to find it." Dodd glanced at Walter before looking back at the elderly archivist. "Especially not him."

"I cannot knowingly hide a crime of this magnitude in my archive," Roul said. He turned to Walter and tears shone in his eyes. "Not even for a friend, and that is how I think of you, no matter your opinion of me, sir."

Walter's jaw trembled, but he clamped it tighter until a headache began to form. His emotions flipped back to wanting to strangle Michael with his bare hands for hurting this many people.

"Sir, I am not asking you to bury evidence. Walter brought this to us, myself and Lieutenant Lex. We need it protected while the Consorts investigate...the individual involved. And," Dodd glanced at Walter, "well..."

Walter forced words past the lump in his throat. "I don't trust myself right now."

Roul nodded. He protectively pressed both books against his chest. "Then I shall protect them with my life. Thank you, Walter Cram, for choosing this path. I suspect it was not easy for a man with your power."

Walter wanted to snort, to say something rude, but honestly, he had no energy left. "What choice was there? I found it with those two standing right there. I didn't have any choice."

"Yet, you walked with Lieutenant Dodd here. You could have killed him, both of them even, and taken the book. You could have killed me, right now, as I stand here. I am no match for you," Roul said. "You did not. You did what was right. I commend you."

Walter opened his mouth to say something, to say how he was not the monster they all assumed he was, but noise outside of the entrance caught their attention. The three men turned in time to see the doors swing open. Two bloody, panting Consorts staggered into the room, swords dripping gore on the historic carpets. Their eyes met Dodd's and instantly relaxed.

"Get them in here! Hurry!" one called out.

DeLancey and Devonsire hurried in after them, the fastest Walter had ever seen the two elderly women move. Three members of the Cathedral came in after them, along with two footmen still in livery, each with swords. All covered in blood. Finally, the two guards who'd been in the corridor when Dodd and Walter had arrived.

Where in the name of the abyss did the servants get swords?

Then the two archive guards, Her Highness's own soldiers who'd been standing watch over the place, said they'd go clear the corridor and slammed the doors.

Walter didn't remember the Consort; she'd been one of the ones who'd stayed behind during the winter. She looked at Dodd and said, "Bonacieux's men are inside the barricade, inside the inner sanctum. We cannot get to the main barricade, to let people in to help us. They're killing everyone, even the servants."

Chills went through Walter's body in the shocked silence that followed that declaration.

Dodd demanded, "How? How did they get in?"

"We think the clerical passages," one of the footmen said.

"How?" Dodd demanded again. "I don't even have a key to those!"

That was when Devonshire, still leaning heavily against DeLancey and the guard, said, "Vanida has them."

CHAPTER TWENTY-FIVE

ALLEGRA GLANCED AT the clock. It was far later than she'd planned to be dealing with her domestic servant issues, but there was still one final issue that had to be dealt with before she could go visit Rupert and Pero. Stanton was there, keeping her friends company at least, and they'd either hold supper if they could, or she'd simply have cake and wine until her stomach hurt.

However, the sun had long set and Calm Seas was still nowhere to be found, so poor Nadira went in search of the girl. Allegra took the time to go over a stack of issues with Nathan and Ysabeau. Serafina showed up, too, to provide an update from the archives. Nothing critical, though the previous news from that quarter still shook her to her core. It wasn't common knowledge, however, and they did not even discuss it in front of Nathan and Ysabeau. Eventually, those two left, leaving Serafina and Allegra alone to discuss and gossip, and speculate.

Serafina left when Nadira arrived with a chagrined Calm Seas, whose clothes were rather dirty for someone who was supposed to be resting and nursing injuries. It came out that Nadira had found the girl on her hands and knees scrubbing the old rectory's floors because Lex had said there were grease stains near the fireplace and had nearly fallen earlier in the day.

"I am certain Lieutenant Lex did not mean for you to do that," Allegra admonished. "In fact, I am certain Lex had, at most, meant for you to alert the necessary servants who take care of such things."

"I know, Your Ladyship, I know, but I was bored." She dragged out the word bored until it became a whine.

"I fear you risk re-infecting your face if you are scrubbing floors." Allegra used the gentlest voice she could manage, as she had no wish to scold the poor girl. No doubt she'd already received an earful from Nadira on the trek back to Allegra's apartment. Allegra sighed. "If I had my way in this, you'd not even work."

"We tried that, Your Ladyship," Nadira said. "We caught her cleaning Walter Cram's fireplace."

Calm Seas' eyes brightened at the mention of Walter, and the youthful flicker of unrequited affection flashed across her face. Lord God, had she ever been that young? She kept her face neutral and did not laugh or point out the obvious. After all, she most likely looked at Walter with the same big, brown eyes, too. A very long time ago.

Nadira's expression was different, as she only ever had one expression whenever some silly girl was fluttering about the rebellious mage: discreetly rolling her eyes. As she did right now.

Allegra's neutral expression faltered, as she tried not to laugh at Nadira's reaction.

"Miss Calm Seas," Nadira said in her commanding tone. Whenever she used the "miss" everyone knew the law was about to be laid down. The girl's shoulders immediately straightened, preparing her fortifications for whatever was to come next. "With Her Ladyship's permission, you shall assist me with the daily orders and messages. You will get to walk about the Cathedral and out to the encampment, as you have been ordered to do every day for the improvement of your constitution. Then, you might avoid taking a scrub brush into your hands."

Calm Seas' eyes filled with tears. "I am not purposely being disobedient. I have...memories. Cleaning helps."

"We know healing is more than burned flesh and broken bones," Allegra said. "Truly, we all understand. But your skin *does* need to heal."

"Cleaning helps," the girl whispered. "If I keep my hands busy, my mind...I don't...I don't see the demons in the corners of the room."

Allegra sighed. She understood that everyone dealt with mental wounds differently. She knew that, in her heart, and knew they all had their ways and methods. But she also knew Calm Seas could not be on the floor, elbow-deep in ash and grease with her burned flesh still healing.

"What about the silverware?" Allegra blurted. "It's cleaning with her hands, and surely there is enough work in this place to keep anyone busy."

Nadira sighed. "It is an excellent idea, Your Ladyship."

"But?"

"The upper butler assigns that task to the footmen as a reward, so they are known to be...unkind to outsiders."

Orsini politics. Even the damned servants were full of it. "So you are advising me not to poke my nose into things, as it would only make it worse for the girl?"

"I would have never used those words, Your Ladyship," Nadira said. She wasn't smiling. Allegra knew she was in her heart, though. She stared at her oldest, dearest servant long enough for Nadira's mouth to flicker towards a smile.

"Well. We must do something. Nadira says you cannot scrub floors, and I agree, and you say you must clean something, with which I also agree." Allegra sighed. "I do not understand girls these days. At your age, I'd have loved an order to stand all day watching the shirtless young men in the construction zone."

Calm Sea's protective veil could only partially obscure the rising flush on her neck and face. "Your Ladyship, I want to be useful. Nadira, honest, I'll clean anything. I need my hands busy or my mind...I start thinking about..."

The girl started crying with that last bit, and Nadira put a supportive arm around the girl's frail body. "There, there. None of that. You cannot expect to be in the Contessa's service without receiving proper medical attention."

"I'm sorry my face is like this," Calm Seas said between her tears. "I'm so sorry."

Allegra's own eyes stung with tears now. Nadira, however, had things well in hand. "None of that," she said, sternly enough that Allegra's own shoulders snapped backward out of childhood reflex at the tone. "You are alive, are you not? Well, there is no point to undo the good work by the healers and the surgeons and let you die from infection. As for your face, my dear? You listen to me, and you listen good. Anyone, I do not care who or what important title they hold, who only sees these scars and not the hard working, trustworthy, good-hearted girl you are, well, they are not worth the air the Lord God Almighty allows them to draw. Do you hear me?"

In that moment, Allegra was a little girl again, bereft of her parents, alone in the world. Her younger brother whisked off to be with relations. She left alone to be raised by servants and an ever-rotating collection of relations who only saw her as the heir of property and not as a person. Nadira had given her several of the same talks.

A commotion caught their attention and Allegra could've sworn she heard fighting in the corridors. Shouting, grunts, screams of pain. The sound of metal against metal.

Allegra protectively stepped in front of Calm Seas, as all three women stared at the door, waiting, worrying, praying to the Lord God the demons were not back. Nadira grabbed the letter opener from Allegra's desk and hurried to the door, saying she would lock it. However, the door flung open to admit a bloody Rahna. She pushed against the door herself, screaming incoherently. A booted foot was wedged in the door, and then an arm. Rahna screamed as she pushed fruitlessly.

Allegra rushed to help, but it was Nadira that sunk the letter opener deep into the offender's forearm. That brought cries and cursing from the owner of the arm, and Allegra froze in place.

Cartossian. The person was Cartossian.

The clashing in the corridor grew louder, and Nadira stabbed the intruder a second time, dragging the letter opener as she did. Blood sprayed everywhere. Calm Seas screamed. Allegra snapped for the girl to cover her eyes as she rushed ahead to help the two women at the door. Nadira's bloody attack helped reduce the pressure on the door, though they had to open it enough to push the screaming attacker away. Allegra helped Rahna keep the door closed while Nadira set the lock.

The three women leaned against the door. Calm Seas carefully approached them, sobbing, desperate for comfort. Allegra, the only one not covered in blood, enveloped the girl in her arms for the support. Shouting, pounding, shaking. Someone was trying to get in. They all pressed hard against the door, for the lock was not designed to withstand this kind of abuse. The paintings upon the walls shook. A vase filled with hothouse flowers danced precariously across a ledge.

The door rattled on its hinges, and they pressed harder. Then, it stopped suddenly, replaced by the clang of steel and shouting.

"What is happening?" Allegra whispered.

"Bonacieux's men are inside the Cathedral. I don't know how many. Beatrix is dead. They killed her while I tried...she said I should. Oh Lord God, not again." Allegra reached out a hand to comfort the soldier, but Rahna stepped back, sucking in a breath. "We need to get you to safety."

"There are no servant passages in this room," Nadira said. "We are trapped, unless you wish to climb the balcony into Mother Cateline's apartment. Her room doesn't have a passage, but it's away from the fighting at least."

Whoever had tried to prevent the soldiers outside her door from entering had given up their lives in her defense, for the rattling at the door started again. Allegra nodded at Rahna and they began to make their way to the back of the suite. However, nails began groaning, as metal pulled away from the wooden frame.

More pounding upon the door. Rahna stepped in front of them, one woman between them and the swords on the other side of a door not built to keep them out. "Your Ladyship, get Nadira and Calm Seas to safety."

Allegra exhaled and put her hand out to stop the guard. "No. I shall stay. Get them to safety, then help as many as you can."

Nadira whispered, "*Allegra*, no. You mustn't."

A nail popped and hit the floor. Allegra turned to the most trusted companion of her life and smiled. Of course, Nadira knew, and still stood by her all of these years, risking her own life in the process. "Try to find Serafina, and Nathan, and Kia. Try to keep them safe, but only if you are safe yourselves."

"Your Ladyship," Nadira said, and she curtsied deeply. Then, she said, her voice not quavering, not even when the second nail hit the floor, "Rahna? Calm Seas? Across the balcony. Do it now."

Allegra did not look back, for she knew her heart would falter. Even now, her hands shook with fear and worry as she heard Nadira's ever calm voice say, "Brave up now." More fighting started outside in the corridor again, but finally she heard Rahna shout, "Contessa! We are safe! Hide!"

Allegra walked to the middle of her suite, giving her enough time to see whoever came through her door before she mustered the courage to burn men alive. Fire terrified her, the kind of fire that covered walls in flame and sent ceiling beams crashing.

She reminded herself, even as her heart painfully objected to the terror beyond her door, that she could always retreat, especially if she caught the front of the suite on fire. She could run, just as the others ran. No one would have proof it was her.

All that worry turned out to be pointless, for when the lock finally gave way, flying across the room, three men stumbled into the room, tripping over each other and hitting the floor. Lanterns and candles flickered in the hallway beyond, and she could see, and hear, the fighting.

What surprised Allegra the most was the abject fear that paralyzed her, even as the soldiers lurched to their feet. Her common sense screamed to do something, anything, and yet she could not even lift her hand. She would die here, sliced into pieces. Moments from now. Stanton would find her body, mangled and cold.

Allegra gasped as a man pushed his way into the room, plunging his sword through one of the Cartossian soldiers. She turned her head away for the rest; she'd seen far too much blood in her lifetime already. She did not need to see more and have it ruin her fondness for the room.

However, she soon opened her eyes at the lack of dying and fighting. She stared at the pooling blood on her polished wooden floor and sighed. She wouldn't be able to return to this room to sleep after this.

Ginny walked into the room, gave Allegra an appraising look, then nodded sharply. "Good."

"Where's Rainier?" The man who'd entered the room first, who'd killed the soldiers...

"Renouf?" Allegra asked. She did not recognize him. One side of his face was caked in blood, and some of his hair was missing. A rather noticeable lump on his cheekbone distorted his features, even from this distance. "Stanton's with...Rupert, Francois. I was working late and missed supper. What is happening? Who are these men?"

Ginny distractedly looked out the door, into the corridor, while answering Allegra's question. "We think Bonacieux's men got into the inner sanctum through the clerical passages, in an attempt to assassinate the Holy Father. So far, there is no sighting of the general, but his men are crawling everywhere."

"The servants have been locking and barring doors, which is slowing them down, but that means they're spreading out everywhere trying to find a route through," Renouf said. "We keep finding pockets of them."

"We believe Vanida gave them his keys," Imogen said. She drew in a long breath before a hard exhale. "We need to get you somewhere safe. Until we are told otherwise, we are assuming the entire senior Cardinal's council, you, Walter Cram, Rainier, and myself are all targets. We assume Cram is still alive, and I am alive, obviously, but we don't know about the others."

Allegra glanced up at the ceiling. The building was still standing, so one assumed Walter had not been found. "We need to get to Rupert."

"What is this *we* business?" Renouf demanded.

Allegra had frozen when it mattered the most. She knew that, and Renouf most likely saw her. However, she also knew her presence would be important. And she did not wish to be alone if she was going to be completely and utterly frank with herself. "I am the Constable of Orsini, the Arbiter of Justice, and the Contessa of Marsina, and quite frankly, completely out of patience. You will escort me to the Holy Father. Immediately."

"My dear Lady, you cannot..."

"Reny, not now," Imogen snapped. "Allegra? Do not step outside of our ranks, do you understand me? We cannot risk a mage uprising if you are harmed."

"I will follow every order you issue," Allegra said, inclining her head.

Allegra stepped out of her suite, stifling a cry as she stepped over Beatrix's mangled form. Even with the blood and injuries, she recognized the person who had once protected her. Who had defended mages and the innocent. Who'd died trying to protect Allegra's door. She recognized others, though, amongst the dead. The footman who kept the wall sconces in this entire wing lit and burning safely, now lay buried under Cartossian bodies.

Allegra silently accepted a lantern, hardening her wits as soldiers fell in around her. Renouf took position in the rear, Imogen in front. Not all of the soldiers around her were Imogen's; she recognized some of the usual corridor guards from the militia. But that did not matter right now. They walked in a gore-splattered corridor, so much so that Allegra had to be careful with every step.

"Allegra? Do you know any quicker route to the Holy Father's residence?" Imogen asked.

"I've only taken the same way." It occurred to Allegra that the Cathedral, built and expanded over centuries, had been designed for this very moment. The hidden entrances and exits, always used by servants. The clerical paths, to quickly get a priest from one area to another, without needing to mingle in the main corridors. The locks, keys, heavy wooden posts.

Imogen issued orders for them to move. Allegra hoped Stanton was not fighting off an assassination attempt alone.

CHAPTER TWENTY-SIX

SWEAT DRIPPED DOWN Lex's face, but they did not move. The closet where they currently hid, hoping to the Lord God they weren't found, wasn't deep enough to hold a human being, not even someone as lean as Lex. They pulled the door as close as possible, but not even with two hands could they get the door to latch. The shelving dug into Lex's back. Lex ignored it and concentrated on breathing as quietly as possible.

Three people, by Lex's count. One-on-one, sure. Lex could even take two, if they played dirty, which Lex absolutely had no issue doing. Three? Three was a death sentence.

However, Lex found themselves straining as they recognized one of the voices. Lex carefully opened the door, not wanting to spook anyone. Not risking their head, they whispered, "It's Lieutenant Lex."

Cardinal Rigi let out a relieved sound when Lex stepped out to join him and Sisters Bianca and Margarite. He held an ornate rapier, and Lex recognized it as one of the decorative, historic pieces in one of the other corridors. "Do you know what's happening?"

Lex shook their head, back to survey the servant passage in either direction. So far, there was no one else there. When Lex had mapped the passages, they'd not realized they'd need them to save their life. "I saw Cartossian soldiers and started running. I was trying to get to the Contessa's room, to warn Rainier, but I got cut off. Half the doors are barred. I thought I'd try to get downstairs, to the archives. But..."

Sister Bianca said, in a low voice, "One of the footmen tried to get us out through a servant's door, but a soldier killed him. Cardinal Rigi saved our lives."

Rigi flushed, and Lex knew the meaning of guilt across his face. He'd not saved the servant, and that wasn't an easy burden. "We're also trying to get to the archives now, since we cannot seem to find our way outside, but the main corridors are full of..."

The dead. Lex knew what he meant.

"Where is everyone?" Sister Margarite asked. "Shouldn't the militia be in here by now?"

"I don't know. I was only here because..." Flashes of Father Michael's journal flipped through Lex's mind. "Dodd and I, and Walter, we found something, and I went to get the Captain. And then all this happened."

They decided to start moving, trying to weave their way down to the archives. Lex had only been through parts of the servant passages, and only once. Without a map or notes, everything started looking the same. Eventually, they found Kia, who had a small gaggle of the younger servants with her, trying to get them all toward a prayer room Kia said she knew had a wooden barricade on the other side.

They veered off to help her, relieved that the Cartossian soldiers had not made it this deep into the Cathedral's servant ways. Lex didn't want to admit aloud they were relieved not to be fighting, but Rigi thankfully said it for himself. He confessed he only knew how to fence, to fight for fun and exercise.

They found the prayer room, a small closet that could only comfortably hold six chairs, but they stacked those chairs and stuffed the children inside. Lex instructed Kia to stay there, and then told both sisters that they'd feel better knowing they were with them.

And then to slam that beam down as far as they could into its brackets and to not open unless they knew the voice on the other side.

"Don't believe anyone knocking on the door begging for help," Lex cautioned. "If you don't know them, you don't open the door."

Margarite began to cry, saying she could never leave Rigi. Rigi looked at Lex, unable to tell the woman he loved the things that needed to be said.

"Sister, the children need protecting," Lex insisted. "More will try to get in here, and you can control who comes in."

Margarite wailed, and everyone shushed her. Then, Sister Bianca put an arm around the young woman and said, "They both have their duty. We must do ours."

"Actually, Kia? Anyone who uses the code phase Lex smells or Dodd smells, let them in."

Even in the near darkness of the prayer closet, Rigi's confused expression was recognizable. Lex let out a grim laugh. "It's a code phrase the Consorts use during training. I don't know if anyone will remember it, but..."

Kia gave them her keys, as she could access parts of the Cathedral that many others couldn't, given she was part of the Contessa's staff. Rigi gave Margarite a swift kiss, told her he loved her, and told her to be careful.

And so on it went, with Lex and Rigi trying to find their way back through the maze of passages, and hearing sounds of fighting, but not knowing how to get to it. Occasionally, they'd come across dead servants or priests, and even a few Cartossian soldiers. They'd search the bodies, as gruesome as it was. However, all of the servants carried keys, and if they had them, well, the attackers did not.

There were so many secret passages in this place. Lex knew of some, but had never used any of them. After all, that had been the point of so many hidden passages; this place had been built in a time of endless war and had been designed with those lessons fresh in mind. But that meant Lex and Rigi were now going in circles, having been cut off. They could hear fighting, sometimes in the next room, and yet could not find a way to assist.

Lex's heart pounded, guilt pulled at them that they could not find a way to help, and their scars ached at the memory of battle, but nevertheless they pressed on. The pair had to cut back several times, switching back through servant passages, and retracing steps, trying to find their way either through to the archives or even to the Holy Father's wing; for this part of the Cathedral, those would be the heaviest defended locations in Lex's mind.

Lex motioned for them to circle back to a servant's passage, convinced there was a path through there. Sure enough, a simple tapestry hanging out of place, in a darkened corner of the passage, and Lex found an unlocked door. They stepped through and came in on the flank of two soldiers trying to get to yet another door. There were three footmen defending the door. One was armed with the long metal pole used to hang the decorative tapestries the Cathedral was so fond of, while the other two hurled priceless vases, glassware, and whatever else they could find to concuss the soldiers.

Lex and Rigi were able to make short work of the soldiers. Somewhere in the fight, an artery had sprayed bright red blood across a painting of Tasmin, her sword held aloft. Lex stared, even as the others tried to get their attention. There were rules for battle and warfare. Everyone knew you tried to avoid killing servants, healers, surgeons, and the priests. There were simply people that were to never meet the sword.

But as Lex stared at that blood-splattered painting, they knew this place would never be the same, not after this. At least the demons were only following their nature; a person always had a choice.

"Lieutenant Lex?" Cardinal Rigi sounded like he'd been repeating that, trying to get Lex's attention.

Lex shook off the morbid thoughts. Right now, they all had to stay alive.

"Where does that door lead?" Lex demanded.

A footman said it would connect with the clerical passage, and loop over to one of the prayer rooms before descending several flights of stairs to come out close to the archives. Lex gave the directions back to the prayer closet and instructed them to use the code phrase, "Dodd smells." The eldest of the footmen snorted. He gathered up the other servants, and it was then that Lex realized the adult servants were protecting four of the young chambermaids, who were hiding behind a chaise.

Lex stared at the girls, none of them older than twelve. The footmen hurried back through the door Lex and Rigi came through, leaving them alone with the bodies.

Thankfully, there were no bodies in the next passage; most of the doors were locked from inside. Good, Lex thought. Lex had seen enough dead servants for a lifetime. They had three more skirmishes awaiting them once they exited the servant passages, and were both exhausted and heaving when they stumbled into the archives' back room through a false bookshelf.

Rigi stared back at it and made a thoughtful sound. "I'd never known that was fake."

Swords pointed in their direction, which were quickly sheathed. A lot of back slapping, relieved sounds, and so on came from them. There were three Consorts, two Amadore soldiers, and a lot of others in the archive. Lex pressed a hand against their midriff, expecting their hand to come back covered in blood. It did not.

"You injured?" Rigi demanded.

Lex shook their head. "No, just feels like it."

The old archivist greeted them. "You just missed Walter and Lieutenant Dodd. They have gone toward the Holy Father and to find more innocents to send back to us."

"Only two of them?" Lex demanded. They didn't bother to acknowledge the hypocrisy of such a statement. To Cardinal Devonshire, Lex asked, "Why are you all here?"

"It's the safest place we could find, my child," the elderly cardinal said.

Lex supposed any room behind Walter Cram would probably be one of the safer ones. Provided he didn't bring down the roof to make himself into a martyr.

Shouting and the sound of rushing footsteps caught their attention. A large Cartossian soldier came through the broken double doors and swung at Lex. Rigi lost his balance trying to parry the blow, and DeLancey tried to trip the soldier with her cane.

Blood blurred Lex's vision as they fought. The others joined in against the other attackers who rushed them, and Lex could not spare a moment to wipe their eyes. Finally, four attackers were cut down, and that was when the wailing began.

DeLancey was on the floor with an injury that no one recovered from. The old woman had not been wearing her cardinal's amulet, or any of her rings that Lex could see. Lex's jacket was full of healing buttons, blessed thread woven into the fabric, all of it. Lex hesitated, though. That was a lot of blood.

Rigi was sobbing, thanking the old woman for saving his life. Begging Lex to help.

DeLancey met Lex's eyes and managed to whisper, "Save the buttons, my child." Those were her last words on this earth.

Lex closed the elderly cardinal's eyes and put their hand on her shoulder, the one that was still whole and not cleaved in two.

Rigi managed to whisper, "May the Almighty greet you and cherish you, and give you rest."

"May the Almighty greet you and cherish you, and give you rest." Lex pushed themself to their feet. "We need to get to the Holy Father."

Rigi eyes were red and rimmed with tears. "She saved my life."

"I know, Your Grace, but we have to go."

"Call me Rigi," he whispered. "Just call me Rigi."

"All right. Listen to me, Rigi. There's enough people in this room to protect themselves. If Bonacieux's men are in this deep, and all over the place, it's because they are trying to find their way to the pope. We know the route there from here. We need to get there and help whoever is currently protecting him."

"We can't leave her," Rigi said. "Maybe she's not...she's still warm."

Cardinal Devonshire bent over and placed a hand on Rigi's back. "You must go help the Holy Father now. She would've understood, I promise."

"I cannot go," Rigi whispered.

Lex wiped their sword against their pant leg. "All right. I need one of you to come with me. We have to make it to the Holy Father. If he's safe, we'll come back. Otherwise, he'll need our protection. That's where they're all going."

"No," Rigi said sharply. He pushed himself up to his feet. "They need to stay, to protect the children. I'll go."

"Can you manage it?" Lex asked. It sounded cold, even to their own ears, but it had to be asked.

Rigi inhaled deeply and let the breath out slowly. Then, nodded. "Yes."

Devonshire pulled off a scarf from her neck and advised Lex to wrap it about their ribs. At first, nothing happened, but soon a warmth spread throughout Lex. It was subtle but eased the pain enough that it was easier for Lex to push it to the back of their mind. Lex gave a sharp nod to the others and said it was time to go.

"Wait," Rigi said. He passed Lex his sword long enough to remove his blood-soaked cardinal's robes. Underneath, he wore simple clothes: a regular tunic, simple trousers with brown suspenders. He carefully draped his robes over DeLancey's still form. Then he took back his sword, and they walked into the corridor to make their way after Dodd and Cram.

CHAPTER TWENTY-SEVEN

ALL THOSE WITHIN the Holy Father's suites had begun the task of fortifying themselves. Those who'd made their way to the area, either for protection or to protect, were ordered to begin barricading the various doors and passages. Stanton lost count at thirty-seven routes to get to the Holy Father's bedroom, the only room without an escape. Pero then informed him about another seven hidden passages that Stanton had never known about. Apparently, the wall tapestries weren't only for decoration.

Stanton recognized Giso and Vittorio's bickering seconds before they were escorted into the private breakfast room. Stanton, Rupert, and Pero had been pushing the furniture closer to the doors, making makeshift barricades, as most of the doors did not even lock. Those that did were flimsy, and Stanton estimated he could take them down with a couple of well-aimed kicks.

With no time for pleasantries, Stanton ordered Giso and Vittorio to the back of the room, near the bedroom doors. The militia who'd come with the cardinals said they would guard the outer entrances into the suites. Even now, Stanton could hear fighting. Stanton asked if they needed his help, but one said no, as the Holy Father needed protection. A soldier turned to Pero and she asked, "You can still fight?"

Stanton looked back at Pero, a man who'd once been in Amadore's army. Once, a very long time ago. Who hadn't trained properly in years. Who only picked up a sword for a little exercise and showing off. But Pero drew in a breath, even as Rupert put a hand on his husband's arm. Pero nodded sharply, even though his face said he was uncertain.

The corporal accepted a sword from someone behind her, and then handed it to Stanton. "For Pero. Fight well, Captain."

"We will barricade the doors behind you and make our stand here."

She nodded sharply. "I understand, Captain. May the Lord God Almighty bless you."

He traded grips with her, hating that he knew so many of them were about to die and he could not even remember her name. "Good luck."

She closed the door behind her, and he knew he'd never see any of them again in this life.

He exhaled a long breath and then handed the still-bloody sword to Pero. He took it gravely, staring at the blood, but only for a moment. Then, he wiped it clean against his trouser leg, put it in easy reach atop a small shelf, and said, "Giso? Bring the spirits cart over here."

Vittorio helped move the cart, both men grumbling it was a crime against the Lord God and nature to smash antique glass and crystal to slow down godless murderers. Some of the doors and corridors had no one in them to slow attackers, so Stanton and Rupert moved furniture to create as many obstructions and blockades as possible. Nothing would stop an army, but at least slowing them would give them the hope of not being overrun at once.

Stanton tried not to think of Allegra as they worked. If they were lucky, she was stuffed in a locked closet somewhere protected by Consorts. Or had been successfully smuggled out of the city. However, Stanton's mind kept racing through how any Cartossian soldiers got into the city. Surely there were not that many, or else the bells, the warnings, something would've happened.

So, there were only some that had gotten in. Perhaps during the refugee evacuation? That was always a worry. And they had to still get inside the Cathedral itself, in past the servants, guards, everyone.

"I've always hated this chair," Pero said as he cracked one of the legs over a table's edge, allowing him to better wedge the chair into a tangled mess of furniture in front of the main doors.

They were working on like that when Vittorio said, "Vanida, that snake."

"We do not know it was him," Giso said.

"Who else could get Cartossian soldiers into the Cathedral under everyone's noses?" Vittorio demanded.

Soon, Pero and Rupert joined into the argument, and Stanton finally said, "I only pray it is a small force that has surprised us."

"I cannot believe he would purposely let soldiers inside the inner doors, to this sanctuary, where he lived most of his life," Giso said without conviction.

"Perhaps it is the mage," Stanton said. When they all looked at him, he clarified, "Perhaps the mage who caused the demon portals is behind this."

That delayed blaming Vanida, though the conversation still frequently turned back to him. His keys had not been confiscated, after all. He knew the inner passages. He knew the path.

"Then why were some of Bonacieux's soldiers running in our area?" Giso demanded. He was panting hard now. They all were. Moving furniture was exhausting. Stanton felt for the servants who did this every day.

No one could answer Giso's question. Stanton guessed it was because Bonacieux sent his men in first, to test out the defenses, to soften resistance, and basically save his own hide from the real fighting. There would be almost no one in the hallways at this time of night; everyone was back to their rooms after prayers, or out at the taverns or brothels. The nighttime servants weren't working yet, and the day servants were already gone to bed.

Stanton's stomach churned. In fact, the only individuals in the Cathedral corridors right now would've been the evening servants and a few dozen evening guards at key entrances.

Finally, Giso and Vittorio both collapsed on a chaise after having dragged it to the door. There were now seven blocked doors between them and the fighting. Would it stop an army? Of course not. But it might discourage or confuse a small group, and it would slow everyone else.

And it would make it easier to kill anyone trying to get through.

The clock said it was another twenty minutes of waiting before he could hear fighting. The sound grew closer. He could hear the shouting, swearing, and dying. Then a lull, and sometimes more fighting, only closer. That meant the first crew had fallen, and reinforcements were arriving. And dying.

As they grew closer, Stanton pushed aside all worries to consider the moments at hand. He tried very hard not to think about how he'd been in this situation before, protecting Rupert and other members of the clergy from bandits.

He heard Pero say, presumably to the priests, "Grab a wine bottle. Bash it over the head of anyone who gets past us, and keep bashing until either the bottle or the head breaks."

"I will not be doing violence," Vittorio said.

"Then you can die, Cardinal," Pero said flatly.

"Are you threatening me, Pero?" Vittorio demanded.

"Vittorio, enough," Giso said.

"No, I will not be silenced!"

"Gentlemen!" Stanton shouted. He sucked in a breath at the stunned silence behind him. He did not look back. Still focused on the doors before him. "We are all about to be murdered where we stand, so if you would kindly shut your mouths so that I can concentrate, I'd greatly appreciate it."

"There's no call for that," Vittorio muttered, but he was silent after that.

The sound of dying men finally ended. Stanton gulped. It was their turn soon. He could hear the grunts and cursing of men trying to pull apart the barricade to enter the adjacent room. His back ached from the tension, and he tried to loosen his shoulders to no avail. Shouting, fighting, more grunts. Well, at least people were still making their way here to protect the Holy Father. It would be too late, but at least people were trying.

A ring of tables was all that was between the barricade door and him. Pero crouched a couple of times, then kicked out his legs and moved his arms. He took off his jacket, passing his sword between his hands, and did the movements again. That seemed to satisfy him.

They were pounding on the locked door now, trying to break the lock or remove the hinges. It was hard to tell through all of the cursing. Stanton turned enough to meet Giso's eye and said, "Lock yourselves in the Holy Father's bedroom."

"No," Giso said, rather defiantly for a man who complained constantly about being old and frail. He lifted his chin. "If it is the Lord's will that I die here today, then I shall die standing, right here, in the place that I choose."

Vittorio sighed dramatically. "You old fool." He made no effort to move, however.

Rupert shrugged at Stanton's insistent glare. "If these two old men won't go, I very well cannot go hide under my bed."

The door listed to one side. They were taking off the hinges. Stanton said quietly, "I cannot protect you when I fall."

"Roo, I'm begging you," Pero said, "I don't want you to see me die."

Rupert smiled at his husband and then reached over his head to the sword displayed on the wall. The blade itself had been repaired or replaced over the centuries, but the grip, guard, and decorative pommel were said to all be from Tasmin's original sword. The one she'd left behind when she charged into the demon portal.

Rupert held it and said, "I wonder if I remember my sword lessons."

Pero argued as Rupert stepped in front of the two old men. He ignored his husband and said, "I'll take care of these two old fools. You take care of each other."

There was no time to argue; the bottom hinge gave way.

CHAPTER TWENTY-EIGHT

As a general rule for his own sanity, Walter rarely compared himself to others. In his experience, most people were good at something, and he was not so egotistical as to assume he was the fount of all wisdom and knowledge. Because of this, he rarely experienced jealousy or envy, and when he did, he could easily recognize it as such.

So, watching boisterous Dodd, fun-loving, card-playing, hat-wearing Dodd, hack his way through human beings with a grim expression and a skill that Walter did not even know he possessed filled him with envy.

Walter could not use his magic here; especially not now as he grew physically exhausted. He had to rely upon a sword he'd taken from a corpse who was no longer in need of it. He'd been in enough scrapes and situations where he knew how to use a sword. And, like any man with a decent upbringing, he'd learned how to use one. But he struggled to keep up with Dodd's trail of moaning and oozing victims, and Walter was painstakingly aware of the difference between knowing which end was the pointy bit and watching someone who was raised for greatness.

Through this violent, gore-filled trek through the main corridors, it was no longer possible to pretend Lieutenant Dodd was just a normal kid.

It had been an image he'd cultivated, while laughing, drinking hard, and playing harder, and Walter was reminded in this moment that he had also fallen for the curated image of Dodd. Just like

Walter, demon lover, was a curated image: both were false, a way to help them live in the world with their choices.

But Lieutenant Dodd was the son of a gentleman. He'd been trained as such, with all of the privileges and opportunities that afforded. And even with their flight through the woods after Borro Abbey's destruction, they had not been fighting non-stop for their lives, and Walter had forgotten that to become a Consort, one first had to be amongst the best of the Orsini militia.

Walter did not even know this side of his friend existed, and hoped deep within his soul that he never did a single action to have this side turned upon him.

Thankfully, a few of the militia, along with the servants they'd been protecting, burst from a locked room to assist them, and the last of the Cartossian bastards were dead. At least, for this section. Dodd ordered the militia—young members who didn't look old enough to be allowed in to see the dancers yet— back into their room, to lock it, and not to open it for anyone who didn't use the code phrase, "Lex smells."

Walter smirked. Well, maybe the curated image wasn't *completely* manufactured from the imagination.

Walter's arms and shoulders ached as they stood in the middle of a slaughterhouse to catch their breath. Both he and Dodd were soaked in blood, and worse. Walter knew better not to look behind them, knowing whatever was there would haunt his memories, a scene that would replay over and over. And yet, he turned to look back.

"Stop. Don't look," Dodd said, and his voice was colder than Walter had ever heard him speak.

Walter decided to obey for once. Though, he did look upward, toward the ancient frescos, and thought about how some poor artist's assistant would have to clean all that with a tiny brush as not to damage the artwork. Everyone would have lifelong scars after this, including the wrecked saps who had to come clean up this mess.

A little voice, one he'd rarely ever heard, and one he resolutely refused to ever obey, whispered over and over in his mind that he should stay, and just for once clean up his own mess.

Thankfully, shouting, and a lot of it, approached. Walter sighed, and his back screamed in protest as he readied himself once more for battle. Perhaps if he were very lucky, he'd die here in defense of this abyss-forsaken place and he'd not have to face the consequences of his own sins.

ALLEGRA'S TEETH CHATTERED from fear. Never in her life had she witnessed such concentrated carnage, and she hoped to the God Almighty that she never would again. As she stood in the midst of soldiers, in her second-best gown, she watched it repeat over and over, as people fought and died. Even as she thought this, blood painted the wall and ceiling nearest her.

Then salvation came running from around the corner. A small cry escaped her, and she had to clamp her hands over her mouth to avoid making any distracting noise. Dodd's stocky form came barreling into the corridor, cutting down four Cartossian soldiers from behind. His green uniform hid the evidence of violence from this distance, but his once-pale hands and face were reddish-brown, and his hair was plastered to his scalp.

Walter was only three steps behind Dodd. He took on the one soldier who turned to swing at Dodd. Walter looked at though he'd rolled around on the floors, and she quickly looked away as they continued fighting hard. She could not bear seeing either of them injured, could not allow her mind to have anymore terrifying images for her nightmares. The screams were already enough.

As people fought and died around her, she knew in her heart Walter had been right all along: she should've learned how to control her fire.

Even now, though, even at this moment as Imogen, Renouf, and everyone else fought to protect her, trust did not come naturally or easily to Allegra. She found herself thinking if they'd seen her unleash elemental fire, they might've turned on her, handing her over to Bonacieux for public execution to stop this bloodshed.

An adjacent door swung open and more Cartossian soldiers rushed into the corridor. All men, all huge, all angry. One managed to grab Allegra's arm in the ensuing fight, and she screamed when he knocked her to the floor, preparing to drag her back through the open door. Fire began rising in her heart, and she fell silent, concentrating all of her might on keeping her magic under control, if even just until she was behind that door, where there would be no witnesses left to breathe the tales.

An arm fell next to her. Then, the owner of the arm a blink later. Allegra let out a short cry. She clamped her eyes shut, only realizing that meant she'd be startled by someone else grabbing her, so opened them to see Imogen standing directly in front of her, taking on two attackers at once. She was tiring fast, too, as Allegra had never seen Imogen move so slowly, and there was no one else to help her.

So, yes, it was rather undignified to be crawling about the floor, smearing God Almighty only knew what all over her gown, but Allegra grabbed a broken piece of decorative ceramics, most likely one of the vases that had hit the floor early. Allegra stabbed it into the shin of one of the men fighting Imogen, and she used both hands to push it deep. Allegra took a knee to the face somewhere in that, and the tears streaming down her face made it difficult to see.

Renouf finished off the man he fought and turned to his left to assist Imogen. Allegra tried to crawl out of the way, but Imogen stumbled trying to avoid her. While she managed to stay on her feet, she'd let down her guard. Renouf slammed sideways against the man, ramming him hard with his shoulder, and his killing blow missed Imogen.

His second one, however, did not miss Renouf.

Allegra frantically clamped her hands over Renouf's wound. She had nothing magical on her to slow the bleeding. She glanced about her, to see if there was anything she recognized to use. Everyone had magical healing items except her, and yet now it seemed like she couldn't see one.

She did not know if the smell came from him, or those around her, but there was a lot of blood bubbling between her fingers. This was not going to be the gut wound that lingered, giving them the chance to find a healer. Tears streamed down her face, and Renouf tried to touch her face, but his hand missed completely. He tried to speak, but she told him to save his strength.

Dodd rushed over, pulling off his jacket as he dropped to his knees. He slammed it down hard on Renouf, but it was too late. Allegra tried not to weep. So many people had died already. It seemed wrong to cry for this one man, right now. And a man she didn't like all that much. But he didn't deserve to die like this.

Dodd sighed and put his jacket back on, blood and all. "You died well, Renouf." Dodd put a bloody hand on Allegra's shoulder before standing.

Imogen crouched beside Renouf's body. "Oh, Reny. Your mother is never going to forgive me for this."

Imogen whispered a short prayer and then stood. She offered Allegra a hand to stand up. She turned to Dodd and Walter. "Thank you for the assistance, Lieutenant Dodd. Mr. Cram."

Walter gave Imogen an incline of the head. No sarcasm. No insults. That scared Allegra more than anything else. How bad was it elsewhere in the Cathedral?

Dodd gave Imogen a curt bow. "Your Highness, we left the senior archivist, some Consorts and militia, Devonshire, and DeLancey in the archives, along with a large number of servants, mostly young maids and the boys who do all of the deliveries. Cardinal Devonshire and DeLancey fear Vanida let Bonacieux's men into the inner sanctum through the clergy passages. We've been trying to get to the Holy Father's suites, but everything is locked, and there's fucking chaos everywhere."

Walter fiddled around underneath his tunic before pulling out a string of keys all tied together. "We've mostly been going in circles for what seems like hours now. Then, we keep finding a random door open or broken down, so we keep trying to find our way forward."

"That was our theory, and plan, as well," Imogen said. "We have some keys, too. Let's see if we can make some headway."

"But what about Renouf?" Allegra asked, even though she already knew the answer. She still had to ask, though.

Imogen's face was grim. "He's with the Lord God now. He doesn't need us."

STANTON FOUGHT FOR his life. Attackers came at them, a constant stream of panting, often bleeding or stumbling soldiers, all angry they'd had to weave through broken glass, furniture, and tripping hazards. While this made it easier to stay alive, Stanton grew exhausted with each wave of attackers. His back announced it was not as young as it used to be, and Stanton regretted all of the paperwork his position had made him do. His shoulders ached, and the mental focus of hyperawareness of his surroundings tired him.

An attacker rushed past Stanton while he fought a burly man. Stanton could not risk pivoting back to assist, but he heard a distinct *thunk* before a body fell backwards in his peripheral vision. This distracted his own attacker for only a heartbeat, but that was all Stanton needed to end the fight. Then, Stanton finished off the moaning, bloody man. He glanced back to see Vittorio holding a wine bottle by the neck, having proved yet again that wine bottles were stronger than most skulls.

In the blessed lull that followed, Stanton struggled to calm his heart. Somewhere in all of this, he'd pulled his rib muscles, and each breath brought a sharp pain. Massaging the area only made his eyes water, so he twisted and stretched. Several pops came from his back when he arched it, and he unhappily agreed with Dodd, who'd said the other morning that Stanton should've been out practicing with him and Lex more.

Stanton asked a fussy Rupert to move so he could check over Pero. Like himself, mostly superficial cuts and bruises, though Pero had a terrible slash across two of his fingers. Stanton offered to use one of his healing buttons to help ease it, but Pero wanted to save it in case of dire need.

Dark stains caked on Rupert's blade said he'd helped in the fight, and Stanton hated that the priest, this man who had been called by the Lord God, had to kill in defense of his own life. Still, he checked Rupert over, even as they heard fighting and shouting from further in the suites.

"Everyone must be coming here," Rupert said as he swatted Stanton away. "Stanton, stop fussing. Check on the other two."

Stanton found Giso and Vittorio gore-splattered and traumatized, but physically fine.

As he stared at Vittorio, ensuring none of the blood was the priest's, a dark, angry voice inside Stanton snarled that maybe Vittorio finally knew what was done to the mages he bought and sold like cattle. Stanton turned away, quicker than necessary, and alerted Pero to come back to the ready.

More boots sounded in the distance. More shouting. More metal against metal. Stanton stretched his shoulders, neck, and back as best as he could. He heard the grunts and curses of people trying to maneuver around furniture, though with the speed of approach, Stanton assumed someone had finally moved it away from the doors in one of the previous attacks.

Stanton didn't believe his eyes at first when the slow approaching figures ahead came into focus: Lex.

"Is that Cardinal Rigi?" Giso demanded.

Stanton's shoulders slumped from relief at not having to fight.

TRY AS LEX might, they were stumbling now from the pain. Devonshire's sash had been exhausted during the last fight, and Lex had used it to wrap Rigi's forearm with a healing button, to stop him from bleeding out. However, without the pressure of the sash against Lex's muscles, everything ached.

As they approached the papal suite, they met up with seven more militia, all protecting servants, and trying to get to the Holy Father. Lex told the servants how to get into one of the fortified prayer rooms they'd just passed, with the code phrase, and the militia stayed with Lex and Rigi. Together, they made their way through the destroyed remains of what had been one of the most beautiful areas of the entire Cathedral.

Many of the doors were hanging off their hinges. Some had their locks smashed. Pieces of what had been historic furniture were also smashed and strewn everywhere. Each step they took crunched from all of the broken glass.

But it was the bodies that bothered Lex the most. Cartossian. Orsini militia. Amadore. Consorts. Servants. Clergy of all ranks. So many had given their lives trying to protect the entrance to one man. So many had given their lives to kill one man. This place would never be the same now.

"Do you think anyone is still alive in there?" Rigi asked. He whispered the question.

Lex found themself whispering back, though there was probably no need. "I don't know."

The handful of times Lex had been here, they'd been brought through a different set of doors than their current path, but it proved easier to simply follow the destruction. They both were startled by the sound of fighting deeper within the premises; someone must've come through via another passage.

When this was over, Lex was going to insist they be given maps of this place, and *all* of the keys. This was ridiculous.

They weaved their way through the various connecting rooms, following the trails of blood and moving furniture from their path. Lex stopped by the body of Kingsley. He'd always had a goofy smile, and Lex hoped he was at the side of the Almighty, right now, telling jokes. Lex had no tears; the shock had dried them up. Instead, they used a broken bottle to cut off Kingsley's buttons. Lex pocketed some, then had the rest passed around.

At the confused expression of one of the Amadore soldiers, Lex said, "Consort buttons are imbued with healing magic. They're good for stopping the bleeding. As long as there's time enough for them to work."

Onward they pushed, cutting down any attacker in their way. They slashed, stabbed, and fought dirty. Lex wasn't ever going to be considered physically imposing, and playing dirty meant Lex got to live. They were fine with that. Just turn off the brain and live. Lex would deal with the rest later.

Coldness spread over Lex as they calmly pulled off buttons from Consorts—their friends, their colleagues, their gambling rivals. Rigi knew the magical items the priests carried and dug those out. Ditto Lex and the Orsini militia. They stopped to administer aid whenever they found someone still alive, but they did not linger. Wrapped a magic item in place, moved them away from the tangle of bodies, gave a word of comfort, and then move on.

Lex and one of the soldiers were helping wrap the broken leg of a servant, and tending to a rather nasty head wound, when Lex clearly heard their name from beyond the room. Then, someone else shouted Rigi's name.

Lex left the footman to the care of the others and followed the voice. A little cry escaped Lex when they saw the Captain standing there, alive. The pope was alive. Pero still stood straight. Rigi rushed past Lex to embrace Giso and Vittorio, and the old men enveloped the young man in a supportive circle.

Lex wanted to hug someone. Lex wanted to be hugged. The Captain's jaw was firm, unyielding, and they understood both that expression, and that Rigi would've said Lex wore the same one: the look of grim determination not to think about the abattoir they'd walked through.

Unfortunately, that caused Lex to think about it, to really think about it, to stare, to process. Uncontrollable retching overtook them, though nothing came out. That set off the Holy Father, who still had something left in his stomach.

The sound of approaching footsteps. A lot of them, boots crunching on glass, cursing as they weaved around broken furniture. They all tensed, even as Lex tried to bring their guts and mind under control.

And then, the sweetest sound in the world sounded: Dodd's voice as clear as day shouting out asking, "Is anyone alive in here? Anyone?"

CHAPTER TWENTY-NINE

REPEATED HORRORS HAD worn down Allegra, so when she finally stepped into what had once been Rupert's private breakfast room, she could not even smile when she finally looked upon Stanton and her own eyes confirmed he yet lived. Part of her wished to wrap her arms about him, but the set of his jaw and twitch of his head told her no, this was not the appropriate place.

"Allegra," he said, and his voice cracked. He cleared his throat. "To the back with Giso and Vittorio. I doubt we're done."

She nodded, restraining herself with all of the lessons of her youth. This was not the time to pull him from his duty. His attention must be on defending them. She understood that. She walked by him, giving him a soft smile. He reached out and touched her arm. Allegra stopped, just a brief moment for them to stop to smile, to know they were, for now, still alive in this world. It was enough.

She joined Giso and Vittorio, who Lord God bless them, stepped in front of her to form a living shield. She protested, and Vittorio told her to learn when to stop speaking. Giso, with significantly more tact, said, "The good captain does not need the distraction of worrying about you. It is good to see you, though, my dear. So very good."

Imogen was amongst the last to walk into the room, hissing with each step. She looked about the room, and when her gaze landed on Rupert, she nodded. "Good. Does anyone have a healing stone?"

Lex immediately went to Imogen's side, and they spoke too low for Allegra to hear. But Lex ordered Imogen to sit down on the sofa, which she did begrudgingly, and Lex rolled up her pant leg to expose an angry wound that dripped blood to the floor. Cardinal Rigi and Dodd went to help, and all three got two of the Consort buttons into place. Allegra watched as the buttons faded, their shiny finish dulling with contact to the wound.

While this was going on, Stanton asked, "Has anyone seen Renouf? Or any Consorts?"

"Renouf is dead," was Imogen's reply.

"Cardinal DeLancey is dead," Lex said.

"Lord God Almighty, save us. Who else?" When no one spoke immediately, Giso raised his voice and said, "Who else?"

"I think I counted seven Consorts. Maybe eight. I lost count of militia and servants," Lex said.

Rupert let out a pained sound. "Servants? Mine?"

"All of them," Walter said. "They killed everyone in their path. We tried to save as many as we could, but..."

"I counted eight Consorts, including Beatrix. She died so that Rahna could alert me," Allegra whispered.

Stanton swore and gripped his sword tighter. "Do you think they're finally done?"

Imogen got to her feet with help and began stretching out her injured leg. She asked Lex to adjust the bandage slightly, so while Lex did that, she said, "I doubt it. As far as I know, Bonacieux isn't even inside the building yet."

"He should be here soon," Walter said. When Allegra asked him why he thought that, he said, "That's his standard way. He sends his troops in to weaken the place, get their hands bloodied. Then, he shows up with the final ultimatum. Then, usually someone loses control of their elemental powers, revealing themselves as a mage, and then the building is burned to the ground with everyone trapped inside."

"How many times has this happened to you?" Vittorio asked. Allegra noticed the uncertainty in the man's voice.

Walter turned his entire body to face the cardinal. "Too many times to count, priest."

Someone was shouting in the distance. Running footsteps. Shouting if anyone was alive. Allegra was shocked to see Father Michael, alive and well, in mostly clean clothes, stumble into the room, out of breath and wide-eyed. He stared at them all, nearly feral.

"Father Michael!" Allegra exclaimed. "It is good to see you."

He waved his hands in the air, pointed and gesturing. He seemed to swallow air, desperate to force out words. Then suddenly, he shouted, "Bonacieux is coming!"

OVERWHELMING RAGE GRIPPED Walter's heart at the sight of Michael. The others did not know, of course they did not. Lex and Dodd did, though, and both put their hands on their swords, turning to look at Walter. Silently asking what to do. What Walter wanted to do and what Walter should do were the same thing, but he did not say anything as kindly Giso coaxed beloved Father Michael, the innocent, the man they trusted, the good one, to the corner to stand with the others.

The floor shook under Walter's feet. The last remaining paintings upon the walls tipped as Walter stared at the man who had betrayed everyone. Michael turned to face him, to look him straight in the eyes. The chandelier above their heads rattled.

Dodd grabbed Walter's forearm. "Not now."

"Wait until we can see him, Cram," the pope said.

That pulled Walter away from his anger, more than anything. Dodd was looking straight at Michael, whereas Rupert was looking toward the doorway. Walter brought his magic under control and continued to stare at the fucking priest who'd stabbed him in the back.

Michael's shoulders slumped, and he nodded. Slowly, at first, but then he straightened and gave Walter a sharp nod.

Dodd said again, "Later."

Walter nodded and turned to face forward. "Later."

"Try not to kill us all," the pope muttered.

Oh, the irony of that statement was not lost on Walter.

The sound of nightmares approached: heavy footfalls, walking with confidence, knowing none could stop them. That sound haunted many of his nightmares, lost in a labyrinth, running with no place to hide, and the sound of boots coming ever closer.

Bonacieux finally walked into the room, calm and clean. Spotlessly so, excepting his boots. The rest of them were soaked in gore, the dirty work that Boncieux did not do himself. No, he believed in finishing the job. He had people to do the hard parts, exhausting everyone by carving a path straight through to the pope. Soften up the militia that would be inside the inner sanctum. Make it impossible for reinforcements to get in.

Walter shook off his thoughts. Now was not the time to figure out how this happened, and how to prevent it from ever happening again. Right now was for staying alive.

Bonacieux did not speak yet. No, of course not. He had to get his lackeys into position. After all, this needed to be a grand moment of conquest for the bastard.

Walter took the opportunity to take in the room's details. He could not guarantee he knew how to kill Bonacieux without killing all of them. As it was, he might bring down the rest of the building in his current state of exhaustion.

He made his choice: he would do it, but only as the last choice. But if pressed, he would.

So, to rub the salt into bleeding wounds, Vanida stepped through the doorway to join Bonacieux.

"You lying sack of shit!" Vittorio screamed, startling everyone. Walter waited, but no magic came from him. Disappointment hit him more than anything. It would've been rather vindicating if Vittorio turned out to be one of those self-hating mages. Alas.

Vanida shook his head. "I am very sorry, my old friends, to do this, but—"

Walter glanced about the room. There were a lot of soldiers in this room right now, and yet...no one was fighting. Bonacieux was letting Vanida run his traitorous mouth. He knew this was Bonacieux's way, and he was used to running in the opposite direction, but this was strange.

"How could you?" Rupert demanded. "How could you betray us?"

"You dare speak of betrayal? After I was kicked from here for having an opinion!" Vanida said.

"You would've had Allegra hanged outside our front gate!" the pope shouted.

Bonacieux decided to speak now. "Oh, rest assured, priest, I still plan to once you're all dead."

And in the midst of Her Highness and Rainier both shouting the order to hold, the verbal saber rattling, with Walter shaking the floor for drama's sake, Michael rushed Bonacieux.

Walter screamed at Michael, screamed with all that was in him. He failed to grab him, tripping in the process, and bounced off the pope before gaining his feet once more. If Michael died bravely right now, no one would believe the truth. They would always remember him as the hero who valiantly threw himself at the monster. Michael was taking the path of martyrdom. He knew it well because he had dreamed of this moment his entire adult life. To throw one's body upon the sword, to radically change the course of history.

Dodd grabbed at Walter, trying to stop him, and so help him God Almighty he'd have skewered Dodd in the process if he hadn't dropped his sword when he stumbled.

Then, as Dodd and Rupert held him back, Walter watched the butcher's sword go through Michael and straight out his back. Walter screamed and fought against the new hands holding him back. The floor shook beneath their feet as Bonacieux thrust against the sword, pulling himself close to the now dying priest.

Walter wailed, and the vibrations beneath their feet became irregular as Walter fought against all of the people pulling him down to the floor, even as he vowed to bring this entire building down upon them if he had to stop this man. He would kill every single person in this building, friend, foe, innocent, monster, he did not care in that moment. Bonacieux lived his last day, Walter vowed. As soon as he gained control of himself.

Then, Michael did not do what Walter expected. Too many times, he had seen them grab the sword, to show defiance in the end. Or one last blast of fire. Or, sometimes, nothing, because the shock and surprise overwhelmed their last heartbeats.

Michael grabbed the general's sleeve. Then, right there, under his God Almighty forsaken feet, a demon portal opened, and Walter's last sight of the man he...he...he...

Michael did not scream. Walter wasn't even sure if Michael was alive by the time he fell from view. Bonacieux, however, was very much alive, and his desperate cries echoed, growing further and further away.

In Walter's logical, sensible part of his mind, he knew he needed to crawl over to that portal and close it fast because demons would be coming for them. He had at least Lex, Dodd, Pero, and the fucking pope on top of him, and he was convinced someone was sitting on his legs. He had to kick free to close the portal.

But all he could do—all any of them did—was stare in stunned, horrified silence.

And then the familiar shrieks filled the air.

CHAPTER THIRTY

RUPERT STARED IN horror as the best of men and the worst of men both plunged into the abyss. How did it all come to this? When good men threw themselves at swords, simply to stop other men? He has seen violent death before, but not in his own home. This place would never be his home again. It would always be a battleground, no matter how brightly they papered the walls.

No one fought. That struck Rupert the most, for two sides bent on killing one another stood in this room, and no one moved. Only Bonacieux's screams to let them know he was soon to be no more. And now, the shrieks of the demons in the distance overtook Bonacieux's voice.

Had Father Michael always been a mage? Or, had Bonacieux opened the rift to the abyss? Had someone else in the room?

Allegra flung herself at the rift, slamming both hands on the edge of it. Life drained from her face, and she squeezed her eyes shut. Sweat or perhaps it was tears, dripped down her face. Another tremor nearly pushed her in, and two militia—Rupert did not know their names—collapsed to the floor to grab her by the ankles and held tight, ignoring the bodies and bits all around them.

His own grip on Walter Cram also tightened. The mage was about to throw himself into the hole. Reason no longer had any room in Walter's mind. He could see it in his face; all that he could think of was the grief in his heart. Even though he could not stand the mage, Rupert gripped him so tightly that his fingers ached, and

Walter sucked in a gasp of air against the pain. That caused the tremors underneath their feet to cease.

Rupert let up and the floor shook again. He dug his fingers into Walter's ribs, begging his forgiveness the entire time, until he found the tenderest spot. Then Rupert pulled back to punch Walter as hard as he could. He knew he did not break a rib; the angle was awkward here on the floor, hitting a man. But it was enough for Walter to gain control of himself for the briefest moment.

"Walter!" Rupert shouted into his ear, so close it must've hurt him. "Help Allegra with the portal!"

"Walter Cram!" Rainier shouted near him. "Help Allegra!"

They all knew Walter had to do something, anything, but grief had overtaken his senses. The first of the demons came through, the tiny bat-things, and everyone with a sword readied themselves, leaving him to keep Cram from throwing himself into the abyss.

That first demonic swarm went straight to Bonacieux's men, by the simple nature of their position relative to how the bats exited the portal. Her Highness shouting for him to slap Walter until he was either unconscious or could help them.

Walter managed to sit up on his knees, but was still unable to see the current danger, only his grief. Rupert shook him, shook him hard, staring him in the eyes. "Walter! Walter, look at me! Do something!"

Walter's words, the ones Rupert could make out, were filled with rage and venom; grief came out in its own ways, he knew that. Walter was saying he'd kill Bonacieux. He didn't even know the man was already dead.

With an eagle-sized demon after him, Vanida came running toward them, screaming for mercy, screaming for protection, demanding they save him. Rupert picked up his abandoned sword and stood. He missed the demon the first two swings, but Lex and Pero got it.

"Kill them!" Vanida was shouting at Lex and Pero. "Francois! The demons!"

What Vanida found was not demons, nor protection, but the end, and the middle, of the sword of Tasmin.

Rupert started at Vanida's shocked expression. He staggered away from the dying man, half of his sword still straight through him. Vanida fell to the floor. Rupert didn't remember doing it. Not really. Not wanting to do this. Just the overwhelming urge to stop this man who had killed so many by his actions this day.

Vittorio stepped to his side, and Rupert expected the lecture and condemnation that he rightfully deserved. And yet, he felt no true shame, nor guilt. Only the regret that he had done it in instinct and not conscious thought.

Vittorio, however, did not speak. He bent down and snatched the necklace and pendant about Vanida's throat and ripped it from his body in one, harsh tug. The healing items removed, Vanida took his final breath and went to face the Almighty.

He turned to see Walter crawling across the dead bodies to get to the portal. And then Rupert saw the claw.

ALLEGRA COULD NOT keep her eyes closed, for she had to see the rift before her. All around her was chaos. Walter was still screaming for Father Michael, even as the demons flew about them. Allegra was on her belly, gown be damned, trying to make herself invisible amongst the dead on the floor. She had to push one body away; the eyes of the dead woman before her, her Amadore uniform soaked in blood, made her sick everywhere. The body slid into the pit, and Allegra nearly went after her from the despair that washed over her in that moment.

But she held on.

Around her, the Cartossian soldiers died. From this angle, she could see that the adjoining room had been full of Bonacieux's soldiers. The first wave of demons came into this world at an angle, and flew straight into the next room, massacring those beyond. Soon, they'd find their way back to this room.

A large claw emerged from the tear between the two worlds and Allegra's heart and courage sank. She had seen this unfold before. They had barely survived. Many did not. The soldiers around her were exhausted, and there were still too many demons in this room. She could not fight. She could not use a sword. Walter was useless. There were no other mages in this room. She had to help.

In that moment, she looked about to see if elemental fire could help because, if it could, she would have used it. But she had fought a demon like this before, and it took far more mages than the two in this room. No, she could help best by closing the damn portal. She pushed every single drop of magic she could find within her soul. At times, flickers of flames danced about her fingers. She pushed harder, no longer caring.

"Back to the abyss with thee, foul reflection of mine sins!" she shouted, and fire erupted from her hands.

A roar so loud the floor vibrated, and two more digits shot through the portal, cutting off the ability for more of the flying demons to rush out at them.

Fire erupted from the cracks around the clawed hand coming through, and Allegra flinched. More fire. That was *not* her.

Walter collapsed next to her and slammed both of his hands down at the portal's edge, not even caring about the very visible flames coming from inside the abyss. As far as Allegra knew, the abyss was not supposed to spew fire. She mustered what was left of her courage and her strength and joined him. She felt the portal's edge buckling every time Walter screamed, and he was screaming a lot. So much so that his voice cracked. He vented all his rage with total abandon now.

Imogen and Stanton stood over them, boots landing close to the edge of the portal itself. Swords came dangerously close to Allegra's head a couple of times, and she flattened herself as much as possible. She could see Lex and the remaining militia fighting the small demons. Dodd jumped into the fray near Walter and began stabbing the demonic forearm that reached out.

"Get us more mages!" Rupert shouted. Three Amadore soldiers ran out of the room.

She could hear Giso praying near her. It would do no good, she thought, unless prayer repulsed demons. Then, Dodd cried out in that high-pitched wail of life-shattering pain that Allegra had heard far too often that evening. One of the claws had impaled Dodd's thigh and was shaking him, trying to rid itself of the horrible human. Dodd screamed, screaming as much as the demons in the abyss wanting to escape to destroy this world.

"Dodd!" Allegra shouted.

"Ally!" Walter shouted at her. "Concentrate!"

Everyone she knew and loved was going to die.

THE DEMON'S SCALY flesh was like hacking at armor, but Stanton managed to get his sword wedged enough to use it as a handhold. He fumbled the first sword tossed up to him, but caught the second without cutting himself. Then, pushing up so that one booted foot was wedged safely between sword and flesh, he started sawing with the second sword. The demon roared and shook its finger, and Dodd screamed more, still firmly speared.

Unfortunately, the demon's hide caught the sword and he couldn't get it out with only one hand. He shouted, "I need another sword! Or a hammer!"

Walter and Allegra closed more of the portal, and the demon roared once more as the edge cut against its flesh. It veered to the side, and Stanton nearly lost his footing. Then, the demon thrust its arm straight up and Stanton ducked out of the way of the chandelier. The demon's fist went upward, through the ceiling, and Stanton held on for dear life. Dodd let out another pained sound, and then went limp.

"Stanton!" Rupert was trying to climb the demon.

"Get back!" Stanton yelled.

"Roo! Stop!" Pero was shouting.

"Take the sword!" Rupert shouted. He was trying to pass him the sword of Tasmin, the one he'd taken from the wall at the beginning of this fight.

Stanton did not hesitate. He snatched the sword in time, as the Holy Father lost his footing when another wave of fire came from the edges of the portal. He knew that wasn't Allegra, nor was it Cram. Was it Father Michael? Was it Bonacieux? Which of them opened the portal?

No time to think, for Stanton had to duck falling ceiling tiles. He climbed around, his wedged sword now a handhold. He got to the talon that impaled Dodd. The boy was mostly silent, the shock and blood loss finally winning the war against the healing buttons, thread, and the healing lining in his boots. The buttons were fading quickly now, right before his eyes. There wasn't much time.

"Your Grace! I need leather! And any Consort jacket!" Stanton shouted down.

He'd meant it to Giso, but Vittorio tossed up a sword belt that was on the floor, and Rupert flung a green Consort jacket that Stanton had no idea who owned, since it was so filthy. It didn't matter. Vittorio also tossed a pendant, shouting that it had healing magic. Stanton caught the items one by one. He put the pendant in his palm, and then wrapped the prayer stole and belt around it, and then the Consort's jacket. Then, he wrapped what was supposedly Tasmin's sword on the opposite side of a talon, locked his legs into place, and started pulling with both of his hands. He'd cut his left hand off if he had to, but he was not going to let Dodd die without a fight. He'd seen too many good people die for one day.

The blade pressed into his hand, pressed against the circular pendant, but the leather and the stole held the pendant in place, and the jacket kept the sword in place. Stanton slipped a couple of times, and he ended up wrapping both of his legs around the talon and pulling harder. He could not get leverage, but it was the best he could do.

Lex managed to crawl up the side of the talon without slipping; Stanton soon realized Lex had used two carving knives as handholds. Cardinal Rigi came up behind Lex, passing up a sack or maybe it was just clothes. At this point, everything was too dark with dried blood to identify. However, Lex managed to grab Dodd's limp arm, and he and Rigi pulled Dodd close enough for Lex to press the sack against his leg.

Dodd screamed in pain. Rigi and Lex both slipped when Dodd bucked, and a rain of dull buttons fell to the floor. Dodd was still screaming, though, and Lex's plan had managed to give the boy a few more minutes.

Imogen made it up the side of the talon. She dropped her sword to the floor, wrapped her arms about the talon and began kicking Stanton's sword, thrusting it deeper. Stanton lost his grip twice, and it was only his legs keeping him attached. He was exhausted beyond all words. His hands were numb, the tingling sensation overtaking him and making it difficult to grip the sword once more.

The portal ripped open. Stanton's heart sank. They were all going to die.

Then, several figures emerged from the abyss. No, that wasn't right. Several figures were running up the side of the demon's arm from the abyss. Dirty, sun-burned, caked in black ichor, fire erupted from their hands, in precise arcs that sliced into the demon's flesh. One of the newcomers, with what was once most likely light hair plastered against her face and skull, jumped expertly to grab the demon's finger. Just as her hand made contact, her hand turned to fire, and smoke filled Stanton's nostrils. He coughed from the stench of burned flesh, and the demon bucked him loose.

He fell atop Walter and Allegra, sprawling across them. Both were so exhausted that they didn't even make a sound, at least not one he could hear over the fighting.

Overhead, the demon's talon erupted into flame before crumbling into dust. Dodd fell, and fell straight into the abyss. Stanton shouted, reaching out his hand, crawling over Allegra and Walter, all the while knowing he could never reach him in time, and trying all the same.

Even before the tears could fall from the grief of having lost yet another, hands, bloodied and bruised, lifted up Dodd's body, carrying him up the side of the demon's arm, passing him up along the long chain. Lex reached Stanton's side, and both of them grabbed Dodd, pulling him back to their world, dragging him over Allegra and Walter's unconscious forms.

Stanton managed to take a glimpse into the abyss; there was an entire army snaking down the body of the demon.

Vittorio and Rupert dropped to their knees, pressing two different pendants directly against Dodd's leg wound. Giso pulled off his own from around his neck and passed it to Rupert. Dodd gasped for air, his eyes wide and wild. He jerked when Giso's third amulet was pressed on his leg, let out a harsh cry, and passed out.

The demon began its retreat into the abyss, now badly burned. Some of the other newcomers who had been fighting the stray demons in the room bowed before jumping back into the abyss. The light-haired woman who'd saved Dodd jumped off the demon to stand before them. She looked about the room, eyes wide. She turned to Stanton, then glanced down at the sword of Tasmin. It had broken sometime during the battle. He didn't remember when. She spoke something he did not understand, though she smiled when she said it.

Vittorio let out an audible gasp and collapsed prostate to the ground. "Gracious Lord God Almighty, forgive me this day."

She gave him a curious expression. Allegra and Walter were near delirious from exhaustion, both with their hands still against the portal edge, though it was doubtful they were doing anything now. She placed a hand on each of their backs, even as Giso knelt beside Vittorio, who whispered, "It cannot be."

She muttered something to the pair of mages, but again Stanton did not understand what she'd said. She moved their hands to their sides, keeping them away from the rift's edge. Then, the shriek of demons sounded once more, as the large demon finally retreated. There would be more soon, and their mages were too exhausted to do anything.

She jumped into the rift, but she did not fall. She hovered just below the tear's edge, as if magic held her up. Then, she mumbled something, and the tear sealed above her, as easily as lacing a pair of boots.

Pero and two soldiers disappeared in the back bedroom, only to return with blankets. They tossed them over Walter and Allegra. Imogen had a gash across her forehead and blood all down her face. She tried pushing herself to her feet but collapsed to her knees.

Everyone was injured, but some not as badly as others. They all began pulling off as much of their magical items as possible, including pants and shirts if they had any healing elements sewn into it. All were pressed to helping the dying or severely injured.

Stanton pulled the laces off his boots and handed them to Giso for Imogen. Head wounds always looked bad, but she was retching every time she tried to stand.

Vittorio wept, even as Rupert instructed him to hold a pendant hard against Dodd's leg. The bleeding had stopped.

"Why are there people, actual living people, in the abyss?" Lex demanded while pressing healing items against two different people and also muttering for Dodd to stay alive. Or else.

"Did anyone understand what she said to me?" Stanton asked as he removed the laces from the other boot.

Vittorio nodded, gasping and weeping. "She said to you, 'My sword yet lives to fight the abyss. I regret that I broke it.' To the...the...mages, she said, 'My kin continue to fight in this age. Good.'"

Chills went through Stanton's body. "No, it cannot be."

"Tasmin? Are you saying that was Tasmin?" Rupert demanded. "She's dead. She's been dead for..."

Vittorio could not answer for he retreated into sobbing prayers of forgiveness. Stanton suddenly found himself on the floor, next to Vittorio. Pero was holding his hand, wrapping something about it. He hadn't realized his hand had been bleeding all this time. No wonder he felt woozy.

Pero helped him roll over to rest against Allegra's hip. He could feel her breathing, steady and strong. She was alive. He was alive.

Stanton wept for those who did not make it.

CHAPTER THIRTY-ONE

THE VIGIL WAS around Dodd's bed this time. Walter stared at his friend—for Dodd was his friend, no matter how much he protested against having attachments of the heart or soul—and felt the heaviness of it all. Lex was snoring, having been quietly drugged by Cardinal Devonshire.

"The boy has been through enough," the old woman said sternly. "And if you do not get some rest, Walter Cram, I shall drug your tea, too."

They discovered Michael had filled three more journals. The pope had ordered them all brought to Walter before they were given over to Roul for protection. Walter had refused at first, saying he did not want to know, did not want to understand, but Rainier had come to sit with him. To steady his heart. To help him find the courage.

Michael thought the Lord God was talking to him, telling him this was the proper path. But he'd never meant for any of it to happen, not the way it did. He did not know he'd been creating portals. He honestly had thought someone else was doing it.

Once he realized, he had convinced himself for a time that it was the Lord God's will. He had convinced himself of the lie so fully, so completely, that he continued his work in secret, continued trying to learn how to summon demons.

He'd thought he could summon Tasmin. He believed the theories that time in the abyss was different than time in this world. He thought bringing forth demons would unite the world.

He'd known about Tasmin, all this time.
He should have just told Walter. He'd have helped him.

I cannot face Walter. The sight of him now enrages me, even though the man has done nothing to harm me. It is my guilt, seeing him reminds me of how arrogant, how stupid, how dangerous I have become. I have destroyed all I wished to achieve. I should leave, disappear, and go far away. But I have no skills, no money, no way to support myself.

Of course, what is all of that when I am a murderer. And not just the regular kind, like Walter, or any soldier of our acquaintance. No, I am the kind who slaughtered innocents for my own ambition.

I am nothing more than a demon.

And so it went. Michael had accidentally opened a portal in his bedroom, and Lex had found the mess. Michael nearly told Lex that day, but could not find the courage, or so his diaries said.

Why does the Lord God spare my life, except to torture me? I must leave this place, for I am a danger to all within. No matter what I do, no matter what I try to accomplish, all I achieve is making things worse.

I should've never gone to Walter's door that night. It had been out of selfish need, of wanting comfort. And, as much as I have tried to pretend otherwise, it was to keep my thumb upon the gossip. For why go to Walter, and not Lex or Dodd, or Rainier, or anyone else? No, I chose Walter for I knew he would open his door, and his bed, to me. And I used him in so many ways.

And I loved every moment that we were together. I should have told him when there was a time he would've protected me. I could have still had this, and him, and more, and help.

And now, the worst of it, is that I struggle to open anything to the abyss, now when I wish to fling myself into the darkest pit and be rent apart by the demons, an end too swift for my sins.

And my heart, even now, whispers, I love you.

Walter wanted to throw the book across the room. Foul fiend. He knew, one day, he would be discovered and that they would all read this. This was a part of his manipulations. Even now, even after he was gone from this existence, he used words to twist.

Walter never felt so tired as he did right now. He had enjoyed Michael's company, and not for the obvious reasons. He had enjoyed having someone about the room, laughing, talking, cursing, taking up space. Seeing Allegra again, seeing her happy, seeing Rupert and Pero fighting, seeing Lex and Dodd figure out what they wanted...it made him lonely. So very, very lonely. And then, Michael knocked on his door.

And, sure, that first night had been naked passion, of not caring about rules or priestdom, or anything else. It had been throwing each other down on the floor, never even making it to the bed. It had been raw and fevered, and full of need.

And then, it started to change. To become comfortable. To leaning against him while he read one of his damnable banned books that he loved.

Of course. That had been how he'd gotten himself into this mess. For all that Walter knew and understood about magic, he had not understood demons, or the portals, or the demon marks. Even now, Walter felt he knew even less than when he'd found the demon marks that day at Borro.

He missed Michael, right now, in this moment by candlelight and firelight. Had Michael died? Or had they healed him? Was he now condemned to live a life fighting the demons, like Tasmin and her army? Had that been what held back the demons for so long, and why so few marks even existed?

Because Tasmin had been holding back the tide.

Maybe Michael, his beloved Father Michael, was doing the same. Making up for mistake after mistake, and unable to simply trust. Or maybe he was dead.

"I did not love him," Walter said out loud. He'd startled Rainier, who had been on the cusp of sleep. At Rainier's confused expression, he said, stronger, "I did not love Father Michael."

Rainier stared at him for a moment, before whispering, "I did."

A pitiful sound escaped Walter's throat. He had not expected that.

"I knew him. I played cards with him. Shared my meals, and my wine. I shared my secrets, my heart, my stories. I loved him the way that a man loves a friend." Rainier's voice cracked. "His betrayal, his choices, his lies cut me, and my anger at him is because of that friendship lost."

And it hit Walter, squarely in the chest just as if Rainier—*Stanton*—had punched him. He had loved Michael. He had trusted him. And he'd been betrayed by him. Walter buried his face in his hands and wept. Grieving sounds of his soul ripping apart escaped him. Stanton's strong arms soon wrapped around him, enveloping him in friendship. He knew Stanton had done it to comfort him, but it only made Walter sob harder.

Soon, Walter felt Lex's thin, bony fingers rubbing his back, whispering how it would be all right in the end, to let it out, and that he was in the company of friends.

Dodd awoke somewhere in there, as Walter wailed for Michael, completely lost in grief, and unable to stop the images of what the demons were doing to him. Despite his leg, despite being half dead, despite it all, Dodd dragged himself from the bed, swatted them all away, and pressed his barrel of a chest against Walter, crushing him with far more strength than a man nearly dead a couple of days before should ever be able to accomplish.

He might never understand, not truly, why Michael just didn't tell him. And his heart broke for not knowing that. But at least, right now, he was not alone. That would have to be enough.

EPILOGUE

IT DID NOT come as a surprise to anyone who knew him when Rupert officially stepped down as Holy Father two weeks after the scene in his apartments. He had not worn his robes since the attack, even while ordering about the servants and militia; he'd told Allegra the robes choked him. Vanida's death had been hushed up, as much as such a thing could be, but no one blamed him. Vanida had made his choice and had faced the consequence.

Later, Rupert told Allegra that he suffered waking nightmares whenever he even thought about moving back into the papal apartments. Pero said he was also relieved to never return to them. There had been too much blood, too much...it had all been too much. They were offered a quiet establishment in Amadore by the king, in thanks for all of Rupert's sacrifices. Pero was offered a position with the army, either in active duty or training, but Pero kindly refused. They would stay in Orsini for the election of the new pope, and then they would accept the kind offer of a small estate for their retirement.

The election for the position of pope had been fierce. Devonshire's name came up, but she declined, as she did each and every time for the last four decades. Though, this time, she did it with a voice that finally sounded her age, laced with grief and sadness, and a heavy conscience. No, she'd said. She was too old, too set in her ways. Let others carry the weight of the world upon their shoulders. She said she would retire her cardinal's robes. She wished to live her remaining years serving the healers, dispensing knowledge, and caring for the lingering wounds and scars of battle.

Giso won the position of pope by one vote: Vittorio's. It was his last act as cardinal, before stepping down to become a regular priest. He surrendered his robes of power for the horsehair of repentance and sin. When he'd told his wife he was donating all his wealth, she took her share according to their marriage agreement and left him. He let her go without protest, without complaint. What was left to him he gave away, all of it, to various charities, individuals, and even the Cathedral. All for the support of mages fleeing the Cartossian conflict. To feed the poor and clothe the naked. All to reverse a lifetime of errors and regrets.

Giso broke tradition and kept his name. He did not wish the separation between himself and his post. He wished to rule the way he had lived his life. No one who knew Giso, either the man or his reputation, was surprised by his first act as Holy Father: an end to the enslavement of mages. His second act, however, perplexed many outside of the new Holy Father's immediate circle: he ordered a translation of every single scrap of writing in Orsini's archives.

Rumors of Tasmin's return, of Tasmin's sword, of Tasmin's status as a mage or warrior or incarnation as the Lord God Almighty spread through Orsini like the flames had at Borro Abbey. Giso said he would release the documents, to not censor the books, and to allow the world to know all of mage history. For now, he wanted them to exercise care as they slowly spread the news through the translators and scholars, through the upper ranks of the clergy. But, Giso promised them all he would officially tell Serna the truth when the translations were done, but also he did not stop anyone from speaking on it. No. There had been too many secrets. He only asked they did not speak of it from the pulpit before he did.

For now, there were more pressing concerns. As the civil war in Cartossa raged, the Cathedral stood as a physical beacon, its partially-repaired spire calling out for all those who were oppressed and hungry, to come inside their protective walls. For not even the armies of the abyss could defeat it. Refugees, migrants, and newly-free mages poured across the border and toward Orsini. Giso opened the gates to all, though admittedly, there was no room left inside Orsini itself.

The encampment beyond Orsini's north walls grew, along with the small farming villages all about the countryside. The Orsini militia worked to keep order as best as possible, and various clergy members organized work placements, apprenticeships, schools, and healing clinics. There was plenty of repair work, at least, and whenever the clerks cried that they were running out of ready coinage, Giso ordered another piece of gold filigree from the Holy Father's destroyed apartments to be used to pay excellent wages. Reconstruction would continue, Giso had declared, and those who'd taken the vows of poverty did not require gold leaf on their chamberpots nor gold mosaic ceilings in their prayer rooms.

Allegra chuckled when he'd said that, for she remembered him complaining about subpar wine.

Change came on a more private level, too. As was now obvious by how Nadira fussed about Allegra's red gown, tutting and fretting about non-existent wrinkles. Allegra had resigned as Arbiter, as Constable, as everything. Stanton resigned his position as captain two months after the attack, though he'd let everyone know ahead of time. There was too much heartache tangled in those positions, for both of them. The King of Amadore offered Stanton any position he wanted at court; Stanton kindly turned him down.

It was Imogen, who perhaps understood his feelings more than anyone else could, who offered him a place with her, training the Amadore army on how to work alongside mages. Allegra accepted an offer, too; though her role was to provide guidance to the army on their treatment of mages, and how to build trust with the people. Stanton's role was to help them keep each other alive.

But no fighting. He had told Allegra, late one evening, he did not even know if he could hold a sword again without agony. He still struggled with the nightmares, the sight of the corridors dripping in blood and gore. She understood, as did Imogen, even if she'd made a different choice. However, Stanton thought this job would be good for him, so Allegra supported him. She did not wish to live here anymore, either.

With Stanton's retirement, Lex was appointed Captain of the Holy Father's Own Consorts and tasked with the unenviable job of training up new members, of rebuilding after the collective trauma, of learning to live with the grief. With Imogen called back to her duties for the king, Dodd was named Captain of the Orsini militia. They were both young, perhaps too young, for the roles in which they were thrust, but truthfully, so many of the more senior officers were now dead or too mentally scarred to safely do these jobs. So, as always, the old friends stepped up to do what was right and necessary.

Walter complained on a near daily basis that he was disappointed they had not become the greatest love story for the ages, but he appreciated their friendship and promised Allegra he would only tease them on a weekly basis.

Walter winked at Allegra as Nadira slapped the back of his head, complaining his hair wasn't cut properly and demanding someone hand her the scissors.

Poor Walter. She knew he'd be angry for her thinking that, but she did. No one blamed him, which seemed to only stoke his anger toward himself. Amongst their circle, they took turns in the ensuing weeks keeping Walter company, insisting he join them for meals, inviting him to cards, prayers, recitals, or even good, old-fashioned manual labor. It wasn't until Vittorio began bringing him meals and sitting in silence next to him that Walter realized it was time to let go.

Eventually, Walter declared he had taken root. Orsini was his home, and he wished to stay. He asked to work with Dodd and Lex, for the three were inseparable friends now, and Giso found he did not have the heart to decline the request after all Walter had done for the Cathedral. Walter would train mages who wished to serve Orsini, be it with the militia or Consorts. After a lifetime of running from destruction, Walter decided to stay and build.

Most of her servants and assistants, save Nathan, asked to come with her and Stanton to Amadore, and Allegra accepted. Happily. Nathan had been named Chief Auditor of Accounts by Special Order of the Holy Father, meaning he was to be unleashed upon centuries of mismanagement, overindulgence, and hoarding.

Allegra gave him her blessing and said she pitied the clergy, for that boy would be relentless with the accounts.

Little Gopher, apparently, had been the one to alert Imogen about the Cartossian soldiers inside the Cathedral. He'd managed to also round up many of the other runners, and those children risked their lives escaping through servant and runner passages, to try to find help. For their bravery, they were all given medals, and permanent positions as apprentices in any job they wished at the Cathedral. Little Gopher asked to be a Consort when he grew up, but for now, he wanted to keep being a runner.

Nadira told Dodd to stop snickering as she cut Walter's hair, or she'd take the scissors to his hair next, too, and that shut him up.

Allegra had offered Nadira a full retirement, with both a pension and the means to settle wherever she wished. Her old servant refused, and honestly seemed rather offended by the offer that Allegra would treat her like the hired help. "After all I've done for you, Your Ladyship," she'd said, which made Allegra laugh. She couldn't help it. No, Nadira had said, the only place she wished to be was by Allegra's side. After all, Nadira did not endure demons and dirt to see her mistress appear before the king of Amadore looking *shabby*.

And so, Nadira remained, and fussed at Allegra's escorts. She complained Walter did not know the meaning of standing up straight, and that Dodd's jacket had a stain on it. Allegra laughed and said Stanton might change his mind if Nadira delayed them any longer, for which Nadira huffed indignantly. If Stanton could not wait a few minutes more for the love of his life, then he did not deserve her.

Allegra could not find a rebuttal for that.

She smiled, for she had survived. She had not been burned upon a pyre. She had not been found swinging from the city gates. She'd not even landed herself in the depths of a mine. She had emerged untainted and unbranded.

"Nadira, my good woman, enough!" Rupert exclaimed. "She is perfect as she is! Not even the Lord God would find fault with her gown. Let this wedding proceed before the mages riot!"

Nadira dabbed her eyes, though she scowled as she gave the former Holy Father her severe inspection. She picked off three long strands of hair, suspiciously the length of Pero's. She tutted and said, "You are now somewhat presentable, *Sir* Rupert."

Calm Seas handed Nadira one of the thick silk ribbons tied about Allegra's waist. It was red, with gold thread throughout. Nadira dabbed her eyes and began weeping silently, but accepted the ribbon. Dodd grinned as he accepted the white ribbon, with the red embroidery. Walter kissed her cheek and accepted the blue ribbon, with the silver thread. Rupert accepted the green ribbon with the white embroidery. He went to hug her, but Nadira slapped him away for fear he'd crush her gown.

It had taken six months for them to get to this wedding, the first of two, and Allegra found herself laughing, even through the nerves bubbling inside her. They would leave here and do this all over again, this time for Stanton's family, for her family, and for the nobility and royalty of Amadore. But this wedding? This one would hold a special place in her heart, she knew it.

Nadira, like the general she was, ordered them to spread out and inspected the ribbons before declaring them straight, taut, and not interfering with her mistress's gown. Nadira nodded to Kia, who beamed and ducked out from the tent formed around the old rectory's entrance to contain their party.

Kia and Serafina pulled back the curtain, revealing the bridal procession to the world. Allegra's stomach clenched when the cheers went up. The crowd cheered as she stepped out in her red gown, embroidered head to toe with gold thread. It took some time before she saw Stanton, but there he was, in his Consort uniform, for the last time. Her heart fluttered seeing his smile. Lex, Pero, Imogen, and Stanton's mother (who refused to miss this event, even though they were leaving the next day for their second wedding at the king's court) held Stanton's identical ribbons.

She caught sight of Nathan and Little Gopher, the scamp, who had been helping Stanton get ready. Little Gopher was nearly as tall as Stanton now. She forgot who'd made the wager he'd be as tall as Stanton. A flicker of a memory, of a time when these people wanted to murder the lad.

She pushed it aside. No, today was about celebration. Of survival. They had all survived.

As both groups slowly made their way through the parted crowds, to stand in front of Giso and all of the senior cardinals, she glanced in the direction of the four plaques that gleamed on the south gate. She could not read it, not from this distance, but she knew what was on it: the names of those who had given their lives. She was glad they were here in memory.

Giso began the blessing, greeting all of them, and Allegra found herself in reflection. Giso's voice, and that of the crowd faded. If the Lord God Almighty were to appear now, in this moment, to inquire if she held any regrets, if her sacrifices had been worth it, she knew within her heart she held no regrets. For even though none of them would know who and what she truly was, it had been worth it all.

For her people.

For her kind.

For peace.

She had always planned to take her secrets to her grave, and now she found true peace with that. It was what mages deserved. It was what she deserved.

For this was a good life, and she planned to live it in joy and love.

THE END

Did you enjoy this book? Please consider leaving a short review to help other readers know if they might enjoy this book, too.

Want to know when the next book comes out? Sign up for my new release email at **kristadball.com**

ABOUT THE AUTHOR

KRISTA D. BALL WAS born and raised in Deer Lake, Newfoundland, where she learned how to use a chainsaw, chop wood,and make raspberry jam. After obtaining a B.A. in British History from Mount Allison University, Krista moved to Edmonton, AB where she currently lives.

Somehow, she's picked up an engineer, two kids, six cats, and two very understanding corgis off ebay. Her credit card has been since taken away.

Like any good writer, Krista has had an eclectic array of jobs throughout her life, including strawberry picker, pub bathroom cleaner, oil spill cleaner upper and soupkitchen coordinator. These days, when Krista isn't software testing, she writes in her messy office.

ALSO BY KRISTA D. BALL

The Dark Abyss of Our Sins Series
The Demons We See
The Nightmare We Know
The Sins We Seek

Spirit Caller Series
Spirits Rising
Dark Whispers
Knight Shift
Mystery Night
Dead Living
Blood Family

Collaborator
Traitor
Fugitive
Rebel

Ladies Occult Society
A Magical Inheritance
A Ghostly Reqest
In the Society of Women (*forthcoming*)

Tales of Tranquility Series
Blaze
Grief
Interlude (short story collection)
Fury
Schemes
Liberate
Ambush

Nonfiction
What Kings Ate and Wizards Drank
Hustlers, Harlots, and Heroes
Appropriately Aggressive

As Dinah Lewis
First Impressions
Love in the Spotlight